# Money

BY THE SAME AUTHOR

*Cash!* (Prix du Livre, Summer 1981)
*Fortune*
*Popoff: The Red Banker*
*The Green King*

# PAUL-LOUP SULITZER

*A NOVEL*

*Translated from the French by Susan Wald*

LYLE STUART INC.     SECAUCUS, N.J.

Belmont

Published by Lyle Stuart Inc.
Published simultaneously in Canada by
Musson Book Company,
A division of General Publishing Co. Limited
Don Mills, Ontario

Queries regarding rights and permissions should be
addressed to: Carole Stuart, 120 Enterprise Avenue,
Secaucus, N.J. 07094

Manufactured in the United States of America


Library of Congress Cataloging in Publication Data

Sulitzer, Paul-Loup, 1946–
  Money.

  Translation of: Money. 1980.
  I. Title.
PQ2679.U457M6613    1985        843'.914        85-9792
ISBN 0-8184-0373-X

Any resemblance to real persons or events is,
of course, purely coincidental.


*To my father*
*To my friends: J.-F. Prévost, J.-R. Hirsch, Olivier B., J.-P. Rein*

*Making money is also an art, a passion unrelated to its object,
a permanent quest for the unattainable. . . .
It is an ironic dance, distant and hopeless in the face of Time.*
—P.-L. SULITZER

# 1. A Fierce, Merry Elation

# 1

I guess the story might just as well begin on that morning of November 23, around 11:30, in the house on Old Queen Street bordering St. James's Park in London. Why not? That was when it all started—perhaps not exactly at 11:30, but after 11:30, and in the five or six hours that followed.

On November 23, 1969, at around 11:30 a.m., the Scotland Yard detective sat down in front of me. I can still remember the pattern of the tweed jacket he was wearing. He was about forty, with the face of a redheaded Scot, and thick, curly hair parted by a straight line on the left and falling into a double corkscrew on the right; his name was Ogilvie or Watts. He watched the furniture movers.

"Are you leaving this house?"

"It's leaving me. They're repossessing everything I haven't finished paying for. I haven't finished paying for anything."

The phone rang. I picked it up, and it was the bank again. Now the second check had bounced. They found the situation "unbearable"; they demanded to know what I meant to do, what time I would be there, the sooner the better, and did I know what a protest bill was?

"I'll be there as soon as possible."

"When?"

"In an hour."

I hung up. The detective's pensive brown eyes were still fixed on me. I was sure he had heard and understood who was calling me and why, but he pretended that he hadn't.

"Right," he said. "I have an idea. Why don't you go back over what you did that night, step by step. You don't have to, but it would save time. And you would be free sooner to go about your business."

I stood up, my legs feeling heavy. "Let's go."

The movers were doing a good job. They had started on the third floor, emptying it completely, and continued on the second floor, emptying it also. Now they were on the ground floor. They were taking everything, absolutely everything, even the little ink drawing of the house in St. Tropez.

"How old are you?"

"Twenty-one. Twenty-one years, two months, and fourteen days. A man."

"When did you rent this house?"

"Two months and fourteen days ago."

"The evening before last—was it the first of that sort?"

"Not the first."

There were a few steps between the second floor and the living rooms on the first floor. We climbed them. I turned around one last time to catch a glimpse of the drawing, but the man who was carrying it had reached the street and the vans.

"Not the first—but definitely the last."

"Were you celebrating anything in particular?"

"My bankruptcy."

We were on the staircase leading to the second floor. I said: "I was downstairs in the drawing room on the right. I saw Annaliese go up the stairs. She turned around, right here. She looked at me, waved, and went on."

"No particular expression on her face? Nothing to make you suspicious?"

"No."

"Were there a lot of people?"

"I'd invited fifty people, and three times that many came. It was crazy."

"The time?"

"I would guess three in the morning."

We reached the second floor landing, and stopped. I went on: "After that, thirty or forty minutes went by. I was still downstairs in the living room. I wanted to go upstairs too, to be with her, but it was hard to fight my way through that crowd. Everybody knew me, everybody spoke to me. They held me back."

"But finally you did go up?"

"Finally, I went up."

A sudden surge of memory, the image of that same staircase— now empty, stripped even of its carpeting—but which had been buried under that exuberant crowd, that mob, those clusters of people clinging to the steps and shouting as I passed: "Happy bankruptcy, Franz!" It lasted barely a second, not even that. Immediately, the staircase reappeared as it really was: silent, echoing, and deserted.

"How did you know exactly that she was on the third floor in this part of the house?"

"She was the only person besides me who had the key to my room, which I had locked for the party."

"You'd had a quarrel?"

"No. Yes. A small one."

"Did you know she was taking drugs?"

The third floor landing.

"Yes."

We walked down the corridor. We came to the door of my room, which was open now but had been closed then. The second surge of memory, in which sound mingled with the image. Suddenly, I saw myself at this same door, thirty-two hours earlier, trying in vain to turn the knob.

"What about you? Drugs, I mean."

"No. No, never."

*Annaliese. Annaliese.* I never knew her last name. She didn't tell me and I never thought to ask. Or where she came from or where she was going. How did we meet and come together? Who knows? Young people find each other though the entire world seems set against them. They give off a passion like a scent that leads the male to the female; in our case, it was Annaliese who found me, found me and took me. Could she have been more than seventeen? I doubt it. Her breasts were too small and too firm, her body like the osiers that grow around the shaded ponds in the south of France. Without her thick black eye makeup she had the face of a child, of a twelve-year-old girl. And yet, for seventeen, what did she not know about sex! No forty-year-old beauty, with a world of experience behind her, could ever make love with the ferocity and frequency of little Annaliese. I thought that I myself knew a thing or two, but I was an infant in Annaliese's arms. Not for long though. It's astonishing how fast one can learn with a good teacher.

Yes, she took drugs. She took them as she took life, as she took passion and Gitanes cigarets and sticky glasses of red wine, for the thrill, for the mood swings, and because they released her sad little soul from her nervous little body. She gulped down everything whole, little Annaliese, without chewing, just swallowing, swallowing. When we met she was already on the needle, and nothing I could say or do would keep her from her bathroom rendezvous with those precious vials of colorless liquid or white powder. Afterward, she would stretch out naked on my large bed, inviting me with her arms and her lips, those tiny hard breasts and long, thin thighs.

"Drink me, my darling," she would murmur, as the high enveloped her, heightening her senses. "Drink me."

And I would fling myself upon that child's body and bury my mouth in the deepest part of her, while she caressed my hair with fevered hands.

I was at the doorsill and could not bring myself to cross it. I simply couldn't. My throat and stomach were in knots.

"I couldn't open the door. She had locked it from inside and left the key in the lock."

"You knocked."

"I knocked, and all those idiots on the stairs rushed to imitate me, thinking it was a game, a—"

"A lovers' quarrel," the detective said, impassively.

The words were on the tip of my tongue, but to say them aloud was another matter.

"They were making so much noise all around me. She could just as well have screamed from in there, without my hearing her."

*14*

"So you went round."

I was sweating large drops. The feeling of malaise was growing stronger by the second.

"I went around by the balcony and I entered the bathroom through the skylight."

Seeing that I still did not move, the detective gently pushed me aside and crossed the threshold himself. He crossed my room and turned sharply to the right to enter the bathroom; he disappeared from sight. But I could hear his voice:

"This skylight, here?"

"There isn't another."

I leaned my shoulder and forehead against the door frame. I was literally soaked with sweat. I heard the detective:

"Why were you in such a rush? Why the acrobatics? You might have broken your neck. Maybe she just wanted to be alone, to brood. Could she have hinted that she was going to kill herself?"

"No."

I heard him open the skylight, hitch himself up to the opening, and come down again.

"But you thought that since she was naturally high-strung, and after the quarrel she'd had with you, with the drugs she must have taken and the wine she'd drunk—you thought for all those reasons she might try to kill herself?"

"Yes."

He opened closets.

"And yet you waited thirty or forty minutes before you began to worry about her?"

Smarting from the implication—from the injustice of it, but also because it set off that feeling of guilt in me—I took a few steps toward the bathroom. I went in. Then my memory erupted for the third time, like a crimson sun, and this time odors joined the images and sounds—the sickly odor of the blood she had splashed everywhere, staining the walls, the bathtub, the marble washstand, and even the frosted glass of the skylight, when she madly slashed her wrists, ankles, stomach and breasts with a razor, and then hanged herself.

And I had just enough time to rush off and vomit.

\* \* \*

The same day two hours later—or about one-thirty—I was on

15

Charles II Street at the entrance to the bank whose claims department had been calling me all day yesterday and all this morning. I entered the lobby, and it was only at the very last second that I turned on my heels and went no farther.

The rain, meanwhile, had begun falling again as I crossed St. James's Square, a fine, cold rain that followed me into Pall Mall and across Green Park. It stopped for a few moments when I got up to Hyde Park Corner, but began again further on, as I came out of the Knightsbridge underground station, where I stopped to look at the map. I couldn't miss it, it was straight ahead, down Brompton Road and then Old Brompton Road—a little over a mile and a half to go.

Walking did me good, despite my fatigue and the rain that was turning into a downpour. My nausea vanished. In fact, it was then that it happened—inexplicably, but with a remarkable strength and clarity. The previous second I had been at the end of my rope, crushed, defeated. Then suddenly, I was like someone plunged into water, who sinks and then, when he hits bottom, bounces up with a kick and shoots to the surface with a wild energy he doesn't know he possessed. It came from deep within me. It was a rage, a fierce, merry rage. It was the irresistible feeling of invulnerability. It had nothing to do with my age, with being twenty-one years, two months and fourteen days old; it was more powerful, more permanent. The feeling lasted all that day, and it would return later, in the months and years to come. At the time, it even changed my gait. Despite the rain and my forty-odd hours without sleep, I floated on air that seemed lighter, my step became a dance.

I arrived at Brompton Cemetery shortly before three o'clock. Annaliese's family was there already, huddled under a sea of black umbrellas. I didn't dare approach them, I didn't even know their names. I took what shelter I could under a kind of canopy supported by the columns of a tomb. I was completely drenched, and shivering, standing about thirty feet from the grave. I saw the coffin arrive, saw it lowered. Then came the slow parade of consoling mourners. Another twenty minutes passed before the crowd of relatives and friends dispersed completely. I waited until the lane was completely empty before finally venturing toward the grave.

I spent several minutes in front of it in the rain. I was sad, of course—more than sad, shattered; and yet, at the same time, I felt that kind of rage and near-elation that had come over me a little while earlier on Old Brompton Road. I would recognize the signs of it later, each time it overcame me.

What I was remembering now, as I stood beside the fresh grave of my lover, was not the red of her blood, but the white of roses, heavy, full-blown roses whose perfume filled the crannies of one's senses. She had loved white roses, Annaliese. She loved to make love in a room where white roses filled the vases everywhere. What she always asked for, laughing, was a bed consisting only of the drooping blooms of fully-opened white roses. And I had promised someday she would have it. I hadn't delivered, and now it was too late. Now there was nothing left. Not the room in which we had so often lain together, our naked bodies so entangled that one could hardly tell where she began and I left off. Not the heavy Royal Vienna vases heaped with the flowers she loved so much. Not the house, nor the bed, nor Annaliese herself. There was only me, and the odor of the roses that filled my nostrils even here, as I stood empty-handed at her grave.

Outside, an elderly man who had left the cemetery a few yards ahead of me started to get back behind the wheel of a Vauxhall. I approached him.

"I'm going near St. James's Park. Can you take me part of the way?"

He started to shake his head. Then his gaze fell on the cemetery we had both just left. He inspected me, with my drowned look. If I'd been crying, it wouldn't have shown, so wet was I with the rain.

"A relative of yours?"

"A girl I knew."

"How old was she?"

"Seventeen. She would have been eighteen in three weeks."

He shook his head.

"Me, it was my wife."

He made up his mind and opened the door for me.

"You said St. James's Park?"

He dropped me off in front of the Guards Chapel, and even though we hadn't said another word to each other, we shook hands and said good-bye as though joined in a secret complicity. The house on Old Queen Street was now empty. They had even removed the carpet in the living rooms, leaving the house extraordinarily and dismally resonant.

The only piece of furniture—if you could call it that—which hadn't been removed was the huge mirror over the mantel in the library; it had been inset into the wall when the house was built. I went over and stared into it, although I can't think what I expected to see other than my own face.

There it was, my own face, Franz Cimballi's face. From some angles it looked fifteen years old, from other angles, thirty. I am dark, of course. With a name like Cimballi, what else would I be? I have too much hair. It grows thick and curly on my head, and it's like a fur rug on my chest and belly. Not too bad, my face, masculine at least, white teeth and a deep cleft in the chin. My nose is hooked, but whether that delightful feature came to me from my Italian father or my Austrian Jewish mother, I leave for you to guess. I don't care one way or another.

Sometimes I hate my eyes. They are too large and too brown, like Bambi's. They make me appear vulnerable, even childish. On the other hand, there are times when this is no small advantage, such as when you are face to face with a deadly enemy or a beautiful woman. Anything that can compel either to underestimate you is a couple of extra points in your favor.

I was a large, lusty baby and a well-developed boy, tall for my age. Then, when I reached fifteen, I stopped growing. That's it, *rien va plus*. My important documents, such as my passport, describe me as being five feet eight inches tall, but don't you believe it. Five feet six and not a centimeter over. Well, well, at least I am sizable where it counts the most. Even today, if you gave me my choice of where the inches would go, it wouldn't be the top of my head.

Women have always gone for me, and I for them. They think I'm cuddly, until they find out different, and then they are too satisfied to complain. Because they were so readily available, I never gave women too much thought, but made love to them happily and shut the door on them happily. Until Annaliese. The first woman who made a lasting impression on me. What a laugh. Cimballi the loser, dancing on the ashes of his very short life.

The letter's whiteness gleamed on the polished oak parquet. It had been slipped through the mail slot in the blood-red painted door. It contained only a few words in German, telling me that the man was waiting for me at the Dorchester, sent by Martin Yahl.

The man who was waiting for me was called Morf.

* * *

"Alfred Morf. From Zurich," he added, as if that would explain everything.

He was slightly taller than I, something that is not unusual, since I'm not gigantic. He had a sharp face, eyes a bit slanted, prominent cheekbones, and hollow cheeks, hollow as a skeleton's. He looked me up and down; to be sure, I was dripping wet. To get to the Dorchester on Park Lane, I had walked across St. James's Park in the rain for the second time that day, and Green Park too. The Buckingham Palace guards must have known me by sight, having seen me go by so many times.

"You're soaked," said Morf, pursing his lips.

"Sharp eyes, eh? It's perspiration."

I sat down under the dismayed eyes of a waiter. A pool immediately formed under me, and I was steaming like an ox which has just been brought back to the shed. I smiled at the waiter.

"Don't worry, the others are on their way, I swam past them off the Irish coast. Champagne for me, and make it snappy, old chap."

I turned back to Morf. It wouldn't take much to make me hate this guy. I disliked him already.

"I am an authorized representative of the Martin Yahl Bank of Geneva and Zurich," he said. "Your father was one of our major clients. Mr. Yahl has instructed me to settle matters with you once and for all."

"Mr Yahl is a crook."

The pool at my feet widened, spread, and attracted the attention of an elderly lady in mink. I smiled at her; she withered me with a glance. Morf continued:

"Mr. Martin Yahl, the president of our bank—"

I was still smiling at the lady.

"And still a crook—"

"For shame," gasped the lady in mink, shocked.

I nodded. "No kidding."

"Mr. Martin Yahl, for the sake of his long friendship with

your father, is prepared to help you again, for the last time. In accordance with your father's wishes, you received, less than three months ago, on your twenty-first birthday, the sum of one hundred three thousand pounds sterling, which was the remainder of your father's estate. You—"

"And sixpence. One hundred three thousand and sixpence."

I was trembling so badly with cold that I nearly dropped the champagne glass. I drank a little wine. Again, the urge to vomit. And the rage that rose at the same time in dull throbs. I said to the lady in mink, whose back was turned:

"They robbed me, Mr. Yahl and his cronies. I'm a poor cheated orphan, dear lady. . . ."

"You squandered that money in a little more than two months. You haven't even a shilling left. Furthermore, our investigations show that you are in debt for an amount of approximately fourteen thousand pounds sterling."

"And sixpence."

"I have been instructed to reimburse all of your creditors, to the extent that I find their claims valid. In addition, I am to give you ten thousand pounds sterling. However, this only on condition that you leave Europe within six hours. And my orders are to accompany you personally to the plane."

Suddenly, I was no longer there in London, at the Dorchester, overlooking the lawns of Hyde Park on a rainy, cold afternoon in late November. I was at La Capilla, the house in St. Tropez, and it was August. The beach at Pampelonne was nearly deserted, except for three naked girls who were looking at my father and laughing. For my father was there, crouching beside me, less concerned with the naked girls than with trying to start the half-horsepower engine of the five-foot-long red Ferrari in which I was sitting. I was eight years old, and the warm, lightly vibrant air was filled with the oily but heady scent of arbutus and rockrose. And I could have wept for happiness.

I put down the champagne glass. I was still cold.

"And if I refuse?"

"There are those bounced checks. The one you gave the jeweler in Burlington Arcade, and the other, which is held by an antique dealer in Kensington Mall. The bank has agreed to wait until tomorrow morning. After ten o'clock tomorrow, a complaint will be filed."

I was still staring at the back of the outraged lady in mink.

"And now they want to send me to jail. What do you think of that?"

"That's enough, young man," said the sixtyish companion of the lady in mink.

"You have no choice," said Morf.

"And can I choose my destination?"

"Provided you leave Europe within six hours, starting from this minute. Where do you want to go?"

The bar of the Dorchester was slowly filling. Everyone's glance slid over me, over all that water with which I was flooding the carpet. More and more I had the impression that I smelled like a wet dog; I probably did smell like a wet dog. "And a stray." I finally happened to glance at a brochure lying on a nearby table. A name and a picture struck me.

"Mombasa, Kenya."

I was practically certain that Kenya was in Africa. It had been there the last time I looked, probably below the Sahara; you turned left at the last oasis, or something like that. The name was vaguely familiar, I must have seen it on a movie poster; but except for that, I was completely ignorant. Morf had silently disappeared, with the furtive shuffle of a cashier. I emptied my champagne glass, shivering more than ever.

"I'll never make it to Kenya alive; I'll die on the way, falling off a camel and forgotten by the caravan, whose train will vanish over the peak of a dune." I clearly saw the camel train disappearing; the champagne was apparently wreaking havoc with my empty stomach.

Morf returned.

"There's a British Airways jet leaving London in just over three hours, heading for Nairobi, Kenya. In Nairobi there's a connection to Mombasa. I reserved a seat for you, we'll pick up your ticket at the airport. Come on, there's a taxi waiting."

He paid for the champagne I had drunk and the mineral water I hadn't touched, and he was already at the door before I could move. Sensing that I had not in fact followed him, he stood motionless, but did not turn around, waiting for me. Well, there was no doubt about it now: I hated this guy.

Just as the taxi was starting towards Heathrow, Morf changed his mind.

21

"You can't travel like that. They might not let you on board."

What worried him was not that I might get pulmonary congestion and then suffocate in Africa in my custom-made combed wool suit. No, he was afraid that my appearance might offend British Airways, which would then bar me from its planes. Without asking my opinion he ordered the taxi to change directions and stop on Oxford Street West, across from the Bond Street station. Twenty minutes later, we came out of Michael Barrie together, then Lilley & Skinner; I was newly clothed, underclothed and shod, having chosen the lightest, most tropical wear they had.

"Do you like me, Alfred? Alfred, tell me that you love me." The champagne had left me light between the ears.

He didn't even turn his head. I had a strong urge to punch him in the jaw; for one thing, it would have warmed me up. The taxi took off again, darting to Marble Arch, toward Kensington, on the way to Heathrow. It was then about five-forty, and night was falling on London, which was glistening with rain. I was leaving it without having resolved to, without fully understanding what was happening and what had happened. The sudden surge of an oppressive, painful sorrow made me lean my head back against the seat, close my eyes, and bury my hands in my coat pockets. I guessed that my life was about to change from top to bottom; that I would wake up tomorrow very different from what I had been only two days before. It was not merely a change of direction, it was a complete metamorphosis, a rebirth. What was more, either the champagne or fatigue or the thought of Annaliese lying under the ground in the rain caused my head to go spinning.

"Sign here, please."

He gave me some papers, spread out on a brown leather attaché case. He explained:

"A receipt. I am to give you these ten thousand pounds, and report back to Mr. Martin Yahl. And then there are the customary formalities. Today is November 23, 1969. The trust established by your father expires at noon today. From now on . . ."

I was barely listening, racked by nausea, still unable to open my eyes.

". . . As of today, you're on your own. Here's your check for ten thousand pounds. Be careful, it's made out to cash. Sign here. And here."

For what was perhaps an extraordinarily fleeting hundredth

of a second, I had the feeling that a relentless trap was closing over me. Or perhaps I imagined it later, when I learned the truth. The fact is that I signed where he told me to.

The airport.

"Would you like something hot to eat or drink?"

Now he was worried about me. But he was as cold as ever. He was dressed in ready-to-wear, and what was worse, actually looked like he dressed in ready-to-wear. He had on huge leather shoes, the kind you buy because they wear well, and carried a fob watch, which he consulted frequently, as though he had absolutely no confidence in the lobby clocks.

I didn't answer his question. Morf took me to one of the B.O.A.C. counters, where he paid for a London-Mombasa ticket with a Diners Club card. "Yes, one way." But he held the ticket instead of giving it to me, and together we went to the gate of the duty-free zone, which was restricted to passengers.

I chose that moment to bolt. I lost myself in the crowd, hidden by a turbaned group of Pakistanis, and darted into an airport florist. The young woman running the flower shop had soft, stupid blue eyes, a flat blouse, and the large red hands of a laundress.

"Can you deliver flowers? White roses, it's for a girl."

I wrote the name and address for her and gave her a shock.

"Brompton Cemetery?"

"Row 34 West. They buried her this morning."

No, no card and no message, just white roses.

I endorsed the check and gave it to her.

"Ten thousand pounds. I want ten thousand pounds' worth of white roses. And sixpence, which I have here. You'll have plenty of time to make sure the check is good. Plenty of time. As for the sixpence, it's also authentic, I personally guarantee it."

I took the receipt she eventually gave me, just as Alfred Morf, a bit lost, a bit winded, caught up with me. I told him what I had done.

He was stunned.

"Come on, Alfred, old chap."

He turned around twice to look at the flower shop, probably wondering if there was the slightest chance he could recover the money. Now it was I who had to drag him along. At the check-in counter he presented our two tickets, mine for Kenya, his for

23

Zurich. Side by side, we entered the duty-free zone. I headed for the little bookstore. Good things happen by chance: I found the admirable book *Out of Africa* by Isak Dinesen, which I had not yet read at the time. I took the book and said to Morf:

"Pay up, old chap, you know I have no more money, not even a sixpence."

Seventy-seven minutes later, the plane carried me off, breaking through the ceiling of clouds. I began to read. I was hungry, immensely hungry, like an animal, a hunger I hadn't felt for many days. It was like returning to myself, a sign that everything was becoming normal again, after these months, no, years of madness. It was eight-ten or eight-twenty. I opened the book I had bought and read the first few lines several times: "I had a farm in Africa, at the foot of the Ngong Hills. The Equator runs across these highlands, a hundred miles to the North, and the farm lay at an altitude of over six thousand feet. . . ."

Isak Dinesen's African farm was in Kenya. In Kenya. I vainly looked for a map, which I should have thought to buy before leaving Heathrow. Where the hell was Mombasa relative to the Ngong mentioned in the book?

The plane finished its climb, the purring of its engines quieted, the rows of seats before me became horizontal again. My mind was empty, blank, a bit like the light bathing this anonymous cabin. I thought about flowers, perhaps. About white roses, a mountain of white roses. Kilimanjaro? I didn't know. Anyway, I had finally kept my promise to Annaliese. A bed of white roses for her to lie . . . under.

My hand crept into the gaping emptiness of my pocket.

Then, like a soft, raw wound: never, never again this. Nothing can make me accept this emptiness. My hand closed suddenly on a burning fabric, soft and terrible, a pocket full of nothing.

I felt my lips form the word.

I heard my voice name it: "Money!"

I had never confronted money; it had never concerned me. That had just changed, once and for all.

\* \* \*

I have a bright, resonant name, a name that dances. At least, that's the way it seems to me; I have always imagined it accompanied by an almost barbarian music, in any case wild, fierce, very cheerful, dancing. And this hasty departure from London, on a November evening, toward the African sun, was the real beginning of the dance for me.

My name is Cimballi, Franz Cimballi.

## 2

At the Mombasa airport, a yellow bus, loaded with passengers and luggage from an East African Airlines plane.

It started down a poorly maintained road, filled with potholes, the asphalt eroded by rains. I had expected crushing heat; it was merely warm, that was all. On the other hand, the air was sticky and filled with countless odors, not all of them appetizing. The people around me were black, of course, in their great majority, but not all of them; there were those lighter skins that seemed to belong to Indians, at least two Arabs, and one European. I tried to catch his eye, and when our glances crossed, I gave him a timid smile, but he turned away without answering me.

The bus stopped and everyone got off. "Terminal," the driver announced, solely for my benefit, seeing that I didn't budge. I stepped down.

It was almost noon on that November 24. At Nairobi, while waiting for my connecting flight, I never left the airport. I passed the time reading Isak Dinesen and saw almost nothing of Kenya. To this day, I've hardly seen any more of it, except, on the road to Mombasa, a village resembling a housing development, with round whitewashed huts, conical thatched roofs, women dressed mostly in pink, wearing skirts of what appeared to be bath towels, with blue turbans; they had wide nostrils but were not ugly, and to my great regret did not go bare-chested.

Getting off the yellow bus, I came into direct contact for the first time with this country into which I had plunged. I saw a

25

large busy street, lined with stores and shops, which I soon learned was called Kilindini Road, the main street of old Mombasa. Everything I owned was on me, I didn't even have a suitcase: what was worse, not even a toothbrush.

"The time has come to make a fortune." The wild elation of Old Brompton Road was still with me. The farther down you sink, the faster you bounce back and the higher you go. I wondered who had said that. Me, perhaps. In my case, my rise should be meteoric; I had nothing. Zero. What exactly was the currency of Kenya? Pearls? Pocket mirrors, or travelers checks? The Barclays Bank sign a little further on caught my eye. I went over to inspect the exchange table, and learned that I was now obliged to make a fortune in something called the East African shilling, which was worth about seventy French centimes, so that there were eighteen and a half shillings to an English pound, and seven shillings to a dollar.

A fat lot of good that did me!

I went back out to Kilindini Road and wandered around, peering into the shade of the shops run by Indians. The men had soft, liquid women's eyes and shiny hair, and looked as though they were ready to sell themselves at a handsome profit. I finally found what I was looking for. He was about my age, about my height, even a bit shorter than I, and still relatively inexperienced, which was also true of me.

"My friend, here I am," I told him. "I came on purpose, all the way from London, on the fastest plane, just to make you the bargain of the century. This superb watch I'm wearing can be yours—no, you're not dreaming, it's true—can be yours for six hundred dollars, even though I paid three times that for it at Boucheron's in Paris. Call them right away if you don't believe me."

He had never heard of Boucheron, that was obvious, and what's more, couldn't have cared less. But the main point was elsewhere—probably in that gleam of merriment deep in his liquid pupils.

"Among all these shops, yours was the one I picked, I'll have you know. It was love at first sight."

I had guessed right. I smiled broadly; he began to grin in response. I broke into laughter, he did likewise; we all but poked each other in the ribs. A couple of pals.

26

"Come on," I persisted, "it's a very good deal, not the kind you're likely to see again, don't let it slip by you. And since you're so anxious to buy it from me, I'll let you have it for five hundred fifty."

He laughed his head off; he was laughing uncontrollably. He moved away from the threshold and waved at me to enter; you don't leave a customer as hilarious as me standing on the doorstep. Ten minutes later, I had recounted my arrival from London and the smallest details of my situation; I had played the card of frankness, of future camaraderie; he had offered me tea and gooey cakes dripping with sugar; and my watch was passed from hand to hand, inspected by a father, uncles, brothers, and cousins in turn, who had been called in to lend their total expertise.

"One hundred dollars."

"Four hundred fifty."

Off we went again into uncontrollable laughter. We drank more tea and my watch went off on a second round.

"One hundred twenty dollars."

"Four hundred."

"One hundred thirty."

"Three hundred eighty-four and seventeen cents."

I was having a really good time; it's always like that at first. But forty-five minutes and six glasses of tea later, having kidded long enough, we came to an agreement, Chandra and I: one hundred seventy-five dollars, plus a razor and three new blades (one of which was really, really new), plus a pair of white cotton underpants like the kind worn by the Indian Army for bathing, plus a toothbrush, plus a map of Kenya.

Chandra, meanwhile, had become my friend, practically a brother. He held me affectionately by the shoulder, while I watched his hand on the off chance that it might stray into my pocket (I was wrong; Chandra proved to be scrupulous). He pointed out a hotel, the Castle, which was just behind the two huge cement elephant tusks at the entrance or exit to Kilindini Road.

It was a vaguely Victorian building, with a Spanish-Moorish balcony tacked on and an outhouse at the back of the courtyard. A room there cost me twelve shillings, almost two dollars, and, upon emerging from the single shower open to guests, I stretched out on my bed and unfolded the map of Kenya to finally see what it looked like. Not much, frankly, at least on paper. At best, it resembled a kind of funnel with the top leaning on the Indian Ocean. Facing inland, you had Somalia to the right, then Ethiopia, then Uganda and Lake Victoria, and finally, all the way to the left, Tanzania. I looked for Kilimanjaro, with its snows and its leopard. No Kilimanjaro; I found only Mount Kenya, which peaked nonetheless at five thousand two hundred meters. Could they have stolen Kilimanjaro? Finally, I spotted it by accident in Tanzania, not far away. They must have moved it; I'd always thought it was in Kenya.

I suddenly felt lonely, very lonely, and far away, in every sense of the word. Stretched out on this bed of theoretical cleanliness, in this noisy room where the fan wheezed like an asthmatic, I had a touch of the blues.

It didn't last. Old Brompton Road again, and that strength I had found there. I had one hundred and seventy-five dollars, I was twenty-one years, two months, and fifteen days old. If worse came to worst, I had enough to last me a month and a half, although hardly enough to keep me in luxury. I would have found something by then, I was sure. I didn't know what; I had never worked, never earned a dime, had been kicked out of various Parisian lycees and sent to schools in the provinces, then Swiss boarding schools, then English public schools. Franz Cimballi, the life of London or Paris parties, of Swiss ski resorts, of "in" spots on the Cote d'Azur; ladies' man, good-for-nothing, capable of jauntily tossing out the window, in two and a half months, one hundred seventeen thousand pounds sterling, which—I had never denied it—wasn't very smart.

But a different Cimballi was in the making. The time had come to make my fortune.

I gave myself a week. As it turned out, it took me seven days to run into Joachim.

\* \* \*

Joachim looked down at me from his height of six feet and a few inches, with his tiny elephant's eyes, twisted and unblinking, sunk into a face that could terrify a Masai warrior. He asked:

"Did you think I was after your money?"

I burst out laughing.

"Half and half."

He frowned without understanding. Then, as the penny dropped, he blushed like a girl. He shook his head.

"Oh, no, I like women."

"Me too."

He was Portuguese; he was quick to tell me that he had spent four or five years in Mozambique and had been in Angola before that, remaining in uniform up to the time when—he told me in a shy whisper—he had left the army, or rather, deserted. He really had a mug that could scare the daylights out of you, especially at night, with a long nose, hooked and bumpy, and two deep, scarlike wrinkles in his pockmarked, leathery cheeks. His real name—the one he went by in Kenya, anyway—was Joachim Ferreira da Silva plus fourteen or fifteen other patronymics.

"Did you know a soccer player named Eusebio?"

"Never heard of him."

"He was the best player in the world, better than Pelé. You know Pelé?"

"Vaguely."

"Eusebio was much better than Pelé."

"No kidding."

"You don't believe me?"

"Who says I don't?"

I saw no reason to contradict Joachim on that score. I had met him in the airport on my seventh day in Mombasa. I had spent the previous six days walking around the city. "City" is a compliment; two estuaries, rias, surrounded by the sea, and between them a peninsula, several feet above the water, on which the slave-hunting Arabs and Persians, and later the Portuguese, had built forts, mosques, and churches. To the northeast was the old Arab port with its dhows and sailing vessels from Arabia; to the south was the modern port of Kilindini, filled with cargo ships. That was where the railroad supplying Nairobi and Uganda began. Between Mombasa and the continent was a toll road. If you take it and head north, you will follow a large, wonderful beach, beyond the sailboat harbor, along which are a string of brand-new luxury hotels and the private home of Jomo Kenyatta, the facade of which I would unfortunately soon come to know in detail.

So much for the setting.

It didn't take me weeks to discover its limits. The modern port? Any Arab or Indian forwarding agent knows a hundred times more about it than I ever will. Trade? Which one? And anyway, I was sure of one thing, if nothing else: I had no intention of getting involved in one of those patient climbs that take at least twenty or thirty years of work and your life. The time had surely come to make a fortune, but it had to be made fast. This was presumptuous, but that was the new me.

Moreover, I had an asset, even if I didn't know it yet, and it was Joachim, as a matter of fact, who revealed it to me. I had noticed Joachim for the first time on the patio of the Castle Hotel. With his unemployed killer's physique, he had few chances of going unnoticed. I saw him again the next day, and twice on the following day, and then, in the course of my Mombasan wanderings, I ran into him more and more often; yet, he kept avoiding me with maidenlike shyness. A shyness that surprised me, and even put me on the wrong track: I thought he had designs on my virtue, and I found that anything but charming. For two cents, I'd have stuck my fist in his face. Two things kept me from doing it—my natural good temper, and the fear that he would hit me back and pulverize me.

"It's true, I was following you," he said, shifting his weight from one foot to the other like a big bear. "But it's because I have a deal to offer you."

He explained. He was basically shy, a victim of his menacing appearance, with the heart of a pimply teenager under the skin of King Kong. He made his living organizing safaris. Not luxury safaris.

"Mainly for German customers, and sometimes Swedes or Danes, Englishmen in a hurry, who want to bag a buffalo before their next plane."

Joachim spoke English, or tried to, anyway, haltingly and with an atrocious accent. We understood each other better in a Franco-Italian-English gibberish with a dash of Spanish thrown in.

"How much do you get from them?"

"Ten thousand shillings."

Seven thousand French francs. A little under fifteen hundred dollars.

"And what do you need me for?"

Joachim explained that because I was young and good-looking (I agreed), and in addition to French and Italian I also spoke English and German, I could deal with tourists for him.

"Me," said Joachim, "when I approach German tourists, I frighten them."

Joachim offered me two thousand shillings for every customer I brought him. We compromised on three thousand. We drank a Coca-Cola in friendship, since Joachim didn't drink alcohol because of a promise he had made to Our Lady of Fatima—I stared at him, dumfounded, but he was as solemn as a pope. My imagination was beginning to race. Supposing I found two, and why not four or five, customers a week? That would make fifteen thousand shillings a week, and would obviously mean hiring other Joachims, since this one could no longer do the job. But if I hired the future Joachims, I would no longer get three thousand, but let's say six thousand shillings per customer, and if I got thirty customers a week, times the number of weeks in the month, supposing, just in theory, that the entire Kenyan jungle were populated with hundreds of thousands of German tourists, millions in fact, in columns of five, I could easily get up to six hundred sixty-nine thousand four hundred twenty-four shillings a month, as a strict minimum, and I could then extend the business to neighboring countries, maybe even to Senegal. . . .

I came down to earth almost as soon as I had done my calculations. The truth was that tourists getting off the plane are dreaming of beaches on the Indian Ocean, of exoticism, of Mombasa the slave port, Mombasa through which a certain Stanley passed in search of the famous Dr. Livingstone. They are not dreaming of safaris, or at least not much. The market, as the economists would say, was not viable. I concluded that after a few days of trailing every newly deplaned tourist from the foot of the gangways, following them step by step as they wandered stupidly, buying horrible carved wood pieces and genuine fake Masai weapons . . .

And yet.

In Joachim's offer to me I began to glimpse the outline of an idea. It was true that my assets were being white, being able to talk to tourists, to inspire confidence in them. Not to the extent of selling them safaris they didn't want—but was it really necessary to *sell* them something?

*31*

I went back to see my friend Chandra, I had gone back to his shop several times since our first meeting; we were now more or less friends, especially since he had already resold my watch at a profit so great he didn't dare confess the amount to me. His answers to my questions corroborated my first idea.

The way to make a fortune?

Well, I think I found it.

\* \* \*

My first customer was a South German from the Munich area, I remember, a lawyer or doctor.

He stared at me from my very first words.

"Where did you learn German?"

"My mother was Austrian."

No, a safari didn't interest him, he wasn't a hunter. No, he didn't need a guide, much less an interpreter. "And if I need a woman, I can find one myself." I raised my arms in surrender.

"I'm not offering you any of that. I merely wanted to tell you something. You're going to change money, let's say, a hundred dollars, for example. For a hundred dollars, the change bureau over there will give you seven hundred shillings; that's the official rate. I can give you seven hundred fifty. You gain fifty shillings, or a little less than thirty deutschemarks. For two hundred dollars, a hundred shillings, sixty deutschemarks. For a thousand dollars, five hundred shillings, three hundred deutschemarks.

He had blue eyes; my youth and glibness amused him, yet his blue eyes took on a mistrustful expression.

"Where's the catch?"

I laughed. "There isn't any catch. Seven hundred fifty shillings for one hundred dollars, and there's no catch. And no policeman will appear."

"*Ein moment, bitte.*"

He went over to the exchange bureau, and in perfectly proper English, inquired about the rate. He returned, still a bit hesitant. "And your shillings are in valid currency, of course?"

"Have the bills checked at the bank, if you wish." He finally made up his mind, and changed four hundred dollars. I motioned to Chandra, who had stood off to the side up to then. He took out of his kind of saddlebag, and carefully counted, three thousand shillings in worn bills. I had insisted to Chandra that the bills should be worn, thinking that new bills might arouse suspicion. Of course, the bills were perfectly good, but I was not especially eager for the employees of the Kenyan Central Bank to pay too much attention to my exchange operations.

After my Municher had gone, Chandra paid me my commission, as agreed: two hundred shillings—twenty-eight dollars. At the official rate, dollars were bought not at seven shillings, but at a little less than eight and a half. And at that price, there were ready buyers. The large Indian colony of Mombasa, like that of Nairobi, was getting ready to complete its first exodus begun in 1968, in which thousands of Asians, especially Indians, returned to their ancestral country in response to measures taken by Kenyatta, who was trying to eliminate them from the controls of domestic trade, which they had taken over. For Chandra and his relatives, buying dollars, even at eight and a half shillings, even at nine and ten, was the only way to realize acquired property and savings prior to a possibly hasty departure.

It was this difference between the two rates, and the high demand for dollars, that I had decided to take advantage of—and fast.

What favored me was a new phenomenon that the Indians themselves had not fully perceived—the sharp growth of European, particularly German, tourism. And I had to move quickly, because sooner or later I could expect to have problems with the Kenyan authorities, even though what I was doing, was not yet illegal.

Chandra was smiling from ear to ear. Even deducting my commission, he had paid three thousand two hundred shillings, instead of three thousand four hundred, for the four hundred dollars he had just bought. He was ready to begin again, to bring me a large number of his countrymen. I warned him:

"On one condition—you and they will deal only with me."

He swore it on somebody's life. Not mine, I hoped.

"Another thing, Chandra: don't tell a soul. In return for your silence I'll sell you dollars at a preferential rate, that is, eight shillings instead of eight-and-a-half."

In other words, to everyone but Chandra, I would sell at eight and a half shillings a dollar that I myself had bought at seven and a half. Hence, a shilling profit per dollar. Provided I could find other Munichers. In the next two days, I never left the air-

33

port. For hours no luck at all, and then I hit my first jackpot. These guys were also German, and there were three of them, plus their wives, who found me cute. I changed two thousand two hundred fifty dollars for them, half of the sum redeemed immediately by Chandra, the other half resold to a merchant on Kilindini Road. Net profit: one thousand six hundred eighty-seven shillings. Two hundred ten dollars.

This was it! For the first time in my life I had earned money, and it was simple! Fantastically simple! I'd had an idea, and that idea had turned into hard cash. Of course, it wasn't an extraordinary idea; neither were the profits. Yet. It was only the beginning; I had no way of imagining what was waiting for me at the end of that road that I called and shall always call my dance.

In my euphoria, a preposterous idea came into my head. On returning to Mombasa, I bought a postcard with the picture of a jackal. I addressed it to Martin Yahl, His Banking Highness Himself, president and chief executive officer of the bank of the same name, a private bank on quai General-Guisan, Geneva. The message: "You see that I haven't forgotten you." A prank? To be sure. Harmless, in any case. At least, I thought so. And I would think so for a long time, until the moment when a staggering reply would reach me.

\* \* \*

I had even found a customer for Joachim, actually two: a young couple from Zurich. Their names were Hans and Erika. He did something in the postal administration, and she worked in electronics, an engineer, I think. They were charming and very much in love. Said they to Joachim: "We don't really want to kill anything. Take us around and show us the countryside." When they first saw Joachim, they seemed to draw back, alarmed by his appearance; now, touched by the gentleness of my big tame bear, they got along perfectly.

From Mombasa, the four of us headed north, toward Malindi and Lamu, following the coast lined with coral reefs just above the water, which cut out fantastically calm, transparent lagoons. Hans and Erika swam in the nude and I was quick to join them. Not Joachim, who, turning pious at the sight of the young Zurich woman in her birthday suit, went off grumbling and indignant. That evening, kneeling before his cot with the holy statue of Fatima above it, he prayed for us sinners who swam in the nude.

34

After Lamu, which was about sixty miles from the Ethiopian border, Joachim turned his old Land Rover toward the west. We went back by way of an inland detour. We made camp on the banks of the Tana before going off to scale the high Masai plateaus. No jungle, but at best a forest of giant ferns, heather, and bamboo, all covered with vines; the rest of the time, a savannah made up of acacias with strange horizontal, layered foliage, more infrequently planted with baobabs and euphorbia. It was thick with animal life, and Joachim was forever pointing his thick hairy fingers. He had been a hunter, even a very good hunter, I'd been told; now he no longer liked it, and I knew he enjoyed this trip on which there was no need to kill.

The altitude increased further. We were in Tsavo National Park, where we would spend two days. This was my first real view of Kenya, and it took my breath away. The sky is never entirely blue, but rather bright white, constantly crossed by pink or golden cloud caravans in endless motion. The earth is ocher or red or violet, sometimes crimson after the rain, when the cactuses burst into bloom; the sunsets are flamboyant and unbelievable, the dawns just as miraculous at the moment when herds of buffalo emerge silently, like phantoms, from the morning mists. The two nights we spent in Tsavo will always be Kenya to me, wherever I go and whatever I do later.

That evening, dining on quail and guinea hens killed by Joachim, we talked mainly of Switzerland. Hans and Erika had thought me Swiss. I enlightened them:

"I have French citizenship. I was born in St. Tropez."

They greeted this with exclamations. They had been in St. Tropez, the summer before. They had swum in the nude at Pampelonne.

"The house where I was born is on that beach. Or was."

They were that close to remembering the house—which they had probably neither seen nor noticed; they politely searched their memories in hopes of finding an image: "A big white building? or a kind of castle, with turrets?"

"No, it's right on the water's edge. There's a stone wall, and behind it a patio with palm trees." The images suddenly flooded me. Why had I kept such a precise, such an extraordinarily clear memory of a house I had known only as a child, where I had never returned since my father's death?

"How old were you when he died?"

35

"Eight."

"Cimballi is an Italian name, isn't it?"

"My father came from Tessin, not the Swiss Tessin, but on the other side of the border, just the other side. A few hundred yards closer, and he would have been born Swiss."

Joachim took out his guitar, and his thick fingers stroked the strings with surprising delicateness.

"And your mother passed away as well?"

"She died when I was eleven."

My mother died of cancer. Not just anywhere: in Paris, rue de la Glacière. The name alone would be grotesque if it weren't tragically accurate. There again, I remembered. I remembered the final months of that agony, that hellish round, that despicable minuet of our old banker, acting on instructions from Martin Yahl, besieging the dying woman's bedside, urging the doctors to do everything possible to prolong her life—and her suffering—not out of concern for her, but so that she would live long enough to sign all the papers the bank needed. The fierce hatred I bore Martin Yahl did not, of course, stem from that period—I had always felt it instinctively—but during those weeks of spring 1960, it found a material base on which it had grown ever since. I hated that man with a violence that even to me seemed inexplicable at times, that had impelled me to practically destroy everything he had given me, education or money, a violent hatred that at times seemed almost to border on pathological obsession. It was as though I could bear nothing—not even an inheritance—tainted by Yahl.

"His father was very rich," Joachim said in his deep voice, pointing his chin at me. "Father very very rich."

He smiled at me, his face glowing with a baffling friendship. He shook his head.

"Very rich. And then finished."

He began to sing *A Micas das Violetas*, his favorite *fado*.

Hans and Erika put their arms around each other, and I contemplated the Southern Cross.

\* \* \*

But back to work. Every tourist, German or otherwise, but usually German, changed an average of eight hundred dollars upon arrival. I earned nearly eight hundred shillings, or a little more than one hundred dollars, per tourist. In the two weeks

*36*

that followed my discovery of this gold mine, I was able to dispense with Chandra's services as a financial backer; that is, I put my own shillings to work. These were the profits obtained from the Indian merchants who bought my dollars.

After exactly twelve days—I remember the date because it marked the end of my third week in Mombasa and in Kenya—I was able to put together four times in a single day the six thousand shillings necessary to buy the dollars of four tourists from the same plane. Four hundred twenty dollars net profit for two hours of work! Not that such a windfall happened to me every day; actually, that day deserved a gold star, at least at that stage of my operations.

One thing was sure: I could now live on what I earned. And more. On December 22, two days before Christmas, I left the Castle Hotel—its noisy fan, its walls studded with crushed mosquitoes, its urine-stinking communal shower at the end of the corridor. I moved into the White Sands Hotel, not very far from the residence of Jomo Kenyatta Himself. Before me was the marvelous white beach and the coral splendor of the Indian Ocean.

I began to feel completely at home in Mombasa, nearly a month after my arrival.

And then, a bombshell.

The letter arrived on December 23. It was in my name, spelled correctly, with two *l*'s and an initial *c*, and bore the simple address "Mombasa, Kenya." I will never know by what miracle the Kenyan post office managed to deliver it to me; but Europeans living in this city of two hundred thousand or so inhabitants were not so numerous, especially the non-British.

I opened it, after noting that it had been mailed from Paris eleven days earlier, on December 12, at 4:15 p.m., rue Beethoven, in the sixteenth arrondissement. The envelope contained only one sheet of paper, size 8½ x 11 inches, with no watermark. Its message was typewritten: "At the time the trusteeship ended, you received approximately one million French francs, representing the remainder of your father's estate. In reality, that estate consisted of fifty to sixty million dollars, of which you have been robbed."

No signature.

Frozen, I stood holding the letter in my hand, unable to move, unable to do anything except read it and re-read it until I knew every impersonal and wretched word by heart. My head echoed with Hamlet's line as he learned of his father's murder: "Oh, my prophetic soul!" Yes, my soul, too, had been prophetic.

Somewhere inside me must have been this knowledge, or else why should I have so purposefully destroyed the paltry sum that had been allotted to me? Why had I felt such contempt for my so-called "inheritance"? But who had dared to rob me so openly, to treat me with such disdain? I had suspicions, but I had to make sure. I had to make very very sure.

# 3

Christmas Eve I spent in conference with a Somalian who had superb breasts and was further endowed with a sloping back that could outclass Niagara Falls. She was sweet, cheerful, and full of good will, though somewhat lacking in initiative.

Joachim was indignant; he wanted me to go with him to midnight mass. This Portuguese surprised me every day—this former mercenary who admitted having burned a few villages here and there in Mozambique, Angola, or the Congo, sometimes forgetting that women and children were still in the huts. This former cutthroat was a fanatic Catholic, carrying a rosary in the breast pocket of his shirt, ready to pray at the drop of a bead.

One evening I had the curiosity to go see where he lived; I was horrified. I discovered a squalid shack on the outskirts of the African ghetto (African by contrast with the European, Arab, or Indian districts), furnished with a narrow cot, a table, a wooden bench, and a metal trunk sealed with innumerable padlocks, on which the military inscriptions it must have borne had been covered with black paint. On the dried mud wall, six prints of Our Lady of Fatima, and the autographed photo of the aforementioned Eusebio in soccer uniform, and another three or four yellowed photographs taken years earlier, in Lisbon no doubt, judging by the tiled streets; they showed Joachim an innocent child with an already ugly face, together with an old woman in black.

"Why didn't you ever go back to Portugal?"

He didn't reply. Probably because there were several answers and therefore none: his situation as a deserter, the fear of finding his relatives poorer on his return than when he had left. Or the difficulty of tearing himself away from Africa. I felt friendship for Joachim, and a little pity, too.

In my money exchange operation, things were going faster than I had ever dared to hope. The Christmas holidays and the vacations in Europe sent streams of tourists who debarked by the planeload. Not just by the regular airlines; there were also charter flights, more and more of them, on planes leased by organizations like Kuoni.

On December 26, thirty-two days after I had arrived myself, I set a new record: seven clients served in the same day, six hundred ninety dollars profit. Two of them were tempted by a camera safari with Joachim as guide, and the Portuguese insisted on kicking back my middleman's share, which brought the sum of my earnings to nine hundred dollars for that day alone.

I returned to my room at the White Sands, and there I remember I spread out the bills, all the bills, on the bed, and gazed at them, incredulous, elated, fascinated.

I went to the bathroom mirror. I was still me! I returned to the bed and collapsed on the carpet of money. A real swan dive. . . .

The time to make money. It was coming.

Especially since in the next few days the trend continued, as they say on the stock exchange, still as a result of the winter vacations. In mid-morning, short on shillings after six exchanges in a row for a total sum of twenty-nine thousand shillings, I had to fall back on Chandra again, who rushed to my aid with wonderment.

And on the 31st of that month of December—to celebrate the New Year all alone—I bought myself a white suit, shoes, a suitcase, and various items. Large expenses, yet my capital went climbing above ten thousand dollars for the first time.

In the following days, I naturally expected a drop among the tourists, heading back to their Bavaria, their Mecklenburg, their native Würtemberg. Nevertheless, it was a rude blow when, from

*39*

ten to twelve customers a day, I suddenly fell back to one or two. When I could find customers at all. Once, I went as long as three days in a row without a nibble. I was already thinking of taking on Chandra as partner, but that was out of the question, for now, anyway. I was furious, and purely to calm my nerves, I called a plenary session with my Somalian, suggesting, as an extra precaution, that she bring along her younger sister, whom she had praised extensively for her talents . . . as a lecturer.

Thus it was that, on that day in January, the three of us were frolicking happily in the shower when someone knocked on the door. The hammering sound naturally made me think of the Portuguese, with his thick hairy fists. I cried:

"Coming, Joachim!"

I did have a towel in my hand, but merely for the fun of irritating the prudish Joachim I wrapped it around my forehead. I went to the door with a clownish grin, my naked Somalians standing at attention; I opened it, and found myself face to face—so to speak—with a gray-haired Kenyan wearing a crewcut, squinting behind his glasses, who informed me curtly that he was the chief of police and that he had come to arrest me.

He looked me up and down.

"You're completely naked."

"One usually is, in the shower."

The Somalians vanished on tiptoe into the bathroom. The water was turned off. The policeman glanced in that direction, then returned to me. Suddenly, I remembered his face. Joachim had spoken to me of this man. I turned away and slipped on a pair of Bermuda shorts, trying to maintain my dignity.

"And why?"

"Why what?"

"Why are you arresting me?"

"Violation of the currency laws."

Normally, he should have waited until I had finished dressing before taking me away. Instead, he barged right into the room, marched to the bathroom, and ejected the two girls with a few words in Swahili. The Somalians took off like two black streaks of lightning, amid a quivering of breasts and buttocks. The policeman shut the door behind them, and I understood. I sat down. This was indeed the man of whom Joachim had spoken, or rather, whom he had warned me against. I'll call him Wamai. He wasn't much to look at, short and skinny, with an ashy complexion, wrinkled skin, the black pearls of his eyes lightly flecked with blood.

"I've seen you often, Mr. Cimballi. I've seen you often in Mombasa."

"No doubt you enjoyed the sight."

He had as much sense of humor as a sponge. He didn't laugh at all. A Kenyan's average income was fifteen to twenty dollars a month. As chief of police, this guy must earn eight or ten times as much, I figured. Fine. I was prepared to go up to a hundred dollars. Maybe even a hundred fifty.

"You're in big trouble," said Wamai. "Very big trouble."

Joachim had warned me: Wamai was in cahoots with the judge, they worked as a team. It was better to pay them both right away, rather than rely on their justice. Okay, I'd go up to three hundred dollars, a hundred fifty each. I asked good-naturedly:

"And what do I have to do to get out ot it?"

"I can intervene on your behalf," said Wamai.

Meanwhile, in my own mind, I had decided to begin the bargaining at twenty-five dollars, fifty for the two of them—a quantity discount. Twenty-five? Why not twenty? That would give me another stage in the negotiation, which I suspected would be lengthy.

"Of course," said Wamai, "there will be costs."

I gave him the big sad smile of someone who would if he only could. . . .

"The problem is I'm short of funds. I hardly know how I'm going to pay for this room—"

He shook his head.

"Five thousand dollars, Mr. Cimballi. Pay it every month and you'll be left alone."

Thereupon, I made a comment about his sister.

And he hauled me off.

\* \* \*

Up to the last second, I thought he was bluffing, that he was merely trying to frighten me. I believed it while he paraded me through the lobby of the White Sands between two policemen. As I passed the reception desk, I couln't resist making a joke: "I'm seeing these gentlemen home and coming back."

41

I still believed it as he made me climb into the back of a Land Rover, with his two henchmen still on either side of me, but this time with handcuffs on my wrists. I believed it a little less—that is, I was beginning to have doubts—when, having brought me to the police station, he left me all alone in a big cell that didn't smell very good, together with half a dozen individuals who spoke only Swahili, and who seemed curiously disturbed by the presence of a white among them.

I tended not to believe it at all any more when they made me get into the strange paddy wagon I had seen passing once or twice through the streets of Mombasa. It was an ordinary truck; on its bed they had built an iron cage that opened only from the rear. A steel bar was bolted to the floor across the length of the truck. Attached to this bar were the chains they put around my wrists and ankles and those of my companions.

There were a good fifteen or twenty of us in the cage, and we were driven through the city as though for the fun of it. For the residents of Mombasa, the sight was not so unusual, though it always drew glances; they were used to seeing the paddy wagon go by. But apparently it was the first time they had seen a European in it, wearing cheap white Bermuda shorts and a shirt decorated with pink and blue palm trees.

Naturally, I had never been in chains before, much less locked in a cage. I didn't like it a bit, not one bit. For a few fleeting seconds, I felt a mad panic, the demented rage of a trapped animal. If Wamai had been there, I would surely have strangled him. I felt like yelling at the top of my lungs, struggling hard enough to wrench my hands off. Fortunately, that didn't last very long; I managed to pull myself together. "Look at you, Cimballi, look at yourself from the outside, can you see your face?"

I managed to sit down on a kind of wooden bench; I put my head between my knees, sinking my teeth into the muscles of my forearm. Soon it was nearly all right. I raised my head just as the truck, turning none too gently, entered Kilindini Road.

We filed past a sidewalk filled with shops; I knew each of the owners. A series of faces, aghast, shining, all turned toward me with the blank look of people on a railway platform as the train is leaving. We were about to pass the Castle Hotel, under the cement tusks, and that was when I spotted the woman. She was

European, a brunette, thin, lively, with superb green eyes and a red mouth with a mocking pucker. Our eyes met, held, could not pull away.

Mechanically, as a pure reflex of pride, I straightened myself, raised my chained fists in greeting, and smiled at her. Without the chains, I would have waved to her like a winning prizefighter. As the truck rolled on after a short halt, I leaned as far as I could so as not to lose sight of her, to hold onto her as long as possible, and I saw her crane her neck also to follow me. I had time to see her smile. I did not know her, I had never seen her before, and nothing in her manner suggested that she knew me either. Yet we were already intimates. A turn finally separated us, as the paddy wagon rolled northward.

*   *   *

The courthouse was a three-storey building with a balcony surrounding an inner courtyard in which the paddy wagon came to a halt. They made us get out, our feet in irons and with kicks in the ass, except for me, 'cause I was so cute. And it did seem to me that I was being given special attention. I was quickly separated from my fellow chainees and forced to drag myself, still chained, up to a small room on the second floor, where, behind a table, sat an Indian, pudgy and sweating like a melting candle.

"You have committed a serious violation of the exchange laws. It is very grave."

I had time to say "Listen" and "I want a lawyer," after which he handed my bodyguards a sheet he had apparently signed before our interesting discussion. I was lifted bodily under the arms and propelled outside. I found myself in the paddy wagon before I could understand what was going on. Other prisoners joined me, and, shortly afterward, the vehicle was set in motion and began rolling northward.

We went past the luxurious beach hotels—including mine, the White Sands—then past Jomo Kenyatta's residence. We traveled some thirty kilometers due north and arrived at the prison. I had gotten a glimpse of it when I went to Malindi and Lamu with Joachim and the Swiss couple. It hadn't made a lasting impression on me; as a tourist attraction, it wasn't worth a detour. I now saw a kind of camp, with permanent huts, surrounded by walls of bamboo vaguely decorated with barbed wire. The flat-roofed

43

buildings were built of cement blocks that no one had bothered to plaster over, much less paint. The stink that escaped in thick layers from the openings, through bars reinforced by grates, was absolutely, appallingly suffocating.

The gloom inside these white-hot huts was dotted by faces straining toward the light, streaming with sweat, and heavily caked with filth. During the few seconds in which I imagined being locked up in there, I suffocated in advance, shaken by disgust and, frankly, fear. Therefore, I was filled with immense relief when I discovered they were taking me away.

I hobbled on the uneven ground, my ankles by now bruised from the steel against my naked flesh; not only was I wearing Bermuda shorts and a Hawaiian shirt, but I had only rubber sandals on my feet. I stumbled, and hardly had time to worry about where I was going.

I discovered the grate at the last second. It was set into the ground and sealed by a padlock.

They opened it for me. They set up a kind of ladder—really a wooden beam with bars nailed unevenly to it.

"Down."

Below I found six men, piled in this hole in the bare earth. It was round, nearly fifteen feet deep and six feet wide; we were wading in an abominably nauseating sludge, the composition of which was only too obvious. I sank into it up to my ankles, nearly weeping from the waves of nausea that racked me; I stumbled around before finally finding a place in the shadow, my back to the wall. Above my head, the grate was locked again, and the policemen went away.

At first, I could make out only faint outlines around me, because of the darkness. Then I was staring at my six fellow detainees, who stared back at me. Four of them regarded me with surprise; the two others barely gave me a disdainful look. These two were unbelievably tall; the top of their skulls all but reached the edge of the hole. They had the same shaved crown, the rest of their hair hidden under a kind of red hairnet; they wore multicolored necklaces; they were impassive, lordly, stiffened by an animal pride. They were Masais.

And they stank abominably.

The four others were Kikuyus, with faces like bandits that could give you nightmares. They frightened me more than the

Masais; their suspicious whisperings in Swahili, the insolent boldness in their eyes—none of that was reassuring.

I decided to move, wading further, raising a puff of stink at each step. I crossed the no-man's land in the middle of the trench and slipped in between the Masais. I must have looked like a quarterback between two linebackers. The Masais didn't blink in the slightest. An hour passed, and the light began to wane, along with my courage. The first bites made me jump, the following ones stung me. In the growing darkness, I discovered that my feet and legs were literally covered by a swarm of brown caterpillars busily eating me alive. I stamped my feet and jumped up and down, half out of my mind. The Kikuyus howled with laughter; the Masais paid me no more attention than if I had been invisible and five thousand miles away. And it was to be that way all night.

In the morning they brought us up. They served us some meat that looked blue and stank like a corpse, which I didn't dare touch. Judging by the sun, it was about seven o'clock in the morning when, after a long wait, they loaded us—not just my fellow prisoners and me, but dozens of other prisoners as well — into five or six regular trucks. We returned to Mombasa. But my immediate hope of reappearing before the judge, before the chief of police, before anybody I could scream at, quickly vanished. Now they were making us get out, truckload after truckload. And a few orders made it clear what they expected of me: I was to repair a road, fill in its holes, and carry stones to do it with, lots of stones, enough stones to build a city, it seemed. And the road I was privileged to rebuild was directly opposite the residence of Jomo Kenyatta, the president of Kenya.

The home was posh as hell.

* * *

Joachim appeared late in the morning. He looked worried, dared not come close, and waved signals at me that were difficult to interpret. Apparently they meant he was taking care of me.

Lunch was eaten right on the edge of the road, under a leaden sky. I was ready to drop, drunk with fatigue. I'd eaten nothing for twenty-four hours and had not slept, having spent the night fighting off those damned caterpillars and watching the Kikuyus. Every time I thought of the coming night, which would no doubt be exactly like the previous one, I was willing to die.

*45*

But around three o'clock, a small Austin stopped in front of me. Down stepped Wamai the policeman.

"Have you thought it over, Cimballi?"

I wanted to crush his head with a stone and jump with both feet on his stinking corpse.

"Not for five thousand dollars."

He turned away, appearing to get back into his car, and my heart jumped into my mouth. I would call him back! Another second, and I would have done it. But he froze; he came back.

"Let's say three thousand."

My legs felt like cotton, my back was aching, my head spinning, and at times my vision was blurred. But my blood was up. No Kenyan policeman was going to get the better of me. I took the time to move a stone from one pile to another; I stepped back and regarded my handiwork with proud and visible satisfaction; at least, I did my best to make it visible.

"Five hundred. That's all I can do and you know it."

"Two thousand."

"Fifteen hundred."

"Two thousand."

I had been on this goddamned road for eight solid hours. I was beginning to dislike it. And I thought of the four Kikuyus chuckling in their sewer, staring at me with their eyes like live coals—not to mention the rest, which was equally incandescent. I also thought of the caterpillars. I tried one last stand.

"Okay, two thousand. But you'll give me a receipt."

That took the wind out of him. His eyes widened. I explained with dignity:

"A receipt. A piece of paper on which you state that you have received money from me. It's for my tax assessor."

He still couldn't get over it, and was wondering if I were completely crazy, or if I were putting him on.

"I will never do that," he said, finally.

"Okay, a thousand."

Which he could share as he liked with his buddy the judge. I wouldn't get mixed up in it, that was for sure.

I read in his eyes that he was going to give in, and the hardest thing at that moment was to resist the impulse to beat him to death with the shovel. He saved face:

"Twelve hundred."

46

I leaned on my shovel. I could have wept with relief. I said: "Okay."

* * *

"I did what I could," Joachim said. "You know I don't have any money, and they just barely tolerate me here. I went to tell Chandra. One of his cousins is the cousin of the brother-in-law of the uncle of a cousin of the judge who sentenced you. Normally, they should have kept you for a week. You were sentenced to a week."

For the last twenty minutes, I had been in the shower in my room at the White Sands Hotel. The water was boiling hot, and I used a stiff bristled brush on my skin. Of course, as I had expected, the room had been searched from top to bottom. Forget it. I hadn't kept a shilling there, my money was safe and sound at the bank, a little in an account, a lot in a safety deposit box.

"Chandra intervened. He gave his cousin a gift, and the sentence was shortened to one day in prison, which you served."

"And I'm free. Thanks, Joachim."

"It was Chandra."

"I'll thank him, too."

I had been released two hours earlier. Before leaving, I had wanted to know what my fellow prisoners were charged with. For the sinister Kikuyus, it was merely a matter of poaching. They were pussycats. As for the noble Masais, with whom I had felt so safe, they were guilty of murder; they had killed an entire Indian family, hacked them to pieces with unbelievable savagery. My famous intuition. I also learned what the pits were for: it was where they kept the short-term prisoners, like me, or those charged and awaiting heavy sentences, like the Masais. A strange mix.

But I was already far away from all that. And I had to be, if only to pay my tax of twelve hundred dollars—which I had done on the very evening of my release. By the next day, the 5th, I was back at what I now called my work at the airport. The result: two customers. Another result: I discovered that this episode hadn't hurt me. The incident sharpened me like a blade, stripped all weakness from me, and exposed an efficient, cold aggressiveness which I had never dreamed existed until then. And the kind of lull that had followed the Christmas holidays began to dissipate, business picked up.

47

Deducting my costs, I made nearly ten thousand dollars profit in the month of January. Then, in February and March, I went over the top. I doubled it in March, when I recorded twenty-five thousand dollars net profit, despite the twelve hundred I continued to pay the policeman and the judge, despite the fact I had taken Chandra on as an assistant—he cost me two thousand dollars a month. He divided his time between the money-changing operations and running his shop, where I took my customers in return for a twenty-five percent commission on everything they bought, a brokerage system that I developed around the middle of March, extending it to all the businesses that agreed to pay me that commission—and there were more and more of them.

The best part was that, in addition to getting twenty-five percent on the selling price, I also took twenty percent on the purchase price (the second commission being paid directly to me by the buyer), and despite this double-dipping, the tourist was still gaining. With my system, he paid thirty to forty percent less for a statuette, weapons, rhinoceros or elephant tusks, or any piece of jewelry than he would have paid if he had made the transaction alone. In short, I was a philanthropist.

The income from this sideline? Fifteen hundred to two thousand at the beginning, later around fifteen thousand—a month.

Toward the end of April, during a short trip to Nairobi where, with the help of one of Chandra's cousins, I was setting up a branch of my money-changing operation (which soon became as profitable as the first), I bought on credit four Mini-Mokes, small convertible jeeps made by British Leyland. I intended to rent them in Mombasa. Joachim, whose safaris were bringing in decidedly less and less, agreed to take charge of this new activity.

It was true that except for weapons and their uses, mechanics was one of the few areas—along with liturgy—in which he had some knowledge. Three weeks later, the turnover of the cars proved to me that I had been right. I immediately expanded, ordering four more vehicles. All in all, by the end of my stay, Joachim would manage a fleet of sixteen cars.

In May, all activities combined and all costs deducted, I realized a profit approaching sixty thousand dollars. I remember that my capital exceeded one hundred thousand dollars by April 21. I had been in Kenya for five months, give or take a few days.

And I again ran into the young woman with green eyes who had smiled at me—I hadn't forgotten her—as they were taking me away in my Bermuda shorts in the paddy wagon.

* * *

She told me she was twenty-four years old. She had been in Mombasa since the beginning of January, and had arrived, in fact, the day before my arrest; her name was Sarah Kyle, and she worked at the White Sands Hotel, as an administrator. Barefoot, she was as tall as I, but she loved to wear high heels, just to annoy me. She also spoke French.

"I took hotel management courses in Lausanne."

Whenever her green eyes fell on me, I read in the depths of her pupils a kind of vast amusement, as though I were the funniest guy you could possible meet.

"Am I all that funny?"

"Rather. You amuse me."

I said: "So far, so good. It's better than making you cry."

"What were you doing in that cage?"

"I thought I was a canary who had seen a cat."

"An error of justice."

"Exactly."

"It's the first time I've seen an error of justice in Bermuda shorts."

With her triangular face slightly tilted back, her cool gaze filtering between half-closed eyelids, she gauged me, evaluated me. I had the uncomfortable sense of being fifteen years old. How in hell was I going to get her into bed? But she left me no choice; I would never have one with her. On January 7, right after my release, during our first conversation, I had asked her to dinner, an invitation she declined. The next day, I ran into her, apparently by chance, in the corridor leading to my room. Which she entered. In order, she said, to make sure I was comfortably settled. She checked the functioning of the shower and bathtub, the toilet, the electric lights, the air conditioning; she made sure the French windows and the drawers locked tightly. I said:

"The problem is the bed. It's hard."

"That cannot be" she snapped. "Let me try it."

Taking off all clothes, Sarah lay down on the bed, crossing her ankles and placing the brown nape of her neck in her palms.

Her body was long and slender, with a high ribcage and a flat belly. I studied it with interest. Her breasts, although not large, had surprisingly prominent nipples, and these were already hard, sticking up like twin invitations. The hair on her mound was silky and long, curling in tempting tendrils onto her belly and thighs. I felt my . . . interest . . . quicken and grow greater. Much greater.

She bounced her hips up and down a few times, and the bedsprings worked perfectly. I said:

"Why, that's remarkable! as of this morning, it was still hard. May I?" I touched my shirt buttons with the greatest delicacy.

"Please," she said.

Undressing was no great achievement in that heat; a shirt, a pair of shorts, underdrawers—all on the floor in a matter of seconds. She never took her eyes off me, and I approached the bed and stood close to her, so that she could get a better look.

A small smile played over her lips, and it was no smile of contempt, believe me. She held out one finger and traced the hair on my chest with tantalizing slowness, around my nipples and down the center, toward my belly and groin. Her coolness had the opposite effect on me; I was a smoking pistol, ready to go off.

When her finger reached my groin it turned into a hand, then both hands, as she grasped and caressed me, forcing a moan through my lips. Her touch was like fire! I could see her thighs part, revealing the treasure between them; at once, I turned into a pirate.

I threw myself on the bed beside her, my lips already hungry for her breasts. Now it was her turn to moan, as I licked and sucked at her nipples, my hands pushing her thighs apart and plunging deeply between them. She was ready, very very ready, and so was I. That first time we came together was furious, a coupling of two caged beasts who'd been starved for days. It had nothing to do with love, or making love. It was purely hot fucking, and it didn't, it couldn't last long. We were both too close to the edge.

When it was over, when both of us lay sweaty and gasping and fulfilled, I began to make love to her slowly, with infinite patience, exploring her body like a cartographer assigned to map its terrain. Not an inch of her went unkissed or untasted; the small of her back particularly fascinated me; where it dipped and then swelled into her round white buttocks were two delightful little dimples. I could have tongued them for hours, but her whimpers of passion were too insistent, so I rolled her onto that magnificent back and began to pay some very heavy attention to her front.

"Franz," she whispered. "Franz," she moaned. *"Franz!"* she screamed.

It must have been some two hours later that I decided that Sarah had been right. The bed wasn't hard at all, and I had no complaints to make to the management.

* * *

Seventy-eight thousand dollars in July, in a single month. My Nairobi agency was working at full capacity. But above all, July was the beginning of the gold era, the full and brief gold era as I would know it.

I had met Walter Hyatt in Nairobi during that trip I had taken at the end of April. I hadn't been overwhelmed by our meeting, and would probably have forgotten it, if Hyatt hadn't landed in Mombasa two weeks later.

"How are the cars doing?"

It was he who had sold them to me. We were at the bar of the White Sands, but, wanting to speak to me, he led me to the beach, where an entire planeload of Dutch people, the color of lobsters dipped in boiling water, were frolicking with elephantine grace.

"I've heard of you," Hyatt told me.

I gave him a quizzical look.

"From that Indian who represents your interests in Nairobi, and from other Indians here in Mombasa, who call you the Little Boss."

And he gave me names. He explained that he was impressed by my rapid success; he thought we might be able to work together. As a matter of fact, he was looking for a partner.

"It involves gold."

"Why me?"

"Because with two of us, there won't be too many. You can put money into the business."

*51*

"Why don't you?"

"Who said I wouldn't? I will. And the Indians trust you."

Events would go very fast now. They were only waiting for me. We did our first operation together, Hyatt and I, less than two weeks after having agreed on it. The matter was simple, anyway: it involved our selling gold that came from South Africa to Indians arriving from Calcutta or Bombay by boat, waiting for us at the theoretical limit of territorial waters. Why did they want gold badly enough to sail all the way from India to buy it illegally? Because the entry of gold on to Indian soil was strictly regulated, while the Indians themselves have always been very fond of gold jewelry. And given the size of the Indian population, the market was obviously significant.

The gold arrived in ingots or bars via Rhodesia, Zambia, and Tanzania, as contraband. In Mombasa, it was graded as to quality by an expert recognized by all parties, in this case a Jew born in Amsterdam, possessing dual British and Israeli citizenship, and making round-trips between Tel Aviv and Nairobi.

Once appraised, the gold was melted down, made into mast-holders, anchors, anchor chains, even mooring poles. Two percent of the sum of the transaction was paid to the expert, eight to ten percent to the melter. Still to be carried out was the trickiest, perhaps the most dangerous, part: to swap the gold on the high seas for dollars from Bombay or Calcutta. To arrive with one's arms full of yellow metal and one's heart in one's mouth is risky, particularly in the middle of the night.

Tradition in such cases required a complex system of hostage exchanges, of bills cut in half and delivered in two stages. The ups and downs didn't much appeal to me; I would not spend much time in this traffic, a bit too flamboyant for my taste. Hyatt, to my surprise, was perfectly at ease. Physical danger tended to elate, even exalt, him. But the whiskey he imbibed by the liter had a lot to do with his relaxation. He always agreed to be the hostage, a role to which I hardly aspired. He did it each time, and each time was so drunk that he didn't know what was going on. Had they pointed a cannon at him, he might have placed his own head in the barrel, singing "Tipperary." On occasion, I had a great deal of trouble getting him back, he had grown so fond of his temporary jailers.

I did five operations in all. One at the end of May, three in

June, and the final one in July. On each one, the profit margin was a little more than thirty-five percent. The first time, I gambled thirty thousand dollars. To see. I saw. In the following operations, I staked the near-total of my available capital; for the July affair, my last one, this meant a profit of some eighty-five thousand dollars for an investment of two hundred forty thousand.

I had been in Kenya for seven and a half months.

Through the network Hyatt told me about between his drinking binges, a network which used a bank located on an island with an ominous name—Mafia Island, off Tanzania—I transferred the near-total of my assets to the Hong Kong and Shanghai Bank. Three hundred forty-five thousand dollars. In addition to what I carried on me, as a kind of pocket money.

As for me, the time had come. On July 7, telling Sarah, Joachim, Chandra, Hyatt, and all my various cronies, agents, and friends in Mombasa and Nairobi that I was going to the Seychelles for a few days to look at land for investments, I actually crossed the Tanzanian border. A no doubt useless and slightly ridiculous precaution, but I preferred that no one know what I was going to do. And to take a plane from Nairobi, under the noses of my crew of money-changers operating out of Embakasi Airport, would have been much too obvious.

Now at last I could carry out a plan I had been developing for a long time.

I finally took that plane from Dar-es-Salaam, heading for Cairo, from Cairo to Rome, and from Rome to Nice. I paid for my plane ticket in cash; I also paid cash for the car I rented at the Nice airport. I had about twenty-five thousand dollars on me.

Late in the afternoon of July 9, I arrived in sight of St. Tropez.

# 4

My father died on August 28, 1956; I was born September 9, 1948. So I was a few days less than eight years old at the time of his death.

My father's name was Andrea Cimballi, and he was born in Campione. This is an Italian city which is not in Italy but in Switzerland; it's a tiny enclave on Swiss soil. I had been there. I found a small, quiet town without pretentions, where the gambling rooms of a small casino existed side by side with a baroque church dedicated to the Madonna dei Ghirli, Our Lady of the Swallows.

If you climb the church's short flight of steps, in whichever direction you look you see Switzerland, and Lugano, with its lake, is in front of you. And yet, you are in Italy, subject to Italian law. The first Swiss town is three kilometers away, and is called Bissone, on the other side of the dike-bridge that did not exist when my father was born, and that now supports the road, the railroad, and the highway at the same time.

Had my father been born three kilometers to the north, it would have changed everything; he might even still be alive. Certainly I wouldn't be selling gold in Kenya to make a buck.

My father's family was from Florence, financially comfortable though not rich, of Lombard descent, I believe. A family of shopkeepers, with a teacher or two, two or three attorneys; traditional. The house in Campione was bought by my grandfather just before World War I, a way of escaping from the Austrian cannons by placing himself in the shelter of Swiss neutrality, without, however, leaving the national soil.

My father was born there in 1919. He was evidently a remarkably intelligent man. He had time to finish his studies, just barely—he was an engineer and a bachelor of law—before being shipped by Mussolini to Libya and Tripoli, where he was wounded and taken prisoner. At the beginning of 1946, he was back in Italy, after nearly a year's stay as a P.O.W. in Canada and the United States. He came back from this trip with an idea which he thought could make him a fortune. It involved a series of real-estate operations aimed at purchasing, developing, and leasing lots for mobile homes and trailers such as exist on the

North American continent. A single drawback: it was an idea which could be realized at that time only in the United States and perhaps in Canada.

My father possessed a small amount of inherited capital. He was ready to risk it. So he made an application to the Italian authorities for withdrawal of funds. Had he been born in Switzerland or Germany, this application would have been a mere formality. In Italy or France—supposedly liberal countries—such a request, coming from an unknown, automatically provokes snickers from the administration.

The request was denied. And that refusal would change his life and mine.

* * *

I awaited nightfall in Sainte-Maxime, on the other side of the bay, and it was not until around ten o'clock that I restarted my car engine. I didn't go into St. Tropez itself; I took a right, toward Ramatuelle, then a left, and by a maze of back roads I rejoined the road to Pampelonne, surprising myself by the ease with which I found my way. In the last few years, in between my frequent academic failures, I had gone back to St. Tropez several times; never had I gone as far as La Capilla. Something had always held me back. The house no longer belonged to me, and up to now I had always rejected the very idea of seeing it owned by someone else, my memories transformed into something different.

At one place on the small road you cross a tiny bridge over a stream. Then a right turn and a straight line, pines on the left, vineyard on the right. I left the car at the head of a road.

With the engine shut off, the silence was total. It was a still, soft night; the scents—arbutus, mimosa, bougainvillea, hibiscus, the sea itself—were heavier than in my memories. The first incline: there was a path there that I found again with the greatest of ease, as though I had walked it only yesterday instead of 13 years ago. The ocean and the beach were seven hundred yards from me; the house was therefore slightly to my left, if it still existed. A low jungle of scented arbutus. The path now ceased to rise; to the contrary, it sloped and began its descent toward the beach.

Something bothered me. Normally—unless, once again, my memory deceived me—I should now have the house in full view,

55

and see its lights. Despite the oleander bushes. Yet I saw and heard nothing. Not the dimmest light, not the faintest noise.

Another two hundred yards—and suddenly I sensed it, there in the shadows. I sensed it as you sense a woman lying next to you in the night. My home. The only real home I'd even known.

Was it occupied?

*　*　*

Less than a week after the Italian government's refusal, my father was in Lugano. There he met a Swiss banker slightly older than he, Martin Yahl, of Zurich. Yahl had come to Swiss Tessin to open a branch of the private bank founded in Zurich and Geneva by his grandfather.

My father was sufficiently persuasive, and Martin Yahl agreed to help him financially, either by finding a way to move my father's Italian funds into Switzerland, or by lending him his own money. Whatever the case, the two men would work together. More than that—Martin Yahl would simultaneously become the bankroller, shareholder, of the company my father founded, and the manager and trustee of that company.

It was a holding company, that is, a corporation set up specially to control and manage a group of companies of the same nature—in this case, worldwide—operating in the same sphere of activity. And Martin was officially in charge of managing the holding company by virtue of what is called an act of trust—he was therefore a trustee. Martin Yahl was the man in whom confidence was placed, the only one who appeared publicly, the only one who really knew who owned what, who had established what, and who was really behind the holding company.

My father had an absolute need for such secrecy. He had defrauded the Italian treasury to a certain extent, even though the money he used to found his company was his own, and on which he had paid his Italian taxes. But he had been officially prevented from using his money as he intended, and he had gone over their heads; that was his crime. He could have lost it at the racetrack or used it to paper the walls of his house in Campione, but could not export it, not even to found Du Pont de Nemours or General Motors. Unless he belonged to the establishment, was the C.E.O. of a large multinational, in which case he could certainly have made some arrangement with Heaven.

My father needed this secrecy and he made use of it. And of Martin Yahl. Then, with the passage of years, he could not go back. It would have been hard to go to the Italian treasury and say: "I committed fraud, would you kindly wipe the record clean—at what price!—and allow me to officially resettle in my native country as the founder of an empire?" Especially since in the meantime my father had settled in France, where he had married a young Austrian Jewish woman whom he had met at the Yahls', and acquired legal property on which he dutifully paid his taxes. Among this legal property, in addition to the two construction companies, shares in various companies, buildings—including one on rue de la Pompe in Paris, where he legally resided—were the seventy-five acres and the house on the southwestern coast of the peninsula of St. Tropez.

Main activity of the holding company: real estate construction and high-yield investments—housing sites, land purchases and real estate in general, together with large interests throughout the world in construction and building materials companies.

Someone once told me: "What was really unusual about your father was the way he had, once he had detected an opening, the glimmer of an idea, of plunging into it with astounding rapidity, and immediately widening it, developing it." They added, "He simply thought faster than anyone around him. No sooner had they begun to understand what he was building than he was already somewhere else. There are two ways to succeed: with patience, and the lightning speed of the gambler. Your father's was the second way."

In ten years, my father's success was phenomenal. Yet he wasn't satisfied with it. During the next fifteen years he struck out in other directions, everywhere. In the last months of our short life together, I remember that one day he showed me a piece of metal, saying, "It's still not used very much in industry. A day will come when it will be essential. And on that day I'll be there—we'll be there, you and I—among the few men in the world to control its availability on the market. . . ."

I know only that the holding company consisted of a corporation registered in Curaçao, in the Dutch Antilles. This Curaçao company, before suddenly disappearing one day in September 1956, held all the shares of other companies registered, respectively, in Nevada, Hong Kong, and Lichtenstein. These companies, in turn, held all the shares of a third tier of companies registered in the United States, Argentina, Luxembourg, France. . . .

A fabulous pyramid, crowned by Curaçao, itself managed by a discreet subsidiary of the Martin Yahl private bank.

And in 1956—in August 1956—everything pointed to the fact that this pyramid was made of pure gold. How had it changed to lead?

\* \* \*

I was ten feet from the house, and I still couldn't see anything. To the left, the low building consisting of garages and sheds, and the small lean-to where my half-horsepower scale-model red Ferrari had been kept. All the wooden doors were locked, sealed by chains and padlocks. You couldn't see anything inside.

In front of me was the house itself. It had twelve or fourteen rooms, I no longer remembered how many. A U-shaped building, opening toward the sea, its double-paneled front door now only a few feet away from me. I went up to it and raised the knocker. The dull thuds echoed in the silence of the night, but without any result, even after several minutes.

I decided to switch on the flashlight I had bought in Sainte-Maxime. It lit up the big oleander hedge to my right; the arbutus seemed to have grown taller, and I suddenly had the impression that the garden had been abandoned.

Who had bought the house when it had been put up for sale?

I went around the building, the smell of the sea in my nostrils. The garden was there, with its palm trees, its agave, its bougainvillea, its yucca, its oleander, its burning bush, and its masses of hortensea in a compact heap. The swimming pool should be on the left, and way at the back, no doubt, was the stone wall, ten feet high, with its metal gate and its staircase leading to the beach and the dock.

Turning around, I climbed the steps leading to the center of the U, to that kind of half-patio where we dined in the evening on nights vibrant with moths. The six French windows were likewise shut, and as the beam of my flashlight outlined the three façades, the closed shutters, the frieze of ocher tiles sticking out from the roof, I was permeated by the certainty that these French windows, these shutters, had not been opened for years.

*58*

Was it possible that not only was La Capilla empty—in this month of July when summer is in full swing in St. Tropez, each square foot of space occupied not once but twice over—but that it also had not been changed?

I rediscovered one of my childhood itineraries: I would climb to the roof of the lean-to, to that of the highest shed, and from there, clutching the roof and advancing onto the tiled frieze, I'd reach the dormer window, which lit up the attic bright as day.

The hook that held the shutter lifted as easily as before; a minute later, I was on the second floor, increasingly gripped by a dull anxiety and the feeling of a mute presence. Yet I would have sworn the house was deserted. But at the same time . . .

To my left, on the corridor, the big open space where you discovered the huge living room; to my right, the bedrooms. My room was at the back, at the end of the corridor; you could see the sea through the windows. My parents' room was in the other wing, so that from one balcony to the other, beyond the twenty-five or thirty feet of patio, my mother smiled and spoke to me each morning when I awoke.

Hesitation. But something drew me downstairs. Step by step on the staircase, I had the feeling of immersing myself in a universe both familiar and strange. A fascination grew in me; I felt it without understanding it. Almost in spite of me the beam of my flashlight traveled to the door of that room in the left-hand wing perpendicular to my parents' room. The door was slightly ajar. A stream of memories: we were on the beach, my father and I, a few minutes after the visitor's departure. There were three pretty naked girls, looking at my father and laughing. He spoke to them in his deep voice, with that slight accent he had when speaking French. We left the beach, climbed the stairs, crossed the garden. My beloved little red Ferrari stood on the patio amid the lounge chairs. I climbed into it. My father ruffled my hair, walked past, and entered that room on the left-hand wing, which was his office. We were alone in the house, he and I. My mother was out; the servants, Pascal and his wife, were off duty for the day. My father was in his office on the telephone. He was speaking German. I tried to start the Ferrari, without success. A dull thud and a muffled cry; it took me a moment to understand and to act. I went into the office and saw my father on the floor, crawling toward me, his face turning blue, his eyes bulging. He dragged himself and stretched out his hand to me, trying to speak. I was only eight years old, but I knew he was dying. I began to yell, and because no one else was at home, I rushed to the beach.

The three naked girls had started walking away and were already three hundred feet from me. I ran also, to that part of the beach where the sand was damp and firm, and when the four of us returned to the house, my father was already dead, lying on his back, his mouth wide open, holding in his hand a jet-black obsidian Buddha. The Buddha was potbellied, naked; he held both arms stretched out in front of him, his fingers almost perpendicular and spread wide; his head was leaning on his shoulder, his eyes were closed, and he smiled with an air of mysterious ecstasy.

I pushed open the door and went into the office, my flashlight leading me. Everything was in the same place as thirteen years ago; everything was intact, unchanged, exactly and fantastically the same—the phone he'd been speaking German to when the heart attack came, the carpet that had rumpled beneath him when he fell. Time froze and I was eight years old. I slumped back against the door, which I had closed after me.

With my head against the wood, I began to cry for the first time in thirteen years, my face in the dark, the flashlight beam focused on the little obsidian Buddha placed on a corner of the desk, giving me his impenetrable smile of boundless happiness.

\* \* \*

My father died on August 28, 1956, of a heart attack, in the office of his home in St. Tropez, as he was phoning someone whose name was still unknown. He was thirty-seven years old.

In August 1956, by my father's expressed wish, my mother and I were his sole heirs. On my mother's death, I should have taken possession of the Curaçao company, or at least the bearer shares which represented its ownership. Nothing was clearer on this point than my father's will, which named as executor Martin Yahl. The executorship concerned the total assets, official assets in France and Switzerland, or the holding company as defined by the act of trust.

Theoretically.

I did take possession of those bearer shares. I saw them, they were shown to me, and when I reached the age of twenty-one, they were even delivered into my hands. But they were worth nothing by then, weren't even worth the paper they were printed on. It was explained to me that everything stemmed from the way my father had built up his wealth from the beginning. "Your father," His Banking Highness Martin Yahl told me, "was an exceptional man, gifted with a real genius for creating. But creating implies administering; digging a tunnel implies that you shore up as you go along. Despite my urgent entreaties, your father would never shore up. And one day, everything collapsed. It is unhappily possible that the heart attack that killed him may have been caused precisely by his feeling of failure. . . ."

Thus spoke His Banking Highness. Him and his "urgent entreaties." I didn't think there was any man alive I could hate as much. I hadn't seen him in years; with me he always dealt through his underlings.

As for my father's Swiss and French assets, I was told that they had been used in their entirety to absorb losses suffered elsewhere. Yahl had proof, naturally, and was ready to face any examination by any specialist, in the event—absurd hypothesis— that the executor's integrity should be doubted. "Franz, I have taken care of you, even spoiled you, perhaps too much," said the letter that accompanied my inheritance. "You are now twenty-one years old; you are an adult under French law. I have decided, for the sake of the friendship and affection I felt for your father, despite his rash disregard of my advice, to dig into my own money and set up a fund to start you out in life, since your studies have unfortunately not been very successful."

I took the check handed me and I left Switzerland for England. In London, because of my crazy Annaliese, who was now dead, I thought I wouldn't be completely alone. I left Switzerland, half crazy with the hatred—inexplicable at the time—that I felt for that man. And I was more than half crazy—I spent that money in two months and fourteen days, in a suicidal frenzy.

*   *   *

Now I was back home, but the house was no longer mine. If the anonymous letter burning a hole in my shirt didn't lie, this house had been stolen from me, along with many millions of dollars. Instead of being the master here, I was nothing but a trespasser, a lawbreaker who came in the night with a flashlight, to climb over roofs and into windows.

I sat down at my father's own desk, in that high-backed black leather chair of his. The Buddha had his back turned to me. I turned him around, and we looked at each other, even though he had his eyes closed. From the breast pocket of my shirt I drew the letter I had received in Mombasa, two days before Christmas. I read it for the thousandth time: "At the time the executorship ended, you received approximately one million French francs, representing the remainder of your father's estate. In reality, that estate consisted of fifty to sixty million dollars, of which you have been robbed."

My father died in August 1956, here in this office. He died of a heart attack and according to Martin Yahl, he died penniless. So broke that it was necessary to sell everything, including the house where this office was located, including La Capilla itself. Nevertheless, out of love for my father, His Banking Highness had financed my youth, spoiled me—rotted would be more accurate, and I saw now that it was not out of kindness—and he had even, on my twenty-first birthday, generously dug into his own pocket in order to set up a dowry for me.

That was his version.

It was false, I was now convinced.

For the next three hours, I searched every cranny of the house, hoping that my father had left something for me, for me alone, a trace, a sign. If he had sent me a warning from beyond the grave, it would be hidden in this house or nowhere. He loved La Capilla, and wouldn't have traded it for anything. That should have alerted me: in the teeth of the worst disaster, my father would certainly have found a way to save this house. He hadn't done so. For me, the conclusion was clear.

I left the house with the first glimmers of dawn on the sea. I took with me the ecstatic Buddha, which I had stolen.

\* \* \*

At nine o'clock, I arrived at the Carlton in Cannes. After my shower I made a series of phone calls. It took me less than an hour to reach a notary.

"I am interested in a property in the town of St. Tropez, near the Pampelonne-Tahiti beach. It's called La Capilla."

"That property? I know it well. It is not for sale."

"I am prepared to pay a high price."

"Sorry, sir. Selling is out of the question."

"But I was told the property had been abandoned."

There was a short silence, and then "You have been misinformed, sir."

The voice was polite but firm, tinged with a slight Provençal accent.

"May I at least meet the owner? I would like to get in touch with him directly, for personal reasons."

I went as far as I dared without giving my name. No use.

"Sorry, sir."

The notary was a steel wall. After thanking him and hanging up, I spent a few seconds looking at the receiver. What if I had tried a bribe? Information can always be bought if it wasn't to be had for free. But somehow I was convinced that the bribery attempt would have failed.

I was irritated, and also puzzled. Why the mystery? Who had bought La Capilla, only to leave it intact, almost religiously intact, just as it had been thirteen years earlier when my father died?

Martin Yahl? Ludicrous.

Yet the person whom the notary described as "holding the ownership rights" had made a large financial commitment at the time of purchase. Even thirteen years ago, seventy-five acres on the St. Tropez peninsula did not come cheap, especially with a fourteen-room house built on them, with a swimming pool and outbuildings and a private dock. The buyer had means. He had them still—to the point where, even today, he didn't need this dammed-up capital. My mysterious owner was very rich.

I left Cannes that afternoon. The evening of July 10 found me in Paris, staying at the Ritz. Since that hotel had not been one of the hangouts of my dissolute years, there was a chance that I might pass unnoticed there. Once more to the telephone. The man I needed was dining out this evening, but his office would not tell me where. I tried pleading, cajoling, even threats. No dice. At last I played my trump card.

"What," I inquired, my voice dripping ice, "do you suppose Monsieur will say when he learns that more than a million American dollars have slipped out of his grasp because I could not reach him for an appointment? Do you think it will make him happy with you? Will he give you a bonus? Put extra francs into your pension plan? Or do you think you'll be looking through the Help Wanted columns, while the secretary of Monsieur's closest competitor is enjoying a juicy raise on that windfall million? Think about it. You have ten seconds."

"Restaurant La Bourgogne, avenue Bosquet."

*"Merci mille fois.* I guarantee that you have done nothing wrong or indiscreet, and a raise in pay will be coming in your direction very soon."

The man I wanted wasn't too pleased to be pulled away from his veal cutlet to answer the telephone. Especially since he'd never heard of me before. He listened to me grudgingly, then with surprise. At last, when I pulled out that tired and overworked (not to mention nonexistent) million, he agreed to meet me after his dinner, Trocadero, near avenue Georges-Mandel.

"How will I recognize you?" he asked.

"I'll be the one in the Rolls."

That reassured him a little; who would stage a kidnap in a Rolls-Royce? He was on time for the meeting, and drew his Citroën up alongside the Rolls. He hesitated, then, seeing my youth and realizing that I was alone, he came and sat down next to me, commenting:

"You're very young."

"Don't worry. It's not contagious."

I handed him the wad.

"Ten thousand dollars. On account."

He laughed a bit nervously, and later we would laugh together over the circumstances of that first meeting.

"If you're looking for a hired gun—"

I gave him a notepad and a pencil.

"The Martin Yahl Bank, main office avenue General-Guisan, Geneva."

I told him everything I knew about Curaçao. I told him my suspicions, in fact my certainty, that there had been an embezzlement, thirteen years earlier. He let his breath out with a whistle. After so many years! The trail would surely be cold!

"I want to know, first of all, if this embezzlement did in reality take place; secondly, if it is still possible to prove something, in other words, if the plot can be exposed. Finally, I want to know who besides Yahl is likely to have taken part in it."

"If there was indeed a conspiracy."

"Believe it. I want you to check it out for me, but with the utmost discretion. I don't want Yahl to know he's being investigated, and above all, I don't want him to hear any mention of my name. My intention is to take him by surprise when I eventually make my move.

"Understand that I am determined to recover what he has stolen from me. You and you alone have I trusted with this secret. You are the best man for the job, the *only* man for the job and I intend to make it worth your while. I will pay you three percent of the money I recover; that could easily be more than the million dollars I mentioned on the phone. I'll pay your expenses of course, plus five thousand American dollars a month."

I could feel his eyes boring into my face. My mouth was grim, my eyes were masked by sunglasses, and the interior of the car was dim, so he could form no clear picture of me. He thought it over for a minute or two, sifting the information in his head in that organized way of his I would come to know so well and depend on so utterly. At last he spoke.

"How did you get my name?" he asked cautiously.

I named the last person in the network I had gone through in fifteen or twenty phone calls. He was no less than a minister in office.

"I will check, of course," he said.

"Of course."

It was clear that his apprehension of a few minutes ago was now mixed with curiosity. The mystery with which I surrounded myself intrigued him. I had to admit, for my part, that I liked him well enough. My new partner's name was Marc Lavater; he was a man of about fifty. He had been one of the top officials in the French internal revenue administration, managing an inspection team on rue Volney; he had then crossed to the other side of the barricades, offering his counsel to those he had previously pursued. I had heard him praised for his effectiveness, the extent of his connections, even internationally, and what the last person I had spoken to called his "reliability."

He was a gray man, this Lavater, totally gray. His hair was thick and gray, his eyes were gray, his skin had a grayish cast, and he wore a three-piece suit of Oxford gray. Completely anonymous, he could slip through a crack and you would never notice he was gone. If your life depended on it, you couldn't give the police a description of this man. He was exactly what I wanted.

"The problem," Lavater said, "is that your affair is mainly based in Switzerland. I'm less comfortable there than in France. On the other hand—"

"Do you accept? Yes or no?"

"Let me finish. On the other hand, this would be a rather difficult investigation in France, especially if it had to be carried out without alerting the interested parties . . ."

"Yes or no?"

"On the other hand, I still have many friends in the Swiss treasury department. . . ."

"That's three hands."

He looked at the bills. I said:

"One million dollars at the end of the road. When I have my answers."

Lavater laughed.

"I will accept," he said. "Not for the money. Although I wouldn't turn it down. No, but because your story interests me."

I didn't believe him at the time. I was wrong. I would find that out later. I added now:

"And there's something else. . . ."

I told him about the house in St. Tropez.

"I want to know who bought it. And if the current owner is the same as thirteen years ago."

He asked me a few questions. No, he could not get in touch with me, it was I who would contact him again. He smiled, now completely at his ease:

"And may I ask your name?"

I returned his smile.

"Franz Cimballi. Call me Franz the Dancer."

\* \* \*

The next day, July 11, drooping a bit, I was back in Mombasa. To Sarah, I explained:

"The Seychelles without you are like cheese without a meal."

And a bit later, to Hyatt:

"You suggested we leave together for Hong Kong? Agreed. For me, Kenya is now history."

# 5

One thing about Hyatt; he knew Hong Kong. Why not? He'd been born there, and he spoke Chinese like a native; it was clear that he was more at home there than in Kenya.

Four days after my return from Europe, Hyatt and I left Mombasa. My business interests there would be well-looked-after by Chandra and Joachim. The only hard part was leaving Sarah.

"Come with me," I begged. We were lying side by side under the mosquito netting that canopied her bed. Bathed in sweat, our bodies were slick with our ferocious lovemaking. What a reunion! Every time I saw that face with its impeccable bone structure, that tall slimness of her body, I ached to strip her bare and devour her.

"Mmmmm," she replied noncommittally. Idly, her long fingers tickled my groin, winding around my penis, limp after hours of the most delicious exertion. "We'll see."

"No, be serious." Reprimanding somebody when both of you are stark naked is a bit ridiculous. "I'm leaving in a matter of days. We have to make our plans."

But Sarah wasn't to be distracted from this little labor of love, futile though it would be. "I *am* serious," she said. "What in hell would I do in Hong Kong?"

"The same thing you do here. Make wonderful love. I'll take care of you, Sarah. You won't have to worry about a thing."

Sarah's fingers tightened on my private parts, and I winced. "And if I don't want to be taken care of? Suppose I prefer to earn my own living and keep my independence?"

"Well, then, we'll find you a job. I'll miss you so much," I pleaded.

She shook her lovely dark head. "It won't be me you miss; it'll be this." And she slid down my damp body and closed that magnificent mouth of hers around my futile limpness.

Suddenly, it wasn't so futile any more. She was talented, that girl.

When we parted two days later, we said "au revoir," not "goodbye." Maybe she'd join me in Hong Kong later, maybe not. That was Sarah Kyle all over.

Now we had been in Hong Kong two weeks, Hyatt and I. Checking out the lay of the land. Hyatt set up appointments for us, but so far nothing had panned out. Still, he had confidence. And he had contacts. Confidence and contacts, combined with Hyatt's intelligence, made me sure that we would hit on something big pretty soon.

\* \* \*

In Hong Kong, in Central, Victoria Island, I walked along DesVoeux Road, following a route I had already traveled twenty or thirty times since my arrival. Soon I emerged in front of those two creamy gray buildings, geometric and ugly but impressive nonetheless, the Bank of China on the left, the Bank of Hong Kong and Shanghai on the right. That was where the three hundred fifty thousand "Kenyan" dollars I had deposited were resting, for the time being.

Kenya now seemed like a dream. Had I really earned so much money there in so short a time? Was the experience unique, or could I possibly do it again? I was still several months short of my twenty-second birthday, and the road ahead seemed not only perilous and filled with hazards, but also unclear. Whom could I trust? And what was the next step going to be?

I found it difficult to sleep at night; Hong Kong was very noisy, especially after dark, but it was also doubt and depression that kept me awake. I had less faith in myself than I did in Hyatt. He might dig up something wildly profitable for us to do, but I wasn't sure I could handle my end of the deal.

The cable railway leading to the Peak was a few hundred feet away, behind the Hilton. The climb was amazingly steep, but as the car—they were two, in fact, they counterbalanced each other—gained altitude, a breathtaking view was revealed: first, St. John's Cathedral, and the hills bordering the shore line; then, coming into view on the left, the Zoo; then, as the fabulous panorama widened, the tall towers of Victoria, the harbor and the Happy Valley appeared, then Wanchai and Causeway; and opposite, beyond the strait, Kowloon Peninsula, the tip of the Chinese continent, deeply scored by the rectilinear tracing of Nathan Road.

I had earned three hundred fifty thousand dollars. By luck or not. I could stop there, settle down, buy a bar and grill, marry someone, Sarah maybe. I could also gamble away every penny, and start over again as in Mombasa.

I thought I had a handle on my depression. It was partly due to missing Sarah more than I imagined I would; it was also due to the anxiety I felt when I thought about what I had set in motion in Europe with Lavater's help. Above all, it was due to Hong Kong; it was not a city in which I felt comfortable, that endlessly flowing Asian horde oppressed me. And finally, what was there to do? I had let Hyatt convince me to join him. Now that I was here, I could grasp the gigantic complexity of what we were undertaking.

I felt nostalgic for Mombasa, for my rides down Kilindini Road at the wheel of my Mini-Moke, waving to my customers and friends, to whom I was the "Little Boss." Here, I was nothing, and could scarcely see a way of becoming something.

Getting off the cable car, I reached Lo Fung, a restaurant on the third floor of the Victoria Peak tower. Waitresses moved back and forth between the tables, carrying dozens, if not hundreds, of different specialties, in the multiple baskets hung around their necks. According to Hyatt, Lo Fung was a dim sum restaurant, a Cantonese smorgasbord, and dim sum meant "little heart" in Cantonese. Hyatt, was already there, waiting for me.

"You look terrible. Is something wrong? At least try to smile at the guy who's coming. He may only be a sales manager, but a lot depends on him."

He launched into an enthusiastic description of the future in store for us, and almost immediately the man with whom we had an appointment arrived. A slim, elegant Chinese, he was dressed in cream-colored shantung, and he spoke English like an announcer for the BBC. He was very mildly condescending toward Hyatt, who either didn't notice or pretended not to notice. With me, the man acted differently. My youth intrigued him. And he made use of a short pause by Hyatt to ask me:

"Have you been partners for very long?"

I smiled. "Years. We were in the army together."

Some two hours later, the three of us were rolling across the Chinese mainland in a BMW, across Kowloon, toward the New Territories. I took my bearings; we were going northwest. I spotted an island on the left.

"Tsing Yi," commented Hyatt. "That's where they moved the shipyards that used to be in Hong Kong."

We filed past the interminable properties of the San Miguel brewery, which was flooding the Asian market with Tsing Tao beer. A bit further on:

"Here we are."

The factory employed six hundred people. Not a single Westerner; we were among Chinese.

"Toys, Franz," commented Hyatt. "I've got it all: the drop-off points in Europe, contacts with the distributors, everything. You know how much a doll made here costs in comparison with the same one made in Europe? Not even half. Maximum! It's a piece of cake. We work three or four months a year, and the rest of the time . . ."

A big wave of his chubby little hands. For Hyatt, that was the future: peaceful, guaranteed, a short three months of work, and then the *dolce far niente*, sweet leisure, the rest of the year. In a word, retirement.

"You don't seem too enthusiastic. Do you have something against toys? Christmas is coming?"

I had nothing against toys, nor against leisure. But I couldn't see myself spending my life in Hong Kong, in the middle of that sea of humanity where all the faces looked alike to me. We filed past the workshops, people smiled pleasantly at us, a foreman or the equivalent let loose a flood of explanations which Hyatt translated for me. Me, I thought of Sarah, of her slim, nervous body, of that sarcastic look she let slip between her half-closed eyelids. . . .

"Here is our design office."

I saw all kinds of battery-driven things, animals, vehicles, other dolls that cried and said "Mama" in thirty-six languages. We had been in that factory for at least two hours, and I was dying of boredom. Just as we were finally on the point of saying good-bye, something at last caught my eye. It looked like a back-scratcher. It *was* a backscratcher.

"But it's electric. You put it on your back and it runs by itself, so you don't have to move your arm. It's only a gadget."

Our sales manager, with whom we had lunched, was named Ching Something Unpronounceable. I asked him:

"And do you have other things like this?"

He shook his head, laughing.

"It's our young people in the design office who were having fun. It's only a gadget."

"Do you sell them?"

Another smile: "No, of course not. It's only—"

"It's only a gadget, I know."

For a dumb idea, it was a smart idea.

*    *    *

Back in Hong Kong. Ching, at my request, agreed to talk to me about those "young people in the design office who were having fun." Two of them, the nuttiest, it seemed, lived in Central. They worked mainly in films, in special effects, and were among the leading specialists in that fake blood that flows by the bucket in all those Kung Fu and horror films made in Hong Kong. That same evening, I met them in a Wanchai restaurant. Their names were Li and Liu, or the reverse; I could never manage to tell Li from Liu, or vice versa. They were about my age. When I told them of my idea, they howled with laughter.

"And you're planning to sell our electric backscratcher on Carnaby Street in London?"

"And elsewhere."

They laughed so hard tears rolled down their cheeks. We drank a kind of Chinese sake, called *hsiao shin*, or something similar; it's a wine the color of urine, exactly, made from rice and warmed before our eyes in a double boiler. After three or four sips, I had to hang onto the table. We met again the following morning, this time in the lobby of the Chamber of Commerce, and the three or four gadget ideas I suggested to them sent them off again into peals of laughter, which was definitely not caused by the *hsiao shin*.

There are no real customs formalities in Hong Kong for imports, much less for exports; there are only indirect taxes on a few products such as tobacco, liquor and gasoline. For my gadgets, no problem.

The Trade Licensing Section of the Commerce and Industry Department gave me a patent for free, immediately and with a smile. My exports would then be duty-free. Nevertheless, I would have to pay certain rights, rather modest ones at that, since it was often a question of materials—chiefly plastics—that were taxed, being manufactured locally and then directly exported from a factory belonging to the Colony. Later, I would even manage to nullify that provision. We were not at that point yet.

On the afternoon of the same day, the Commerce and Industry Department agreed in principle to grant me, for products that did not yet exist but would soon come into being, the obligatory certificate of origin. This was called a Generalized Preference Certificate of Origin, and would enable me to export as I wished to the six initial countries of the European Common Market, plus the United Kingdom, New Zealand, the Republic of Ireland, Sweden, Switzerland, Austria, Japan, the United States, Denmark, Greece, Canada, Australia, and several other countries.

"But you don't have Beluchistan, nor Burundi, nor Samoa either," Hyatt remarked acidly.

Hyatt thought I had flipped out. At that point in the business, I could hardly say he was wrong. I tried to explain to him, I told him what I had felt, on Carnaby Street in London, as it happened, before a display of nameless thingamajigs, without rhyme or reason, which people snatched up with all the more frenzy the more useless they were, in those open-air stalls near the Mary Quant boutique.

"There's a demand for things that don't serve any purpose. Or if it doesn't really exist yet, we'll create it."

"Not *we*. Count *me* out."

I tried as hard as I could to convince him, but I couldn't shake him. Hyatt dug in his heels. He clung to his idea of three months of work for nine months of vacation, and he wouldn't give in, he said. But I needed him, or at least his money. Ching's factory agreed to produce in surprising quantities the Glowing Shoehorn for Putting On Your Shoes Without Waking Your Wife, the Cold Scissors for Cutting Ice, the Talking Cigarette Lighter That Insults You Each Time You Light a New Cigarette, the Drunk Whose Red Nose Blinks Whenever Your Glass Is Empty, the Banana That Screams When You Peel It—the factory was willing to mass-produce all of that, on condition that I sign a firm order with them. Meaning that I had to commit my total capital to the business. But my savings were limited—especially since I might have to pay a bill for ninety thousand dollars that Marc Lavater might send me at any moment.

It's damn expensive to play Monte Cristo in a Rolls, even if I had had fun at the time. Then, too, I needed money to lay the groundwork in Europe, to set up the necessary contacts; and I still needed money to live on, in Hong Kong or elsewhere, while waiting for profits to develop.

If there were to be profits.

Hyatt's refusal left me at sea on a raft. I needed a hundred, or maybe as much as a hundred and fifty thousand dollars. No bank I consulted had faith in the gadgets, at that loan level.

"Hyatt, at least lend me money."

Tucking his chin into his neck he replied, "I offered you a gold-plated venture, three months of work, nine months of vacation; you weren't having any. Now it's my turn to say no."

And the days sped by. We were between the 15th and the 20th of August. Twice I had phoned Paris, and each time, Marc Lavater's secretary told me that Lavater was away and that there was no message for me. It might be true that there was no news to tell me yet, and it probably *was* true; I could hardly imagine him pocketing my money and forgetting me the next day. But this silence exasperated me.

Sarah's response also irritated me. I had cabled her twice, telegraphed and phoned. "You wouldn't have five hundred thousand dollars to lend me?"—or, more often, insistent: "Come here. I miss you."

"It's not easy to find a job in Hong Kong if you're a nice girl," she said.

"For God's sake, who's talking about a job?"

"Me, I am."

And Ching, who, each time we met, politely informed me that the factory was waiting on me. A final attempt with Hyatt. Nothing doing. He declared that even if he wanted to, he could no longer invest with me; he had sunk his money into transistor radios. I went back to Ching.

"Listen, Ching, there must be some way to see eye-to-eye."

"You can't change the work schedule of an entire factory without a guarantee."

It was a discussion we'd already had ten times.

"But your company could take some risks. The toy market is saturated; the gadget market is ready to be tapped."

"You think so? Truly?"

"Who would decide on your company having a possible interest in my business? Who gives the orders?"

"Not me," said Ching.

"Then who?"

One evening, Hyatt had uttered a name in my presence. Now the name came back to me.

"Mr. Hak?"

A surprised look from Ching.

"Mr. Hak is an important man."

"I would like to meet him. Can you arrange a meeting for me?"

"Impossible! Mr. Hak is a very very important man."

I insisted. Reluctantly, he agreed to try.

The following night, for the third time, I called Paris, where, because of the time difference, it was ten-thirty in the morning. This time Marc Lavater came to the phone.

"I have some of the information you asked me for. First, the house. It was bought on October 11, 1956, one and a half months after your father's death, by a notary acting on confidential instructions, for the sum of only four hundred thousand new francs. A bargain! The official owner is a company registered in Lichtenstein. They call this an *Anstalt*, an establishment, in Vaduz. Total discretion, impossible to find out more."

"Is it still the same owner today?"

"The same."

"The activities of this *Anstalt*?"

"None. Absolutely. But each year, someone pays the small tax claimed by the Lichtenstein government, as well as the fees of the Vaduz attorney with whom the *Anstalt* is officially domiciled.

"I attempted to follow the trail: the funds come from Switzerland, a numbered account. Don't ask me how, but I went beyond that: I came up with a second lawyer in Geneva—silent as a carp—who is paid by automatic withdrawal from a second numbered account that is regularly replenished. I couldn't get beyond that. One thing is certain: the owner is not your banker. He himself, a few years back, made an inquiry identical to mine and fell flat on his face."

Martin Yahl had tried to discover the identity of the buyer of the house . . . . I digested the news.

"And the other matter?"

"It's shaping up," said Lavater.

At a distance of nearly six thousand miles, I heard a kind of excitement in his voice. Looking out on the illuminated Hong Kong night, I suddenly felt a fever that all but made me tremble.

"Listen," Lavater said, "this is a fantastic embezzlement scheme. Mind you, I have no proof. And if you want my opinion, I'll never have any. Nevertheless I have an impression, almost an absolute conviction. It's unlikely that your father died penniless. Our investigation is positive—"

"Positive!" I exclaimed, interrupting. My heart pounded.

"There was manipulation, embezzlement, despoilment, misappropriation of a legacy, call it what you wish. Fifty or sixty million dollars, your anonymous correspondent wrote. In my opinion, that could even be an underestimation. We may be speaking of double, maybe even triple that amount."

I tried to digest this information, but it stuck in my throat, suffocating me. At last, I managed to croak out, "Any chance of a lawsuit?"

"Without fresh evidence—zero. Unless someone agrees to talk. And I don't believe anyone will."

"Why?"

"Because the scheme was fantastically well constructed."

"By whom?"

"Even if I had names to give you now, I wouldn't say them over the phone. But whoever authored the scheme had accomplices on all levels. We only suspect who they are. One thing I *can* tell you. There are men who, thirteen years ago, became richer than their greediest dreams, and overnight."

"I want their names."

"I'll try. Give me some more time. I need money."

"I'm sending you forty thousand dollars."

"Not to me, please. To the account number I gave you."

"Yes, of course. The remainder when I receive what you're sending."

"I don't have your address."

Unhesitatingly:

"My name, care of Miss Sarah Kyle, White Sands Hotel, Mombasa, Kenya. A little while ago you said you were going to explain why I'd never have a chance to prove the embezzlement. Why?"

"Because I'm almost certain that it's the same man who designed the plan for your father's company, who then, with virtual genius, dismantled everything, erased everything, rebuilt it all elsewhere, without leaving the slightest trace or the smallest evidence. I'm not afraid to use the word: the guy who did this was a genius. It was prestidigitation, magic. I am personally filled with admiration."

*If you think it's impossible to hate a man you've never laid eyes on, hate him so much that every bone in your body aches with the will to destroy him, then think again. I assure you it's possible. All you have to do is remember your beloved father's face turning blue as he gasped for the life-giving air which eluded him. And your mother, hounded in her very death-bed, unable to leave this wretched world in peace. Remembering those desecrations, and all in the name of money, how is it possible not to hate, not to live only for revenge?*

"Do you know who it is?"

"Did you ever hear your father speak of a man named William Carradine?"

"No."

"How about Will Scarlet?"

"No . . . yes . . . that name sounds familiar."

"The two are one and the same. At Harvard many years ago, the students nicknamed William Carradine Will Scarlet, because of his bloody reputation. Even as a boy, he was a shark. He was a classmate of Martin Yahl, and the two remained associated. It was Scarlet who performed the manipulations. He was a genius at it."

So far, Lavater had refused to name any names, and yet here he was talking freely about a "Will Scarlet." I didn't get it, and I told him so.

Already a plan was beginning to form in my mind, taking shape slowly. My strongest ally was my youth. Yahl thought me a child, a fool, a wastrel, a bankrupt. A boy with nothing more than milk teeth. Good. He would learn that those milky white teeth could turn into venomous fangs. But he would not know it was me until the very last moment. I would draw a circle around him, circle of money, and, inch by inch, the invisible circle would draw tighter and tighter, a noose of wealth and power that would eventually strangle him.

I would not seek him out, no, nor would I confront him. That would be too easy. Why give your enemy a warning? Instead, I would stay as far away from him as possible, so that his suspicions would be diverted and I could act with more freedom. I would use men like Lavater to draw the circle for me, while I remained anonymous. And money was the answer. More money than I had ever dreamed of. More money than Yahl had stolen from my father and from me. It would take time, but then time was on my side, *n'est ce pas?* I was so young, so very very young, while Yahl was getting older by the minute.

I laughed into the telephone, startling Lavater. The dance was about to begin.

"Ah, yes," replied Lavater, and his voice was tinged with irony. "That's because Will Scarlet is dead."

Well, there it was, in a confirmed nutshell. I had been cleverly and systematically robbed of everything that should have been mine. Everything that my father had worked so hard to ensure would be mine. Like Hamlet, my father's ghost was pleading with me for revenge. And my own young hot blood cried out for vengeance. One of my enemies had already escaped me by dying.

Because of my youth and my impetuosity, I wanted nothing more than Martin Yahl's wrinkled throat between my angry hands. I wanted to see his eyes bulge, hear him gasp hoarsely for mercy. And I would show no mercy, even if I had to hang for it. But no, that was not the way to go. *Kill your enemy with his own weapon*, spoke a voice in my ear. *Carry the battle into his own fortress, where he least expects to see you. It will take time, it will not happen tomorrow, but you must be patient. Besides, don't the Italians have an old saying: "Revenge is a dish that people of taste prefer to eat cold "?*

Yes, I would take my revenge, but slowly and with infinite patience. And it would be a vengeance that Yahl would recognize and fear, for it would be taken with a weapon made of money. Money! I despised it, even while I recognized its usefulness and power. But Yahl worshipped it, revered it enough to steal it and amass it and kill for it. It warmed him, protected him, shielded him . . . or so he thought. Yahl believed that money, piled high enough, would assure him of immortality. He was wrong.

\* \* \*

Phone call from Ching.
"Are you available tomorrow evening after six o'clock."

"Sure."

"Let me pick you up at the Mandarin Hotel. Five-thirty."

Nothing more, but I understood: I was going to meet the "very, very important" Mr. Hak. I asked Hyatt to fill me in about him.

Hyatt looked at me in surprise: "I'd be amazed if you ever managed to speak to him."

"What's so special about him? He lives in heaven and sits on a cloud?"

"He's very important."

"Shit. I'm important, too. I'm the most important guy I know. Is he that rich?"

"It's not a question of money. Not entirely. This is Hong Kong." And Hyatt looked at me as though he had given me crucial information. Some days, I could kill him.

The huge Mercedes picked us up at the Star Ferry landing. We zoomed toward the Kaitak airport, where we boarded a small tourist plane. Heading due north, that is, toward mainland China. At my side, Ching did not blink. The flight was actually very short, about ten minutes, and soon I glimpsed, under our wings, in the waning light, a mountainous island, which seemed inhabited by only a tiny fishing village nestled in an inlet.

"Are we in China?"

"We're still in Hong Kong, in the New Territories. But China is over there."

A line on the horizon, barely a few miles away. The plane touched down, jolting along a short concrete runway. A Land Rover with a Chinese chauffeur. A road wound, climbed, bumped over two or three hills, and the vegetation suddenly appeared, replacing the somewhat sinister rocks and bare earth. I recognized Chinese banyans, camphor trees and pines, which hadn't grown there by themselves. Somebody had planted them. A little farther on, at the end of a double row of eucalyptus forming a driveway, in a sea of white camellias, dwarf magnolias and azaleas, a verandah appeared. Getting out of the Land Rover, Ching and I marched between a double wall of orchids. The ground was of perfect, uncracked concrete without a step of any kind. It was very beautiful and extraordinarily quiet, bordering on oppressive.

Mr. Hak's house was in front of me. Awaiting me was one of the most surprising encounters of my life.

# 6

My eyes were drawn, first, to his hands. They were long and thin, elegant, even graceful. On each one, the nail of the little finger was disproportionately long, more than four inches.

But very quickly, my attention was drawn elsewhere, even turning to fascination—to his legs. Mr. Hak wore a black silk dressing gown which parted at mid-thigh level and revealed two strange, shiny metal devices. They were cylinders; no one had even bothered to give them the shape of real human limbs. Such indifference to esthetics, to convention, was impressive; at any rate, it impressed me. On the steel, at the place where the knee would normally be, I could see grooves intersecting at right angles, forming eight small squares. And likewise on the other leg. Mr. Hak remained seated. Could he stand on fake gleaming metal legs?

"Would you like something to drink, Mr. Cimballi?"

I turned; Ching had silently vanished, leaving us alone. We were in a living room, but the many neighboring rooms, were defined by light partitions, possibly movable. The floor appeared to be of genuine marble, an almost black marble veined with silver gray. No staircase was in sight, everything was flat. There was very little furniture, but what there was seemed to be ultra-luxurious. I noted particularly the stunning screens of black and geranium red lacquer.

"Would you care for some champagne?"

"Yes, thank you."

I expected to see a servant appear. But we remained alone, and it was Mr. Hak's hand that moved. He placed it on his left thigh. The nail of a little finger went into one of the grooves and lifted a tiny flap; a microscopic dial appeared, containing four buttons as big as the head of a pin. Mr. Hak's fingernail brushed these buttons according to a prearranged code. The flap closed again.

Mr. Hak rose, and as he walked I watched with trepidation; he advanced, keeping his chest, and indeed his whole living body, perfectly still; I would have sworn that the line of his shoulders was perfectly horizontal. And yet, he advanced, he moved, like those marvelously adjusted electronic toys, whose metal base is the only thing that moves. The movement was similarly smooth, of the same technical perfection.

We came into a room with a rear wall that was completely semicircular. Armchairs and sofas occupied the center, all facing the curved wall.

"Sit down, please . . . ."

A very slight motion behind me. Moving in total silence on the marble floor, a rolling table with rubber wheels came slowly toward us, without any servant pushing it. It was remote-controlled, coming to rest gently at Mr. Hak's side, like a pet dog.

"Which of these champagnes do you prefer?"

"That's more than I hoped for. Please choose for me?"

Mr. Hak sat down. It was apparently the only movement that was hard for him; he let himself fall backward. As soon as he was seated, his hand opened other microscopic flaps, this time on his right knee. Then several things happened. Another rolling table appeared, just as silent as the first, offering several rows of tiny patés, fish tidbits, shrimp, cuttlefish, fritters of all kinds, small filled rolls, and other savory delicacies. At the same time, music filled the air; it was western music, richly harmonic, Brahms, I'm certain.

Simultaneously, the black lacquer panel on the semi-circular wall slid back silently. Revealed was a glass partition eight feet high and forty feet long, and, behind the partition, the sea itself. The water was lit by projectors with multicolored lights that changed continuously, and the living creatures in the water's depths were outlined by bursts of color as they glided or darted by. The entire room was under water! I couldn't help a gasp of admiration.

"I'm impressed."

"Thank you, Mr. Cimballi."

He served the champagne himself. Then he asked me about Kenya. I didn't know what he knew about me but I had nothing to hide. I told him the circumstances of my leaving London and of my money-changing venture. I even told him about the gold. His keen, intelligent gaze never left my face.

"Why Kenya?"

I shrugged. "It was on the map."

He smiled:

"All right. Tell me about these . . . things . . . you want to manufacture."

"There's not much to tell. I believe there is a market, a large one. I believe I can develop and exploit it. That's all."

A few minutes earlier, I'd been ready to launch into impassioned explanations, in short, to sell my idea in the best way possible. Since facing this half-artificial man, I knew that would be useless. Perhaps it was that very discretion which convinced him; or perhaps everything was decided in a few seconds, as often happens. In any event, he informed me that evening that the factory of which Ching was sales manager belonged to him, to him, Hak, personally; that it was not the only factory he controlled, that there were several others, making various products, and that he was willing to cover my investments in the gadgets up to the sum of one hundred fifty thousand dollars, and perhaps even beyond that.

He did not tell me that evening what I learned later, that Mr. Hak was in fact one of the major semi-official businessmen allowed to operate in mainland China, and that, as such, he controlled and managed substantial goods and capital, not only in Hong Kong, but throughout Southeast Asia and even a bit farther. His importance would become crucial to my future and would one day come to a startling ending.

When I got back to Hong Kong—that is, Victoria—nothing now prevented me from throwing myself into this venture which Hyatt had rejected. All the same, by the end of that August—perhaps shaken up by the support I had miraculously found from Mr. Hak—Hyatt agreed to help me. The European sales network of which he had boasted in fact did exist, and it was agreed that he would accompany me to Paris to set up the contacts I needed. I suggested one last time that he become my partner; again, he refused. He preferred, he said, to be on a regular retainer.

It would be the worst decision of his life. In eleven months to the day, the creation, distribution, and sale of the "gadgets" would realize a net sales figure of nearly eight million dollars.

My share, after deducting Mr. Hak's: one and a half million dollars.

The dance, Franz—the dance continues.

Faster, faster.

* * *

We had been in London for several days, Hyatt and I—London, where the contacts Hyatt boasted of finally proved useful, perhaps less so than Hyatt claimed, yet more so than I had expected.

Obviously, I had no intention of calling on every retailer in the United Kingdom with a briefcase filled with samples, like a door-to-door salesman peddling novelty items. No, modern times call for modern methods, and the most modern of them was Ute.

Six feet tall, a Scandinavian by birth and a nudist by religion, Ute Jenssen was one of Europe's leading fashion models. She would stride down the runway, shaking her non-existent hips and throwing back her mane of butter-colored hair, and buyers would scribble furiously on their order pads, sure that whatever Ute was modeling would set their stores on fire. She could sell anything.

When I explained to her about the T.N.T. Bottle Opener and the Pedal-Operated Alligator Caddy, as well as my other beloved pieces of nonsense, she raised one golden eyebrow, tilted her head on one side and took a large bite out of an organic carrot; she carried sacks of them around with her at all times.

"Maybe you're crazy," she said in her Greta Garbo accent. "Maybe not. Ve'll see, von't ve?"

"How much is all of this going to cost me?" I asked her cautiously. We were sitting over tea at the Dorchester. I preferred to be sitting in her presence, since she towered over me like a lighthouse.

"You can't afford me," she laughed, showing very white teeth. "I get top rates, 150 pounds an hour. But for you, I vill vork for nothing, ja? Absolutely free."

"What's the catch?" I asked her amiably.

"You pay me a commission on sales, that's all. These are idiotic little gadgets, ja? Trashy . . . absolute rot. But these are trashy times, ja? Ve should do verrrry vell vit them. Especially if *I* do the demonstrating." She batted two inches of mink eyelashes at me and I was her captive. That Danish girl could sell anything, as I said before. If she sold my products the way she sold me . . .

"Let's go to my suite and discuss it, ja?" I asked her.

Ute shrugged her gorgeous shoulders and took another bite of her carrot. She had left her scones and jam roll, her buttered toast and little sandwiches, completely untasted while she chomped on her horse-fodder.

When we stood up, I felt like a dwarf beside her, but as she passed through the Dorchester lobby to the lift, so many men cast me looks of heartfelt envy, I was a giant by the time we reached the door to my room.

But Hyatt was there, looking frightfully disapproving, and, when Ute and I began to discuss business, he waved his arms and shook his head no-no behind her back. He didn't want her aboard, that much was obvious.

What Hyatt didn't see was that his every gesture could be seen by Ute in the large gilt-framed mirror on the wall where the two of us were sitting. With a grin, my Danish pastry stood up, grabbed Hyatt by the arm, and ushered him out of the suite, locking the door behind him.

"There," she said. "Now ve can talk. I may look like a control tower, but I'm not a complete idiot. This business is going to put a lot of lettuce on my Danish china. I want exclusive rights to the British Isles and Denmark."

She took off various things she had on, and what I'd heard about her was absolutely true; she didn't wear underpants.

"I'm never cold," she explained.

"Especially your eyes. The British Isles and Denmark? And what else?

We stretched out side by side on the bed, and her feet went six inches farther than mine, even though our heads were together.

"I could ask you for Sweden and Norway, but no, I'm reasonable. And I only want ten percent."

I snorted.

"Half a percent will suffice."

The first interruption. For such a beanpole, she had amazingly large breasts. I began to investigate them, first with my hands, then with my lips and tongue.

"Five percent," she said.

"Nuts." The word seemed to give Ute some ideas and there was another, longer interruption.

"I have lots of business ideas," she said a bit later, out of breath. "I could form a squadron of girls. For example. Without bras."

Interruption. Her skin smelled like jasmine, and there was plenty of it. I finally said:

"One percent is okay."

She got up, opened the window, put the air conditioner on high, and seeing that I was freezing, decided to warm me up.

"Three percent."

"One-and-a-half."

"Two."

"Rape! Rape!"

\* \* \*

Paris.

After the usual laborious calculation, I realized it must be three o'clock in the morning in Hong Kong, the time when Li and Liu were usually at the top of their form. I put through a call. By some miracle that would never be repeated, the telephone worked instantly, and I had Li or Liu, one or the other, at the other end of the line. I had gotten some new gadget ideas in London, and had quickly filed for patents, namely a Laughing Bag (a bag that gives off a vampire-ghost laugh whenever you pick it up), and especially the Phantomas Bank, a piggy bank which shoots out a hand to grab the coin from your fingers, which would become one of my most popular items. Li and Liu went into intercontinental hysterics.

"For the sake of unity, take your time," said Hyatt, who was growing more bitter by the day, now that he saw the gadget business beginning to take on amazing proportions. He could smell success on the way; the reaction in France only strengthened his belief. He realized it even more at a meeting with American businessmen. My gadgets interested them, and I held the patents.

Quickly, we signed contracts, or agreed to do so. Either they would buy directly from me in order to resell, or they would manufacture themselves under my license. It was decided that Hyatt would go with them to the United States to settle the final details, while I would take care of Europe. Normally, Hyatt would have remained while I crossed the Atlantic, but I wanted to see Marc Lavater.

\* \* \*

"I still don't have much news," Lavater told me. "Did I mention the Leonis to you?"

"No."

"They're a couple who were hired ten or twelve years ago to care for La Capilla, in St. Tropez. They were hired by the notary.

*84*

I interviewed them myself; they don't know anything, never saw anything, except once a car registered in Switzerland, a Mercedes, they think, which arrived after nightfall and left again before sunrise. The notary had informed them beforehand, asking them not to interfere or try to identify who was in the car. And the fact is that they didn't see anyone."

"When was this?"

"August 28th, three years ago."

The tenth anniversary of my father's death.

Lavater cocked a brow at me.

"I even wondered if it hadn't been you."

"Very funny. I'm howling."

"Relax. The Leonis know nothing. The orders they receive are to keep the house in order, without changing anything."

Rage was mounting inside me. Who was the owner of the house in St. Tropez? *Who was it?* The mystery was driving me half-crazy. I asked Lavater:

"And the notary? Can't we buy him?"

"Also funny," said Lavater. "My turn to howl."

He smiled at me, soothingly:

"Come on, don't look so tragic. It will all clear up in the end. Why don't you join me for dinner, one of these evenings?"

"And what about the rest? That list of names you promised me?"

"I was going to send you an initial report in a few days and mail it to you in Kenya. But here you are in Paris. You'll have to wait a little longer. Would you like me to return your fifty thousand dollars? I'll give it back to you right away, if you wish."

Our friendship had probably started earlier, but it officially began at that moment. I managed to smile at him, despite the rage that continued to knot my stomach.

"Okay, I'll wait. Not patiently, but I'll wait. And I'll come to your house for dinner one of these evenings. Gladly."

Two days passed, in which I never stopped running. On the basis of Hyatt's network, which turned out to be quite useful, I set up a European organization, with men whose relations with me would outlive the gadget business, and whom I would meet again later on; such as Letta, in Rome.

Adriano Letta was a mongrel, a little of everything—part French, part Italian, a little Arabic thrown in. He was originally

85

from Tunis, but now he lived almost exclusively in Rome, which he regarded as something of a private domain. He knew everybody, and everybody knew him.

Letta resembled nothing more than a Barbary pirate, with his crooked teeth bared in a wolfish grin, and tufts of hair growing out of his ears, he was nevertheless a gentle and very intelligent man, with a raffish sense of humor very like my own. He would prove an invaluable friend in times to come.

The triumph of my new venture was not enough to rid me of that raging, near-anguish which Lavater's information had instilled in me. Hyatt had left for the United States and I was alone, two days before my birthday when I would be twenty-two years old. I had holed up in my hotel room dead with fatigue, after ten or twenty meetings and discussions. I picked up the telephone, toying nervously with the tape recorder-cigarette lighter which, each time you open it, thunders in your ear: "You're gonna get cancer, you poor bastard!" Subtle as hell, and in good taste, besides . . . . But the worst part was that it would work. Work? It worked already. We had sold tens of thousands in three days. I dialed London direct.

"Ute? Take the first plane and come here."

"Only if I feel like it, little chum."

"Do you feel like it?"

"Yeah."

"Okay, see you later."

She arrived at ten-thirty, straight from a taxi, a plane, another taxi; she carried two volumes of the *Encyclopaedia Britannica*, and, hanging from her shoulder, a full sack of carrots, like a horse of the National Guard bringing his own meal to a picnic. I took her to dinner on Place de la Madeleine. We sat down and I assumed a pitiful air:

"I'm sad, Ute."

She opened her shirt, and while various waiters choked, showed me one of her breasts: she had painted a daisy on it, with her nipple as the flower bud. It was very pretty.

"And the paint is nearly indelible, and when you lick it, it tastes like raspberry. Want a lick?"

I looked at the maitre d', the sommelier, the waiters, and the twenty or thirty customers who were staring at us. I gave them an imbecilic smile, and answered:

"Raspberry doesn't go with lobster tails, does it?"

She stroked my cheek.

"Are you still blue?"

"Not in the least. Put your tittie back now."

When we returned to my hotel room, Ute undressed briskly, almost clinically. She hated clothing, and would have been happy frolicking on some frigid beach on the North Sea, totally in the nude. She was a Viking, that one! I looked at her with appreciation—that incredibly long line of creamy skin from her shoulders to her ankles, the prow of a Norse ship. Her eyes were cat-green, her nose snub and tilting upward, and her jaw rounded and dimpled. The picture of health, thanks, no doubt, to carrots, but I just wasn't turned on.

Once more she offered me a lick of the daisy on her breast, but I shook my head and sighed.

"What is it, Franz? This isn't like you, little one."

"In the first place, I'd rather not be called little one, thank you," I retorted in a chilly tone. "And in the second place . . ."

"Ja?"

Now I drooped, a forlorn flower. "Today is my birthday, and nobody remembered . . . nobody phoned . . . nobody wrote." I milked the sympathy bit for everything I could; it didn't occur to either of us that probably nobody on earth knew my birthdate except myself and the Bureau of Records.

"I vill give you a present, Franz. See here?" Ute threw herself on the bed, and let her thighs fall temptingly apart. "This you can have if you vant it . . ."

I let a sigh escape me, but I eyed the golden fur between Ute's thighs with some interest. After all, it was the only birthday gift offered me the entire day. I took possession of it. First, I merely cupped it in my palm, letting the soft warmth of my present tickle my hand. Then I began to explore it gently, then more seriously, while Ute panted and moaned under my exploration. The sound of her whimpers and the feel of her golden pussy worked on me, and soon my passion was equal to hers. But still I kept all my clothing on, preferring to watch Ute come to climax, as she did, again and again. The bedroom lights were bright enough to see the color of her erect nipples grow darker with excitement as she writhed on the bed.

First, I made her come only by using my hand. Then I did it again with my lips and tongue. Finally, she lay still, bathed in a love-dew.

"And you, Franz? It is your birthday, not mine, ja?"

Very slowly I stood up, and pulled my garments off one by one, Ute's eyes on my body. I was very excited, erect and hard as stone. Ute saw my stiffness.

Carefully, as though the girl were made of glass, I lowered myself onto her, taking my weight on the heels of my hands on either side of her. Our bodies didn't touch; our only point of contact was our genitals. Now I thrust hard into her, all the way, and she cried out.

Furiously, I stroked again and again, all my nerve endings concentrated in my penis, which had swelled larger than I'd ever seen or felt it.

She rose up to meet my every stroke, her narrow hips and bony pelvis matching me in ferocity. All my frustrations, all my expression, my pent-up hatreds, all were concentrated just *there*, between my legs, and I beat at the girl with a jackhammer that moved faster and ever more furiously, until both of us screamed in surrender, and I collapsed on top of her, all passion spent.

Later, we made love again, but this time more like friends; it was cozy and snuggly and satisfying and when it was over, I fell sound asleep, and slept until late morning, the first good night's sleep I'd had in weeks.

\* \* \*

"Where would you like the tray?" asked the chambermaid sarcastically. "On the table or on your face?"

I knew that voice. I opened my eyes.

"Hi, Sarah, what a surprise."

She stared at Ute, whose head and feet alone were sticking out, at the two ends of the bed.

"Holy Jesus!" she cried. "Did you put two together, or is it all the same one?"

Pushing the sheet away from her face, Ute opened one sleepy eye and gave Sarah the same long, calculating look that Sarah was giving her. Caught in the middle, like the pickle in a sandwich, I wished I were back in Mombasa, Hong Kong, anywhere but here.

"So, shorty," hissed Ute. "Vere were you ven he needed you?"

"On my way," snapped Sarah. "It's not just across the street, you know."

Ute shrugged. "Vell, now that you're here . . ." she pulled the sheet back invitingly.

88

Sarah didn't have to be asked twice. She put the breakfast tray down and was out of her clothes and into the bed before you could say "sex" three times.

And once more I was caught in the middle, like a pickle in a sandwich. Only this time I loved it.

\* \* \*

The day after next, a Friday, in the evening, we landed in Geneva, Sarah and I. In Cointrin, I rented a car, and crossing Geneva without stopping we entered France by way of Anne-masse. The road quickly began to rise. In Cluzes, I bore left, toward Morzine; the Parador was about to close, but they had agreed to wait for us and receive us there, warning us that we would be alone and that the staff would be reduced. Sarah's sarcastic green gaze between her eyelids.

"And whence this sudden passion for mountains?"

"I had enough of the Kikuyus, the Chinese, the tropics. I wanted to see some cows."

"Then we should have gone to Normandy. Normandy is full of cows."

She was no fool, and had never been and would never be one with me. She asked:

"When do you want us to go to Geneva?"

"Who said anything about Geneva?"

"My eye. When? Today? Tonight, with big capes and black velvet masks on our faces?"

"Tomorrow. No, the day after tomorrow."

"Because it will be Sunday and there won't be a soul on the streets. It all becomes clear. By the way, you fool, happy birthday. Why do you think I left my twelve African lovers? Happy birthday, Franz. There are times when I almost like you, you know."

\* \* \*

Everything happened as she had foretold. Sunday morning around nine o'clock, Geneva was nearly as deserted as our hotel had been. As a final precaution that made Sarah chuckle, I had parked on the other bank of the Leman, and we crossed the Rhone on foot, over the little Bergues Bridge, with a stop in the small garden of Rousseau Island. From there we could easily see the bank and its façade; you could even read the name Yahl on it.

89

It made me tremble. Sarah took my hand, and leaned her shoulder against mine.

"You're nuts, Franz. Are you going to spend your life trying to get even with that guy? Who ever heard of getting even with a Swiss banker?" She knew something, had guessed even more.

Her hip against mine also. Sarah had a thin body, constantly and completely tanned, she was naturally dark, her hair in fact almost black; she was slim but muscular, nervous, her breasts were small and hard. Making love with her was not necessarily gentle, but more often a battle, which I won only occasionally.

"Franz, forget everything and let's go to Hong Kong together. Your future is ahead of you, what can I tell you? You're going to be rich. Forget that man. You may be richer than he is one day. And then you can give him the finger."

"Shit."

"I want some coffee."

"Let's walk past it, at least."

"And pee against his door."

We finished crossing the Rhone, crossing, too, the square leading into Mont-Blanc Bridge; the fountain was on our left, the bank's façade on our right. Sarah whispered:

"Maybe he's in there now, crouching in the shadows, waiting for you with his jackal's black eyes."

"Blue, his eyes are blue. Like two pieces of glacial ice."

"What about my coffee?"

Across from the Touring Club, we bore right to return to the rue de Rive. It was over. Taking a look at Yahl's bank hadn't accomplished anything, of course. But I was still ill and shaky from it. Sarah was alarmed by my pale face. "My God, Franz, is it that bad? You're crazy. And I'm serious."

We went back to Morzine, and there, it was she who made love to me, with unaccustomed tenderness. Afterward, she went back and forth in the room with that busy look that women are so prone to get inside what they consider their home, be it merely a hotel room. I asked her:

"Did you really believe what you told me, that I'm going to make a fortune?"

She burst out laughing, and I got the green flowing look I knew so well.

"Yes. And you'll get fat, you'll wear three-piece suits, own a yacht, and two electric razors in case the first one gets broken. Now let's get going or we'll miss our plane."

* * *

I called Hong Kong and confirmed that things were going well. Ching's factory was working at peak production, and the resources of some of Mr. Hak's other factories had been called in to handle the overflow. My silly gadgets were pouring off the assembly lines.

With Sarah at my side, I made some feverish airline reservations. We went to Germany, Italy, Spain and Scandinavia. We also flew to Egypt, Morocco and Greece. It was an odd time for me, poised on the brink of events, with everything just about to happen. I attended sales meetings all over the globe, presenting the prototypes of the inventions, garnering orders and contracts until my attaché case was bulging and couldn't close. But still I continued to travel, it was as though I couldn't sit still.

At night, back at whatever hotel Sarah had booked us into, we made love until we were both drained. I couldn't sleep. I kept trying to penetrate the future, to see around the closed doors to what was to come. By day, a dynamo; by night, an anxious boy of twenty-two.

Hyatt was returning from New York and California, and we arranged to meet in Rome. He came in flushed with success, but underneath his pride and apparent triumph, there was a thin strain of bitterness. None of the profits he generated were going to be his; he had missed an opportunity not once but twice. I was tempted to re-make our deal to include him in the profit-sharing, but something stayed my hand. After all, he was a grown man with the power of choice. Wouldn't it be wrong to treat him as a child, to be given a lollipop whenever he cries?

He had made his decision and it was a wrong one. It would be insulting to pretend that his decision had never existed, or could be cast aside. I *would* give him a hefty bonus, though, as soon as the money came in. He had earned it.

I was so busy at this point that I had neglected to call Marc Lavater, as agreed. I finally reached him, not in his office, but at another number he had given me, in a house near Chagny in Burgundy.

"I wondered what had happened to you—"

I suddenly knew there was news.

"—especially since I didn't know where to reach you. Well, I won't waste words, I have your list."

Silence. My hand gripped the phone as if to break it.

There is pleasure in hatred.

"How many are there?"

"Six."

"Including Martin Yahl?"

"Naturally. As far as I could, I classified these gentlemen in their order of responsibility for what happened. And Yahl comes first. As you suspected he's traitor number one."

I had called Lavater from Rome, and was preparing to return to Hong Kong, where Ching had been clamoring for me for days. Now I thought quickly and said to Lavater:

"Miss Sarah Kyle will be at the Ritz in Paris this evening. Can you have the list delivered to her?"

He agreed.

Sarah frowned. She didn't care for me to decide for her like that.

"Thanks, Marc."

I was about to hang up when Lavater said, "Cimballi? Franz?"

"Yes?"

"Make it as hot for them as you can. They're a gang of rogues who don't expect to have to face consequences."

I smiled at the receiver. Rising in me like an irresistible tide, I felt the fierce elation of Old Brompton Road, more powerful and fiercer than ever.

Oh was I going to make them sweat!

# 2. Operation Golden Dragon

# 7

With excitement bubbling in my blood, I flew back to Hong Kong. Sarah accompanied me. At this point, we were very close, and not only physically.

Was I in love with her? I can't say. If my life hadn't been so complicated by business and revenge I might have settled down with her and been happy. As it was, she was like an afterthought. When she was gone, I missed her, but when she was around I paid little attention to her apart from sex. Still, we were close. It was as though she could read my mind, as though I didn't need to talk to her for her to know my thoughts and feelings. She herself was independent, and always wanted—and took—time out from our relationship.

We had decided to share digs.

Personally, I would have chosen to live in Kowloon, in that part of the peninsula that goes from the Star Ferry landing to Jordan Road—that is, Tsimshatsui. It's damned lively, and practically never sleeps, but I like that, and who in hell needs to sleep so much? And it's full of shops and international hotels with slinky bars.

"Exactly," said Sarah. "I see enough hotels, thank you. Anyway, there's nothing stopping you from going to live in Kowloon alone. We'll see each other once a week, on my day off. If I'm free."

The little bitch. As it turned out, she chose a villa in the Stanley district, on the island of Hong Kong proper. Through the windows you could see a beach and a not very big harbor with junks and sampans. We were at the end of the world, but my office, located in Central, was hardly a dozen miles away.

"As for the rent," Sarah also said, "we'll share it, of course. I'll keep the books, if you don't mind."

She had found a job at the Repulse Bay Hotel, one of the three biggest in Hong Kong along with the Peninsula and the Mandarin, and was absolutely bent on preserving her freedom. The first few days I was continually fuming. "Supposing I want to sleep with you?" With that angelic smile she must have given her hotel guests: "Ask me for a date, darling." That very evening, I laid a Hong Kong ten-dollar bill on her bare stomach, about ten French francs, two dollars. I explained: "A present." The filtering look of her green eyes. She grasped the bill between her thumb and forefinger, put it very carefully in her handbag, and came back with another bill, exactly identical, which she rolled up and wrapped around my penis. "A present," she said. And she lay down again next to me.

These skirmishes aside, we lived together. Strangely enough for a woman who helped to manage a thousand-room hotel, she wasn't the domestic type; you could have painted her living room purple without her noticing. I know; I did it. We lived well, very well, in fact. My capital reached one million dollars for the first time on March 14; you'll see why I remember the date. I had not seen Mr. Hak again since my return to Hong Kong, but he had sent me his compliments by way of Mr. Ching.

And then there was the list. Lavater's list. I never let it out of my hands. I read it and re-read it, until I knew every name and every scrap of information on it by heart. It was engraved onto my brain, written there in the icy letters of cold rage. Each of the names was a man, a man who had betrayed my father's trust, and had robbed his widow and child. Each of these men had been valued by my father, and each had proved worthless. By becoming my father's enemies, they had become mine.

There were actually seven names on the list, not six, but two of them were partners and so intertwined and interconnected that Lavater had counted them as one. I did, too. Studying the list, becoming so expert that I could pass any examination on its contents with an "A," I also could see the makeup of my father's empire more clearly, and marvel at its complexity.

At the top stood Martin Yahl, Geneva banker, unimaginably wealthy and powerful. He had been the most trusted of all, therefore his crime was the greatest. Him would I save for last, for him I hated the most. I wanted him to feel the noose grow tighter and tighter until his eyes bugged out and his tongue turned black, Only then could I relax.

Compared with Yahl and Will Scarlet, who was dead and out of my reach, the others were small potatoes. Nevertheless, they would not go unpunished, not while Franz Cimballi lived.

There was Alvin Bremer, whose name rose up out of my boyhood memories; he must have spent time at St. Tropez. No doubt he had patted me on my childish head, while figuring out how best to beggar me. His present address was a luxurious residence on the shores of Lake Michigan in Chicago, not far from the Loyola campus. Bremer's cover was that of president of a construction materials company; capital, twenty million dollars.

The two whom Lavater and I counted as one were John Hovius and James Donaldson, an unlikely pair. Hovius was an Argentinian, and Donaldson a Scot from Glasgow. Both were deeply involved financially in Latin America, especially Chile, and the partnership was tied to the Yahl bank by a subtle but real network of companies.

And there was Sidney H. Lamm, a real estate developer in San Francisco, an American, who had his fingers in a great many California pies, including the political.

At the bottom of the list was a Frenchman, Henri-Georges Landau. He lived in style, this Landau, with a large apartment in the 16th *arrondissement*. He owned some real estate, but the darling of his heart was the restaurant-pub, a sizable brasserie, on the Champs Élysées. He pulled a lot of money out of French appetites, and fancied himself a four-star restaurateur.

So. Yahl, Scarlet, Bremer, Hovius and Donaldson, Lamm, Landau. Scarlet was dead so there was one down and five to go.

97

Lavater had become my friend by telephone. I sensed a deep honesty in him, a warmth, and an outrage as the facts were pieced together and the design of the conspiracy became clearer.

I wanted to see him, sit down with him and talk, without the damned telephone wires between us. I invited him and Mme. Lavater to spend the Christmas holidays with Sarah and me in the Hong Kong villa, and they accepted.

The Lavaters arrived on December 23rd, for five days. While Sarah took Mme. Lavater to peruse the famous shopping streets of Hong Kong, Lavater and I discussed strategy, sifting through the new files he'd brought with him. I had the strong feeling that he looked on me as a father would a favorite son, and it almost brought tears to my eyes. I had been so alone for so long.

"I recommend that you begin with Landau. He seems to be the most vulnerable of all of them. You must have met him, either at St. Tropez or at your parents' apartment on rue de la Pompe. He knew you when you were very small."

I studied the photograph Lavater handed me. It showed a man of about fifty, well-dressed and respectable. In his lapel, the ribbon of the Legion of Honor. Snowy hair, soft, full, womanly lips, yet something in the eyes . . . cold, mean. But no bell rang from the dark recesses of my memory. I didn't recognize him.

"For Landau," said Lavater, "we have all the bank information necessary. We even know that he placed a little money in Switzerland, in 1968, and that it's still there; the sum must be around seven hundred thousand Swiss francs. More official assets: two apartments in Paris, one on avenue du Maréchal-Lyautey with a view of the Auteuil racetrack, and another older one in the Cité; that's where he keeps his mistress. He also owns a villa in Cannes . . . I forgot: the apartment in the Cité is in the name of the said mistress, Amanda Fernet, whose real name is Marthe, but there must be a paper somewhere legalizing her name change. So much for the nonproductive property. The source of his revenues: a large brasserie on the Champs Elysées, the value of which is estimated at eight to nine million francs. He bought it for a quarter of that amount in April 1957."

"Eight months after my father's death. Where did the money come from?"

"At that time, he presented claims which were paid to him, cash on the barrel, by the Martin Yahl Bank, Ltd. Three million current francs. Up to then, he was a man who earned a very good living working with your father, but no more than that."

As always when I'm focused on something, I walk. Rather than remain sitting in my office, we went out, Lavater and I, into DesVoeux Road. Lavater talked while walking and enjoying the amazing street sights. I took him to the Central Market, Fabric Alley, Eggs Street.

"Three million francs' worth of Judas money."

"Everything's going up nowadays."

"What role did Landau play for my father?"

"He had the merit of being the first person to back your father when he moved to France. But Landau was never a genius. Your father put him in charge of managing his French interests. Someone told us that in 1971, just before his death, your father was thinking of getting rid of Landau, who wasn't competent enough. But that's only hearsay."

"What shape is his brasserie business in?"

"It's gone through ups and downs; at first, he didn't pay enough attention to it. Right now it's a going concern. A few months ago, he started major renovations."

"Financed by whom?"

Lavater smiled. We had just left Aberdeen Street and were walking toward Ma Mo temple. A fortuneteller brandishing a colorful bird in a cage slipped between us. Lavater shook his head.

"You're sharp. You've hit on his Achilles' heel—the renovations he undertook and the borrowing he did to finance them."

"How much?"

Marc Lavater stopped before a street barber, working by the ancient method; each hair of the beard is pulled out singly after being tied in a microscopic silk slipknot.

"About four million French francs," said Lavater finally, fascinated by the spectacle.

We walked on. We wound up in the famous Cat Street, the high Thieves' Street, with its numerous steplike alleyways. Lavater inhaled deeply, visibly delighted to be there.

"It doesn't seem possible to me, but you don't like Hong Kong, Franz?"

"No." Hong Kong's streets had lost their fascination for me. I kept thinking about Landau.

"Shall we talk about Hovius and Donaldson now?" asked Lavater sympathetically.

I literally trembled with anger. I shook my head.

"Later. First Landau. I'll start with him."

# 8

Paris, February 20, eight-fifty in the morning. I had been on the Champs Élysées for more than an hour already, and I was freezing, despite my lined overcoat. The sky was overcast and gray, snow weather, said the waiter in the bistro on rue du Colisée, where I drank my fifth or sixth cup of coffee since rising. One more almost sleepless night. The night before, I'd flown in from Hong Kong. Now I waited.

And I had to wait another twenty-five minutes before the car finally appeared. It was a large BMW, sparkling clean. Landau was seated in back, reading *Le Figaro*. The car came to a halt within three feet of where I had been told it would stop.

Having waited for his chauffeur to open the door for him, Landau got out and continued on foot. *"As a rule, he never has them stop right in front of the brassiere. It's his way of getting exercise. He sometimes goes down to the Place de la Concorde, but in general, he never goes farther than the Théâtre des Ambassadeurs. There he makes a U-turn and goes to his office."*

That morning, he didn't walk as far as the Ambassadeurs, only to within sight of the theater. I followed him twenty feet behind. He read while walking. A few minutes, and finally he did an about-face. The following instant, we were face to face.

"Excuse me, sir, would you know where the avenue de Marigny is?" I asked innocently.

He already had his eyes on the traffic lights, waiting to cross the street. Now he lowered his eyes to me. With a wave of his hand:

"The avenue right over there. You can't miss it."

"Thanks a lot."

Exchanging nods, we glanced away from each other; *he* looked away, at least. The light changed to red. Henri-Georges Landau crossed with an even step. I stared after him. If he turned around, it meant that he recognized me, or simply that my face struck him in some way or other; I do resemble my father, being about the same height and certainly having his voice. But he didn't turn around. He continued onward, up the Champs Elysées, once again buried in his newspaper, at a steady, calm pace, with the serenity of a peaceful conscience. After a moment, I hailed a taxi.

\* \* \*

At Heathrow Airport in London, there was Ute. She pressed her breasts into my chest as she kissed me. I snickered:

"Aha! We're cold, aren't we, after all, Danish or not."

She wore a fur coat. She opened it. Underneath, she was totally naked. Two Pakistanis who were passing by tripped over their own suitcases. Ute asked me:

"What have you done with your green-eyed Irish girl?"

"Back in Hong Kong."

"Are you going to marry her?"

"Mind your own business. How *is* business?"

"In the buff."

"You mean in the pink."

"I sent you the latest figures. The pre-Christmas sales were smashing."

I had received what she called the latest figures, and they were truly spectacular. The Phantomas Bank, in particular, was an extraordinary success.

"I'm a good saleswoman, huh?"

"Get your hands out of there."

The accountant with whom I had flanked Ute had written to me to underscore the necessity, in his view, of a structure more solid than one made up of a giant often-naked Danish girl, trailing a squadron of other girls behind her. I had no intention of following the accountant's suggestion. The success of my idiotic gadgets wouldn't last forever, and I wanted no part of any organization that could later hamper my freedom of movement.

"Tell me I'm a good saleswoman or I'll rape you."

"Fuck off."

She had bought a Jaguar XKE with her new money. We got into it. I asked:

"What time is my meeting?"

"He's waiting for you at ten tonight sharp."

"Tell me about him."

"We could go to my place. We have time."

"Tell me about him."

\* \* \*

"He" was called simply the Turk. He lived in a luxurious villa in Hampstead Heath; the garden is small, but superbly tended. The house itself appears from the outside to be a typical North London pseudo-cottage, impossibly rustic for a city setting, and self-consciously adorable.

I left Ute in the Jag and went up the front steps alone. At my ring, the door was opened by a petite brunette wearing little more than her modesty and a pair of sapphire earrings.

"Mr. Cimballi? You're early." Her teeth gleamed like tiny pearls hidden in a bed of roses.

I must confess that I was taken aback by her near-nudity, not to mention the perfection of her small body. It's not every day that a naked maid takes your coat and scarf.

"Do I have to strip, too?" I asked her mischievously.

She pretended not to have heard me.

If the exterior of the house was English expensive country chichi, the inside was overwhelmingly opulent. No Englishman ever lived in this florid a style. Genuine gold leaf on the walls, and gold thread in the filmy draperies. From the ceiling hung many-branched crystal chandeliers, whose hanging prisms caught the light a hundred times and refracted it, sending it back a thousandfold. Oriental splendor if I ever saw it.

The nearly nude girl ushered me into a drawing-room whose luxury outshone that of the entrance-hall like a summer sun outshines a winter moon. I sank down into an overstuffed lounge chair, and gazed at a solid gold tobacco humidor on the marble table next to my chair. It was filled with Montecristos and Romeo y Julietas and I could almost wish that I smoked.

After no more than a three-minute wait, the girl reappeared to usher me up a magnificent paneled staircase. The sight of her little round buttocks only inches away from my teeth was somewhat unnerving, yet I managed to follow her without losing too much of my cool.

"This way, please."

I could hear the familiar clicking before I saw them; teletypes. A large business office filled with six or seven teletype machines, all spitting out quotations. These, I would learn, were the Turk's umbilical connections to the major stock, commodity and currency exchanges of the world. Tending these machines like nurses in an intensive care ward were half a dozen ravishingly beautiful young women, whose severely cut business suits and pulled-back hair did nothing to disguise their ripe loveliness. The look in their eyes was all business, though, and they barely glanced at me as I was led past them to the room beyond, the inner sanctum of the Turk himself.

A double door with panels of leaded glass, totally opaque. Beyond that, a trip to Ankara on a magic carpet.

The ceilings were draped in silky fabrics, like the walls of a sheikh's tent. There were no chairs or sofas to sit on, only heaped-up pillows of satin and velvet at the side of tiny tables with incised brass tops. The floor was created out of Persian carpets, piled one atop another until your feet sank into a fortune in rugs. At least a few hundred thousand dollars' worth.

The room smelled of sandalwood, and little cones of sandalwood incense burned in pierced brass holders. It was a scene from another century and another way of life.

But nothing I had heard from Hyatt or Lavater prepared me for the sight of the Turk himself.

A giant of a man, with a belly big enough for three men, he wore long, black, oily moustaches and had a front tooth made of solid gold, set with a huge diamond. He was dressed in a satiny shirt of pink silk, with loose green silk pants tucked into high boots of shiny black leather as supple as fabric. He was reclining on pillows, and small tables around him bore the necessities of his life: a water-pipe containing a sweet sticky substance that smelled suspiciously like the finest Lebanese hashish, a tiny cup of coffee, and a plate of sticky nougats and other sweetmeats.

One of the pillows moved suddenly. I must have looked startled, because a hugh roar of laughter came rushing out of the Turk's throat.

The pillow was a girl! In fact, several of the pillows upon which the Turk reclined were girls, as beautiful and as bare as the girl who'd answered the door. This was no room, this was a harem!

Lord of all he surveyed, the Turk laughed mightily at my confusion. I took a closer look at him. His eyes were slanted, bright and black as two buttons. His neck was powerful and thick, and the head it supported was entirely shaved. From all the reports I'd heard, he couldn't have been more than forty years old, but it seemed to me that he was ageless, had always been and would always be. If he'd ever had a name, it was lost now in the mists of history; he was simply the Turk.

Now he took a shrewd look at me, and saw me sizing him up. "So, do you like me?"

"Not enough to marry you," I answered dryly.

"How is Hyatt?"

"Wonderful."

"What did he tell you about me?"

"He said you were somebody to go to when I have a short-term need for a lot of cash; that you lend money, taking risks no bank would take; and that I'd better pay it back if I don't want trouble."

His slit black eyes, with their kind of feminine languor, gave me a long stare.

"What's your name again?"

"Cimballi."

"Nice name. Makes you think of cymbals, slightly wild music, dancing. I've heard of a Cimballi before, who was in construction."

"My father."

The double glass partition that separated us from the teleprinters opened for a girl carrying a piece of paper to the Turk. The Turk nodded, and told the girl: "Twenty thousand." I could barely take my eyes off all these female bodies, all absolutely magnificent.

104

"Hyatt also told me you were a racing buff, that you follow the track hour by hour all over the world, and that you wager huge sums of money on the horses. One of those teleprinters out there is linked to the tracks."

"I understand you had some business to offer me," said the Turk.

Lying on her back, her thighs spread with utter indecency, a girl smiled at me. She was sixteen or seventeen years old and blond, with a radiantly clear complexion.

"Five months ago, you lent money to a Frenchman by the name of Henri-Georges Landau so that he could finance renovation and construction work on his brasserie on the Champs Elysées. I want to buy the promissory note."

"Do you know the amount?"

"Four and a half million francs. I'm offering you five."

"Cash?"

"Cash. Any means of payment you wish."

"Where did you get this money? From your father?"

"I earned every cent of it."

I anticipated the next question. I raised my hand to forestall it.

"And I'm twenty-two-and-a-half-years old."

The Turk's hand alighted on the crotch of the teenage blonde who had smiled at me. His fingers hooked the golden fleece. The girl suddenly let out a cry of pain. The big dark slit eyes of the Turk had a dreamy, far-away expression.

"Cimballi . . . I like that name. It's a pretty, dancing name."

"I'm overjoyed."

He was going to refuse, I knew it.

"But my answer is no," said the Turk, his gaze still elsewhere. And his hand still stroked the belly of the girl who had smiled at me and whom he had punished for smiling at me.

"I won't sell you that note, Cimballi, and it's not a question of money. It just so happens that I have promised to keep it. Someone is acting as a guarantor."

Intuition forced me to ask. "The Martin Yahl Bank of Geneva?"

His houri's eyes rested on me, empty of all expression.

"Who is the woman who brought you here?"

"A friend."

"What kind of friend?"

"A friend."

"I was told she's very tall and very beautiful."

I shrugged. I turned around and gazed at the teleprinters. An idea gradually formed in my mind, and I asked, as though of no one in particular: "Is there a horse race on anywhere now?"

"In San Diego, California."

"Has it started?"

"The first race is already run."

From the sound of his voice, I knew he had guessed what I was getting at. I added anyway: "We could do it in the third race." He motioned through the double doors, and they brought us a list of the entries. Eleven.

"You know something about horses?"

"I know that they have four legs."

He handed me the list.

"Choose your favorite."

I read the names, which meant absolutely nothing to me. Really completely at random, I chose: "Silver Dragon. Number Five."

A mental association with the dragons in the streets of Hong Kong during the Chinese New Year? Who knows?

"You could have made a worse choice. He's fourteen to one. You want to make a wager?"

I replied, "I want to make a deal. If my horse wins, you'll sell me the note?"

He smiled:

"Agreed. And how much will you bet on Silver Dragon?"

"A pound."

"Only if he wins. If he places—if he comes in second or third—it doesn't count." He smoothed his janissary's moustache.

"Okay."

Solemnly, he gave the order. Run by a black woman with fabulous thighs, the teleprinter transmitted the bet five or six thousand miles from there.

"I'll follow you," said the Turk. "For me it will be ten thousand dollars. You're really not tempted?"

"No."

The room we were in was suddenly filled with a special, dense silence. To break it, I asked:

"And how long will it take?"

"Ten or fifteen minutes."

The door behind me opened, allowing for a few seconds the din of the teleprinters to penetrate the silk walls. It closed again, and the sound was cleanly cut off. Ute's voice:

"Did you ask for me?"

"Get the hell out of here."

"But you're not bothering us at all," the Turk told Ute. "Quite the contrary. Please stay."

To back up his words, he rose, bracing himself on bellies and breasts. He was my height, or nearly, but infinitely more massive than me, and he must have weighed close to 200 pounds. He began to walk around my Dane, looking her over and leering. The black teleprinter operator reappeared, bringing news.

"The second race results," commented the Turk. "The favorite won, this must be the day for favorites. Your Silver Dragon is in bad shape. Now he's sixteen to one. The distance doesn't help him."

He continued to walk around Ute, and now brushed against her. He was exactly in front of her, his black eyes riveted on the naked skin in the coat's V-neck. Ute smiled at me:

"Take it easy, Franzy," she said. "I'll knock him down when I feel like it, this guy."

The Turks hands rose and gently seized the coat's lapels.

"Swedish?"

"Danish, buddy," Ute said. "Can't you tell?"

Very slowly, inch by inch, the Turk opened the coat, only to be confronted by six feet of Scandinavian nudity. He was dumbfounded for a moment. He shook his head:

"Would you enjoy punching me in the nose, Cimballi?"

"It's something to contemplate," I said.

"But you think you can?"

The Turk moved in closer and kissed each of Ute's nipples.

"I could try, of course."

"But you won't."

I answered:

"No. First, because I don't have a prayer; second, and above all, because you're simply trying to test my nerve."

The Turk suddenly let go of Ute, whom he hadn't touched otherwise. Sitting back on his heels, he smiled and shook his head, and then suddenly got up, with surprising agility for a man of his weight. Ute closed her coat and winked for my benefit.

"You had him where it hurts," she said.

The Turk chuckled.

"I should have bet more on that goddamn Silver Dragon. I'm starting to believe in him. Sort of a hunch."

A silence ensued. Not a heavy silence; a silence of complicity. For him a peaceful wait, for me a kind of blankness. And suddenly I began to be afraid. Pictures appeared in my imagination. I told myself it must be three o'clock in San Diego. A mild, warm sunshine. Certainly a huge racetrack; and an innocent green lawn. Eleven horses at the gate. Eleven unknowns. The starter. They all spring forward. Silver Dragon is black or brown. I don't know. Yes! He's black, black and shiny as a blade. I tried to see . . .

The Turk threw me a lazy, lascivious glance. It was over. I had seen nothing.

The teleprinter clicked. An aloof girl tore off the paper and marched over to hand it to the Turk.

He remained motionless, waiting for a few moments before glancing indifferently at the information, and told me:

"You speak French, huh? Me too. I spent my youth in Beirut; you know it?"

"No."

"We'll go there together, one of these days. What do you have against Landau? He's a loser."

"A personal matter."

"Yahl? He's a different story. I wouldn't go up against him, if I were you."

Then he handed me the paper absent-mindedly: "Silver Dragon first."

Nothing showed on my face, but inside I was dancing in triumph.

Ute had already gone out; she was at the wheel, and was busy making a U-turn with the Jaguar in the narrow gravel driveway. The nearly naked maid with apple-shaped breasts and quivering haunches opened the door for me. The Turk escorted me to the door. He was a hundred and sixty thousand dollars richer, thanks to Silver Dragon; it was the least he could do.

"Listen, Cimballi: if you have a deal to offer me some day, I'm in on it. I want to be in on it, okay?"

I walked in front of the maid, thinking of her cropped chestnut hair, slender, graceful neck, blue eyes and red lips. I grabbed her suddenly by the nape of the neck, crushing my mouth against hers, and hugged her hard enough to take her breath away. As I climbed into the car, the last image in my mind was that of the Turk in pink and green, doubled over, literally weeping with laughter.

In my pocket was Landau's I.O.U.

# 9

The first thing to do was to present the promissory note. This amounted to going to see Henri-Georges Landau, shoving a few papers under his nose, and telling him very politely: "Be good enough to immediately pay back the four and a half million francs—plus interest—that you owe."

Knowing, of course—we knew everything about his financial situation—that he had absolutely no chance of finding the money, at least within the allotted time period.

My emissary (in fact, he did not even know my name) went to Landau's office on February 26, at 9:30 a.m. He was officially sent by the Hung & Chang Bank of Singapore, which was acting on behalf of a corporation it knew nothing about, the Sara Co., Inc., which I had set up in Lichtenstein for the purpose. My emissary laid down his legal ultimatum and withdrew.

In working out our plan, Marc Lavater and I had tried to predict what Landau would then do. He did it, step by step, exactly as we'd figured. He began by calling the Turk in London, wanting to know why and how an I.O.U. that was supposed to remain in London for several more months should suddenly be presented by a Singapore bank. As he and I had agreed, the Turk avoided answering for three days; he was out of town, he had just gone out, he would be back soon, he was ill, he was at the dentist.

The Turk finally spoke to Landau: "My poor friend," he told him, "I know I made a promise to you, but if you knew what a position I'm in myself! Oh, these Chinese!"

"You have to help me," begged Landau.

"And I will, have no fear. Give me some time to get back on my feet."

"But I have to pay in ten days!"

"I promise," said the Turk, "you'll have the money in a week. Four million, that's all I can do, make some arrangement for the rest."

Make no mistake about it: in those last days of February, despite the sudden presentation of the claim, Landau was not in a desperate position. To begin with, he had the brasserie, even if it was mortgaged; but after all, in November of the previous year, a group of restaurateurs had offered to buy it for eight million, and would probably have gone as high as eight and a half. Imagining a normal sale of the brasserie, this would leave him four million, after paying off the mortgage.

To those four million should be added about two and a half million in official real property, the apartment on avenue Lyautey and the villa in Cannes (it was worth more, but he had used it as collateral for a loan). Say six and a half million.

And it was also necessary to add the one million three for the apartment in the Cité, officially in the name of Amanda Fernet. Seven million eight.

Plus the francs deposited in Geneva in a numbered account. Then one had to add the furniture, the paintings, Madame's jewelry, and the cars. A good billion centimes. Such was his real fortune, minus the four and a half million for the mortgage. And if he had been given the time, Landau could have redeemed his I.O.U. himself without too much trouble, merely from the revenues of his brasserie.

But giving Landau time was not part of my plan.

\* \* \*

The emissary from the Hung & Chang Bank of Singapore had granted Landau ten days. The promise Landau had received from the Turk—four million in a week—meant that the brasserie owner felt completely secure. Especially since he was having a few problems—an unhappy coincidence, but Lavater had kept

*110*

some friends—with his income taxes: an auditor arrived, wanting some information about that apartment in the Cité. For example: where had Miss Marthe, alias Amanda Fernet, found the necessary funds to buy it? Why had the local taxes been paid by checks signed by Landau? And also the water and electric bills? And that decorator, that antique dealer, that caterer, all paid by Landau?

Landau fought. On March 5, three days prior to the expiration of the grace period, he succeeded—by scraping the bottom of the barrel, as they say—in gathering some sixty million old francs. Four million new francs were lacking. The Turk had promised them to him. Landau called London again. Another exasperating session of hesitation-waltz on the part of the Turk, who, after having played the invisible man for ten straight hours—told him: "Not today, Landau. Impossible. But I'm waiting for a big payment tomorrow or the day after."

"I can't risk the delay!"

"All right. Ninety-nine chances out of a hundred that I'll be able to give you the money within forty-eight hours."

Landau was reassured, that was part of his character; he was the type who goes for the easiest solution. Two days later, less than twenty-four hours from the expiration of the grace period, he again pursued the Turk, who, enjoying the torture he was inflicting (in this he went even beyond what I had asked him to do, but he was definitely a bastard by nature), prolonged the suspense as long as he could, only, in the end, fifteen hours before the return of the emissary supposedly sent by the Singapore bank, to confess, pretending unhappiness: "Landau, that money I was counting on hasn't arrived. I'm terribly sorry."

"But you told me the chances were ninety-nine percent!"

"That left a one percent risk. Unfortunately . . . However, I feel guilty, and I may have a solution for you. . . ."

A solution that consisted of appealing to an Englishman named Hyatt, who was now "somewhere between Rome and London," bearing huge amounts of Vietnamese capital in search of fruitful investments. "Hyatt can help you, Landau. Provided you get in touch with him in time. But hurry." As though it were necessary to urge a man who now had his back to the wall!

Landau clung to the telephone as to a lifeline; the waters were rising. Where was Hyatt? He called one hotel after another, discovered that this Englishman certainly traveled a lot, that he was in London, had gone to Rome, had stopped over in Geneva, Frankfurt, Brussels. . . .

Returning finally to Rome, not at the first hotel where Landau, wild with anxiety, had first looked for him, but at another one, the Bernini Bristol, piazza Barberini.

"*Ma il signor* he went out," the desk announced placidly.
No, they didn't know what time *il signor* Hyatt would return.

"For the love of heaven, tell him to call me back, at any time of night, I won't leave my office."

Hyatt, who was waiting for the green light from me, did call back, at 11:40 p.m., on the night of March 7.

"But of course, Mr. Landau, I'm quite willing to meet you . . . . Yes, a deal of this nature would interest the people I represent. . . . Tonight? So soon? But there aren't even any more planes, and . . . a chartered plane? Yes, yes, I do understand that you'll pay for the chartered plane, but I still have to find one. . . ."

Hyatt found a private plane (we had actually chartered it several days earlier). He landed at Le Bourget airport at four o'clock in the morning, awaited as he stepped off the plane by Landau, who was hysterical with fatigue and nervous exhaustion.

"Mr. Landau, I was able to reach my clients. They do not wish to commit themselves to such a high amount. Nevertheless, they have agreed to cover the amount of your note. You'll have to go to public auction sale, of course, but there's nothing to stop you from buying back your business yourself. That is the only condition on which my clients will agree to come into the operation."

"But my brasserie is worth at least nine million!"

"Mr. Landau, I also took the time to do a little background check. A restaurant consortium wants to buy your business. You got in touch with them again this morning. If my information is correct—and it is—they declined your offer. They will not take part in the sale, it seems. That means you have a reasonable chance of buying back your brasserie for, let's say, six million. We will act as guarantors for four and a half million. It's up to you to find the rest."

"But I don't have it!"

Especially, since with interest and fees, it was much more than a million and a half that Landau had to come up with in a cruelly short time.

"Don't you have real estate?"

Landau nodded dumbly.

"Yes? Then you must sell it. If I have any advice to give you, that's it: Sell! Sell! Sell! The main thing is to save your brasserie."

Landau didn't know where to sell his Paris apartment and his villa in Cannes on such short notice. No problem. Hyatt knew someone who might be interested, specifically a French limited liability company headed by a retired general, whose financial adviser and authorized representative was one Marc Lavater. Lavater would buy the apartment and villa as soon as the papers could be drawn. He'd pay all of one million four hundred thousand francs. In cash, too!

"It's highway robbery!" Landau shouted.

But after the shouting, Landau had no choice. He took it. Losing one million francs, he sold the apartment and villa to the company, which was immediately dissolved—by me.

The public aution sale was held, and the restaurant consortium did not appear, just as Hyatt had predicted. So that Henri-Georges Landau bought back his own business for six million two—an unknown upped the bidding. Exhausted, Landau thought he deserved a little rest. He was sure he was going to get it.

He was wrong. In reality, the promissory note for four and a half million went from a Singapore bank, the Hung & Chang Bank, acting on behalf of the Lichtenstein company, Sara, Inc., to a Luxembourg company supposedly acting as fiduciary on behalf of Vietnamese clients of the Indochina Bank. In reality, it was me, of course. In other words, I held it, me, Cimballi; I passed it from my right hand to my left hand. That was all.

For Landau things had changed dramatically, though he still owed four and a half million—much more with fees and interest. Hampered by the financial inquiry, he could no longer do as he liked with the apartment in the Cité; he was threatened with the payment of back taxes, and he had sold real estate worth two and a half million for one million four.

Of course, he still had his brasserie, and this was his only hope of coming out cruelly wounded but alive.

On one condition: that the promissory note was not presented to him again, that he was given time to recover.

And, of course, the I.O.U. was presented to him again, on
April 9.

* * *

On that day, Hyatt arrived in the office on the second floor
of the brasserie on the Champs Élysées.

"You cannot be unaware, he told Landau, "of the grave events
now taking place in Vietnam. My Vietnamese clients are worried,
nervous; there's no telling what they might do, and in fact they're
doing it. I am sorry to tell you this, but they want their money
now. Right away. I speak of the four and a half million or so
that you owe them."

The exact figure being—I'll always remember it—four million
eight hundred eighty-eight thousand francs, all fees included.

From that moment, Henri-Georges Landau was dead, financially. Nothing could prevent a second public auction from taking
place. The consortium of restaurant owners—albeit the natural,
logical buyers—did not attend, any more than they had the first
time. And this silence on their part, like the two successive auction sales, and certain rumors that were going around—all meant
that people did not exactly rush to the sale. In fact, a single buyer
appeared—another company, German this time, which declared
itself ready to pay, in cash, five million two hundred thousand
francs in settlement. Landau received this sum, minus the usual
costs, and out of this money from the German company (me),
he paid the Luxembourg company (me) the four million eight or
nine that he owed.

He still owned seven hundred thousand francs in Switzerland.
He made the mistake of trying to bring them back to Paris. His
wife made the journey and was caught by customs officials on
her way back. It happened just as she crossed the border into
France. The seven hundred thousand francs were impounded,
and there was talk of a heavy fine for violating the currency re-
strictions.

After which, to my great relief, he didn't kill himself. With
the jewels and furniture sold, he had some money left. It
amounted to a few hundred thousand francs.

He tried to go back into the restaurant business and went in
on a fast-food deal with a semi-gangster, in which he lost quite
a bit of what still remained to him. Then he went crazy, literally.

114

He was later arrested on the balcony of his former establishment when he suddenly began breaking tables and chairs; he was put away for good when, stripped naked and shouting, he battled the waiters and two gendarmes who tried to subdue him.

At no time did he understand anything; he never even knew what hit him—he was simply crushed to death by Cimballi's dance.

*  *  *

Now as to that restaurant consortium.

In conceiving the plan, I had regarded them, even more than the Turk, as the main obstacle I would have to overcome.

I made contact with them on February 21, the day after I had gotten the Turk to give me the note. Not personally, you understand—I never officially appeared in the Landau affair—but through Marc Lavater. There was a double advantage in this: first, discretion (I did not want Martin Yahl to identify me; I wanted him to go on thinking of me as a young fool wandering about somewhere in Kenya), then the fact that these gentlemen would listen more easily to Lavater, with his solid reputation, than to a kid from Hong Kong. Also, their own tax adviser was a friend of Marc's. From one tax mafioso to another . . .

Marc Lavater to the restaurant owners:

"Last November, you made offers of purchase to Henri-Georges Landau. He said then that he had no intention of selling. Do you still wish to buy?"

"What business is it of yours?"

Marc showed them the note. And added:

"You offered Landau eight million. Let's assume you were prepared to go a little higher. Let's say eight and a half, for example."

Poker faces.

"As a result of certain events that are likely to occur within the next few months, the Landau brasserie will probably become the property of one of my clients, whose name I am not authorized to disclose. One thing is clear: the brasserie in itself does not interest my client. As soon as he takes possession of it, my client is ready to sell it to you for a substantially lower sum than you were prepared to pay in November."

"How much lower?"

115

"Seven and a half million. You save five hundred thousand to one million francs, even more. It is no longer November, and prices have gone up since then."

"What are the conditions for such a purchase?"

"There will be two successive auction sales. You must not take part in either of them."

"In exchange for what kind of guarantee?"

"A blank promise of sale to you signed by my client."

"But that would be illegal!"

A big smile from Marc:

"So?"

Silence.

"I could read their minds," Marc told me later.

"Supposing we go to those auctions just to observe?"

Another smile, downright angelic, from Marc:

"Fine! But if you offer to buy at any time whatsoever, whether or not you have an agreement with my client—who, may I remind you, holds the promissory note of four and a half million—the bidding will continue until you give up. I need not inform you that in such circumstances, one can always make a 10 percent higher bid. Your intervention will therefore have no result except to artificially raise the price of the Landau brasserie. Which my client would resell anyway, even at a loss, to anybody except you."

The meeting with the consortium posed risk. They might warn Landau. But warn him about what? How much did they actually know? Nothing. Above all, we had gambled on the restaurant owners' ruthless business sense coupled with their greed. One is never mistaken in relying on other people's greed.

"Franz, in business matters those guys would frighten sharks. I only showed them the I.O.U. Besides, what were they risking by accepting our deal? Landau had already rejected their offers without leaving the door open. Even after the second auction sale, once you had firm ownership of the brasserie, if you refused to honor your promise of sale, they would still have the opportunity to make a higher bid. They aren't crazy. And they're saving a million or a million and a half with inflation."

The consortium accepted, and their promise was not broken; at no time did they come forward, assisting in the kill with an implacable neutrality. Four days after the second auction sale, I transferred the brasserie to them for seven million two hundred thousand francs (they had earned a discount). That day, I also dissolved all the structures I had used in the Landau affair: Sara, Inc., the Lichtenstein fiduciary, the Luxembourg one, the German company. Finally, I erased the last vestiges of the company that had bought Landau's real estate and had just resold it to my Hong Kong company.

There was nothing left. And the name of Cimballi was never mentioned in the affair.

Financially speaking, I had murdered Henri-Georges Landau. In the killing I had made money, though that had not been my primary goal. The Paris apartment and the villa, which were resold a little later, netted me three million two hundred fifty thousand francs.

My transaction with the restaurant owners added another two million to my holdings.

Nearly three million seven in total—but not all profit. I had to deduct Marc's share, Hyatt's, the Turk's, the costs, and, since we were in France, the thirty percent taxes. These I paid with a smile to my country's treasury.

# 10

The Bahamas lend themselves nicely to the game of setting up companies. You would be surprised at how many famous international enterprises are based in the sunny and uninquisitive warmth of what Shakespeare called "the vexed Bermooths." Also, you can get a great tan there.

I had planned a trip to Nassau even while Landau was choking with anxiety in Paris. There's nothing like a week or two in the tropics to wash a bad taste from your mouth.

I'd expected Sarah (first choice) or Ute (a logical second choice) to come down with me, but both declined. The tourist season was on in Hong Kong, and Sarah was working seventeen hours a day. Ute, bless her long legs, was coining money selling my ridiculous gadgets in London. Someone told me that she had something going with the Turk. There's no accounting for tastes.

So I flew to the Bahamas alone, and there my love life changed forever.

She was rather small, a slightly reddish blonde, and what struck you first about her was her eyes: she had a golden, almost childlike gaze, which fell on me from the first second with what you would call a questioning expression, as though she were really asking about me.

"Franz Cimballi, Catherine Varles."

We'd been introduced by Sally Kendall; Sally and I hadn't seen each other for over a year, but we shared the memory of wild parties in Cannes, Portofino, St. Moritz, or God knows where. The last time I'd seen her was at my house in London, the house on St. James's Park. It had been the night Annaliese died, two days before my departure for Kenya. I couldn't even remember if I had slept with her or not; it wouldn't have meant much to either of us.

The day after my arrival at the Emerald Beach Plantation Hotel, we came face to face. She kissed me sloppily; she was overjoyed to see me again. Where had I disappeared to? She'd heard I was dead, or, worse I joined the Foreign Legion. Did I know she was married? And so on, most of which I ignored. I was watching the girl with her.

I looked at the golden eyes.

"French?"

She nodded. She looked to be sixteen or seventeen years old; actually, she was almost twenty. Sally took my arm and tried to lead me away. "Franz, I'm really thrilled to see you again. Come, I'll introduce you to my husband. And there's Peter Moses, too, who married Anita. You must remember them. We're going to have one hell of a party."

I freed myself gently but firmly. "Are you alone in Nassau?" I asked Catherine.

"No," she said. "With friends." Her voice was low and rich, surprising in so young a girl.

"Are you married?"

She laughed.

"No."

"Will you marry me?"

"No."

I said to Sally: "Go. We'll catch up with you." And to the girl with the golden eyes: "I don't care what we do together, but let's do it right away." An amused twinkle in her golden pupils.

"Sailing?"

"Sailing's okay."

The hotel's private beach had small catamarans. We were both wearing bathing suits, and we climbed aboard. I tried to raise those goddamn sails, I pulled, tugged, let go, balled up all the separate lines within reach. The result was a disaster. She went into fits of laughter.

"Let me do it. Where did you learn to sail?"

"By correspondence. But my mailman hated me."

Her small hands flew gracefully, calmly; in a miraculously short time, there was our twin-hulled liner, skimming along in silence, a true silence that was due not only to the lack of a motor but especially to the fact that I said absolutely nothing.

I merely looked at her, and from time to time, her own gaze left the horizon, the gleaming whiteness of the sail, the raw blue of the Caribbean Sea, to meet mine. The sail lasted thirty or forty minutes, and then she steered toward the beach.

She told me to drag the boat onto the sand, out of reach of the tide; and as far as dragging it goes, I dragged it, while watching her walk away; if no one had stopped me, I would probably have crossed the lobby with it. I then went out to the pool, which was in the far wing of the hotel, and there I ran into Sally again.

"Well, well!" she said, waving her hands like a crazed semaphorist.

"Sally—"

"Now you do make a pretty couple. And she's your height, which must be nice for a change."

"Sally—"

"Both adorable. She's still a little young, but you're both adorable. I was saying to—"

"SALLY!"

"Yes, Franz darling?"

"Shut up."

"Yes, Franz darling."

She kissed me, I kissed her, and we went to find her husband, who was sort of a big jaw full of teeth with an Englishman around it. Nice, though twenty years older than his wife. The Moseses, Anita and Peter, were already there, and other couples, and everybody was drinking champagne mixed with punch, which is an excellent way to get plastered in record time. Catherine Varles was with a young English couple who joined us at sunset, when we all went together to hear the concert given by the Nassau Guards orchestra at the Beach Hotel, then finished the night, after six straight hours of calypso, with a fabulous feast of grilled crab in the early hours of a coral dawn.

I was supposed to leave the Bahamas the next day; Lavater was waiting for me in Paris; we were about to put the finishing touches on Landau's execution.

I cabled Marc to say I'd been delayed, without explaining how or why. I extended my stay by two days, and after that, by another twenty-four. And those hours, nearly all of which we spent together, Catherine and I, stood out in an extraordinary way, so that afterwards nothing would ever be the same.

For our last night in the Bahamas, at least together, I let my imagination run wild. I rented one of those glass-bottomed boats, through which you see the splendor of the coral and schools of multicolored fish. I had asked that the boat be outfitted with searchlights and escorted by two or three other boats packed full of flower-decked musicians playing *moderato* and *voluptuoso*. It began well, it was even well begun, and then, wouldn't you know it, one of those tropical squalls blew up, turning the flowery music boats into pitiful rafts, my orchestras into drenched water rats.

I went back with her to the door of her room. We both looked like sea-wrack washed up on the beach.

"You know," I said, "there are some things in life I'm successful at. I'm not a systematic failure."

Silence. After which I asked her again if she would marry me. She looked at me gravely:

"Not yet," she said.

A "no" I would have understood. That "not yet" was beyond me.

"Because you're too young?"

"That's not the only reason."

She kissed me on the cheek. "You look like someone who's running."

"Who's dancing. Cimballi doesn't run, he dances. That's me, Cimballi."

"Who's running after something that he absolutely must have. Come back when the race is over. Then we'll see."

"And if the race should take twenty years?"

"Dance faster."

Upon which, she placed a light, almost vague kiss on my lips, and shut her door in my face. We'd never even slept together; it had never even occurred to me to ask, God alone knows why. There were other satisfactions I wanted more badly from her.

The following day, I was back in Paris, attending the leading of Henri-Georges Landau to the slaughter, like a sheep. Like a treacherous, murdering, Judas sheep.

And, when I drove to the 16th *arrondissement*, to the address she told me was her family's home, nobody there had heard of anybody named Varles.

\* \* \*

Everything seemed to be running together—Landau, Catherine's golden eyes, the business in Hong Kong—everything was flowing through me at the same time, and it must indeed have seemed that I was somebody running. It seemed to me that I would never stop.

The Turk phoned me in Paris.

"Franzy . . ."

"Don't call me Franzy," I snapped, annoyed. "Cimballi or Franz, but never Franzy. What do you want?"

"I like what you're doing with this Landau business. It's really nasty, just what I love. What I want is for us to go on working together. I want to be part of your next deal."

"There is no next deal."

"Ah, Franzy, you can't fool me for an instant. With you there will *always* be a next deal. And I want in. I believe in you, little brother. Allah is with you."

"Allah be damned!" I slammed the phone down in his ear.

Nevertheless, he had a nose, that beast of a Turk. He could smell out money while it was still around the corner and two blocks away.

121

Not long afterward, I was back in Hong Kong. The gadget business was pouring gold into my account at the Hong Kong and Shanghai Bank. One Friday afternoon, returning to my office on DesVoeux Road, I found a note inviting me to call a certain number in the New Territories. I dialed that number and first got an answering machine which asked me to be patient, then a voice which I couldn't identify right away.

"Hak."

In a flash, the atmosphere was recreated: the strange house partially under water, silent as a thought, and the Chinese with intelligent eyes and legs of steel, gliding almost silently across the black marble floor.

"Mr. Cimballi, I was wondering if you would like to spend a few days with me."

I had not seen Mr. Hak since our first and only meeting.

"There's nothing I'd enjoy more."

"Select a convenient day."

"Tomorrow?"

"Why not? I am infinitely pleased at the thought of seeing you again. And I would be even more pleased if Miss Kyle were to accompany you."

So he knew about Sarah.

Sarah was someone I'd have to deal with, even though I didn't want to face up to it now. Things had changed between us after my trip to Nassau. When I returned to Hong Kong, I threw myself onto her thin body with all the hunger of a famine victim, eating and drinking her flesh voraciously. But, after my physical hunger had been fulfilled, the change became evident. My thoughts were elsewhere, and the eyes I wanted to look deeply into were golden, not green. How could she not notice?

Sarah, being Sarah, held her peace. We continued to live together in the villa, and she continued to commute daily to her hotel job, leaving us little time together. The time we did have was cordial, but strained. We never quarreled, but then, we didn't laugh much either. We were like a married couple when one of them had been unfaithful and was feeling guilt, and the other lacked evidence enough for the all-out accusation.

We still slept in the same bed and, from time to time, we even made love. But whenever I held her in my arms, I would imagine that her eyes were open, and regarding me in the darkness with that same cool, speculative, filtering green look she always gave me when I was behaving like an idiot.

My body was with Sarah but my mind was still in the Bahamas, with Catherine.

\* \* \*

When the little twin-engine prop plane set us down on the hidden airstrip of Mr. Hak's private island, I could see that Sarah was impressed. A jeep met us and drove us over the bumpy terrain that soon gave way to the smooth concrete walks I had remembered, and whose use I now understood. Mr. Hak himself was fond of "walking," or should I say rolling?

The gardens were more beautiful than I had remembered, and Sarah gave a gasp of pleasure and little murmurs of appreciation as she passed the magnificient flowering specimens and the rare plants. A flame tree in full and glorious leaf especially amazed her, and she wanted to stop the jeep so that she could look at it longer. I had to put my hand on her arm to keep her from jumping out of the car.

At the door to the house we were met by two servants, a man and a woman, their faces neutral and unreadable.

"Mr. Hak soon come. You please enter."

Sarah's eyes glowed like emeralds as we walked through the exotic villa, me pointing out some of the rarer of Mr. Hak's extensive collection of treasures. "It's incredible, a fantasy," she breathed. I was enjoying myself just watching her pleasure, but I was also pleased to be back in this Kublai Kahn palace myself.

"Welcome, my young friends."

A gasp from poor Sarah, who had turned white as Mr. Hak rolled up behind us on silent wheels.

"I told you, he moves on a cushion of air, like a *pneumatique*," I whispered.

"I see you have made yourselves at home. That pleases me. But you must be hungry after your journey. Would you care for a small supper?"

"Would I!" Sarah exclaimed. "I could eat a horse."

I refrained from mentioning the possibility that she would be doing exactly that.

The "small supper" turned out to be a banquet so lavish that I wondered what a large dinner would consist of. I can't remember everything that was brought in by a procession of Chinese servants in noiseless slippers, but a few things I can recall were: shrimp stuffed with cassava; frog's legs with ginger; goose in honey; cuttlefish with chicken livers; pigeon squabs stuffed with the tongues, brains and livers of ortolans; chicken steamed in seaweed; sharkfin and bird's nest soups. The so-called *pièce de résistance* of this Lucullan repast was a course devoted to snakes—the meat of python, cobra, dhaman and various other reptiles, topped off by what the Chinese call the Magnificent Trio: Dragon (python), Tiger (cat) and Phoenix (chicken) cooked together and highly seasoned. I have to confess that I couldn't stomach any of the snake dishes, but Sarah's ivory chopsticks never stopped working, and dipped happily into everything on the table. You have to hand it to that girl, she has guts!

The meal was washed down with *mao t'ai*, an exceptional Chinese wine, possessing both bouquet and body. There were four of us at table. Sarah, who looked quite beautiful in the narrow silk *cheongsam* that had been supplied to her, her long legs tantalizing me through the gown's high slits, and her strong young throat rising up out of the high-standing collar. Mr. Hak and I made three, and the fourth place was taken by Mr. Hak's niece, a girl of breeding and education, whose Oriental beauty was only suggested by her name, Blossom of Jade.

Jade spoke perfect English, having been educated at Roedean, among the best of England's girls' schools. She acted as her uncle's hostess, and served gracefully, pouring out the wine and handing the delicate cups of tea around. Mostly, though, she made conversation with Sarah. Jade had recently had a holiday in Ireland, in the very county of Sarah's birth, and the two of them chattered away happily and rather oddly, considering what they were eating and wearing.

"Are we really under the sea?" Sarah asked, her face flushed from the wine. The wall had moved back to give the diners a spectacular view of the illumined ocean depths. As we picked out morsels with our chopsticks, the circling sharks behind the glass were picking out morsels from the ocean. For our entertainment, hunks of fresh-killed meat, oozing blood, had been hung on submerged butcher hooks, to bring us the drama of the sharks' feeding. Even as Sarah spoke, a basking shark that must have been thirty feet long was tearing at the meat with razor-sharp teeth.

"I assure you," breathed Jade softly, "that this is no aquarium. That glass is the only thing between the four of us and a most unpleasant death." As Sarah gave a small involuntary shudder, Jade moved an inch or two closer, and placed a tiny, kitten-soft hand on the Irish girl's shoulder. "It's a very, very strong glass wall," she reassured her.

By the time we left the table, the hour was late, and the strain of the past few weeks, mingled with the powerful wine, made it difficult to keep my eyes open. Rude though it was, I couldn't suppress a yawn.

"It is time for bed, of course. My apologies for keeping you up so late," Mr. Hak said with great delicacy. "My niece will direct you to your room. I trust that all your needs have been anticipated, but should anything be lacking, the servants will answer your summons immediately."

We followed Blossom of Jade's tiny figure into the labyrinthine center of the house. At a black lacquer door, she clapped her hands twice, and it was opened at once by a servant, who glided out silently at a word from Jade in Chinese.

"Holy Mother of God," breathed Sarah, as we stepped inside. I quite agreed. It was the most beautiful room imaginable, hung with silken draperies that shut it off from the rest of the house, and fragrant with sweet incense. The bed, which took up most of the floor space, was lacquered black and red and encrusted with real gold and silver medallions. The sheets were of purest silk. Low tables of lacquer, centuries old, held tiny cups and an exquisite carafe of wine. The carpets on the floor, of heavy silk, dated back to the Ch'ing dynasty and were worth a king's ransom. I did mental mathematics. In silk alone, I figured this room must have cost close to a million dollars. Holy Mother of God indeed!

"You must be very weary," said Jade in almost a whisper. "Your bath is waiting. Come."

A small door led to a large bathroom, where a tub large enough for a harem stood steaming, its waters fragrant with exotic perfume.

"Let me help you undress," murmured Jade, and her tiny hands were all over me, undoing buckles and buttons, pulling at sleeves and trouser legs. Suddenly, I was less tired than I'd supposed.

When I was naked, Jade urged me into the tub. At first the water was almost too hot to bear, but I soon became accustomed to it, and felt my contracted muscles relaxing for the first time in weeks, soothed by the fragrant oils in the water.

"Now, you," said Blossom of Jade to Sarah, and once again her fingers were busy, and Sarah was soon in the tub beside me.

"And now, me," Jade whispered, lowering a tiny ivory-colored body into the heated water. I caught a glimpse of the two smallest, sweetest breasts in the world, topped by twin nipples the size, shape and color of raspberries. Under her flat belly was the merest fluff of pubic hair, and I wondered idly if it was true what they say about Oriental quims. It seemed as though I was about to find out. I closed my eyes in happy anticipation.

But a moan opened them again. What the devil? It was Sarah's lips on those little raspberries, not mine, Sarah's hand buried in that little Chinese muff, while Blossom of Jade, her head thrown back in ecstasy, long black hair floating in the water, moaned her appreciation.

I watched in fascination as the two of them, dark-haired mermaids, sported with each other, kissing with passion, tongues touching, mingling, hands seeking one another's secret places. They paid no attention to me at all, yet I was stiffer and more excited than I'd ever been in my life. This was something my ego hadn't bargained for.

As they stepped out of the tub, streaming water, I determined to get into the act. I grabbed up towels, thick and heavy cotton, and pulled Jade into my arms, kissing her deeply as I rubbed her body dry. She arched against me, and her hands found my hardness, caressing me with skill.

Sarah, meanwhile, fell to her knees and buried her face between Jade's thighs.

We barely made it to the bed.

I was wild with lust, and didn't know which of them to possess first, the petite pearl of the Orient or my ferocious Irish beauty. But they were busy with each other.

I had never seen this in my life, a *soixante-neuf* between two desirable women, and it excited me beyond my imaginings. I wanted them both at once; no, I wanted to watch them forever as they writhed and whimpered with pleasure. I managed to wriggle in between just a little, to stroke and fondle four breasts and suck delicious nipples. The fact that they didn't seem to need me at all was more arousing than demoralizing.

With groans, they reached a mutual climax, and they disentangled themselves to kiss each other on the mouth, and cuddle happily in each other's arms. They were adorable, maddening but adorable.

"Ah, look at poor little Franz," teased Sarah. "all alone and *so* neglected. We must do something for him. Do you agree, darling?"

"Oh, yes," mewed the kitten Jade. "Let's."

In an instant, they were all over me, smothering me in hot kisses and tiny bites; throwing me on my back so that they could get at my belly and my groin. One of them, I don't know which, stuck her tongue deeply into my mouth, while the other, I don't know which, took me between her lips and tongued me expertly.

And then a slender body was riding mine like a jockey, faster and faster, while another slender body was presented to my lips and mouth, which accepted it eagerly. Underneath my back, the silken sheets were ablaze with body heat. In my brief years, I'd enjoyed more sex than most men experienced in a lifetime, and with more beautiful women than they'd ever hope to see, but this was something, even for me. This was the hottest sex I'd ever had.

Then, somehow, we were changing places, and Jade was on her knees, with me behind her and Sarah underneath, her tongue busy with whatever she could find. Then it was Sarah who was lying under me, her hips rising to meet mine, while Jade licked furiously at her breasts. Like a dream unfolding, it went on for hours, perhaps days, with pleasure exploding again and again for all three of us.

I must have slept more soundly than ever in my life, yet I remembered being awakened hours later by the groans and the sweet sucking sounds of sex. The girls were at it again, entangled head to belly, their hands pressing each other's buttocks hard for deeper contact.

Well, let them, I thought grumpily. It has nothing to do with *me*! And I fell back to sleep once more.

* * *

When I came out of my room in the morning, Mr. Hak was already up. I found him playing chess with himself on one of those small rolling tables.

"Some coffee?"

"Yes, thank you."

He began to speak of what he called my alacrity and effectiveness in marketing the gadgets. He added:

"I had several other things to offer you. That network you were able to put together in a remarkably short time could be used, I might suggest, for other commercial purposes. There are other products besides gadgets. But I know that the retail trade in itself doesn't interest you. True?"

"True."

The intelligent eyes stared at me, gauging me. He had something special to offer me, and still hesitated to do it, that was clear. I waited.

"Miss Kyle?"

I had a brief image of Sarah as I'd seen her this morning, sleeping the deep sleep of sexual exhaustion. She and Jade were tangled around each other in a sprawl of delicate limbs, and Sarah wore a blissful smile on her unconscious face.

"If I know her, she won't open her eyes before noon."

He moved one last piece on the chessboard, finally made up his mind, and fingered one of the panels on his legs. Another table approached almost immediately, and on its black velvet was a steel chest. It looked ominous, but Mr. Hak made no move to open it.

"Mr. Cimballi, what do you think would happen to you if I should one day be unhappy with you?"

"Don't tell me. Let me guess."

"I'd have you killed."

"Terrific."

We exchanged a smile. The atmosphere was so heavy that I thought I could feel ringing in my ears.

"Next question," said Mr. Hak. "What do you know about speculation in gold and currency?"

"Almost nothing. No, make that nothing at all."

"I am sure you will come to understand very rapidly."

"I'll do my best."

"I need you for a specific, temporary, extremely confidential operation. Only two persons will know, not that the operation takes place, but that I am behind it. You and I."

And so if the secret got out, it would have to be me. I was having a harder and harder time swallowing. What kind of hornet's nest had I stumbled into?

128

"Cimballi," said Hak, "it happens that I have some information of crucial importance. I intend to use it for personal ends. I cannot act myself, I cannot even operate out of a Hong Kong bank. What I mean to do is perfectly legal; what you will do for me will never put you in an illegal position. If, that is, you accept."

"I don't even know what it's about."

"I'll give you all the necessary technical information."

"But you're not going to tell me what that crucial bit of information is?"

"Exactly. And it goes without saying that you will draw huge profits from your participation."

Mr. Hak had larger eyes than most Chinese; I would rarely encounter a face as intelligent as his. Furthermore, it wouldn't take much to make me feel sympathy, even friendship, for this man; but first I would have to stop being afraid of him.

"Can I still refuse?"

"You can."

He hesitated a little, nonetheless. I said:

"I accept."

He nodded. His metal legs straightened, and he rose. With the unearthly movement of a wind-up doll, he went over to a sofa covered with a superb brocaded silk. He sat down. He touched one of the control panels on his thigh.

"I forgot the coffee you wanted."

"It can wait."

Behind the glass panel, the big basking shark was gone. In its place, a dogfish glided and did half-turns, wheeling around the bloody shreds of meat still hanging from the butcher hooks.

Another table appeared, carrying a porcelain service of coffee cups. But I couldn't take my eyes off the other table, covered with black velvet, with its ominous steel chest. Suddenly, as if in response to my very thoughts, it began to move; it approached me in almost total silence, taking on a weird, almost lifelike quality. It came directly toward me and stopped within my reach.

"Please be good enough to open the chest."

I did.

"One hundred million dollars, Mr. Cimballi. I'm placing it in your care. It would, of course, be best not to lose it."

# 11

Each country has a currency, and these currencies are exchanged for one another. In the distant past, such exchanges were the function of bankers, who performed them on a bench in the street.

For example, you have Dutch florins and you need Spanish pesetas. So you buy the latter with the former, according to the value of those two currencies relative to one another. You turn over your florins, and you are given pesetas. You have completed a cash transaction. Nothing could be simpler.

Where it becomes interesting is when, instead of buying currency—or gold—with cash, you buy or sell it at *term*. This is sometimes necessary for your business, but it can also be a fascinating, dangerous game, in which you can win and lose a lot.

Say you live in Bourg-en-Bresse in France and you raise chickens, beautiful plump, tender chickens with big bright eyes. You sell these chickens, for example, to an American friend who lives in New York. He will pay you for them in dollars, naturally. And since Bourg-en-Bresse is not next door to New York, as well as for a host of other reasons, he will not pay you for your chickens the day you ship them, but, at best, when he receives them, or even later if he has gotten you to accept bills of exchange. In short, the payment can take three months. You have sold a thousand chickens at ten dollars apiece (these chickens have *really* bright eyes), and you should thus receive ten thousand dollars in three months.

That doesn't suit you at all, first because you have to wait three months, then because, in the meantime, the dollar may very well decline in value. And if the dollar declines, that means that in three months, assuming one dollar to five francs at the time the contract is signed, you will not get fifty thousand francs, but perhaps forty-eight thousand, or forty-five or even forty thousand.

That's a risk you take—after all, the dollars might also go up. But if you do not want to take that risk, you go to your bank and explain the situation. Your bank will understand right away; banks are very smart in such matters. It will offer to buy from you *in advance* the ten thousand dollars you are supposed to receive, after, of course, making sure that your American friend is solvent. It will pay you those dollars at five francs, cash, at an interest of one percent per month, twelve percent per year, and an insurance premium. In other words, your bank will then take the risk for you of seeing the dollar decline. It has insured itself a little against that. And if by chance it goes up, the bank will earn a lot of money.

And if, instead of being a banker with a Legion of Honor medal and boxer shorts, if instead of taking this kind of risk—betting on the long or short-term rise or fall of a currency by buying it in advance—in the name of a totally disinterested love of free enterprise; if, rather, you are only an ordinary individual, like me, who mainly wishes to make money—an idea that would never occur to a banker—then you are nothing but a dirty speculator.

Q.E.D.

\* \* \*

In June, on the 11th, I took a plane. Not alone; at the last minute, in a switch that left me positively breathless, Sarah decided to accompany me.

"What about your hotel?"

"It can go to hell."

"Sarah, what's going on?"

"Nothing, nothing at all."

And that diabolical way of looking at me, her face tilted slightly backward, her half-closed eyes shining with a sarcastic gleam, as though I were the most hilarious, not to mention the most grotesque, guy in the world.

"You really mean to say you would drop your work, which has always meant so much to you, merely for the pleasure of coming with me?"

"If you don't like my company, say so."

An image rose up, out of all the others: Sarah's face in the black crowd on Kilindini Road in Mombasa, giving me a smile both mocking and friendly, me, locked in a cage like an animal, a smile all the more comforting precisely because it was mocking and friendly, as if to say: "Go on, this isn't all that serious, it's even rather funny."

"I like your company. I've liked it from the first time I saw you."

131

"Delighted to hear you say it, darling. Of course, I'll pay for my own ticket."

But she agreed that we should take the same plane. And even, as soon as we were on board, that I should buy her champagne, while together we watched the sun set on the islands of Hong Kong, clustered in the China Sea.

Our destination via Rome: Zurich.

* * *

As I said: everything ran together. I left London, shown to the door by Alfred Morf, on November 23, 1969; I arrived in Mombasa the next day, the 24th; I visited the house in St. Tropez by night during the journey I made in the second week of the following July; in that period I first made contact with Marc Lavater; I left Kenya for good a few days later; then Hong Kong, where, after my first meeting with Mr. Hak, I launched the gadget operation in August; stays in London, Paris, and Geneva, I met Ute, Letta in Rome, Sarah joined me in Hong Kong; at Christmas that year, Marc Lavater came with his wife to the foot of Victoria Peak, and together we planned the attack on Landau; the attack was launched in February, after my first meeting with the Turk, at about the time I met Catherine Varles in Nassau, Bahamas. The period climaxed in the weekend on Mr. Hak's island and the oblique proposal he made to me.

A proposal that on June 12 saw me getting out of a car in front of the porch of the Baur Hotel on the Lake, arriving straight from Zurich airport. I got out alone. Sarah Kyle had again furnished me with proof that she was positively unpredictable; during our stopover in Rome, she had suddenly announced, with the greatest calm and even an ironic smile, that she wasn't coming with me to Switzerland, that in fact she had decided to continue on alone to Dublin. "What the hell are you going to do in Ireland?"

"See my family."

"But you haven't seen them in years, and you never write!"

"All the more reason."

Impossible to get any more out of her. A wall—even if her smiling nonchalance never left her. She kissed me:

"I'll call you at your hotel in Zurich."

"I don't even know how long I'll be there."

132

"In that case, I'll get in touch with Marc Lavater. He'll know where to find you, no?"

"Go to hell."

"Yes, my love."

On June 12 when I arrived in Zurich, taking into account my problem with Sarah and her talent for provoking my exasperation, my situation was as follows: The gadget business was moving along superbly; it had enabled me to pay the Turk the five million francs for Landau's I.O.U. and still have left a million dollars and change. Although it was still going pretty strong, I saw the warning signs of a downturn, which would not be long in coming. Others, more attentive, more persevering, more powerfully armed than I, in Japan especially, were in the process of knocking off the same products, to be sold more cheaply.

I owned a million dollars and change. I decided to gamble that million dollars along with the hundred million Hak had entrusted to me. What was good for Mr. Hak must be good for me, right? All Hong Kong was in awe of Mr. Hak's financial talents. To gamble that money represented an enormous risk for me, first because it was all I had left in the till, second because I would have nothing left to live on except the revenues from the gadget business, which would be declining. And worst of all: in tying up my small million with Mr. Hak's, I was leaping into an adventure whose outcome I would not know until August, three months from now.

It was a high-wire act, and I would have to do some fancy dancing in mid-air. And without a net.

\* \* \*

On June 12, in the early afternoon, I presented myself, by appointment, at a branch of the Schweizerischer Bankverein, the Swiss banking association on the Paradeplatz with main offices in Basel. I deposited, or rather transferred to them, the hundred and one million dollars from various deposits in my name at various banks around the world.

The operation I was launching, following Mr. Hak's orders scrupulously (except for my little personal million slipped into the ante), was a dollar and gold speculation. It involved buying ahead, three months in this case, gold payable in dollars. That is, I would ask the Swiss banking association to sign a contract—

*133*

in its name, but at my risk—with an American bank, for example, First National City Corporation, for a sum of five hundred five million dollars. By this contract, the Swiss bank agreed to deliver five hundred five million dollars in three months to First National City, which in turn promised to deliver gold in exchange for those dollars at the *current price of gold expressed in dollars*. If the dollar should meantime fall in relation to gold, just before giving them to First National City, the Swiss bank would itself buy the dollars it had promised to deliver. While First National City, for its part, would willy-nilly have to supply the gold at the price charged three months previously, before the devaluation of the American currency, if it should happen to be devalued.

In both cases, the banks risked nothing; they made the transaction in their name, of course, but not on their own behalf. The real risks were for those who bet against the fall and rise of the dollar (or any other currency, or corn, wheat, copper, or any other product listed on any exchange).

If the client who engages in this kind of speculation is deemed to be solvent, it may even happen that the bank will not ask him for a security deposit, so that the speculator, if he bets correctly, will be in the extraordinary position of making a substantial profit selling millions that he never owned! But in general, of course, the bank does require a security deposit.

Furthermore, the bankers' prudence has invented the margin call, which means that if, while the term is still in operation, the market fluctuations are such that the risks exceed either the security deposit or the client's reputed solvency, the bank can demand a boost, a rise in the security margin: "Add such-and-such an amount to cover us, or you're out and you lose your stake."

Mr. Hak knew all of this and had explained it to me. With his hundred million dollars, he might perhaps have been able to persuade the bank, any bank, to make the amount of the transaction a billion dollars, a hundred million representing a ten percent security deposit. But that posed a much higher risk. He chose conventional wisdom, and a twenty percent deposit, reducing the potential profits by half, of course, but almost completely eliminating the risk of a margin call. "And if there is one anyway, do I call you?"

"Call Li or Liu."

134

I looked at Mr. Hak with surprise: what did those two clowns, who lived for gadgets and cinematic special effects have to do with such an operation? "They happen to be my nephews, Cimballi, didn't you know that?"

* * *

The assistant manager of the Swiss banking association had never seen me before. "Five hundred million dollars?"

"Five hundred five."

Under his professional reserve, a near panic: the sum was not run-of-the-mill, and my youth worried him.

"Would you like to see my passport?"

"If you please."

I was indeed over twenty-one, he reassured himself. And I had indeed said five hundred five million dollars, with a security deposit of one hundred and one.

He examined the various transfers that had enabled me to make up the deposit.

"Owing to the size of the sum, I must consult my superior before agreeing to a transaction like this."

I told him I understood completely. This nervous man in front of me and his superior in charge of numbered accounts would be the only ones, besides me, to know that account number 18.790—on behalf of which the bank would operate for five hundred five million dollars—in reality masked the identity of Cimballi, Franz. Me!

"I'll come back in an hour, all right?"

He said that would be fine. I went out and walked around Zurich; I had come there as a child with my mother, we had taken a boat trip on the lake, and I still remembered the blue Alps of Glaris in the setting sun, the sloping shores of the lake tumbling beneath superb villas. Zurich was the city where my mother, fleeing Nazi Austria, had spent her youth, the city where my parents had met. Now here I was.

A little over an hour later, having climbed up and down the Bahnhofstrasse and seen from a distance, on the same quai General-Guisan as in Geneva, the façade of the Martin Yahl private bank, I saw the assistant manager again. Yes, they were willing to take the risk.

135

I went back to my hotel and phoned the Turk.

* * *

He reacted faster than I had expected. I only had to explain
the situation to him in a few words, he understood immediately:
"Where are you, Franzy?"
"Franz."
"Where are you?"
"Zurich."
"Where in Zurich?"
"The Baur on the Lake."
"That's a mistake. All the financiers are there. You'll be spot-
ted. I'm not anxious to be seen in your company, Yahl is a bit
too muscular for my taste. I'll be at the Dolder. There's a plane
around five o'clock. We'll meet at the Dolder for dinner. Your
treat."

In an upstanding and conservative hotel restaurant like the
Dolders, the exotic Turk stood out like a wild orchid in a field
of daisies. He was sitting in the exact center of the room, alone
at a table for six, and his flamboyant clothing and janissary mus-
tachios made him the exact center of everybody's attention. When
he spotted me, he stood up and in a voice like the bellow of a
rutting bull, shouted "Franzy!"

I winced and came toward him gingerly, one hand already
raised in protest, but it did no good. He threw his meaty arms
around me and, holding me prisoner in his oily embrace, gave
me a wet, smacking kiss on both cheeks. What a moment of hu-
miliation! I could imagine the fish-faced waiters giving surrep-
titious grins into the napkins they carried on their arms.

The Turk, of course, had not done me the courtesy of waiting
for me, but had already begun his dinner. A platter of bright
red lobsters, enough for a dozen big eaters, was on the table
before him, and he had already demolished two, to judge by the
empty shells littering his plate. His lips were greasy with the
melted butter. He waved at me to dig in, while he reached across
and speared a third lobster.

"Tell me everything," he commanded, as he broke off a meaty
claw and cracked it with his strong teeth.

There wasn't much to tell, since I was honor-bound not to
reveal anything about Mr. Hak or his dealings. Without that,

the information was so skimpy that even I, Franz Cimballi the shameless, was ashamed. All I could say that I was in a big-money deal with an important Chinese, and thought it good enough to sink my own funds into it. I told the Turk I was living up to my (unstated) promise to include him in on my next deal.

The Turk's velvety eyes narrowed to slits, and he regarded me long and hard over the broken remains of lobster number three.

"In other words, you're asking me to follow you, to put in some of my own dough, because this Hong Kong guy claims to have confidential information that the dollar is going to plummet?"

"I'm not involving you, I'm offering you. You decide."

"You have so much confidence in that Chink?"

"You see the proof."

"And that slant-eyes would have information that no one else has?"

I had my own idea on the subject: Mr. Hak was not an independent businessman; he was in direct contact with Peking, and there already was a possible source. Later, I would learn of Kissinger's secret trip to Peking, all those mysterious contacts of the time. I would learn about them from the newspapers, like everyone else, and would only have to draw a cause-and-effect conclusion.

The Turk was still staring at me:

"And how much are you putting into this deal?"

"A million."

"U.S. or Hong Kong dollars?"

I shrugged. "American."

He whistled:

"And a few months ago, you paid me five million French francs for a promissory note. Congratulations. How old are you now?"

"Sixty-eight. Turk, when we parted in February in London, you asked me to bring you in on my next deal. You repeated it the next time. I'm sending the elevator back down, we're even now."

"If it comes off."

"If it comes off, okay."

The Turk sucked on a piece of lobster. He shook his head:

"I'm weeping with joy, I'm drowning in gratitude, Franzy."

137

"You give me a pain. And stop calling me Franzy."

He continued to shake his head, wiping his lips to guzzle a glass of champagne.

"Silver Dragon at sixteen to one, shit, I'll always remember that! What was he, that horse? One of Mao's spies? I'm in. But you'd better be right, sonny boy."

He smiled at me, with his eyes like those of a woman. Then he really took me by surprise; his bear paw hooked me by the neck, and before I could react, he kissed me full on the mouth. I fought and hit back with what was near at hand: a knife. The blade lightly slit his cheek and opened his lip deeply. He fell back and howled with laughter, despite the gushing blood.

"I merely wanted to prove my friendship to you," he said between two spasms of wild laughter.

"Do it again and I'll kill you."

His wild laughter suddenly ceased. Not that he was afraid, that wasn't like him. But the very violence of my reaction surprised and intrigued him. He half closed his eyes:

"You get too excited, Franzy. Who are you after? It wasn't Landau. I told you: he's a loser. Then who? Yahl? He's too big for you. He'd be twenty times too big for the two of us put together."

I put my fork down. Contemptuously, I threw some bills on the table and left.

* * *

I had expected to find a phone message from Sarah at my hotel, but there was nothing. I suddenly realized that I knew very little about her; she might not even be in Dublin. Later, knowing the explanation for this silence, I would understand. At the time, I felt nothing but a furious resentment. To leave me at a time like this!

So I didn't have the slightest qualms about dialing that number in Kensington, London, which I hardly needed to search my memory for, I had done it so often before. A sleepy voice finally answered:

"Sally? It's Franz."

"For heaven's sake, do you know what time it is?"

Three o'clock in the morning in London.

"That used to be your best time."

She whispered:

"I'm married now, fool."

"I want Catherine Varles's address."

"She gave it to you in Nassau; I heard her do it."

"She gave me an address in Paris, I went there and found myself in front of a bad-tempered Breton notary who took me for a madman and kicked me out. Sally, stop playing dumb or I'll come to London and tell your husband everything."

"What everything?"

"Think about it."

If she remembered even as little as I did, I had her.

"Evil bastard, I don't even know what you're talking about."

"I want that address, Sally."

She remained silent for so long that I thought we had been cut off. But finally she said:

"Oh, shit! Work it out between the two of you. It's called Fournac, it's in France, in Haute-Loire, near another hole-in-the-wall called Chomélix."

"Sally, if this is some more of your bullshit . . ."

She hung up.

\* \* \*

Fournac was nothing, or at least not much. You had to go around the tree trunks and raise a few clods of earth in order to see the village, if you could call it a village. I found it by following the directions of the town clerk, whom I had phoned from Lyons.

The house was large, nearly twenty rooms. I leaned on my car horn for a long time without any answer. To hell with it. The house wasn't locked, so I pushed open a door and went into a big dark kitchen, and there were two women peeling potatoes. The younger one was sixty. She had moustaches like a Bulgarian.

"I'm looking for Miss Varles. Catherine Varles."

Their eyes were on their potatoes, ignoring me completely.

"Answer me or I'll take off all my clothes and start screaming."

A jerk of the right thumb pressed against the knife blade. "Over there." I came out again into the garden and wound up on a grassy patio planted with hundred-year-old trees, from which you had a magnificent view of the valley. To the right a small path descended; we descended together. An orchard to cross, a short meadow, and then I heard the crystalline sound of a river. The path wound under a covering of trees and emerged in a clearing.

She was there.

She was sitting alone on a tree stump, her profile turned to me, tanned, thin, so pretty you could cry. Lying next to her was a huge dog, a Newfoundland, who must have weighed 175 pounds; he was asleep.

Sensing my approach, she turned her head gracefully, and watched me, mocking merriment curving her soft lips.

"Did you have any trouble finding this place?"

"None at all, after the first few weeks."

The dog was still sleeping. I nudged him with the tip of my shoe:

"Up and at 'em, watchdog."

"His name is Theobald."

The dog opened one eye, blinked at me, and went back to sleep.

"Have you ever thought of putting a saddle on him?"

"Always."

I looked around me; it was really a pretty spot—trees, flowers, a lapping brook decorated with dragonflies, butterflies everywhere, sunshine. Almost a postcard.

"May I sit down?"

Her golden eyes smiled at me.

"Mmmm."

I stretched myself out on the grass, at her feet, facing the river, my neck resting on her thigh. After a moment, her hand slowly lifted and came to rest on my shoulder, her fingers close enough to touch my cheek. The weather was superb. I was completely happy.

# 12

July came and went, and I still had no news from Sarah. I remembered that one day she had mentioned the name of a city in Ireland, and by going through an atlas, I finally found it: Ennis, in County Clare, not far from Shannon International Airport. I did find several Kyles in Ennis, but not one of them had a sister or cousin, close or distant, named Sarah and working in the hotel industry. I really tried everything, even going so far as to contact the White Sands Hotel in Mombasa. I questioned the people she had worked for, or with; I even inquired at the Parador in Morzine, where we had spent a few days together. Nothing. Total silence. She had disappeared without the slightest trace.

Being deprived of the one did not, however, enable me to enjoy the presence of the other. Catherine had plans for the vacation independent of me; a cruise in the Greek islands in July, and a visit to American friends, whose name she refused to tell me, during the entire month of August. And then? Then back to classes at the university. In Fournac, I spent only a short time with her; the house belonged to one of her uncles, and, while the uncle did not regard me entirely with disapproval, he seemed uncomfortable about my being there, so I didn't stay long.

What exactly was happening between Catherine and me? It's hard to say. She offered me no explanation of why she'd fed me a false address in Nassau, and I said no word to her about the wild goose chase I'd been on all over Paris just to find her. Nor did she appear surprised to see me turn up here; it was as though she'd expected me all along.

It *was* surprising that two such healthy young people as she and I didn't have sex. After all, that's what young people in love do, and I was certainly in love with her. Wasn't I? I expected to marry her, that much, at least. It was as though something larger than myself, larger than she, was drawing me to her.

And Catherine? Why was I always cursed with mysterious girls, girls who spoke more with their eyes than their lips? She would never tell me her thoughts, but her golden eyes rested on me languidly, filled with merriment. I seem to be born to amuse beautiful women.

The big difference between us was that I snatched at every moment like a starving animal at meat, while Catherine was content to allow things to happen at their own rate of speed. If we were meant to be together, well and good, the time would ripen eventually. If not, *tant pis*. It was maddening. When I left Fournac, I was no closer to an answer than when I'd arrived, just more enmeshed with Catherine Varles.

The Lavaters had invited me to spend the summer at their country house in Chagny. Not the whole summer; they had made other plans, to spend five weeks in the Yucatan, from August 10 to September 15. They invited me to go with them, but I had as much desire to go to Yucatan as to hang myself. "Franz, the house in Chagny is yours, whenever you want and for as long as you want." Marc and Françoise were at least twenty years older than I; I could have been their son; but I was too old for a babysitter.

A phone call to the Turk. He was excited, he had just heard that the big American multinationals were also selling off dollars at term. "Your Chink's information seems to check out, Franzy. This could be a stroke of genius!" He got on my nerves with his "Franzy"!

I returned to Hong Kong, where the first problems with the gadget business were showing up. The competition, mostly Japanese, was getting stiffer and stiffer, and I was being priced out of the market, perhaps as a result of not having paid enough attention to the problem. I was bored stiff in Hong Kong. I had never felt its supposed fascination, and the idea of leaving began to haunt me. But where to go? My revenues were falling, so was my bank account, my million was tied up with Hak's venture. I was beginning to have to watch my expenses.

Hyatt was also back in Hong Kong, but he seemed cold to me, and vaguely resentful, as though I should have forced him into business with me at the point of a gun. The only amusement I had in Hong Kong was watching the antics of Li and Liu. Everything they touched was a parody of something else, but it possessed an antic genius. For example, they'd made a very low-budget movie, shot it in something like a week. It was a satire on kung fu movies, with comic-strip sound effects and the broadest possible acting. Yet this stupid movie had been showing all over Hong Kong for eight weeks now, to lines around the block, and was outgrossing Bruce Lee movies! And the brothers had made it more for fun than for money! Underneath that comic looniness was a pair of brains worthy of Mr. Hak's nephews.

At the time, I was satisfied with the friendship I felt toward them, which they generously reciprocated. A friendship that would make what was about to happen still more incomprehensible to me for a long time to come.

In July, the 7th or 8th, I believe, I left for Japan. Li and Liu literally dispatched me there, after convincing me that I might have a dazzling future in the sale of electronic contraptions. A fruitless trip; I failed dismally in trying to convince my Japanese listeners that I could help them sell their little wonders across the big wide world.

"You didn't believe in it enough," Li and Liu told me, "that's why. Too bad; you're spinning your wheels right now."

They weren't wrong. I was spinning in the air, if I spinned at all. For the time being, Cimballi's dance was like an old gramophone winding down. I went less and less often to the villa in Stanley that Sarah had wanted so much, with its living room still painted mauve. However, I happened to be there that night the phone call came.

I picked up the phone mechanically, still asleep. A glance at my watch: three in the morning. In Europe it would be nine or ten o'clock, broad daylight.

"Franz?"

I recognized her voice.

"Where are you?"

"In London, but I'm not staying. Franz, let me talk, if you don't mind."

From my bed, from our bed, we could always see the sampans and junks anchored in the small Stanley harbor, and the hundreds of small fires that the Chinese sometimes kindled on certain nights around the Tin Hau temple. Now I watched those same sampans and junks while I listened.

"Listen to me and don't talk, this call is costing me a fortune."

"I won't say a word, Sarah."

"I know I should have been in touch with you sooner, Franz, but I . . . I was pregnant. Not any more, of course, I did what I had to do. I wasn't going to tell you a word about it, but I guess I owe you that much of an explanation. No, don't interrupt. I'm fine now, I really am. Flat as a board. I knew back in February, after you came back from Nassau, that we didn't have much time left together. You were different, that's all, and our relationship was running on borrowed time. We had fun while it lasted, didn't we?"

"Sarah . . ."

"No, Franz, I don't want to hear it. I'm not coming back to Hong Kong. I've found a job somewhere else in the world. Maybe we'll run into each other some day, and we can talk over old

*143*

times. Some day, when you're very rich and have grown a paunch and lost your hair . . ." her voice broke a little, but before I could say a word, she recovered herself. "By the way, when you're a billionaire, don't get funny and try to buy whatever hotel I'll be working at. Because I'll quit, Franz, I swear it."

She stopped speaking, but did not hang up. I heard her breathing. The seconds passed, but I couldn't think of anything to say.

"Franz . . . goodbye."

She hung up. I was still looking at the sampans and junks. We had spent I don't know how many hours here, lying in each other's arms. She had chosen this little villa because of the view, the tiny harbor and the temple, and farther to the right, the big beach, nearly always deserted. I could all but smell again the perfume of her thin, nervous body, fiercely strained during love-making, relaxing only after a very long moment, like a wave that finally falls. Her eyes did not close until the very last second, and she would sometimes remain motionless, her cheek on the sheet, refusing to look me in the face until she felt sure enough of herself to shoot me her sarcastic look. "Not bad, for a kid," she said.

Okay then: here was the kid now, crying.

\* \* \*

I had been in the Lavaters' house in Chagny for a few days; I was reading. At Chalon-sur-Saône, where I had driven in the Lavaters' old Renault 4, I had grabbed up everything I could find on banking techniques, finance—in a word, money. I had even found a book by one of the Rockefellers: *Creative Imagination in Business*. Just what I needed. And since you've got to have something to stir your imagination, I also bought a copy of *The Count of Monte Cristo*, which I'd read about eight years before, and only dimly remembered. I found it fascinating; I was still down in the dumps from losing Sarah and not having gained Catherine, but Dumas's bravura heroics managed to pull my chin up off my chest. I was deeply into the chapter "The Inn of the Pont du Gard," and Caderousse, one of those who betrayed Dantès, was receiving a visit from "a priest dressed in black and wearing a three-cornered hat," when the telephone rang.

I stared at it. It was the first time the damn thing had rung since Marc and Françoise Lavater had gone off to wander among the yuccas of Yucatan. Should I answer it? It couldn't possibly be for me; who knew I was here? And Marc hadn't given me any instructions as to what to tell his callers. Still, you can't just sit there and watch a phone ring.

"Monsieur Cimballi? This is André Cannat, Monsieur Lavater's assistant. I was instructed not to disturb you unless something urgent came up, but I think that this fits the description. Alvin Bremer has just died of a heart attack in Chicago."

"Thanks," I said brusquely, and hung up.

The Lavaters' housekeeper, who spoke French with such a barbaric peasant accent that it sounded like Polish, shuffled in with a tray of morning coffee and croissants and set it on the table in front of me.

Without thinking, I took a deep gulp of the steaming coffee, bitter and black as I liked it best, and bit off a chunk of croissant. They turned to acid and ashes in my mouth. *Bremer dead!* I pushed the table away and stood up, heading for my room.

"Monsieur!" protested Berthe. "Your coffee will be ice!"

"I'll be back," was all I could manage to say. I almost stumbled in the hallway, so eager was I to get away from her shrewd, curious eyes. By the time I reached my room, my brain was frying; everything I saw was the color of blood.

On the wall of my room were pinned all the notes lists, dossiers, photographs I had collected over the last eight months, a map of revenge. Of the names on the list, only Scarlet's was crossed out. Landau—any minute now I would know that he was ruined forever and he, too, would be crossed out. Two down.

I suppose I should have felt glad. It was three down, actually, with Bremer dead, and without firing a shot. But I wasn't glad. I was furious. That son of a bitch had slipped through my fingers, while I was sitting on my ass reading a schoolboy costume drama. Shit!

For Bremer I had concocted a special scheme, more complex and more ruinous than the one I'd used on Landau. He would have died a beggar, and to his heirs, not one penny. As it was, they stood to inherit a fortune. Not like my mother or me.

I took a deep breath, then another, to calm myself. I had been turning my anger inward, against myself, but truly, there had been nothing I could do in Bremer's case. My plan called for money, large sums of it, much more than I had, but not more than what I might earn from this scheme of Mr. Hak's. And

145

whatever could be done in that scheme had already been done. There was nothing left *to* do except wait, sit on my ass and wait.

So why not read Dumas?

I went over to the wall and took up a red pencil. Then, very deliberately, I crossed out Alvin Bremer's name. Three down, four to go.

\* \* \*

Suddenly the waiting was over and things began to happen very quickly.

About three days after I learned of Bremer's death, it was announced that the dollar would no longer be convertible into gold.

This created pandemonium in money circles.

For twenty-five years, the dollar had been the standard currency in the world, the only currency officially tied to gold, the only currency that was worth gold, in the real sense of the term.

The gold standard no longer existed. The first result was, of course, a devaluation of the dollar. This, then, must have been the crucial information Mr. Hak had possessed. Knowing beforehand the exact date on which the American government would announce this decision, he could calculate the term of his purchase.

Even though the dollar's drop in value was small, the profit was fabulous. At the time I deposited the five hundred million dollars in Zurich, an ounce of gold had been officially worth thirty-eight dollars and ninety cents. Three months later, to the day, it was worth forty-two dollars and sixty cents. A tiny margin? Indeed. All in all, the profit realized by Mr. Hak was forty-seven million dollars, from which I deducted, as agreed, the two-and-a-half million dollars that were coming to me in my role of discreet courier, apart from the percentage taken by the bank. Adding this sum to the million dollars I had gambled myself, together with the four hundred seventy-five thousand five hundred seventy-eight dollars interest my gamble had brought me, I found myself in possession, on that 12th of September, of slightly more than four million dollars.

Good. Now it was time to act. First, to finish off Landau. Now that I had the money, it should be only a matter of weeks. Then, start on the others. I was over my disappointment about Bremer; it was time to go on to other things. I was tense as a strung wire, a thousand and one schemes rushing through my brain. But first things first, as the Greeks say.

I phoned the Turk.

"Franzy, I adore you," the oily bugger oozed into the telephone. "You made so much money for me."

"That's one you owe me, Turk, and I'll be coming to collect."

"Actually, my darling, that's *two* I owe you. Hold on a moment."

Another voice in my ear. Sultry, Scandanavian. "Helllooo, Franz."

"Ute! You Danish cunt, what the hell are you doing in Hampstead with that greasy hunk of Turkish Delight?"

"The same things *ve* used to do, my dearest, only much more often. Jealous?"

"Of the two of you? No, amused is a much better word," I lied. "And what about the other members of the harem? Are the 'secretaries' and the 'maids' still in residence?"

"Still in residence, only I am the boss, and how I love to crack that vip!"

"Well, sooner him than me, pussycat. Love and kisses. Will you put the Ankara stud back on the line, please?"

The Turk came back to the phone choking with laughter. I'd never be able to hate him.

"Let's talk seriously for a moment," I said. "I need an introduction. In Nassau, Bahamas."

"Another deal?"

"Personal."

He thought for a moment, then said:

"No names over the phone, I don't like that. When will you be down there?"

A quick calculation:

"End of September, this month."

I heard Ute speak but didn't understand what she said. In any case, if she managed to stay on the line while the Turk and I were talking, it meant, as she had told me, that she really "cracked the vip." The Turk:

"Franz, we'll be in Nassau by September 25, the Dane and I. That doesn't bother you?"

"Not in the least."

"You sure you're not mad about Ute?"

"No. Screw her for me. Ciao."

I recorded a cassette for Marc, who should be coming back soon from his goddamn Yucatan. On the 2nd, I called Chomélix one more time, but Catherine's uncle was away, and no one answered the phone.

I took the plane to Hong Kong.

* * *

I finally tracked Hyatt down at the Bull and Bear, the perfect replica of an English pub. The heavy oak furnishings and stained glass had been brought over by boat from England, piece by piece. Hyatt was not completely drunk. He raised his glass:

"Little Boss is back."

The nickname they had given me in Mombasa.

"I'll buy you a drink," Hyatt went on. "A nice creamy Guinness, made in Dublin with water from the Liffey. How long are you back for, this time?"

"I'm not staying. I even have a deal to offer you: I'll turn over everything on the gadgets to you."

"Everything?"

"Everything. You take it over. Interested?"

It wasn't a bad deal, for him. Even if the business no longer had a chance of bringing in the fabulous profits of the first few months, it was still, thanks to my patents, lucrative and provided a good income for someone who preferred modest but steady returns to high-risk ventures where you can lose everything. Like Hyatt. But his initial refusal was still sticking in his craw. We discussed it for half an hour, talking money. He asked me for twenty-four hours to think it over, and I knew he would accept it, the next day, for eighty thousand dollars. A bargain.

"One last drink?" Hyatt offered.

"No. Seen Ching lately?"

It had seemed to me up to then I could detect a certain discomfort in my Englishman. This time, there could be no doubt. Especially since he played the fool:

"Ching who?"

"You know very well. What's going on?"

"I don't understand."

He looked down at his dark Guinness. I didn't insist, with the uncomfortable feeling deep inside me that something had happened or was going to happen that would affect me more or less directly. I traded a bill for some small change, and began making phone calls. No Ching anywhere, not at his office, the factory, or his home. Worst of all was that silence that followed my question, which someone always finally broke by answering me. No, they didn't know where Ching was. Away from Hong Kong? Certainly not. Then where? No one knew.

I called Li and Liu at their workshop on Kennedy Road. A ringing in the emptiness. That's what worried me the most. It was the middle of the week, my two clowns didn't work alone, they employed a number of underlings, yet nobody answered the phone. I tried their apartment above Bowen Street, on a street whose name I had never known. Nothing. But after several unanswered rings, just as I was putting down the receiver, somebody finally picked up the phone. . . .

"Li? Liu?"

Silence. Yet there was someone at the other end of the line.

"Li or Liu?"

And that someone very gently hung up on me. I went out of the booth. Hyatt had split. I went out in the street; there was the crowd, oppressive, huge, like an ocean. And suddenly it came, inexplicable but all the stronger for that—a thrill of fear.

\*   \*   \*

Hyatt had asked me for a day to think things over; we had an appointment the next day at the entrance to the registration office in Caxton House, on Duddel Street, at eleven o'clock. That left me roughly twenty hours to spend in Hong Kong. And those hours seemed interminable to me. I had a mad urge to jump on the next plane going anywhere, in a word to get the hell out.

I went to Stanley and gathered up the little that remained. There were still a few items and books belonging to Sarah; I put it all in a suitcase and closed the lid. Now I was feeling worse than ever. Back to Central, where I crossed over to Kowloon. I took a room at the Peninsula, among the old ladies who had lived in Colonial India, and the retired colonels, formerly of Burma. And that's when the idea came to me, irresistible and unreasonable. A taxi to the airport; there I rented a small plane, a Cessna, I think, piloted by a young Australian with muscular tattooed forearms. Who stared at me lethargically:

"If you don't even know the name of this fucking island, how am I going to find it?"

"I'll recognize it."

And what if we accidentally stray over China, mister? And what if the Chinks fire on us? And what if I had simply dreamed up this island where I claimed to have landed twice? The Australian grumbled, but got his machine ready, all the same. I pointed him in a direction, and he followed it. The first group of islands.

"There?"

"Farther on. After that kind of big dike."

The Plover Cove Reservoir, said the Australian. We flew very low, a thousand or twelve hundred feet above everything that stuck out. You always think of Hong Kong as overpopulated; yet these lands beneath us belonged to the Colony and were empty, or just about; no roads, but there were paths, climbed, as at that moment, by Hakka peasant women with big hats entirely surrounded by black veils.

The sea suddenly appeared under our wings.

"Well, mister?"

"That one."

According to the map, we were flying over Mirs Bay, at the edge of the New Territories.

"Where do you see a landing strip? A fly wouldn't land its ass on that rock."

But he spotted the landing field even before I had time to answer. He literally plunged to the ground, landed with abrupt casualness, clipped his engines, propped up his left shoulder, and relit his Philippine cigar; the smoke alone would kill an ox.

"I'm warning you: in one hour, I'm taking off."

"I'm not sure I'll be back in an hour."

"Sixty minutes, mister. You'd better get a move on. It's getting dark, and I fly by sight. No instruments and no radar."

I jumped down, and anger made me race the first few dozen feet. And then suddenly I realized what I was doing. What a dummy I was! A glance at the little airplane; the Australian had stepped down also, and was smoking, contemplating the Chinese sky with caustic contentment. I hurried on my way again; that bastard *would* be capable of leaving without me.

Twice already I had come to this island. Both times, a car had brought me from the airstrip to the house. Now I was on foot.

I expected some kind of mad dash, practically a marathon. I was surprised to find that by cutting across rocks and climbing a single ridge, I arrived sooner than I'd hoped at the garden, and beyond it the house.

Silence.

It grew like a fog, in thicker and thicker layers, as I approached. It was crushing as I went down the drive with Chinese banyans and camphor trees. I let out the first yell, which went unechoed. I finished crossing the garden, which gave out a steady fragrance. My foot touched the black marble of the floor at the entrance.

The sliding front door was open.

"Mr. Hak? Cimballi."

The echo of my voice seemed to come back without end. The hairs on my neck rose. I was afraid.

"Mr. Hak!"

He had said: "When the operation is finished, late August or early September, come back to Hong Kong. I may have something else to offer you. Your return will mean that everything went well." I crossed the threshold of the first living room, and there, where on my first visit there had been rugs, tables, and sumptuous, priceless screens, there was now nothing. Everything had been removed. The first living room was empty.

The next room was empty; so were the others, as well as the room where Sarah and I had slept with Jade. A sudden flash of a hot memory. Gripped by fear, but driven by curiosity, I entered the part of the house where I had never gone. There, too, everything had been removed. In the kitchens, which must have been remarkably automated, only the built-in ovens were left, since they were encased in cement. Further on was an alcove, where the strange remote-controlled rolling tables were parked, like sleeping monsters. A few more steps, and I was in the huge room where one entire wall was concave and made of glass. The lacquer panel, painted with red dragons, was closed over the glass, shutting the room off from the sea.

This room too was completely empty. With one exception: on the floor was a rectangular box like those used by model airplane hobbiests. It had many levers. I tried one, then two, then three. At first, nothing. But then three tables rose up like shadows, made of black velvet and shiny steel. They came toward me, stopped within my reach, fascinating and frightening in their docility, like tame beasts.

151

I moved other levers and panels slid open, rose, drew back, created new rooms; music filled the air, tables somersaulted, the entire house came alive and obeyed me like a living creature.

I didn't hear it move; it shifted behind my back, without my knowledge, activated without my deliberate will. But when— gripped by the strange sensation of a presence—I turned around, I saw that the semicircular panel covering the glass wall had rolled back, folding on itself. And the sharks were six feet from me, less; at face level; three creatures, each one nearly eight feet long, giving off the same aura of ruthless ferocity. The halo of the projectors tinted them with a stupefying red glow.

At least, at first glance that's what I thought the red must be.

But a closer look told another story. The flesh on the butcher's hooks, the flesh the sharks were tearing at . . . I shivered with horror. The shape of it was that of a human torso, spinning in the water, the hook through the neck. There had been a head, but it was eaten away now. A severed hand was floating lazily in the water, bloodless.

But what made the strongest shudder of my life grip my limbs was the glint of metal at the lower half of the torso, where the legs would normally have been. A control board for a limbless man.

The torso strained at the hook as another shark took a huge bite out of it. I backed away from the glass. All that genius, all that money, all that power—food for the fishes.

\* \* \*

Hyatt avoided my gaze. I repeated:

"I don't know what's stopping me from breaking your jaw."

"Franz, I didn't know anything. I still don't know anything. Everything was just rumors."

The rumors that had gone around Hong Kong concerned Mr. Hak's availing himself, for his personal benefit, of sums not belonging to him. The money was said to be the property of the Chinese Peoples Republic, or, even worse, of high Peking dignitaries. Hyatt knew nothing more. Maybe it had just been a "loan." Perhaps he had intended to restore the hundred million after his profit had come through; who knows? They never gave him the chance. Instead, they fed him to his beloved sharks.

And me? Did they know about me and my part as courier? Was I next on the Chinese Hit Parade? More than ever I felt the need to get away from Hong Kong. I would have *given* Hyatt my share in the business if he hadn't agreed to buy it from me. Besides, who knew if Mr. Hak's factories would be allowed to go on operating? I was no monster; I made that a condition of the sale. The patents themselves I kept.

"And Ching?"

He shook his head.

"And Li and Liu?"

He didn't know, he swore it. We had a last drink together, the imminence of my departure helping us to dig up the ghost of a friendship that might have been.

"And you're never coming back to Hong Kong?"

"Not if I can help it."

The topless dancers of the Kosukai Club smiled at us.

"You remember those Ethiopian women in Nairobi?" said Hyatt. "And the one you had in Mombasa. . . ."

I remembered. Just as I remembered Joachim, Chandra, the rotten cop and the shady judge, Jomo Kenyatta's house, my friends on Kilindini Road, Ching, Li and Liu, Mr. Hak, Landau. And Sarah. A past past.

I had four million two hundred thousand dollars.

And the music of Cimballi's dance began again.

# 3. Those Men in the Bahamas

# 13

I arrived in Nassau, Bahamas, on September 26, twenty-two months after my departure from London under the guidance of Alfred Morf. It was my second visit, counting the one in February, when I had met Catherine.

In Nassau I found the Turk, Ute Jenssen, and two "maids" in string bikinis—enchanting. The Turk was floating like a dozing sperm whale in the middle of the pool he had rented for his stay—there was also a forty-room house adjacent to the pool.

"What you did to Landau," he said, "Naughty. I felt almost sorry for him."

"You have as much pity as an alligator."

"What have you got against alligators? Okay, buzz off, girls, we're going to talk seriously. We talk, Franzy?"

"Don't call me Franzy."

"Ute calls you that."

"You're not Ute."

"That's obvious," the Turk admitted. "We talk?"

"We talk. Have you seen Marc Lavater?"

The Turk's soft, velvety black eyes gazed at me.

"I saw him. Smart guy, that one. Sharp, even. Like me, that's all I can say. He explained everything to me, everything I need to know, in his opinion. You want my opinion?"

"No."

"You're crazy, both of you. It's a plan that would drive anyone crazy. You don't have a chance."

"Are you in on it?"

"I'm here, aren't I?"

"Where's Zarra?"

"Right here, not far from here. Armed guards everywhere. And equipped, those guys. With big bad eyes."

"Did you speak to him?"

"First on the phone, then I went to his house, keeping a low profile. He agrees to meet you."

I gazed at Ute's immense and splendid naked body stretched on her back ten feet away from us, at the edge of the pool. A short laugh from the Turk:

"Do you fancy that?"

I shook my head. Ute (I saw her face between the twin mounds of her breasts) gave me a wink: "How's it going, my pal?"

"It's going fine, Ute."

"Franz," said the Turk. "Forget it. You're crazy. This Zarra is dangerous enough by himself. But the guys behind him are even more so. Don't mess with that."

* * *

On the right, Robert Zarra.

In the beginning, a financier with a sound backing. At the end, one of the biggest thieves of all time. Those who openly pocket two hundred million dollars are not so common.

Openly and with total impunity.

It all started in Geneva in 1958. A European from New York settled on the shores of Lake Leman with a single idea: to get the American GIs stationed in Europe, overpaid according to the overseas standard of living, to hand him part of their nest egg for purposes of investment in the United States: "You'll be rich when you go back, instead of helping the fräuleins get rich." It made sense and it worked. By 1966, the European from New

*158*

York was already managing six hundred million Swiss francs. And the funds kept pouring in. Everything went perfectly as long as an upward trend continued on the New York Stock Exchange, thereby raising the share of the investment company, which was only the average of all the American shares held by the company in the name of its GI members. But, when the dizzying overhead costs exceeded the amount of the commissions paid for new members, it began to go downhill. The European from New York, for whom the Swiss bankers did not much care, began to have problems. He passed "the baby," as they say in such cases, to someone else.

That person was Robert Zarra.

At the time Robert Zarra took over the reins, the investment company might still have been saved. Zarra may have thought about it, but not for long. He found a better solution. Putting the two hundred-odd million dollars left in the till in a suitcase, he flew the coop with it. In the United States, they were unpleasantly surprised, and Robert Zarra was sentenced in absentia to twenty years in prison.

Zarra didn't give a damn. Why should he? He was set as far as his retirement was concerned: the Bahamas, or more precisely, Nassau, and still more precisely, Paradise Island, a tiny island that isn't one any longer since it was connected to Nassau by a toll bridge. Paradise Island has casinos, and some of those casinos, of course, are in the hands of the American Mafia. Zarra (like everybody else) knew this, and his plan was simple. He injected some of the two hundred million into the Mafia-run economy. In return, he received aid and protection against police of every stripe, the Coast Guard, U.S. Treasury agents, maybe even the Salvation Army—all of them on his trail. Considering the short distance between Nassau and the Florida coast, his enemies were only across the street, watching him through angry binoculars.

On the right, then, Robert Zarra.

* * *

On the left, John Hovius, "officially" from Buenos Aires and possessing Argentinian citizenship; and James Donaldson, officially and really a British subject, born in Glasgow or thereabouts.

On my list they bore the numbers Four and Five. That was a mistake; I should have put them in a category by themselves.

159

One thing was certain. In Landau's case, I might, if pressed, summon up a few regrets for what I had done. But I would sleep with an easy conscience when the news came of the double suicide of Hovius and Donaldson.

They had both been trusted colleagues of my father. I had their dossier in front of me, and read it again, more out of habit than necessity; I knew each line by heart. Hovius was twenty-one years old when he met my father. My father took notice of him while the boy was just a receptionist at a Paris hotel. Hovius already spoke eight languages; he had the stock exchange rates since the end of the war at the tip of his tongue. My father convinced him to leave the hotel industry and sent him first to Switzerland, then the United States. He subsidized Hovius for two years on the sole condition that he learn business and come back, at the end of that apprenticeship, to take his place as chief assistant. Which is what happened. Six years later, in 1951, Hovius was given responsibility for the powerful Cimballi interests in Latin America; he earned five times more than he would have earned had he got as far as Manager of the Hotel Georges V. On my father's death, Hovius turned up as the bearer of forty percent of the shares of the entire South American group of companies.

Forty percent to Hovius, twenty percent to the Martin Yahl Private Bank, and the third slice of the Latin American pie went to James Donaldson. He was an attorney by profession, a Scot. And he looked so much like a Scottish attorney that it bordered on a disguise. I have several photographs of him: here, shaking hands with Hugo Banzer, the dictator of Bolivia; there, arm in arm with General Stroessner, the dictator of Paraguay, or with his good friend, General Godoy, the well-known Peruvian democrat. Physically, he was a sterner-faced Abraham Lincoln, who inspired you with respect and confidence. He had inspired so much confidence in my father that he had made Donaldson his right arm and had given him a copy of the act of trust, so that he might prove, in case of mishap, that the only true owner of Curaçao was Andrea Cimballi. And the loyal Scot had burned the papers that were entrusted to him, pocketing his share, not only accepting Martin Yahl's proposals urging him to betray, but perhaps eliciting them; and, having apparently agreed to this betrayal without a shadow of remorse, had acquired wealth and power to the point where, according to Lavater, he would sooner or later be knighted by the queen. *Honi soit qui mal y pense.*

On the left, then, Hovius and Donaldson.

\* \* \*

And between Zarra and them, me.

After having spent many nights reading and rereading the reports of the investigators dispatched by Marc, I began to explain to him the idea that had come to me. He shrugged his shoulders: "It won't work."

"Okay, then come up with something else." Bubbling inside me was the fierce, merry elation I had felt that day on the Old Brompton Road, and a need to assert myself as a man. Franz Cimballi was no indecisive Hamlet.

"You're sure of our information, aren't you?" I demanded. "It's one hundred percent correct?"

Lavater turned his gray-eyed gaze on me, and spoke slowly, like the conservative man he was. "One hundred percent correct? How could we ever be certain of that? What are our guarantees? But substantially correct, yes. It is the best information your money can buy. But this preposterous proposal of yours . . . to set Hovius and Donaldson at war with Robert Zarra! It won't work, I tell you! Why, the two factions don't even know each other!"

"Oh, it will work," I laughed. "Of that I'm very sure. And we will make the introductions."

"And those political events you're counting on . . ."

". . . Will come to pass," I assured him. "The only thing I don't know is exactly when. My friend, you worry too much." I showed him my strong white teeth in a grin of confidence, but my hand in my pocket stroked nervously at the little obsidian Buddha I had stolen from my father's study in St. Tropez.

*161*

# 14

The September days between Hong Kong and Nassau were feverish, exciting, and often delicious. They were feverish during the second auction sale of the Landau brasserie, my purchase of it, and the sale to the restaurant consortium. They were exciting because my plan of action, a plan dreamed up almost a year earlier, was working out at last.

They were delicious for a reason named Catherine.

She had come back to France from her cruise in Greece, her trip to the United States, her wanderings; and, informed of the day of her arrival at Roissy by the two potato-peeling black owls at Fournac whom I had heavily bribed, I went to meet her at the airport, accompanied by the only Caribbean band then in Paris, and carrying, with the aid of several of its members, a twenty-five-foot sign proclaiming: CATHERINE, I'M HERE!

I had the pleasure of seeing those golden eyes snap open in surprise. Catherine came off the plane accompanied by a woman I took (correctly, as it turned out) to be her mother. She was wearing a light summer dress with a very short skirt, almost a micro-mini, and those magnificent legs of hers were tanned to a deep bronze. Her hair, which was usually the exact color of her eyes, was three shades lighter, bleached by the sun of the Greek Islands. She was so enchanting, that at first I could barely spare a glance for the mother.

Which would have been a major mistake. It is a universally acknowledged fact that, if you want to know how the girl you love will look as a middle-aged woman, you must take a look at her mother. If that law held true, then Catherine at forty would be twice as beautiful as she was now at twenty.

Mme. Varles was, quite simply, the most beautiful woman I had ever seen.

She wore a linen suit, wrinkled from traveling, but the wrinkles clinging to her body in all the right places. A light wrap of a dozen sables clung around those magnificent shoulders as though caressing them. I didn't blame those little dead animals in the slightest. Under a pert and rather absurd hat, her hair was cut short and feathery, whereas Catherine's was, in the fashion of the times, very long and silky, and ironed to hang as straight as a plumbline down her back.

They had the same snub nose, mother and daughter, and identical sets of pouting lips that begged to be kissed and bitten. I had one devastating moment's flash of me between the two of them in one large bed with a white lace canopy.

*Get a grip on yourself, Cimballi, you goat, this is the girl you are going to marry and that is your future mother-in-law.*

While a uniformed chauffeur struggled with at least twenty-two pieces of Louis Vuitton luggage (this was years before every shop assistant began carrying Vuitton), I signalled to my steel band, which broke at once into a deafening and somewhat tuneless rendering of *La Marseilles*. Everyone in the airport stared, and Catherine blushed.

*Maman*, bless her, merely looked coolly amused.

"Franz, you idiot," gritted my Catherine through pearly teeth. "Make them stop immediately! This is mortifying!"

But I was already bent over Mme. Varles's white hand, dropping cooing little kisses on her platinum and diamond rings, as though she were the Pope.

And she blessed me by an invitation to lunch on Thursday, and with the correct address and telephone number of the Varles residence. She also told me to call her Veronique, and kissed me on both cheeks, to her daughter's dismay.

It was the seventh *arrondissement* they called home, an apartment behind Invalides, which already meant money. A very chichi place to live. It was as I suspected; after all, you don't float around the Bahamas with Sally Kendall and her crowd with only a few centimes in pocket money.

The apartment at Invalides was even grander than I had anticipated. I thought, perhaps two servants; there were four besides the chauffeur. A cook, a footman-butler who did the serving, and two homely maids. It was one of those opulent Art Nouveau buildings from *La Belle Epoque*, all iron curlicues and stone flowers and an open-cage elevator that inched its way protestingly up to the fifth floor, where the Varles had fourteen rooms with sixteen-foot ceilings, eight working fireplaces, and a hothouse where orchids grew.

Not too shabby.

I had dressed very carefully, and had even gotten a haircut, so that I would not appear too grotesque. I have a beard like iron; I should shave every hour on the hour, but the barber had subdued my whiskers somewhat with an old-fashioned straight-edge razor, the kind I'd like to use on Martin Yahl's throat.

Veronique Varles had dressed for dinner, and was surrounded by a double cloud of chiffon and a perfume I could not identify. I learned later that it was her personal scent, blended only for her by a perfumer in Jermyn Street, London.

Catherine, the minx, wore a simple apricot-colored minidress, and looked so juicy I wanted to take a bite out of her, dress and all.

I had sneaked a peek into the formal dining room, and shuddered. It was bigger than Versailles, and twice as intimidating; it could have seated fifty without a groan, and there was room for fifty more standing. I had a mental picture of the three of us rattling around at opposite ends of the vast table, shouting polite inanities at one another.

I should have known better. Mme. Varles had ordered a small round table, cosy for three, to be set up in one of the smaller salons. Flowers graced every place setting, and candles threw a soft glow over the china, crystal and silver.

Of the food itself, I can only say that it was ambrosia and that I ate like a farm worker. But whether it was fish or chicken or frogs' legs, whether we had different wine with each course or drank champagne throughout, this I don't remember. I was so busy looking from one beauty to the other and shoving my fork into my face that I never took the time to discover what I was eating or drinking.

After dinner, Catherine excused herself for a few minutes, leaving *Maman* and me to get down to business.

"She is very young." Veronique made the classic opening move.

"Yes." I wasn't risking my pawns.

"And so are you."

"Yes." It was fruitless to argue the point.

"Catherine says you are running after something. Is it money?"

I threw her a reckless smile, Errol Flynn from the poopdeck of his pirate vessel. Tucked away in my jacket pocket was the transfer order for the money I had that very day sent from my Swiss bank to my new bank in Nassau. I took it out of my pocket and placed it gently into Mme. Varles's white hand. Her rose-tipped nails flicked it open and she drank its contents in eagerly.

"Not money, Veronique," I said softly.

"But this is four million one hundred thousand dollars!"

"Yes." It was a supreme moment, and I was eating it up.

She looked at me shrewdly, her golden eyes, so like Catherine's, speculative.

"Did you inherit this money?"

I shook my head.

"Then how. . . .?"

"I earned it, *Madame*. It belongs to nobody but me, and I earned it myself. There are no illegal strings attached."

A silence. Then, "Good Lord!" she said at last, rising and crossing in front of me. A gentle pressure of her hand on my shoulder kept me in my seat. For a moment or two, she stood by the tall window that looked out over the avenue de Segur, her face a mask I couldn't read. Then she came and sat next to me on the tiny sofa.

"You . . . you're still so young, in spite of all that money. Can I help you in some way?"

The very way she phrased her question puzzled me; I wasn't sure I understood.

"Catherine is right," she said. "You *are* running after something, something that isn't easy to get. Be careful, I beg you."

I stared at her, surprised and not a little disturbed. What did she want of me? What did all this concern of hers signify? Was it maternal? Was it for my benefit or Catherine's? I couldn't figure this woman out, but there was a depth to her that sooner or later I'd have to plumb.

Before we could continue our baffling conversation, Catherine came back, her hair freshly combed into a waterfall that tumbled to her waist, and a sweater around her shoulders. She wanted to go out, a movie, then dancing perhaps. A new discotheque with an American deejay.

From that evening until the day I left for Nassau, Catherine and I were never apart for more than a few hours. Her moods were merry, alternating with serious or even sad. She was a young girl attempting to deal with emotions perhaps a bit grownup for her. I must have been her first love.

As for me, only half of me was with her, much as I was enjoying myself. The rest of me was already in the Bahamas, already closing in mentally on Hovius and Donaldson. Vengeance is not only time-consuming, it's *all*-consuming.

We did young, happy things, Catherine and Franz. Paris in the summer—sticky, almost deserted—became our playground. Soon we would be parted, she to attend classes, me to attend to the fate of two traitors, but now we were happy together, holding hands, taking walks, listening to concerts, watching the puppet shows in the Bois de Boulogne, laughing like the little kids.

We didn't go to bed, although we had progressed to many passionate kisses and my hands on her breasts. Not her bare breasts, though. She was afraid of my touch.

On the day I flew to Nassau, she came with me to the airport, although without the benefit of steel band or banner. When she kissed me goodbye, there were tears in her golden eyes.

* * *

I left Nassau about ten o'clock, paid the two-dollar toll, and approached Paradise Island.

The Turk had not exaggerated: Robert Zarra was indeed at the center of an extraordinary defense system. I was stopped once on the road and, after passing the outer wall, I was stopped twice more, and each time I was searched and my identity checked. What the hell was he afraid of?

Meeting Zarra for the first time, you got the impression that there was nothing he was afraid of. His whole demeanor exuded confidence and power; he was a fellow to be reckoned with! Tall, muscular, even handsome, with a broad white smile that froze the marrow in your bones. Those teeth were like a crocodile's, and I felt certain that the blood ran cold in his veins, like a reptile's. He received me with a courtesy that was almost formal, but his handshake lacked sincerity.

"The Turk has told me many good things about you."

"But he doesn't know everything."

"Is that your real name, Cimballi?"

"No doubt about that."

"Italian?"

"French."

"But of Italian descent."

He was pressing me. Did he want to think of me as a paisano? Let him.

"Correct. My father, my father's family was from Florence." I looked around me. There were four armed guards—huge pistols in shoulder holsters and walkie-talkies—just in the area around the pool. I had seen at least six others in the garden, not to mention the men posted at the entrance, and there must have been at least two of them on the second floor of the house, equipped with long-range rifles.

"You have nothing to fear," Zarra told me with a smile.

"I'm afraid for their sake. What if I lose my temper? . . . It's a bit early for a daiquiri," I said, "but I would like a glass of orange juice."

They brought me a glass, some ice, and freshly squeezed orange juice in a huge solid silver thermos.

"I'm listening," said Zarra.

He let me speak for ten whole minutes without interrupting me, asking no questions, showing no particular interest, but almost never taking his eyes off me, not even to light a cigar. Something intrigued me then in the way his hands moved, until I realized that he made each of his gestures without ever looking at his fingers, which acted, as it were, independently of him.

I stopped talking. Silence. He puffed on his cigar, watched the smoke, and finally asked me:

"And who runs this company that you're so anxious to hurt?"

"John Hovius and James Donaldson."

"I know Donaldson a little."

"I know. We checked: you met him in London, three years ago. We checked to see if you had any interests in common with him or Hovius. You don't. And if you have an interest in warning them about what I'm going to do to them, it utterly escapes me."

He smiled: "You're well-informed."

"I never go anywhere empty-handed."

Zarra stiffened.

From the corner of my eye, I suddenly caught a glimpse of the guards, who were standing at attention, their hands already on the butts of their weapons, their faces alert. A few seconds passed in which I almost expected a bloodbath. But nothing happened, the sentries repositioned themselves and settled back into their earlier immobility; dogs stalking game.

"Of course," said Zarra, who hadn't even turned his head, "I can't answer you right away. I need to think, to talk with friends. How long will you be here?"

"As long as necessary. I'm at the Britannia Beach Hotel."

"Give me three days. I'll get back in touch with you."

I nodded. The guards escorted me, and I went back through one line of defense after another, like a negotiator bringing a summons.

I wondered if it was worth so much trouble just to protect two hundred million stolen dollars.

*   *   *

The Bahamas archipelago contains a few hundred islands and islets. The Bimini group, which is part of it, is the closest to the Florida coast, only fifty miles away. The Spanish discoverer of Florida, Ponce de Leon, thought it was the site of the legendary Fountain of Youth. More to the point, it's a paradise for big-game fishermen because of the warmth of the Gulf Stream waters that go through it. Hemingway emptied a few bottles there, and dreamed up *The Old Man and the Sea.*

"Have you ever fished for swordfish?"

"I've never even fished for sardines."

I was sitting in the back of a deep-sea fishing boat, in one of those chairs that are bolted to the deck. Robert Zarra was seated next to me, in a similar chair. They had fitted us out with fishing rods and other equipment; I didn't know how to use any of it.

"You have a chance to catch a swordfish," said Zarra. "Who knows? Or a mere barracuda, a white marlin, a sail, a wahoo, a kingfish, a tuna, maybe even a giant tuna bluefish."

"Don't tell me the menu, I'll take the special. And I mainly want to catch a Scot named Donaldson and an Argentinian named Hovius."

"A personal matter?"

"More personal than you can imagine."

Zarra lit a cigar, putting aside his fishing rod with an air of weariness.

"I have your answer," he said. "We've decided to accept your offer. On one condition, however, you must double your financial contribution."

A thrill of unpleasant surprise. "I don't have that much money."

"That's your problem."

"Where do you think I can pick up two million dollars?"

He handed me gloves:

"Put them on, it's better, at least use the left one."

168

Talking business with him amounted to trying to convince a doormat to become a computer. I put on the gloves, and that was when the outery began. I didn't even have time to turn around to find out what was happening; the two patrol boats rushing toward us at an incredible speed had emerged from their hiding place somewhere in the string of Cat Cay islets. Their bows cleaved the violet water and threw up an impressive spray; they were about half a nautical mile from us. Aboard the yacht, the appearance of these two vessels had aroused, if not panic, at least an almost feverish agitation.

I didn't even have time to exclaim, "What's happening?" or some other equally stupid remark; I was torn from the chair, lifted bodily, and carried to a cabin done all in beige leather and marquetry. Everything happened so fast. Robert Zarra had drawn the first puff on his cigar on the bridge, seated in his fishing chair, and here he was, drawing the second puff on a leather sofa. And dull booms were echoing. The engines of our yacht had begun to pump at full capacity, and as far as I could tell, we were getting the hell out of there at a meteoric speed.

"Fun, eh?" Zarra said to me.

"I'm having a ball. Are they really shooting at us?"

"I'm afraid so. Champagne?"

A black waiter uncorked some Dom Perignon.

"It's the American police," Zarra explained. "Or the Coast Guard, the FBI, the CIA or the Texas Rangers, who knows? It happens every other time. I rather enjoy it; distractions are so few."

He sipped his champagne calmly, and I thought of the crocodile again.

"Where were we, Cimballi? Oh, yes, we accept your contribution of two million dollars. One million payable in advance. Now let me see if I have it straight: a certain company has powerful interests in a Latin American country; it has ties to the present rulers, and because of this alliance, has been able to beat out various rival American companies. Those are the facts. Let's come to your hypothesis: you think that sooner or later, the government now in power will be overthrown; that many people in the United States are already working toward that end, not only in official circles but also in . . . other spheres, to which I have ties. Correct?"

169

"Correct."

"Good. What you hope to achieve then, is that as a result of that overthrow, if it occurs, that certain corporation should not only be ousted from that Latin American country which I have not named, but also that the ouster should be accompanied by the heaviest possible financial losses. Correct?"

"Correct."

"If, for example, these people of . . . various American milieus of whom we were speaking decided to use, let's say, a truckers' strike to disrupt the economy of the country in question, you would like that strike to particularly affect that certain corporation. Correct?"

Silence had returned to the sea. The yacht was slowing down and now it adopted a cruising speed.

"Correct."

"And to that sole end, you are ready to contribute up to two million dollars to this, shall we say, anticommunist crusade?"

Never had my idea seemed as crazy to me as at that moment. But I said:

"If I can come up with another million dollars. . . ."

Robert Zarra smiled.

"You'll find it, I'm sure. You're dealing with people who have the highest respect for promises, especially promises made to them. And, since we are in agreement, one last word: We cannot, of course, guarantee the date of the operation."

"I'll wait as long as necessary."

He inspected me with curiosity.

"Do you know Santiago de Chile?"

I shook my head:

"No."

\* \* \*

My first concern on my arrival in Nassau had been to go to that bank where Mr. Hak's hundred million dollars had been transferred, plus the forty-two million worth of profit from the gold speculation. Even though Mr. Hak was dead, I ordered the hundred million to be immediately transferred to a certain bank in the Philippines, as he'd originally instructed me to do. But the forty-two million was still in Nassau, and for now, I hadn't the slightest idea what I should do with it.

Mr. Hak's orders had been precise: I was to send the initial hundred million as soon as possible back to the Philippines, where he may have planned to collect it in order to return it to its owners. I would never know anything more of this matter, and the hundred million may still, to this day, be in that Manila account where I had it sent.

At first, Hak had wanted me to meet him, with what he called "the profits," in some South American country. He had suggested Argentina; I was the one who persuaded him that the meeting should take place in Nassau. He then told me: "Go to Nassau, check in at the Britannia Beach Hotel, and wait. You will be contacted."

By whom? I had been in Nassau for more than a week, and nothing had happened.

Except that the days were slowly passing. On October 3, I did get a phone call, but it was from Marc Lavater:

"Good Lord, Marc, it's four o'clock in the morning!"

"Sorry. Just wanted some news."

"I met that guy, and we're in agreement."

Silence.

"Well, it's off the ground," Lavater said finally. "And it'll happen when?"

"They don't know."

"I'll be in New York, and I'll be meeting with some interesting people there. You wouldn't feel like hopping over to Manhattan?"

I gave it some thought. "Maybe."

"I'll be at the St. Regis from eight o'clock on, for at least three days. Try to come."

Assuming "they" had contacted me by then! After all, I couldn't spend months or years waiting for Mr. Hak's emissary. I kept thinking of the corpse that somebody had fed to the sharks. And what if all communication were finally severed between Mr. Hak—or his successors, those for whom he intended "the profits"—and me? And—even assuming they had been executed—what if Peking decided to come after me? A cold sweat suddenly rolled down my back.

"Franz?"

"I was thinking. Okay, I'll be there on the evening of the tenth."

*171*

"We'll have dinner. I'll expect you."

When four more days went by, my tension mounted. By now I had pretty well decided to leave Nassau, whether I was contacted or not. I thought of marking my trail for the bank, which would then always know where to find me, but, apart from the fact that this would require a complex system of communication between the bank and the Britannia Beach Hotel, it would practically do away with the kind of near-anonymity in which I had been living for two years. I didn't know what to do.

It was a long time since the Turk, Ute, and their escort of "maids" had left the Bahamas and gone back to London. On the eighth, the Turk called me, to find out what was new. I told him I was fine, an optimistic statement, to say the least; everything was jumbled in my head. The kind of mental anguish that this waiting aroused in me, not to mention missing Catherine and anxiety over this wild adventure with Zarra, his Mafia friends, and God knows who else, combined to make me a little crazy.

On the ninth, I reserved a seat on a plane for New York. It was definite: I was getting out of Nassau. I left instructions both at the bank, where the forty-two-plus million dollars was, and the Britannia Beach Hotel. They were to accept all calls made to me, and I would call them myself every day at eight o'clock in the evening, from wherever I was. Awkward as hell, but what else was there to do?

Two American women looking for a husband, seeing me sad and alone, decided to launch an attack; I put up a fierce resistance, and the three of us were having dinner on the evening of the ninth, when someone came to tell me that a Dr. Foo was asking for me.

"Who?"

"Dr. Foo."

I had to be intrigued, at least.

"I'll take the call in my room."

Upstairs, with the door closed, a bloodcurdling scream burst through the receiver, which I had just picked up. Next came calls for help, then a rattle of machine-gun fire, and finally a death rattle.

Then, at last, a voice, almost human. High and shrill but with a jokester's snicker behind it. "Herro. This diaborical Fu Manchu

172

and his evil accomplice. How is honolable and beroved fliend Flanz?"

Cute. They were adorable, those two. I closed my eyes in exasperation, wishing I had both of them where I could get my hands on them. Still, I missed them, Li and Liu.

"You no-good bastards, couldn't you have called sooner?"

"We're in San Francisco, looking for an apartment. We hear you have some money for us."

"A few bucks, that's all. Forty-two million."

"Hot damn!" And those idiots hung up.

\* \* \*

On the evening of the tenth, I was in New York sitting across from Marc Lavater.

"You have a nice tan," he remarked.

"What else was there to do?"

We had taken refuge in a little Italian restaurant where the linguine was disgusting, absolutely disgusting. "Fifteen years ago it was great," Marc said, to excuse himself. "You should come to New York more often."

"And those interesting people you saw?"

"Deaf, dumb and blind. It's super confidential, top secret. Only *Time* Magazine, the *Washington Post*, and two or three hundred journalists are in on it, not to mention the Director of the C.I.A. That's how unsecret it is. They give Allende a year to live, at most. And they'll use a truckers' strike to set it off. Your crazy idea seems to be coming together."

"Who are 'they'?"

"Read the papers. The C.I.A., ITT, the Mafia, everybody, a whole mess. I can't keep track of it all."

"Stop kidding around, Marc."

"I don't feel like kidding around. I feel more like throwing up, and it may not be the linguine. I feel like throwing up because of what they say is going to happen in Chile. Shall we go somewhere else to eat?" I'd never seen him so emotional; it was unlike Lavater's usual calm.

"I've gotten involved with Zarra, and there's no way to back out. Not with guys like that."

"Why should you back out?" Even assuming you could? There's no reason to. You're taking advantage of a situation, you're not creating it. It would happen exactly the same way without you. Come on, let's get the hell out of here, I really feel sick."

His "incredibly good little Italian restaurant" was not too far from Madison Square Garden, where a mounted policeman was keeping an eye on the fans leaving some kind of game. Marc and I set off on foot toward Times Square, on pavements that were becoming dangerously empty. Taking me by surprise, Marc asked me suddenly:

"Why don't you marry her?"

I must have looked astounded.

"Who?"

"Catherine Varles."

"I didn't know you knew her."

"I saw you together at Regine's. And I know her mother."

The streets of Manhattan were empty, except for a few solitary groups of hippies and Blacks. A feeling of danger. We should have taken a taxi.

"Marc, I'm not marrying her for the simple reason that she won't marry me. Not now, she says. She says we'll get married when I'm finished running after . . . what I'm running after."

We had reached Times Square, which was lively or not, depending on your point of view, and without consulting each other, as though we were betting which one would give in first, we continued as far as the St. Regis. Strange city, where walking the streets after eight o'clock at night becomes a dangerous adventure.

The next day, I flew to San Francisco.

\* \* \*

At San Francisco airport there was a policeman about eight feet tall, and beside him, two small gray sausages, monstrously padded, in Mao-style tunics, wearing bright red conical hats and long pigtails trailing on the ground. The two sausages, who looked like they had been inflated with helium, hurled themselves at my knees, kissing them; they prostrated themselves, kissing my feet and hands, uttering shrill cries, with a feverish devotion that bordered on delirium. They looked like Peking spies and wore thick black glasses. The eight-foot-tall policeman looked at me suspiciously:

"Friends of yours?"

174

"I brought them up. I gave them their first solid food. On your feet!"

The three of us went out, the sausages and me, and climbed into a Rolls-Royce Silver Shadow. I asked:

"Was this circus really necessary?"

"Miserable Li and Liu affectionately greet honorable Franz and welcome him to San Francisco," said Li (or Liu). "Did you bring the money?"

"We would have loved to see your mug in Nassau the other day, when we called you," added Liu (or Li). "Have you got it on you?" And they grabbed for my pockets.

They had a pretty wooden house, built soon after the earthquake at the beginning of the century, on the heights of Telegraph Hill. Two painters' studios were nearby; right next to them was a pop art sculptor who specialized in making nothing but little fingers of the left hand; he had started with a normal-sized little finger, his own, a cast of which he sold for a hundred dollars to a Texan. He sold the next one for five thousand dollars, and it was true that the next one was already nine feet long; he was working on one thirty feet long for which several contemporary art museums were competing; the latest offer was a hundred thousand dollars.

In the house next door to Li's and Liu's was a woman writer, who lived surrounded by dogs; three actors lived across the way, and last but not least, a ballet troupe, which was rehearsing when we arrived. Li and Liu introduced me to everyone and took me into their house. It had three floors, and was sumptuously furnished; on the third and top floor, a huge bay window revealed a panorama of San Francisco, with the view carrying as far as Sausalito.

"And from the other side you can see Chinatown," they giggled.

"Superb. Rented or bought?"

"First rented, then bought three days ago, when you told us about the money."

I looked at Golden Gate, and in a few seconds, the fog which had been absent earlier began rapidly overtaking it. I turned around: Li and Liu had taken off their tunics, which matched the Rolls, and the cushions with which they had made themselves plump; they were once again slender and nimble, and were smiling at me.

"I'm glad to see you again, you clowns. I thought you were dead."

"We're glad, too." Their faces grew serious for a moment.

"Why didn't you tell me sooner that that money was for you? *Was* it for you?"

"It's for us."

This would be one of the few occasions when Li and Liu looked solemn or spoke seriously. They told their story simply, without buffoonery. Uncle Hak had always been a rather mysterious relative, and neither of the boys had ever dared to inquire into his affairs. The success of that silly kung fu movie had made Li and Liu ambitious; they wanted to make real films, even artistic ones. They decided to leave Hong Kong and strike out on their own, in the States.

To their surprise, Uncle Hak said he would come with them, or, rather, that he would join his nephews later. They suspected at once that something might be terribly wrong; why should Hak leave his island, of which he was absolute ruler, to go to a country whose people he had always professed to despise as barbarians?

But China is a land where you don't argue with your elders, and Li and Liu had agreed at once. Then Uncle Hak had become furtive, even mysterious. He'd planned a very roundabout itinerary for the brothers—Hong Kong to Los Angeles by way of London with a stopover in New York. "In case they were followed," he'd said.

Who would want to follow Li or Liu? But dutifully, they'd done exactly as he'd planned . . . hopping from plane to plane and flying half-way around the world, like a pair of spies. Being Li and Liu, they had quite enjoyed it, wallowing in melodrama.

Arriving in New York, they had found a message instructing them not to go to Los Angeles, but instead to San Francisco, where Uncle Hak would meet with them.

"But he didn't come."

I told them about my visit to the deserted house in the New Territories, though I didn't tell them about the meal the sharks had shared. Li and Liu were a lot less nutty than they appeared.

"And Ching has disappeared too?"

"Not a trace."

"Then it's serious."

At their request, I explained the gold speculation business.

"What does that mean, convertibility?"

They looked at me wide-eyed, which isn't so easy for Chinese. So Uncle Hak had "borrowed" a hundred million dollars, for speculation purposes, intending to replace the money when the operation was completed?

"So he didn't steal anything, since he meant to give back the money, or gave it back."

"What he did is not exactly legal. And I don't know if the money has been returned or not."

"And even you couldn't get back the money, the hundred million in the Philippines?"

"I transferred the money to an account which isn't mine, I no longer have any control over it. And I don't want control. That money is so hot it's scalding."

"You think we can go to Los Angeles now?"

How should I know? I could only suspect what had happened to Hak, or the reasons which had led someone to send Li and Liu to northern California rather than southern California.

"We'll stay here for a while," Li and Liu said. "We've heard of a young filmmaker who's thinking about a huge science-fiction movie, something like a battle among the stars. He lives on Telegraph Hill. We might be able to work with him."

With forty-two-plus million dollars, they could not only live without working, but could produce their own movies. Apparently, they hadn't realized that yet, or perhaps they thought that the money belonged more to Uncle Hak than to them. That was their problem. My problem was different. When Li and Liu had told me on the phone that they were waiting for me and their forty-two-plus million dollars, I couldn't help being amazed at the tricks fate plays. What a coincidence!

Sidney H. Lamm, Number Six on my list, was here. Through the bay window on the third floor of my friends' house, in fact, I discovered that Lamm was now within rifle range.

Literally and figuratively!

# 15

His offices were on California Street, not far from the Transamerica Building. He lived in a lovely apartment with a wraparound balcony looking out on amusing Lombard Street, a red brick street that does its best, by slithering like a drunk rattlesnake, to hurtle down head first to the bottom of the hill.

I had already met Lamm, but the risk that he might recognize me was so small as to be negligible. I had been eight years old on August 27, 1956, when he had come to St. Tropez to see my father. Lamm had spoken to him a long time the very day before his death.

That visit remained etched in my memory because of a scene that had particularly struck me. La Capilla, the house my father owned in St. Tropez, the house where I was born and where he died, was shaped like a U, opening onto the Pampelonne beach. My father's office was at the tip of the left branch of the U, as you looked out to sea. Lamm was in this office with my father that August 27, in the early afternoon, and I was in the garden, returning from the pool or the beach, several dozen feet ahead of my mother, who was talking with a friend. At that moment, voices were raised in the office, and my father began to shout, which was very unusual for him. His customary temper was calm. The words are still in my head: "I don't call that negligence! I call that theft! And I'll take care of you as soon as I can!"

My father died the next day; he didn't "take care" of Sidney Lamm. I had asked the investigators recruited by Marc Lavater to find out what in Lamm's past, fifteen years ago, had justified my father's accusations. They had found nothing, probably because all traces were erased by Lamm himself, with full agreement from the executor of the will, Martin Yahl, in exchange for Lamm's silence. It might even have been a way of making sure that he would never talk, and would never bring up the subject of Andrea Cimballi.

And in the final analysis, it didn't much matter. I was convinced that Lamm had betrayed my father, twice instead of once, since he had even tried to rob him while he was alive. The rest was unimportant; I wasn't his judge, but his executioner.

I had already set events in train to entrap Hovius and Donaldson; now I was right here, under Lamm's nose, and the opportunity was too god-given to waste. While Zarra and his . . . Americans . . . were making their plans for Chile, I was supposed to be getting my hands on another million dollars. If I worked this right, I could kill two pigeons with the same rock—put an end to Lamm's comfort and make a few dollars in the process.

My dossier on Sidney Harrison Lamm informed me that he was a gambler and a bluffer, capable of taking the most insane risks. He was possessed of that supreme naïveté of gamblers and sharks: luck always owes them something. And so preoccupied with hoodwinking a victim, he might not notice that he was about to become a victim himself.

Yes, I decided to stay on in San Francisco.

*  *  *

It took me six weeks to set everything up.

We worked out every detail as though we were setting up a movie, and indeed, there were many elements present of a comic scenario, even a farce. We rented a set of exquisitely expensive and extravagant offices in one of the Embarcadero Center skyscrapers; that was our sound stage. Li and Liu had costumes made for me in the form of badly tailored suits of sleazy fabric, with patch pockets and too much shoulder padding. They even bought me a large and flashy "diamond" pinky ring, and this I absolutely refused to wear. But when I looked in the mirror and saw the total effect they had achieved—a nouveau riche boy with more money than taste, and too young to have developed many smarts—I knew they were right about the ring, and put it on. It complemented the nauseating necktie that gave the finishing touch.

I was perfect. You'd rush to buy a used car from me, because I looked so gullible.

The telephone rang, then my secretary answered, and, after the usual delay, my caller stated his identity:

"My name won't mean anything to you, of course: it's Sidney Harrison Lamm."

"I'm sorry, Mr. . . Lamm? I don't know you."

"Mr. Joseph Benharoun . . . are you French?"

179

"That's right."

I did my best to speak with what I thought was a heavy North African accent.

"You don't have a trace of an accent," said Lamm's voice. "I think it would be good for us to meet, Mr. Benharoun. I'm in the real-estate business, I dabble in it, on the side, but nonetheless . . ."

I replied that, my schedule permitting, I would be happy to make his acquaintance, that it would give me the greatest pleasure, and that I was practically overjoyed to learn that his offices were next door to mine—what a coincidence! "I could hop over," he said. He hopped, and there we were, face to face.

Despite the fifteen years that had gone by, I recognized him. He was a very handsome man, slim and elegant, tanned, perfectly dressed, six inches taller than I, and not lacking in charm. But I knew he was a shark, and was sure I would have spotted him as such without even knowing him, by something in his eyes.

What worried me was: would *he* recognize *me?* Oh, I know I had come a long way from my eight-year-old face, but everybody had always told me how much I resembled my father. Now that I was a man, was I wearing Andrea Cimballi's face? And, in fact, an uneasy look came into Lamm's eye as he shook my hand, but I could almost hear his mental shrug. Whatever was itching in his memory, he couldn't put his finger on it to scratch it.

"So young, and in business already," he said. "I'm impressed."

I assumed a falsely modest look, serious and sure of myself. I launched into a big speech about what I wanted to do, my outlook on life; I gave many examples of my wicked cunning, my diabolical subtlety, my phenomenal capacity for work; I called my poor secretary three times to give her unnecessary orders. In short, I really did everything possible to convince him that I was really nothing but a pretentious young idiot, naïve and easy to bamboozle, who mattered only because of the money left him by his uncle, who had gotten rich on the backs of the "wogs" in Algeria.

Lamm listened to me with an indulgent and benevolent patience, at best with a fleeting gleam of irony in his eyes when he glanced at my pinky ring. He managed to appear impressed by what he called my drive. And there he was, not to be outdone, singing a hymn to "America, land of free enterprise," while watching me out of the corner of his eye, and obviously wondering if I was as stupid as I looked. He finally came to the point of his visit:

"My dear Joe—I *can* call you Joe, can't I?—my dear Joe, as it happens, only the day before yesterday, I was driving on the road to Mount Tamalpais. It's a place that's always been dear to my heart."

I looked interested.

You must know that the city of San Francisco is built on a peninsula, pointing approximately north. Across from it is another peninsula, Marin; the two fingers of land are separated by only a mile and the Golden Gate bridge. Mount Tamalpais is in Marin, beyond Sausalito, which is the first city you come to after you cross the Golden Gate bridge from San Francisco.

"You know, Joe," said Lamm, "to me, Sausalito and the whole region around Mount Tamalpais are where I grew up. I'm attached to it for sentimental reasons. When I was a child, my dear father had a big house at the foot of the redwoods. I used to play on the white sand of Stinson Beach. Sometimes we climbed Mount Tam to look at the Pacific and the Sierra Nevada."

I nodded gravely. Of course, I was perfectly aware of everything in Lamm's background. His real name was Sygmunt Lammerski; he was born in Chicago, and when he came out of the reform school where he spent his youth, he had gone on to sell vacuum cleaners, insurance policies, his virility to elderly ladies, before striking it rich in real estate and cheating at it, since my father had caught him with his hand in the cookie jar. And his present wealth was based on the two hundred fifty thousand dollars that Martin Yahl had most likely given him in the autumn of 1956.

But I continued to play dumb.

"And that's how," Lamm continued, "the day before yesterday, as I happened to be making one of those trips to my childhood home, I learned from the Lopezes, old friends, what had happened."

He slapped his forehead.

"I couldn't believe my ears! I simply couldn't believe it! I called Art Becknall, the attorney who handles the affairs of the Elbert family, and I had to accept the evidence: It was true!"

"What was true?"

Lamm raised his hands to the heavens:

"I've been trying to buy that land for months! What am I say-ing—not months, years! And here you show up in San Francisco, where you don't know a soul, and with the first offer you make, they give you what they've always refused to give me! Isn't that enough to drive you crazy?"

I assumed a cold, dignified manner:

"It's probably because I offered more than you did."

He stared at me, rose, began pacing, feigned checked anger, stormy, barely controllable, and feigned it perfectly. I could al-most believe it. He came back and sat down.

"Joe, how old are you? Twenty-two, twenty-three? Please don't get mad at what I'm going to tell you. I'm not a real real-estate developer myself, it's only a hobby with me. With the fortune I inherited from my parents, I could easily live without working. But let me tell you a few things anyway. You paid six hundred thousand dollars for one hundred thirty-seven acres. That's a relatively large sum, even for me."

This time I looked wounded:

"I have substantial resources."

He smiled indulgently.

"Come on, Joe, San Francisco is my city. The manager of the bank where you deposited your money just happens to be one of my best friends, you see what a small world it is. So I know that the six hundred thousand dollars you paid is almost your entire capital. Oh, I bet I know what you wanted to do with that land. You said to yourself that twenty miles from San Fran-cisco, with that marvelous view of the Pacific, the Sierra Nevada, Santa Cruz, and San Francisco Bay, with all those assets, you could do a fantastic business, and that all you had to do was parcel it out, resell your land in small pieces—"

"Don't forget that I got the property. Not you."

With the most charming smile in the world:

"I certainly admit I should have paid more attention to the matter. That's the drawback of being a mere amateur. But you should know that you were incredibly lucky; Becknall put the land up for sale twelve hours before you arrived. And that's not the most important thing, Joe. There are two basic facts you don't know—"

"Who is this Elbert family you're talking about? They're not the ones I dealt with."

He crowed:

"Precisely! Precisely, Joe! That's the first fact I was referring to: you've been had, my friend. You bought your land from a company headquartered in the Bahamas, one of those anonymous deals where you never know who's behind it. Those guys took you for a ride! You paid them six hundred thousand dollars for land they bought for four hundred fifty thousand dollars less than three weeks earlier, from the Elbert family. In other words, they made a hundred fifty thousand on you!"

The situation demanded that I first appear stunned, then become belligerent.

"What business is it of yours?"

"Calm down, Joe," Lamm said, cordially. "If you don't believe me, ask Art Becknall; he's the most honest man in the world. But it gets worse, Joe, there's another basic fact: the land you bought is undevelopable! I've always known that, don't forget I played there as a child. That Bahamas company . . . what was your vendor's name?"

"There were two of them—Koski and Sasplan."

"I don't know them."

(I thought: that doesn't surprise me. On the other hand, if he *had* known them, it would have stupefied me!)

"I don't know them, but those two guys must have been crooks. It's impossible to divide up Tamalpais. That land is only good for hunting rabbits or for nature lovers like me."

That mendacious sonofabitch! But I stayed in character, I was gradually incredulous, suspicious, doubtful, worried, and, finally, crushed.

"I'm terribly, terribly sorry," said Lamm, with a sincerity worthy of an Academy Award.

I played the wretch grasping at anything, no matter how small a hope.

"You said it was undevelopable—what does that mean?"

He shook his head, like an indulgent father at his son's escapades:

"Joe, you were very careless in this matter. If you had taken more time to read the contract that those two bandits—what did you say their names were?"

"Sasplan and Koski."

"That those two bandits made you sign, you would have noticed that according to a provision of Dwight Elbert's will, the

183

land cannot sustain any construction until after December 31, 1975. That's a legal provision which no one can go against. Furthermore, in buying the land, you committed yourself ipso facto to honor it. Why do you think the Elbert land hasn't been sold up to now? Who would invest hundreds of thousands of dollars in a piece of land that will *perhaps* be developed years from now?"

Silence. I did my best to look pale. In reality, the blood was coursing through my veins so hotly that I was sure my face was bright red. This was the first time I was face-to-face with one of my father's enemies, my first real confrontation. Carradine and Bremer had slipped through my hands by dying; I had laid very low during the entire Landau affair so that nobody would suspect my part in it. But this man, bland and silky, was sitting here, within reach of my fingers, obviously tickled to death with himself. His complacency enraged me, but I had to go on playing the fool. My entire scheme depended on it.

"Well, well!" Lamm sighed.

He rose and tapped me on the shoulder.

"We've all made mistakes, Joe. When I learned what had happened, I had to come and warn you. The real-estate profession has a few bad examples of unscrupulous characters in it—that's why I'm an amateur, I'd rather stay out of it. But not everyone has the same scruples. You know where my office is—here's my home address. Take a few days to get over the terrible disappointment you're feeling, and call me. Perhaps by then I may have found a solution for you. I know so many people in this city. So, call me. In three days. And I'll help you. Don't forget. Three days . . ."

We shook hands. He left. I sent my secretary home: "I want to be alone," I said, my throat tight, my face gray, and my tone funereal.

And as soon as both of them were gone, I began to laugh. I opened the door—which had been locked up to then—leading to the neighboring offices, and I brought in Li and Liu, Koski the finger sculptor and Sasplan the painter and a few other friends, including a satirical male ballet troupe in full drag.

And we had a party like you wouldn't believe.

\* \* \*

Of course, Sidney Harrison Lamm was a goddamned liar.

He had, for example, exaggerated the remarkable honesty of Arthur Becknall. Arthur Becknall, in exchange for having Li and Liu as clients—forty-two million dollars to manage, and clover under the table—had readily agreed to tell big lies to the aforesaid Lamm.

Sidney Lamm had lied about his youthful memories; lied about his parents' wealth; lied about his amateur status in real estate. He was a professional who, at the time, was not strictly speaking in a tight spot, but was nonetheless tied up on two other fronts in clean deals for which he had obtained large bank loans. He had something to fall back on. According to the closest estimates of the team of experts hired by Lavater, he was "worth" about one and a half million dollars.

He had lied again in informing me that the land had been bought for four hundred fifty thousand dollars by the Bahamas company from the Elbert heirs. I knew, since the Bahamas company was me. What I had paid was two hundred fifty thousand dollars. And I had resold the land to that idiot Joseph Benharoun—me again—for six hundred thousand dollars; that much was true.

Lamm had lied, because he was preparing to buy the land from me for his own benefit. And because everyone knows that no real-estate developer, even with the most heartrending sentimental reasons in the world, would agree to pay six hundred thousand dollars for land that is hardly worth more than two hundred thousand.

Lamm knew it also, and also knew that if he tried to make Joseph Benharoun swallow a pill like that, even Joseph Benharoun would be suspicious. Whereas if Joseph Benharoun thought that the land was worth four or five hundred thousand dollars, he would not find it improbable that the good Sidney Lamm, with his big heart, his huge fortune inherited from his parents, his childhood memories, and his ecological interests, should be willing to pay, let's say, five hundred or five hundred fifty thousand, which would reduce poor Joseph Benharoun's losses. . . .

It had first been necessary to find the land. The real-estate agents I consulted had first directed me to Napa Valley, north of San Francisco Bay; it's a wine-growing area, which wasn't much use to me. I wanted rocks, not good growing soil. Then they showed me (officially not me, but Koski and Sasplan; I was only their anonymous chauffeur) other properties, this time in the south. I had almost decided on something else when I learned of the existence of Tamalpais, with its strange hereditary clause. A flash.

I bought the land immediately, and just as quickly resold it to myself, for six hundred thousand dollars, which I paid myself, cash on the barrel.

With the six hundred eighty thousand dollars I had deposited in the name of Joseph Benharoun in that little bank whose manager—not coincidentally—was one of Lamm's close friends. After withdrawing the six hundred thousand dollars—a little more for expenses and Becknall's fees—I confided my worries and even my hopes to that same manager—certain that, sooner or later, these confidences would get back to Lamm.

And Lamm had wound up phoning me.

And that was the end of phase one.

*　*　*

The second phase had actually begun shortly before, with the arrival in San Francisco of two Chinese, supposedly from Saigon. They made no attempt to conceal their intentions: they were in the United States, in California, to invest substantial moneys in real estate. They were, they said, representing several of their compatriots and countrymen in Vietnam and Cambodia, who were quite anxious over the gains of the North Vietnamese army. They had met real-estate agents in Los Angeles and southern California, and the prices had stunned them. In the north, they thought, the prices should be more reasonable. By accident, they met a certain real-estate agent who, again by accident, directed them to one of the projects Lamm was involved in. All these "accidents" had cost me twenty thousand dollars under the table.

"We're mainly looking for land," the Chinese told Lamm. "We like San Francisco because it's a city where there are already sixty thousand Chinese-Americans in Chinatown alone. We would like some land in order to establish—not immediately, but in the coming years—a real little Chinese city, where we would be together, with our families; obeying the laws of our new country, of course, but also with respect for our traditions. Ours is a long-term project. We will remain in Vietnam and Cambodia as long as possible, and for many more years, we hope. . . ."

(That was one of the springs of the trap set for Lamm: the Tamalpais land could not be developed until January 1976—there were four long years to wait!)

A question from Lamm: "How much do you want to spend?" In reality, Lamm was not entirely ignorant on this score; both Becknall and the real-estate agent who, through my efforts, had put him in touch with the two Chinese, had fully enlightened him on this point. The reply from Li and Liu—excuse me, the two Chinese from Vietnam: "Two million dollars for the land, if it's worth it. . . ."

A discreet inquiry by Lamm, which convinced him that the two Chinese really did have the resources; they had made deposits up to twenty million dollars in various San Francisco banks, and had already begun to make real investments, such as the house on Telegraph Hill; but they had also bought a building in Oakland and huge warehouses in Berkeley. (These were genuine investments the brothers had made with part of their new money.)

A week later, Lamm and Becknall had dinner together. Lamm mentioned the Chinese, who were looking for land. "What a pity," cried Becknall, whom I had previously coached. "If you had only mentioned it to me two weeks ago! Especially since your friends from Saigon aren't in a hurry to build! Too bad."

"Why?"

"Because you're too late. I had just the right piece of land at Tamalpais, but someone has just bought it."

"Who?"

"A slightly naïve young Frenchman who thinks he's a big shot in business—one Joseph Benharoun. You should see that ridiculous ring he sports! And his ties!"

According to formula, Lamm had to try to contact the young idiot named Joseph Benharoun.

And that was the end of phase two.

* * *

The third phase opened with a telephone call I made on Monday the 14th:

"Mr. Sidney Lamm? Joe Benharoun here."

A silence, as though he had forgotten my name and I was miles from his thoughts—when I well knew that he had been feverishly awaiting my call for six days, hounded as he was by

Li and Liu, who had practically enjoined him to show them that famous piece of land in Tamalpais he had already told them about, and who were even talking—since Lamm did not want to deal with them—of buying those one hundred fifty acres in Half Moon Bay—"Cheap, Mr. Lamm, barely a million five hundred thousand dollars"—that another agency had offered them.

"Ah, Joe! How's it going?"

"Can I see you? Today? Tomorrow, maybe?" My voice was frantic.

At the other end of the line, that scoundrel delivered a really fine performance: "I'm not free today, lots of meetings, you know how it is, and I'm having dinner with the mayor this evening. As for tomorrow, unfortunately—wait! If it's so urgent . . . I'll call you back, Joe. . . ."

And he called me back twenty minutes later, oozing charm. "What luck, Joe, I was able to get away. I'll take you to have some seafood at Aliotto's, since Scoma's is closed at lunch. . . ."

Within the hour we found ourselves facing the charming panorama of Fisherman's Wharf and the Golden Gate Bridge, shrouded in fog; with crabs in the foreground, on our plates. I played to the hilt the role I had devised for his benefit. Alternately the confident businessman, and then, suddenly, the little French kid, a bit too big for his britches and almost pitiful. And lo and behold, as I talked, something happened to me. I saw this same man, emerging suddenly from my memory, his face white as he left my father's office in St. Tropez, going around the house beneath the pines to reach his car, and throwing me a murderous look as he passed. To a certain extent, this man had killed my father, or helped to kill him, and then betrayed him again after his death. For five or six seconds, I was so overcome with hatred that it made me tremble, to the point where Lamm noticed my emotion and fortunately ascribed it to other causes:

"Is something wrong, Joe?"

I drank a little water, my temples bathed in sweat.

"Joe, I guess the last few days must not have been easy for you. . . ."

He said: "Joe, I've been so busy this whole time that I've hardly had time to think about your problem. . . ." What problem?

Come on, he knew what a tough position I was in, with that six hundred thousand dollars locked up for years. "You're stuck, my boy . . . it's sad, but true. Still, for all the reasons you're familiar with . . ."

For sentimental reasons, and also because the wealth inherited from Pop enabled him to leave a totally unproductive investment alone for four long years, he agreed to buy the Tamalpais property from me.

"Five hundred thousand dollars, Joe. That's all I can do. Amateurism and love of nature have their limits. Think of the interest I could earn on half a million deposited for four years." I got up and left.

He called me two hours later at my office in Embarcadero.

"Good Lord, Joe, what got into you?"

We met again, for the second time that day, in a bar on California Street.

"Joe, I've had time to think it over. I tried to manipulate you, and it didn't work; you're cleverer than I thought. Okay, I'll make it up to you. The truth is that I already have an idea of who I might be able to sell that land to in four years, without making a big profit, of course, but I don't do this so much for the money. No hard feelings?"

He smiled, tanned, elegant, charming. I had him over the barrel, but he'd choke before he showed it.

"Six hundred thousand dollars, Joe. The price you paid yourself."

I sulked:

"Six hundred ten thousand. Let me make *something*, at least."

He frowned, and for a second, I was afraid I had gone too far. But he burst out laughing:

"Okay, you sly young Frenchman."

We signed that very day, Tuesday the 15th, and he paid me cash, to the tune of five hundred and fifty thousand dollars to a Panamanian company I had set up specially for the occasion and sixty thousand in cash. "Why in cash?" I mumbled a confused explanation about my uncle in Algeria and money I owed him, and since he knew from our mutual banker that the Benharoun account was nearly empty, he thought the money was going to pay off some deal I had tried and failed to bring off.

*189*

Which reinforced his conviction that I was certainly nothing but an arrant young imbecile and a loser.

Just between us, I had just sold him, for six hundred ten thousand dollars, land that could not be developed for several years, for which I had paid, under the cover of my Bahamas company, two hundred thousand. That was already gratifying, but the game had hardly begun.

And to mark the end of phase three, I let him pay for our drinks.

* * *

Even before he managed to "talk me out of" the Tamalpais property, Lamm was convinced that it was going to be his. So sure was he, that when those two Chinese from Saigon (otherwise known as Li and Liu) put the pressure on him to let them see the land, Lamm gave in and drove them up there. This was six days *before* I had with sadness and chagrin parted with my undevelopable mountain. It was risky business, to offer for sale something you don't own, but Lamm didn't want to let these two wealthy and gullible Chinese slip through his fingers.

He took them in his own car, sitting alone up front like a chauffeur while Li and Liu chattered in Chinese in the luxurious back seat of the BMW. Like just about everybody else in California, Sidney Lamm drove an expensive German car.

The boys had dressed for the occasion. Where they'd picked up their Halloween costumes Buddha alone knew. They looked like a pair of Charlie Chans on cook's night out. They wore long robes of dark blue silk, fastened up the front with a hundred tiny buttons. The robes had wide sleeves, and the boys went so far as to fold their hands and tuck them up the sleeves, as Chinese do only in caricatures of Chinese. On their heads they wore little black silk skullcaps with a button on the top. They had everything except the Fu Manchu mustaches and the pigtails. It was a good thing that Sidney Lamm didn't know that real Chinese businessmen wear three-button gray suits and old school ties.

These outrageous clowns were enjoying every minute of this charade. Each of them was desperate to keep his own face straight while trying like crazy to break the other one up.

Solemnly, they pretended to discuss "business" in the back seat, while actually swapping dirty jokes. In perfect Mandarin, of course. When occasionally they addressed a serious remark to Lamm, it was in atrocious pidgin English.

I couldn't even begin to reproduce it for you accurately, because you might not believe that a man as shrewd as Lamm would fall for their "Confucius Say" act. But greed turns intelligent men into idiots and Lamm's thoughts were more tightly fastened on the Chinamen's bank accounts than on the Chinamen themselves.

It was a perfect day, a rare and glorious day of clear sunshine and soft, fluffy clouds. Leaves glistened on the trees as though they'd been freshly washed. A soft breeze whispered through the boughs of Tamalpais's majestic pine trees. From the summit, you could see for many miles, out over the water, and even into the county beyond. The views were spectacular. The mountain looked as beautiful as a woman when you first desire her. I wish I'd been there, not only to see the natural splendor but to witness Liu's and Li's burlesque. But, then, Joseph Benharoun wasn't even supposed to know that these potential buyers existed, let alone come along for the ride.

"Would you care to go over the property?" asked Lamm suavely.

Would they!

For hours, they ran around the mountain like a pair of fox terriers chasing a rat, while Sidney Lamm panted after them, sweating and out of breath. The boys did everything but climb the trees. Maybe if they hadn't been hampered by their long tight silk robes, they would have done that, too. They investigated every crag, every rock, every gully and every rise, and all the while they kept chattering away in Chinese.

"This byooful property," they told Lamm in pidgin English.

"This guy's gonna drop dead of a coronary occlusion," they told each other in Chinese.

"We want land," they said to Lamm.

"What a turkey," they said to each other.

"We see Half Moon Bay property. We like. We were gonna buy, sign papers tonight. Give money. But we like this more better, you betcha. We buy. Sign chopchop. You sell? But we no pay two million dollar. You ask too much dollar. One million two hundred thousand. Top dollar. No penny more." And they folded their hands up their sleeves and looked inscrutable. The fourth phase had already begun.

191

Note the way they brought the conversation around to the price of the transaction. In actual fact, Lamm had never mentioned a price. And the two partners had been careful not to ask him for one. The only time money was mentioned was when Lamm had merely inquired about their resources. Li and Liu had answered: "Two million dollar."

That day, after their visit to the property, they pretended to consider the figure they had given as the price Lamm had set. When the two clowns and I had rehearsed the scene, Li and Liu did not believe such a misunderstanding was plausible, and I had replied: "What have we got to lose by trying?"

As a matter of fact, when Lamm heard them talking about a million two hundred thousand dollars, he had three possible solutions. One, he could protest, saying he had never heard money mentioned, and settle matters—an honest developer would do that; two, he could keep still, and accept the misunderstanding as a miracle from heaven; and three, he could ask for more. And since Lamm was endowed with a nonexistent moral sense, he chose the third solution.

"I can hardly go below one and a half million," he said.

Li looked serious. Liu looked solemn. One and a half million was no laughing matter. All the while, they were close to exploding with laughter, and only a monumental effort and all the acting skill they could muster up between them kept the charade rolling merrily along.

The partners put their skullcapped heads together and talked business. In Chinese. For a very long time. A very, *very* long time, while Lamm waited, and Lamm wondered, and Lamm broke out in a sweat that was alternately hot and cold. I'm curious to know what Lamm would have done if he'd realized that the "partners" were taking turns reciting an endless 16th century poetic epic in which a heroine is pursued by dragon-men.

At last they broke off, and turned to Lamm. "We pay one million four hundred fifty thousand dollar," they agreed. "But you build wall."

"Build wall?" Lamm looked stupefied.

"Wall all around property," Li and Liu nodded. "Four gates. We want big wall and four gates. And access. You pay costs."

"Well . . ."

"No. You pay, then we pay. We want big wall, four gates. Dragon gates. Like so." And down from Li's sleeve dropped a thinly-rolled blueprint. A massive wall with four huge gates, guarded by monumental dragons. Specifications for the exact dimensions of the dragons were included in the blueprint. Lamm could only goggle.

"Exact same so," insisted Li.

Liu nodded his agreement. "Big wall. Four gates. Dragons. Access. You do first. Put in contract. You pay for work, we pay for land. Otherwise, no deal. We sign contract for Half Moon Bay tonight."

Lamm thought fast. On the one hand, he didn't own the land and couldn't with any legality make an agreement to wall it in, dragons or no dragons. On the other hand, if he said no, he'd lose these two suckers, and somebody else would make a killing. It didn't bear thinking of. On the one hand, the wall sounded expensive, very expensive. It might run him as high as fifty thousand dollars. On the other hand, he stood to make at least ten times that in profit alone on these Chinese. What could a few measly dragons cost, after all?

As it turned out, they cost $295,000. Li and Liu demanded exact replicas of ancient dragons for which they would provide a model, and they wanted not only two at each gate in the wall, but another one stationed every three hundred feet along the wall. The wall it-self was to be fifteen feet high and a foot thick, and to encircle completely the Tamalpais property boundaries. And all of this to be included in the contract, or no sale. For men who were supposed to know practically no English, Li and Liu were surprisingly able to get their meaning across when they had to.

For the time being, Lamm was still ignorant of such details. Another thing was worrying him: He was in the process of selling a property which he did not yet possess, since, contrary to his promise, Joseph Benharoun hadn't yet called. All of this was taking place, on Wednesday, whereas Lamm's purchase of the land from "Joe Benharoun" was not to occur until the following Tuesday. So he felt rather uncomfortable, and this explains his haste to conclude the transaction with me. He asked the Chinese:

"When would you like us to sign the contract?"

"Chopchop," answered the bozos, "we must leave for Saigon chopchop, to see beloved ancestor."

Lamm smiled. He was used to this kind of acrobatics, he had seen it before. He was sure he could quickly get in touch with that simpleton Joe Benharoun and buy his land from him at the

*193*

best price. Anyway, that jerk Joe Benharoun should be calling him any moment now.

No luck. Joe Benharoun would be impossible to find for six days, and would not reappear until the following Tuesday. Lamm did not know this either at the time. He took the Chinese back to San Francisco and heard them ask that construction of the wall and gate begin as soon as possible.

At first Lamm refused: "I cannot commit such large sums without a guarantee. What if you change your mind?"

It was agreed that Li and Liu would make a one-hundred-fifty-thousand-dollar down payment in exchange for a tersely written promise of sale merely stating the whereabouts of the land referred to as the Elbert property at Tamalpais.

"But," said the Chinese, "since we're leaving next Monday, the fourteenth, we must sign before our departure."

"There's not enough time!" protested Lamm.

"At half Moon Bay, they're ready to sign immediately," the Sublime Ones retorted.

Lamm gave in, telling himself that he would get in touch with me before then. He wasn't able to. As we have seen, I did not resurface as Benharoun until the following day, and rather than lose the deal, he signed a promise of sale on Monday the fourteenth, for which he received one hundred forty-five thousand dollars, and was instructed to begin the wall construction under the orders of his clients' business advisers. Since he obviously could not, on the fourteenth, sell a property he had not yet bought, he took advantage of the late hour of the signing to date the document Tuesday, the fifteenth.

*   *   *

Under cover of the Panamanian company, I concluded the property sale to Lamm on Tuesday the 15th. The next day, the 16th, I was in Sacramento, the capital and government seat of the State of California. Wrapped in a towel was the sixty thousand dollars in cash that Lamm had given me. The bundles still bore the paper bands with the logo of Lamm's bank on them.

Just before leaving San Francisco, I set in motion the procedures for dissolving the Panamian company, whose total assets, five hundred fifty thousand dollars, resulting from the land sale, were sped to a numbered bank account in the Bahamas.

In the afternoon, I deposited the sixty thousand dollars cash to the account of the person I will call here the Man from Sacramento. In reality, I did not make the payment myself; that honor went to my friend Sasplan, who sported dark glasses and a false moustache for the occasion. In the excitement of the moment, he wanted to add a false beard, but I refused; he already had the face of a born bandit, they would have thought it was a hold-up.

Li and Liu did leave San Francisco on the evening of Monday the 14th, heading for Tokyo, where they really did have some personal business. This detail of the date and time of their departure is crucial. Their presence on board the Pan Am jet would have been noticed: it's not every day you have passengers on board who buy up twelve first-class seats just for the two of them, just so they can calmly play chess on a six-foot-long collapsible chessboard, with remote-controlled chessmen.

In Tokyo they had meetings as soon as they arrived. Another crucial detail. In addition to their odd behavior on the plane. All of this would prove beyond a possible doubt that they were not in San Francisco on Tuesday the 15th and thus could not have signed the promise of sale, and therefore that the document had been predated, which is not legal.

Li and Liu, again because of matters that concerned only them, would be far from San Francisco for several weeks. Which did not prevent them from pressuring Lamm, through their business advisers, to carry out the terms spelled out in the promise of sale.

Which terms would be carried out by December 21.

\* \* \*

As for me, in the first few days of that month of December, I met the person I referred to earlier as the Man from Sacramento. We met on the haughty summit of Nob Hill, in my suite at the Fairmont Hotel rented in my real name, Cimballi. Joseph Benharoun had ceased to exist.

It was not an easy contest, and without the remarkable work of the investigators whom Marc Lavater's American correspondents had put on the trail, I would have been KO'd in the first round. After less than a minute, he pounced:

"Would you by any chance be daring to blackmail me?"

"You received sixty thousand dollars a few days ago. The money was withdrawn the day before by Sidney Lamm from his bank."

195

This took him totally by surprise, and he denied it vehemently. How could he know that the money, withdrawn by Lamm in cash and bearing the numbers of Lamm's bank, had been deposited into his account? Of this he was totally innocent. Nevertheless, this was no innocent man I had here, but a corrupt and greedy politico. I was following the well-known adage: set a thief to catch a thief.

I waved the receipt showing the cash payment in his face, along with various other papers that did not prove very much, but nonetheless showed that he had a numbered account in a Swiss bank and another one in a Nassau bank. That finally quieted him, even if it did not convince him. I said:

"All I ask is that you listen to me."

"What do you want from me?"

"One, that you take the hundred thousand dollars I am holding for you, by any means of payment you choose. Two, that you send back to Sidney Lamm the money he had the shameless audacity to 'send' you. Three, that you do it publicly, with as much publicity as possible. Four, that you let it be known, with just as much publicity, that that putrid individual tried to buy you, to get you to lend a hand in the matter of the Tamalpais property, which he wanted to have declared fit for building. Five, that you take the strongest, most effective, and most public measures to see to it that the Elbert property at Tamalpais, a symbol of the national and ecological heritage of the United States of America, is declared forever off-limits to developers. This will demonstrate that you are a man of integrity, a defender of the environment and a fierce opponent of mismanagement, which can hardly do your political career any harm. In addition, you get to keep a hundred thousand dollars with the utmost discretion. Vive democracy."

\* \* \*

And then—as soon as the affair made page one of the newspapers—the attorneys hired by Li and Liu to defend their interests came into the picture as planned. They filed a complaint against Lamm for various counts of fraud, for example, for not having told their clients that the land was off-limits to developers (the terse agreement did not mention this point), and especially for having sold them on the 14th a piece of land he could not buy until the 15th, which was neither nice nor legal.

*196*

The situation became thoroughly unpleasant for Lamm when it was discovered that the alleged Joseph Benharoun, from whom he claimed he had bought the land for six hundred thousand dollars, did not exist; the immigration records were beyond dispute. And things got even worse when an evil-minded reporter, tipped off by an anonymous phone call—one of my least expensive maneuvers—suggested that perhaps both the Bahamas company that had bought the property in the first place, and the Panamanian company that had repurchased it in order to sell it to Lamm for six hundred thousand dollars, were invented by Lamm himself.

Why not? Both companies had been dissolved without the slightest trace. And—the reporter further suggested—it might after all be nothing but a means used by the despicable Lamm to hoodwink the unfortunate Indochinese Chinese, already the victims of vicious Vietcong communism. Lamm had, after all, tried to sell these poor people property for one and a half million dollars that had been bought for two hundred fifty thousand dollars less than two months earlier!

What a scandal. Financial columnists could write of nothing else for days on end!

With the elections at hand, the Man from Sacramento went at it tooth and nail. He did a superb job. As for me, I didn't lag behind. I went to Tamalpais, which I had not seen before. There I found a magnificent landscape, which it would be criminal to spoil by any kind of construction. I also came across an old man and his dog, guarding three or four sheep. I did what had to be done: They all went on television—"Here are the ones whose livelihood they want to take away! Here are the ones whom men like Sidney Lamm are after!"—though it meant buying the necessary air time, and I had half of California crying.

That didn't make things easier for Sidney Lamm. Even if the Chinese did show mercy—not out of pity, for Li and Liu, who had never seen Saigon except in the movies, were not anxious to receive much attention—and withdrew their complaint, on condition that Lamm return the hundred forty-five thousand dollars he had received from them and pay an indemnity of the same amount. At the Sacramento end, they were likewise willing to do business, in exchange for a contribution of two hundred thousand dollars to a fund for handicapped children and other good works. Lamm got off with a reprimand.

Thunderstruck, he lost one million one hundred thousand dollars in the affair, according to my calculations. As for me, I had earned only two hundred thousand, but then I had a lot of expenses.

Lamm still owned the Tamalpais property. He was the landlord, after all. And he always had the option of going there to admire several hundred dragons, which were really, but really, HIDEOUS!

As for the rest, the Man from Sacramento thundered: "No construction on that land for the next five hundred years!", his voice trembling with righteous indignation—he, the Incorruptible.

## 16

Robert Zarra and I had agreed on regular contacts. He stressed that he had to be able to get in touch with me when it should become necessary, though conceding that that might take months. We finally settled on a certain number in Las Vegas, which I would call from time to time, just to say where I was and for how long.

Since that eventful fishing trip with Zarra in Nassau, weeks had gone by, then months. I was almost at the point of hoping the matter was dead, and willing to kiss good-bye my million-dollar ante. But I had set in motion a process that appeared to be inexorable. In the first days of December, I was at the Fairmont Hotel on Nob Hill, and I had just finished having that discussion with the Man from Sacramento, when the telephone rang. A strange voice:

"I'm calling you on behalf of the friend you went fishing with in Bimini. Do you remember him?"

"Yes."

"He wants to know if you would be able to hop over to Las Vegas."

"When?"

"The sooner the better. It won't take more than a few hours of your time."

I thought fast. What was the point of waiting?

"I can leave tomorrow."

"A suite will be reserved for you at Caesars Palace."

At least they had class! I arrived in Vegas around lunchtime, and it was as though cameras were following me even into the bathroom; I barely had time to get out of the shower and slip on a bathrobe when they arrived. There were three of them, but the one who led the conversation was a man of about thirty-five, a Latin type, moustache and black hair carefully groomed, very broad-shouldered but hardly taller than I. I'll call him Ximenez.

"Our job, Mr. Cimballi, is to organize and extend spontaneous legitimate workers' strikes. We are currently working in South America and will become more and more active there. We were told that you were personally interested in our work."

He had round black eyes, astonishing and—to tell the truth—impressive in their steadiness, and a bit too close together. He had as much humor as a food processor. If I were so stupid as to interrupt him in the middle of a sentence, he began again from the beginning, with deadly seriousness. It seemed that Ximenez had been ordered to come and report to me for little other reason than to assure me that the million dollars I had already paid had not been thrown away and to remind me of the other million I still owed. And to explain to me how, why, and in what circumstances he and those with him would direct their efforts particularly against all the interests of the Hovius-Donaldson group in Chile. He had an exhaustive inventory of those interests; not a factory, truck, or typewriter was missing.

It goes without saying that I learned more about the degree to which Hovius and his Scottish partner were entrenched in Chile. In the beginning, it had been Hovius's idea. A strange character, this Austro-Hungarian of Argentinian citizenship; though on the best possible terms with the right wing in his own country and nearly all of the Latin American dictators, he nonetheless prided himself on being a personal friend of Fidel Castro and a childhood friend of Ché Guevara, which was questionable, according to the Lavater report. Hovius seemed convinced that the day would come when "American imperialism," to use the leftist term, would collapse. He argued that in Chile, for example, three-quarters of the corporations really belonged to a single American conglomerate encompassing the Rockefeller bank, International Telegraph and Telephone, the Edwards bank, the South American bank, and the theoretical Bank of Chile. He further stressed that the profits made in Chile by American companies such as Bethlehem Steel, Anaconda Copper or Kennecott Copper represented more than four times the country's global revenues.

Perhaps Hovius imagined himself as a missionary, creating Latin American Economic unity around himself, preferably for his profit, at the expense of the North Americans, naturally. Politically, he was as much of a socialist as Robinson Crusoe, but he was playing both ends against the middle. His wife was both Chilean and a leftist, which was something of a joke when you knew that she ruled over twenty servants.

"For the time being," Ximenez said," we have left them alone. So it'll hit them all at once. We're organizing a strike that will paralyze them, these friends of yours, and the strike will go on and on and on. . . ."

Hovius had taken risks, and, which was much more surprising, had persuaded Donaldson to take some. The new regime's rise to power had appeared to him the sign of a new era, the signal of a tide that would carry him safely into port. According to the figures Marc and I had worked out, Donaldson and Hovius had invested more than thirty million dollars in that torn country. Marc Lavater, although disapproving of my reliance on the Mafia, the mastermind—along with the C.I.A.—of the Chilean strikes, nonetheless agreed with my analysis of the situation: "Hovius and Donaldson are deeply committed. They can still get out, with the loss of a great deal of money, but emerging otherwise unscathed. The trick is first to keep them in Chile until the time comes when they will be in too deep to be able to get out. Then it will be do or die for them.

"They'll be enmeshed; they'll have to invest more and more just to keep afloat. Their resources are not endless. With a little luck, Hovius may even succeed in convincing Yahl to intervene, but I don't think so. If the situation is hopeless, Yahl will find it out sooner than anyone. And he won't hesitate one moment to abandon his old partner. He's not the sentimental type. Franz, your participation in this venture may be only symbolic. But who knows? It may also be the straw that breaks the camel's back."

Ximenez looked at me, and I realized that he had stopped talking for several seconds already.

"All I ask," I said, "is that Hovius and Donaldson are forced to go in all the way, without the possibility of return. That's the kind of trap you have to set for them."

His round black eyes, with their positively uncanny steadiness, regarded me with an icy surprise.

"What else have I just been telling you?" he asked.

* * *

A few days before Christmas, the idea of staying alone in California, without Li and Liu, suddenly seemed intolerable to me. The Lamm affair was under way; everything was going forward as planned; the trap had been set and would spring before long; I could therefore leave.

I was still feeling the effects of that conversation at Caesars Palace in Las Vegas; the malaise it had caused me was far from dissipated, in fact it worsened. Christmas was coming, and I was alone. I thought of Catherine day and night.

I flew to Paris on December 20, and the first thing I did was to take a taxi to the apartment on avenue de Segur. There was nobody there. Not even a maid to answer my knock, my ringing of the bell, my almost-hysterical shouting. Where was everybody?

If you are ever in Paris and in doubt about anything, go to the concierge. Hold money in your hand, and your concierge will tell you everything you want to know, from who is sleeping with whom to who murdered whom.

"They are gone, Monsieur," said the concierge at the avenue de Segur, tucking my wad of francs in her apron pocket.

"Very good. We have a beginning. Now tell me something I *don't* know."

She sighed, and brushed one finger over her thick black moustache. It rivaled the Turk's. I understood the signal, and reached for my wallet, peeling off notes until her greedy eyes brightened. But I held them away from her, just out of reach.

"Madame and Mademoiselle have gone to Morocco for the holidays. Marrakesh, I believe."

I handed her the money. "You'd better believe correctly. If I go all the way to North Africa and don't find them, I'm going to come back here and . . . and . . . *shave* you!"

I caught the first plane, and in that cold, gray month of December which did nothing to take away the knot in the pit of my stomach, found Catherine and her mother, both in bathing suits, the one nearly as beautiful as the other, in the marvelous setting of La Mamounia.

For some reason, they didn't look surprised to see me, not Catherine, not Veronique. Even though I told them: "It's really lucky that I just happened to be passing through Marrakesh today, on my way from Bourg-en-Bresse to Sioux Falls."

I had brought gifts for them: for Veronique a porcelain thing that had been painted near Amsterdam around 1771; and Mme. Varles, who was a collector, delightedly identified it as an Oude Loosdrecht or something of the kind. She told me I was crazy and that it was a far too handsome present. And kissed me as though she were almost my mother, which made an uncommon impression on me.

For Catherine, something much more modest, a little ring. No diamond, no hint of an engagement to frighten her off, just a simple antique gold ring, set with garnets, not even very expensive. She looked at me quizzically as I put the ring on her right hand, and the depths of her eyes glowed golden. I think it pleased her.

We were now a party of three, and determined to have fun in the sun. The girls had rented a Daimler, and we went to take a spin on the other side of the Atlas Mountains, due south toward the desert, and places like Quarzazate and Tineghir. At Tineghir, the hotel had a huge terrace from which you had a wonderful view of the oasis and the sunsets. The evening of our arrival, Catherine's mother saw to it that she and I were alone there for a few minutes.

"Franz, I must talk to you," she said urgently. "You appear and disappear so fast that I'm never sure I'll have time to finish my sentences, with you. It's about Martin Yahl. Franz, I know Martin Yahl, and have for a long time. I know what's between the two of you; I know more about it than you can imagine, but that's not the main thing. The main thing is that some time ago, my husband and I attended a dinner at which Martin Yahl was present. Your name, your family name, anyway, came up in the conversation.

"Martin Yahl, fears you and hates you with an almost paranoid hatred, just as you apparently hate him. I don't like this kind of situation, it frightens me. I wanted to tell you two things, Franz. The first is to ask you to be careful; Martin Yahl is a terrible enemy. The second concerns you and Catherine. I would like you to marry her; I believe she herself would not be opposed to such a plan, far from it. But Catherine and I share the same feeling: not now. Not as long as you are in this situation."

I looked at her, stunned, trying to take in everything she had said. That Yahl was aware of me, I knew. Knew, also, that he must hate me as the son of the man he'd destroyed. I was, after all, his natural enemy. But that he *feared* me! I had taken such precautions to keep my profile low, myself out of his sight during all my manipulations, so that Yahl would not suspect that I was drawing a noose around him. The one thing I hadn't counted on was an unreasoning fear of me, a fear arising from paranoia and not from any knowledge of my maneuvers. So he lived in fear of me! Not only rabid hatred, but fear! Although I was at once on my guard, part of me felt like dancing my antic dance. My enemy was afraid of me! Elation coursed through my veins like warm brandy on a winter day.

But wait, there's this matter of Veronique Varles. Just how much *did* she know? Was she teasing me, mocking me, as Catherine often did? Were they alike, these two women? Was she my friend or my enemy? How well did she know Yahl? Well enough to tell him where I was, how much money I had on hand, what feeling I had for her daughter? Was the concern she expressed for me genuine or was she an ally of Yahl's? I realized suddenly that I was vulnerable before this woman; she literally held me in the hollow of her hand.

I opened my lips to answer her, but my mouth was so dry that no words came. Instead, I bent my lips wordlessly to that long, slim, manicured and powerful hand of hers and kissed it on the palm. The kiss burned, and she pulled her hand back with a little cry. We were even.

* * *

In January, I returned to San Francisco. The matter of the

*203*

despicable Sidney Lamm, unscrupulous developer, would be settled in the spring.

Time passed. Li and Liu were working with a young director whom they considered brilliant, who dreamed of a super-big big movie taking place in a mythical future, pitting imaginary worlds against each other in a fantastic battle of the stars, with unbelievable sets and characters out of Never-Never-Land. The project excited my Bozos.

"Didn't you already talk to me about something like this?"

"Yes, but this time we're doing it. We're going to put money into it." They were putting money into everything; particularly in Japan, where they had made contacts with an animation studio that was thinking of creating huge comic strips for television, especially for children's programming. There it involved robots. For that matter, robots were everywhere Li and Liu went. They had filled their house on Telegraph Hill and their warehouses in Berkeley with them. "Franz, come and work with us." I hesitated, and finally refused; I couldn't see myself going into robots.

Time passed, and I was tense, anxious, almost desperate. I went twice to Vegas and received a report, like an advertising agency's client, on the results of my investments. My informants were different each time, but the impression they made on me was the same: an icy efficiency and an amused contempt for the amateur I was. Increasingly, my conviction was that I had gotten myself into an adventure where I didn't belong, that was beyond my scope, and because of which I would certainly wind up as a victim in one way or another. What madness!

My partners told me that all was well, that "in the general context of the deteriorating economic situation in the country," that a certain corporation was in the process of plummeting, pulled downward by a strategy which, I was assured, was likely to swallow up more and more capital.

"Capital that will be lost, rest assured, Mr. Cimballi. This whole adventure is going to cost them a lot of money."

And they emphasized that they would respect the promises made on their behalf by Robert Zarra. Insinuation: Better keep yours, Cimballi, we're not the kind you forget to pay.

I suspected as much.

\* \* \*

In spring, with Sidney Lamm disposed of, I left San Francisco.

I went to the Bahamas. In order to follow what was happening in Chile, I was no worse off there than elsewhere. To keep busy, I speculated vaguely, getting more and more familiar with the workings of the exchange market, playing the mark against the dollar, exchanging Swiss francs for yen, florins for dollars or gold, and starting all over again. It was fun, and I earned a bit at it—nothing spectacular, but enough to pay for my hotels and airplanes.

Robert Zarra left Nassau. Even the powerful protection of the Mafia was not enough for him; he was definitely too visible, and that annoyed the American police. Leading a veritable private army of several hundred men, he took up new quarters on a property as vast as a personal empire, in a small Central American republic, and his financial and military power there was such that it counterbalanced the power of the local head of state, who had even fewer scruples than his guest. And it even got to the point where Zarra was soon contacted by the C.I.A., which had few hard feelings; it explained to the exile that as an American, he had a duty to help his country, namely by helping to keep a tight lid on Communism in the country he had fled to. Zarra, always the patriot, accepted the offer, and used his influence, in exchange for the U.S. government's permitting him discreet visits into the United States.

So much for the C.I.A.–Mafia Connection.

\* \* \*

I traveled; I went to London, where I visited Annaliese's grave in Brompton Cemetery in order to lay more whole roses on it, as many as I could carry. I went to Mombasa; Joachim, Chandra, and many others gave me a royal welcome, which warmed my heart in these lonely times. Joachim had had to sell the car rental business I had left him, but "it's going very well," he said, shifting from one paw to another. I also learned he had become a choir boy, bless my soul!—along with pint-sized Kikuyus. He took me on a safari tour for three days, but stoutly refused to accept a penny from me. I went to see Chandra, who was running his black-market exchange business—mine, that is—with Indian meticulousness. He had done calculations worthy of an Einstein in order to determine what share of his profits belonged to me. "It's your money, Little Boss."

"What about Joachim? He hasn't got a cent, has he?" He nodded; if only Joachim had let him, Chandra, help run things, but I knew Joachim, didn't I? As clumsy in business as in life. "Chandra, I don't want that money. Give it to Joachim, but not all at once; give him three hundred dollars a month."

Ten hours later, I was back at Caesars Palace in Vegas, and there was Ximenez again, the man with hooded eyes like a falcon.

"Mr. Cimballi, I have come to tell you that the end is near. As you must have read, a state of emergency has just been proclaimed in the capital; there has been one military uprising already, and the head of state, who demanded emergency powers, has been refused them. Everything is going just as we anticipated."

It may have been those last words that got my dander up, or this guy's arrogance, or my conviction that I didn't have much to lose; but I said:

"I do not want to pay for something that has not been done. I admit that the people I'm interested in have lost money in Chile over the last few months and are still losing it. What I question is that those losses are the result of a campaign aimed directly at them, which I paid for. They are, in fact, the victims of a general situation."

The dark gaze pierced me.

"And what are your suggestions, Mr. Cimballi?"

"I will not pay unless it's worth it. I want Hovius and Donaldson to lose their shirts."

"Assuming there's a way to do it."

I heard myself say:

"There is a way."

I developed the idea as I went along:

"Hovius and Donaldson, and their company, have invested several tens of millions of dollars, about forty million, it seems. They've already lost a good bit of it, perhaps a quarter, perhaps more. . . ."

"There will be other strikes. The miners are still on strike. And a very large action is going to . . ."

"And they will lose more money, I agree. They'll keep on losing until they pull out. They'll be a lot less rich, but they won't be ruined. And I want them ruined. I'll pay for ruining them and nothing else."

He stared at me, absolutely expressionless:

206

"How?"

"Contact Hovius—either you, or one of the members of the future junta. Hint to Hovius about the possibility of a future 'latinization' of the Chilean economy. Remind him of the possibility for his partner and him, especially for Hovius as an Argentinian, to remain in Chile after a change of regime and be able to make back more than the money invested up to now."

"In exchange?"

"In exchange for ten million dollars payable to the junta or to you. By him, not me."

Silence. There were three of them before me in the room, and I hoped that my face betrayed none of my intense fear.

"And the new government would not keep its promises, is that it?" Ximenez asked.

I bore his gaze without blinking, as well as I could, and did not answer. He hadn't really asked me a question, anyway. He was more or less thinking out loud.

"I know Hovius," he said finally. "He's a man who takes risks."

Another silence, which lasted. The falcon's eyes enveloped me, and for once, I did not read in them the usual slight disdain.

"My orders are to fulfill your wishes," Ximenez said finally.

*   *   *

From then on, events moved quickly. On July 25 there was the huge strike by the truckdrivers and all the bus and taxi drivers in Chile, and, two days later, the murder of the president's closest aide; then a whole series of pressures, sabotage actions, and threats from mid-July through August and the beginning of September. On September 5, the president himself was assassinated. I wasn't happy at the news of his death. Thank God, I hadn't played the tiniest role in it.

The news of John Hovius's death pleased me even less, because it came too soon. Hovius died eleven days after the president. Not in Chile, where all of his company's factories and offices had been requisitioned and handed over to others without compensation, but in Argentina. He fell from the ninth floor of his hotel. It is possible that he killed himself, but unlikely.

As for me, they came to see me at the Britannia Beach Hotel in Nassau one morning, and they literally dragged me out of bed. There were two of them—clean-cut, young, looking like what they were: important and very intelligent lawyers, very sure of themselves and of their case.

"We're here to settle the details of that payment you agreed to make several months ago on the basis of an oral contract."

That the contract was "oral" did not seem to trouble them in the slightest. I nodded: "You're referring to the second million dollars?"

They shook their heads politely:

"You're mistaken, Mr. Cimballi. Because of the additional services you demanded from our clients, the fees amount to three million dollars."

I looked at them. I said: "Give me an hour."

One hour later, I paid. To all appearances, they were fully informed as to what I could pay, almost every penny I had in the bank. And bargaining with them would have been like arguing with the sea, with the exception that the sea does not push you off a ninth-floor balcony.

\* \* \*

I took stock, and I could count my accomplishments on the fingers of one had, with the thumb left over. Hovius was dead. Donaldson was bankrupt, or nearly so. It had cost me four million dollars, nearly every penny I had in the world. Not to mention a brush with the Mafia.

I was back to square one, with Martin Yahl—if he knew I existed, as Veronique Varles claimed he did—laughing up his safe Swiss sleeve at me. I was powerless to cause him any trouble.

Oh, he might be feeling a little pinch; his bank owned about twenty percent of the Hovius-Donaldson South American holdings. But I didn't even have the satisfaction of thinking that Yahl knew that the fingers doing the pinching were mine. He was putting his loss down to Latin American politics, not Franz Cimballi.

So much for vengeance. My success with Lamm and Landau, even with Hovius, were as nothing to my thirst for Yahl's head on a platter. That happy outcome seemed further away than ever.

That month of October in New York was sunny and mild. By day, I walked in Central Park or strolled through downtown Manhattan, like a dog lost at the bottom of the canyons carved out by the facades of the all-powerful banks. I had opened an account at Chase Manhattan for the pleasure of convincing myself

I was their customer; but now it was merely academic. I was somewhat out of sorts, my Black Friday came every day of the week, and Wall Street appeared to me as it really was: a narrow and repulsively filthy alleyway.

Each morning, I told myself I had to try something, anything, use up my last capital to open a restaurant, or maybe found a new religion that would bring me contributions, not to mention that fact that you don't pay taxes once you're a god.

Then something happened which made everything come together with the clarity that lightning gives, for one explosive instant illuminating the universe.

I was following my usual itinerary through the financial district—sometimes I thought my feet must be wearing ruts in the concrete of the pavement—when I heard sirens, screaming through the streets. The excited street talk was that a bank holdup was in progress; the alarm had been set off, and police cars were closing in on the scene with screeching brakes. At least ten police officers were converging on the bank, guns drawn.

From across the street, I watched, fascinated, a cops-and-robbers movie. Pedestrians were scattering in terror, but I was safe. Then, as though in a dream, I saw one police officer turn and look at me. He raised his gun, and I noticed almost idly that the barrel was longer than the usual police special, much longer, and fitted with a sight and a silencer. In the melee, amid the shouts and the confusion, nobody saw him but me. I stared in terror as he took deliberate aim and fired, straight at my heart.

The bullet ripped through my flesh with an impact that knocked me down and sent me sprawling. If my reaction had been a shade less quick—and I was surprised it wasn't, so frozen had I seemed to be—it would have torn open my chest in a fatal wound. As it was, I spun around at the last second, catching it in my left shoulder.

The wound was bad enough to send me to the hospital for six weeks. Which ate up a good part of the little money I had left.

There was an investigation, of course, at which I was present, but said nothing. What was there to say? That a policeman, or a man dressed like a policeman, had deliberately attempted to kill Franz Cimballi? Terrific. What would that have earned me, except a small headline for one whole day? Needless to say, the investigation came up empty.

I had weeks to think about it, lying in that hospital bed. Who had pulled that trigger? Had the Mafia changed its mind about me, deciding that I knew more than I should? In that case, I was a dead man, might as well jump right out of the window, before they came and pushed me, like they did to Hovius. Or had word leaked out about my participation in recent events in Chile? Was it the C.I.A., or refugee Chilean leftists, or Hovius's family, or Donaldson? Could it even be Martin Yahl who had sent an assassin to kill me? And whoever it was, would he try again?

At last I was back on the street, my left arm in a sling and hurting like hell. Even today, it's a reliable weather prophet, and tells me a day before it rains that I have to get out my umbrella and galoshes.

I was more depressed than ever. No money. No Catherine, and now, without a dime, no prospect of a Catherine in the near future. What next?

There are ideas you sense beforehand, guessing at their approach the way you see a horseman coming toward you across the distance of a vast plain. . . . Less poetically, there are ideas that explode in your face.

I was rambling through Greenwich Village, from one bench to another in Washington Square Park, watching the little gray squirrels. They didn't know where their next meal was coming from either. Like my furry little rodent brothers, I was in the process, or very nearly, of becoming a tramp. Cimballi's dance was no longer even a one-step.

Then into my life stepped David Sussman. He called himself an artist and was about as much of one as I was, except that he at least could tell one color from another. He bought me a beer in a bar on Avenue of the Americas, I bought him one on Fourteenth Street; he returned the favor somewhere near Macy's, and I did the same on Fifty-Eighth Street. We went into the Guggenheim before we were completely plastered, looking at things hanging on the spiral-shaped walls.

David invited me over for dinner at his family's house in Brooklyn. They were Austrian Jews, exactly like my mother. The chance that had led me here led me to meet David's brother Leonard, who had also come for a family dinner, since he was alone in New York, his wife having gone to visit her parents in Ohio for a few days. And that was exactly how one thing led to another with the same far-fetched, unpredictable momentum.

Leonard told me with a laugh: "If you're looking for a job, don't come to me, I'm in a slump." I asked him—but I really didn't give a damn, it was just out of politeness—to explain to me what this slump was. He explained, and there it was; the idea I got at that moment literally exploded, like a blow.

Who in hell could have foreseen that such an idea would be worth more than fifty million dollars to me, and the long-awaited honor of a face-to-face confrontation with His Banking Highness, Martin Yahl, himself?

# 4. The Sun Belt

# 17

"It's mostly happening in Florida," Leonard Sussman told me. "Other places too, but mainly on the east coast of Florida; that's where it's the most intense. It begins in North Palm Beach, and the farther south you go, the more you see the slump, the depth and seriousness of it. Go there," Leonard said, "go to the South, go to Riviera Beach, West Palm Beach, all those beaches one after the other—Boyton, Delray, Deerfield and Pompano. Go to Fort Lauderdale. Go to Miami. The slump, Frank, with a capital S."

In New York, I was staying at the St. Regis again, less as a sign of my returning prosperity than as a foretaste of my future wealth. "And you will, of course, keep my suite for me during my absence; I don't know yet how long it will last." In a lordly tone. "Of course, Mr. Cimballi."

I went out looking dignified; I took the wheel of the Porsche I had rented, although only for eight days, and I headed south.

I would spend a total of six days in Florida, and in those six days, I would meet twenty-eight real-estate developers or agents, a specialist journalist from Miami, an attorney and two bankers. I returned with the trunk of my car bulging with four-color brochures and prospectuses.

Each of the thirty-two meetings I had had under the mild winter sun of Florida had convinced me a little more that I really had a solid gold idea.

This was some healthy slump!

\* \* \*

It took me all one morning and a good part of the afternoon to get to see him, but I was finally facing the man I wanted to see. He did not know what I knew about him or why I decided to seek him out. He was Leonard Sussman's boss, at the very top of the ladder. Through the large bay window to the right of his wraparound desk, you could see one of the skeletons of the World Trade Center being fleshed out, with its twin towers reaching up to twelve hundred feet. To the left, another bay window offered an unimpeded view of the U.S. Steel Building, Battery Park, and the distant Statue of Liberty.

The man across from me spoke:

"Mr. Cimballi, I agreed to see you because you were so insistent."

"You'll allow me ten minutes?"

"Not one second longer."

"That will be time enough."

I had rehearsed my pitch like a vacuum-cleaner salesman, going over and over it till I knew it by heart. I recited it as fast as I could, feeling and hoping—not without reasons—that this man was not an idiot.

"First point: the existence of what is known in the United States as the Sun Belt. It includes everything, Florida, New Mexico, Arizona and California, and possibly a part of Texas.

"Someone living in New York, New England, Detroit, Chicago, Oregon, the Dakotas, Nebraska, or Canada, whoever freezes his ears off eight months a year, naturally wants to live in the Sun Belt, especially when he retires. So he begins buying.

"To meet demand, a real-estate building boom began.

"People built like crazy. Developers went to work and piled up fabulous profits. It's a situation that no bank in the world could look at without being tempted. So the banks got involved. They invested through the medium of what you call the R.I.T.s,

216

the Real Investment Trusts. A basic fact to be noted: unlike the European banks, the American banks are not used to real-estate operations; therefore, they tend to rely entirely on the developers. And back them one hundred percent. Banks advance everything: money for the land, money for construction, money for advertising and even money with which to pay interest on the money."

The man setting across from me, Henry Clay Adams, smiled.

"It's so easy that any fortune-hunter can become a developer. And that's the crux of the problem, Mr. Adams. By building tens of thousands, hundreds of thousands, millions of apartments for sale or rental in the Sun Belt, there comes a time when the supply enormously exceeds the demand. You have over-built. On top of this is the recession; even the traditional customers, the New York Jews who often retire to Florida, are no longer investing.

"Yes, the banks hold the mortgages, but what good are these since the developers can no longer pay? And that's where we stand, Mr. Adams."

He started to speak and I hurried on. "Imagine a bank in Chicago or New York. This bank has loaned hundreds of millions of dollars for apartment houses that have indeed been built, which exist, which are splendid, in Fort Lauderdale or Pompano Beach; Corpus Christi, Texas; Santa Monica, California. But these buildings are empty; no one wants them any more, and the few tenants have stopped paying rent, and yet they're not evicted because at least they keep up a semblance of life in those mausoleums.

"Every month, Mr. Adams, every year—since this has been going on now for almost three years—you still have to pay the taxes and the maintenance costs, and each time, your yearly balance sheets show hundreds of millions of dollars of investment with no return. Hundreds of millions of dollars missing, unproductive, going to waste. They create a picture that's not very flattering."

"You have about thirty seconds left, Mr. Cimballi."

Henry Clay Adams had snowy hair, a pink face, and an expressive gaze. I smiled at him. I already knew that this man was going to make me rich; I could have danced.

"I'm finished, Mr. Adams. Except for two things. First, I know that your bank has placed about four hundred million dollars in these currently unsold buildings, mainly in Florida. Second, I know how those apartments can be sold, I know who to sell them to, and how to get fresh money for them."

He didn't blink. Neither did I. We waited to see who could hold out longest. He lost, and he said, in his soft voice:

"You have ten additional minutes. May I have more details?"

I gave him my most radiant smile. What do you know! I explained the details of what I was going to do—well, almost all the details. After a few minutes, he leaned back in his chair, stretched out his arm without turning his head, and picked up the phone:

"We're not to be disturbed."

He returned to me:

"Your terms?"

"A one-hundred-fifty-thousand-dollar advance for my expenses, and twenty percent commission."

"Ten."

"Fifteen."

"All right."

Twelve percent had been my bottom figure. We discussed the details, and quickly came to an agreement. What was a hundred fifty thousand dollars to an Adams, to a bank like his? And he risked nothing else. If I did not find buyers, I would get nothing.

That same evening, I flew to Brussels, and from there to Luxembourg.

\* \* \*

Act fast. My idea was good only because I had had it first. It was also good only because I was dealing with Americans, American bankers, who could teach anybody a thing or two in any field, but who had botched things badly in this specific instance. And they would lose no time in covering themselves, even to the point of edging me out, if need be.

I had to run a speed race. I gave myself six months, perhaps a little more, perhaps less, before those grand gentlemen ensconced in their huge towers of concrete and steel began to look at me cross-eyed and wish me in hell.

My idea was simple. For reasons which I was convinced were merely circumstantial, there were no more American buyers of American apartments in the United States. Fine. I believed they could be found elsewhere. Everywhere. Throughout the world.

There was war in Vietnam, war in the Middle East; Africa wasn't in great shape; Latin America was being torn apart by dictators and revolutionaries. As for Europe, nothing could be simpler: not everyone could smuggle money into Switzerland in the fear of a new May '68, which this time would carry its revolutionary barricades to their logical conclusion. I thought—I was certain—that in all these parts of the world, there were potential customers, people who would have to be interested in an investment in the United States, the symbol of capitalism, the ideal niche for a nest egg, where they wouldn't fear overnight nationalizations.

It was difficult for an American, accustomed to the almighty dollar, to imagine that it might be necessary to find money elsewhere than in the United States. *That* was the weakness of my American partners.

And if an argument as primary and basic as a safe nest egg was not sufficient, I had other assets with which to convince my customers. Those two dozen real-estate salesmen I had met in Florida had proved it to me with figures: the price of a square foot in the United States was less than half what it was in Europe. It was simple. For an apartment of three hundred square feet in a luxury building in West Palm Beach, an American developer, or the bank that has picked up his mortgage, asks sixty thousand dollars. Thus, between two thousand five hundred and three thousand francs per square foot. In the vicinity of Cannes, the same size apartment—exactly the same—costs at least twice as much, maybe even three or four times as much.

Another example? For the price of a furnished room in Geneva, you can get your feet wet in Delray Beach—a very handsome studio of one hundred fifty to two hundred square feet with a pool, the beach, and sunshine.

And you think I wouldn't find buyers?

During those few days I had spent in Florida, I'd had photos taken. Not just any photos: in the center of the picture I naturally had to have one of those buildings I had undertaken to sell, showing off the quality of its workmanship, its trim, its gardens filled with tropical flowers, its pool and beach nearby. Then I asked the photographer to superimpose, on the foreground, a company of the United States Marines marching by, the flag leading the way. The message was obvious: "Look! It's not only pretty, it's not only sunny, it's not only cheaper than in Europe, it's not only an investment in a currency that will never be disastrously devalued, but it's also an investment in the most powerful country in the world, and the United States armed forces will personally watch over your savings!"

I found a printer in Belgium. I gave him the negatives and the text, with a dummy layout. "Five thousand copies, to start."

*   *   *

I had received from Henry Clay Adams more than his agreement and a hundred fifty thousand dollars. We had gone farther. Adams had first refused, with a curt shake of his snowy white head:

"Don't ask too much."

"Mr. Adams, if my information is correct—and it is—you now have twelve thousand unsold apartments on your hands, with the costs going up each month, from Florida to California. Let's take an average price of sixty thousand—"

"That's too much."

"Let's say fifty thousand, then. Multiplied by twelve thousand, that makes six hundred million dollars locked up. And how long has this been going on, Mr. Adams? Nearly three years, if I'm not mistaken. So there you are, for three years almost, with four hundred million dollars locked up, officially represented by twelve percent mortgages. But are these mortgages paid? No. You're not getting a cent, in nearly every case."

"What's your idea?"

"I won't have a chance of finding people who agree to pay sixty thousand dollars for an apartment and whom I must honestly tell they will have to pay maintenance fees on top of it; I won't have a chance unless I can promise them something."

"What?"

"A five percent interest on the money they put down to buy it."

The calculation was simple. A Frenchman who wished to put some money aside in Switzerland had to pay a flat tax of up to thirty-five percent of his deposit. I, in the United States—and the dollar almost equals the Swiss franc where safety and reliability are concerned—would offer my customers five percent more, instead of thirty-five percent less. You should have seen Adams's face:

"And of course, my bank will have to pay them that interest?"

"Of course, Mr. Adams. Who else? Don't look at me like that, please. As for me, I will sell them an apartment for seventy thousand dollars that is worth sixty thousand, and I will tell them candidly why the price is ten thousand dollars higher: because as soon as they have paid at least, let's say, sixty percent of the total price, they will be paid five percent interest each year, that is, three thousand five hundred dollars paid by you, Mr. Adams. And you should pay it gladly, because you know that by paying five percent interest to someone who brings you fifty, sixty, or seventy thousand dollars cash, it is as though you yourself were borrowing those sums in order to be able to lend them to someone else, here in the United States, for an interest of twelve percent and more. You will pay five percent, you'll get twelve. The profit: seven percent. But you know all of this better than I."

A look from Henry Clay Adams:

"How old are you, Mr. Cimballi?"

I laughed. "Just think if you had known me when I was really young!"

* * *

I found my first customers, my first four customers, all by myself. They were Belgians, one of whom had worked with me in the not-so-distant era of the gadgets. He had earned quite a bit of money then, and while somewhat less than grateful, at least he tended to listen to me when I spoke.

And he had friends who were interested in the deal.

Plus a lawyer whom he knew, and who also had clients whom he counseled.

Plus the friends of the lawyers' clients who read my brochure. And it spread like wildfire. My friend Letta in Rome, won over by my first words, went on a campaign, and promised me fast results.

The surprise came to me from Marc Lavater, whom I had consulted because it wouldn't occur to me to hide anything from him, and also because he was better able than anyone to send me clients.

"I know one."

I looked at him, flabbergasted:

"You?"

"Is it a good deal, or isn't it?"

221

"It is."

"So buy five apartments for me, will you? What do you want me to do with all this money you've been giving me for three years?"

* * *

Of course, I never used my own name during this entire business. The company that published my brochure was in Luxembourg, and was locally represented by a journalist who needed a new car. As for the happy new owners of a beautiful apartment in Florida, they themselves were discreetly hidden behind companies headquartered, for instance, in Panama. And those companies dealt with them only through a company I had just formed . . . in Curaçao.

Curaçao is in the Dutch Antilles, off the coast of Venezuela, to the right of Maracaibo. You can't miss it. In those days it was a big nothing; it didn't look like much. I went there to distract myself during the time I was drying up in Nassau. I saw the signboard behind which my father, on the advice of one William Carradine, nicknamed Scarlet, had once built an empire. And without even needing to cross the street, I saw the other signboard behind which—thanks to that same Scarlet, now dead—Martin Yahl had pulled off his fabulous embezzling maneuver.

I saw to it that I was ensconced next door.

His Banking Highness and I now practically shared a nameplate. We were neighbors.

* * *

Now for the fun. I called together some of my old network. Not only Letta in Rome, but Ute and the Turk. They were still together, and still, honest! very much in love. Ute was especially delighted. She, who could sell anything to anybody, was getting bored with doing nothing but making love and bossing the rest of the harem around,

I even thought I'd give Hyatt another chance to make himself rich. He'd never left Hong Kong, where he was earning a decent living on the remains of the gadget business. When he heard my voice on the phone, he tried to back off, once again not wanting to get involved. But I needed somebody on the spot, so I offered him no involvement except five percent commission, and he accepted. He was a born subordinate.

222

But the best worker of all of them turned out to be Letta in Rome. In no longer than a week, that workhorse sent me an entire fleet of serious customers. The rich Italians were being made paranoid by an epidemic of kidnapping and Red Guard terrorism. Miami looked like a haven; besides, you could always hire Mafia hitmen for protection. Italians always feel comfortable when the Mafia is nearby, and God knows they were all over Miami, thanks to the booming drug trade.

On the way back from Brussels, I stretched my legs out and tried to sleep. The plane wasn't too comfortable, even in first class, and my shoulder was paining like the devil. I'd made no attempt to see Catherine in Paris this trip. I was damned if I was going to go to her empty-handed; no, that business could wait. But I was regretting it a little now. It seemed to me that it had been a hundred years since I had kissed a beautiful girl, and a thousand since I'd been laid. After all, I was only twenty-four or twenty-five; all work and no play had been making Franz a dull boy.

"An extra pillow, Monsieur? Something perhaps to drink?"

I opened my eyes. Leaning over me was the stewardess from first class, a stunning blonde, although hardly a natural one. She had a pair of classy legs, which were showing up to the garters, skirts were adorably short that year, and I immediately grew a hardon that was burning through my pants. Her eyes dropped to my crotch, and there the damn thing was, staring back at her. She smiled. No doubt about it, she was coming on with me.

Suddenly, I wanted her so much that I could have torn off her cute little uniform with its silver wings and sunk my teeth into her round behind, right there in the cabin. Instead, I dropped a copy of *Time* Magazine onto my lap, over my crotch, and, taking her hand, smuggled it under the magazine and onto my trousers. She took a tight hold.

"Mercy, I beg of you." I whispered in her ear. "Are you staying over in New York?"

"Yes," she whispered back. "But tonight only."

"I have a suite at the St. Regis in my name. Franz. Cimballi. Let me buy you a wonderful dinner. With champagne."

"Tonight?" She threw me a sly smile. "Will you make it worth my while?" she asked me coaxingly.

Dipping my hand swiftly between her legs, so that the other first-class passengers wouldn't see, I licked her ear. "Yes. In more

ways than you can possibly expect. What's your name, beautiful?"

"Darlene."

"Then until tonight, Darlene. The St. Regis, nine o'clock."

"Great. Now keep this warm for me." She gave my painful
erection another coy squeeze. "Save it for me, mind."

"Save it! It will earn eight percent interest by tonight!"

I had champagne waiting, and steaks on order. Darlene wore
black lace underwear, the merest *cache-sex* and a wisp of a bra,
and on her feet, very high heels. She loomed over me like the
Statue of Liberty, but I found it strangely exciting. Her legs in
their black stockings and garters acted on me like an aphrodisiac.
Modestly, I must say that I was at my best, even with a wounded
shoulder, and brought her to climax four times, each stronger
than the one before. When she left the following morning, I
pressed five hundred dollars cash into her hands, and she almost
didn't take it.

\* \* \*

Back in New York, there I was again, face to face with Adams.
I was dead tired, and no wonder.

"I've sold forty-six apartments for you. That may sound pathetic compared with the twelve thousand you have to sell. But
the main thing is the network I've set up, and its results, which
will grow in profit with every week that passes. But I didn't
cross the Atlantic to get a medal. Let's talk figures instead. I've
calculated that each of those forty-six customers brought in an
average of forty-one thousand dollars and change. For a total
payment of one million eight hundred ninety-three thousand two
hundred twenty-two dollars, from which I have deducted, as
agreed, my fifteen percent commission—that is, two hundred
eighty-three thousand nine hundred eighty-three dollars and
thirty cents. You can check my arithmetic."

Adams looked at me. At times, his face was almost human.
"Unfortunately, I am not free for lunch, Mr. Cimballi, but I'm
sure one of my associates would like to have the pleasure of en-
tertaining you."

I said no thanks, I was tired, and it must have showed.

"May I at least have you driven back to your hotel? The St.
Regis, you say?"

224

At the St. Regis, I had made friends with one of the clerks, who had the same birthday as I. From the look on his face, I could tell he had something to say to me. I took him aside:

"Some men have been asking questions about you, Mr. Cimballi. Serious faces, hard eyes. They went to the management, not to us."

I thanked him in the usual way. I was really on my last legs, and the information I had just obtained did not really sink in. I spent the next ten hours sleeping, and it was pitch dark when, after a shower, I felt more or less like myself again. I stretched out in front of the television, which was showing a football game. "Serious faces, hard eyes." My own eyes were on the players, but my thoughts were elsewhere.

\* \* \*

"Marc? Were you able to do it?"

"Affirmative. Yahl has hired the biggest American private detective agency. They're following you day by day, almost around the clock. They're on top of the Florida thing, the Luxembourg company, and the one in Curaçao. They know about Landau and Lamm, too."

"And the Argentinian and the Scot?"

"Yahl knows. He's ignorant of the details, and the extent of your involvement, but he knows how much you earned from the man with steel legs, and how much it cost you in Nassau. In my opinion, he knows what you've got in your pocket, give or take a thousand."

"And how do *you* know he knows all that?"

He laughed.

"I've got a crystal ball."

He refused to say any more, perhaps because we were on the phone, but that was not the only reason. That sly fox was hiding something from me, and since I had almost total confidence in him, the mystery he made of the source of his information irritated me, but did not really worry me. I would find out eventually . . . .

There remained the doings of His Banking Highness. So, he knew how much I had in my pocket, give or take a thousand dollars? Fine. So what? I hadn't seen him for years, but I could easily imagine him, getting daily reports on the financial status

225

of Franz Cimballi, currently domiciled at the St. Regis Hotel in New York, and worth about three hundred fifty thousand dollars. To all appearances, Martin Yahl feared me in proportion to the money I might have. He wasn't wrong. And I certainly wasn't going to frighten him with three hundred fifty thousand dollars.

Thinking it over, though, he hadn't batted an eye when I had over four million, either?

What level of wealth would I have to reach before he began to be afraid?

A hundred million dollars? Two hundred million?

And even assuming I attained such fortune, what could I do to him? Financially, I would barely be at his level. And I hadn't the slightest notion of how I was going to lay siege to his mighty fortress.

I had just earned two hundred eighty-three thousand, and I knew very well that, at that rate, in the best of circumstances, it would probably take me two or three years to return to the level I had reached with Mr. Hak. Assuming that the bankers, like Adams, left me alone, which was unlikely.

And it was like an electric discharge. I jumped. I danced alone in my room like a madman. I opened the refrigerator, and uncorked a bottle of champagne.

Dummy! Cimballi, you big dummy! You idiot! How come you didn't think of this before?

# 18

It's called leverage.

It's a very American principle—not just American, but practiced nowhere else with as much virtuosity as in the United States—the principle by which, in order to clear a mortgage, it is not necessary to pay the total amount of that mortgage.

Leverage is the possibility—a real one, we shall see—of paying two thousand dollars to clear a mortgage of one hundred thousand dollars on a property or building. And of course, having cleared the mortgage, one is able legally to sell something one has never bought, or, more precisely, to sell it and pay it off after selling it, and thus discharge the total sum of the mortgage—ninety-eight thousand dollars, if one paid only two thousand initially—by dipping into the money you got from the sale.

Your two thousand dollars are a lever and nothing more. But "Give me a lever and a place to stand and I will move the earth," said Archimedes, and in two thousand years nobody has proved him wrong.

And if circumstances favor you, and you manage, for instance, to sell that same property, bearing a hundred-thousand-dollar mortgage (of which you have paid only two percent, or two thousand) for two hundred thousand dollars, your profit will be not merely one hundred percent, but one hundred thousand dollars for a two-thousand-dollar investment, hence *five thousand percent*.

So much for the first system I would use.

*　*　*

There was a second one.

Within all those boards of directors of all those banks mired in the Slump, and the insurance companies which had invested on the same terms and in the same places, the distress was such that they were at the point of agreeing to anything in order to get rid of the passive irritant which those tens of thousands of unpaid mortgages represented. So much frozen money gave those bankers sleepless nights. There's nothing a financier hates more than immobile, unproductive money. It gives him ulcers.

To the point where many of those banks and insurance companies were ready to literally sell off their mortgages.

At half price.

And that's where it became the stuff of hallucinations.

Imagine—and it's happened, more than once—an apartment building in Palm Beach, Florida, whose developer has gone bankrupt because he can't find buyers. This developer's bank—say, the National Illinois Company of Chicago—lent him ten million dollars, and has held a mortgage of ten million dollars since then. In other words, the building is worth ten million dollars. The bank has held this mortgage for three years. It's sick and tired of it, it doesn't want to see that mortgage in its financial statements any more, especially since it's hardly the only one, there ai : thousands of others.

That's the point at which the National Illinois Bank of Chicago is ready to assign its mortgage at half price.

Say five million dollars instead of ten.

And what if the leverage principle were now applied to that five million dollars?

\* \* \*

I needed at most five hundred thousand dollars, in order to have the right to put a building worth ten million dollars up for sale. After the sale, I would pay the bank the four-and-a-half million dollars covering the remainder of the mortgage transfer price. That was what it came down to, in a nutshell.

At that time, which was immediately after I had set up my apartment-selling network in Europe and even in Asia, thanks to Hyatt in Hong Kong, I did not have five hundred thousand dollars; I had two-thirds of that, and could scarcely think of investing it; after all, I needed money to live on and travel.

I could borrow the five hundred thousand dollars. There was no doubt that, upon hearing my leverage argument, any New York bank would advance me the money, including Adams' bank. But that was just it—it was all too simple. I wasn't at all eager for my idea to get around the corporate offices. And then I had another reason not to do it, at least equally compelling: borrowing money would mean coming out of the shadows into the daylight. It would be tantamount to screaming in the ears of those private detectives whom Martin Yahl had tied to my footsteps: "Watch out, I'm about to pull a fast one."

The truth was that, even if I did not yet know how I would one day go after Martin Yahl, my intention, my will to go after him, was unshakable. Revenge was the single force behind all my manipulations. There was no doubt that I would need money for that, lots of money. And the weaker he thought I was, the longer he went on believing that all I had to live on were the revenues—comfortable, of course, but still out of proportion to his own means—of my brokerage commissions from Henry Clay

Adams, the more surprised he would be when I went on the offensive.

I needed five hundred thousand dollars, and I did not want to approach the banks, or the Turk, or even Marc Lavater, both of whom would have been quite willing to lend me that amount. No, what I needed was a system that could be used more than once if necessary, each time I had a chance to clear the mortgage on another building.

Of all the men and women, such as Ute Jenssen, whose talents I had made use of in the gadget business, there was one person who had made a special impression on me because of his intelligence, his capacity for work, and his near-ferocity when it came to snaring a contract, a contact, or a commission. This was Letta. I met him in Rome at the end of an improbable journey that had enabled me—I thought then—to throw any possible follower off the track, even if he belonged to "the biggest private detective agency in the United States." I had planned a trip to California, then dashed to Montreal, from there to Chicago, where I took a plane to Geneva, where I rented a car and drove to Lyons, where I boarded the train to Rome. I told Letta:

"I need ten people as soon as possible who can each pay fifty thousand dollars cash for an apartment."

"Ten?"

"Ten."

He didn't flinch. He was a bit hunched, his head sunk on his shoulders, his hands sometimes waving with the gestures of a croupier raking in the lost chips. Normally, he looked up at the person he was talking to from under his bushy brows, as though he were trying to guess the price of him per pound. He took his dusty notebook out of his pocket, and made a few calculations.

"Italians? Or do you have a favorite nationality?"

"I couldn't care less."

"I can find you ten Italians. They all have cousins or parents in the United States; I know, I sounded them out because of that. It creates ties. I can find them for you in forty-eight hours. Maybe less. I have to visit them one by one. You don't discuss such things over the phone.

"By the way, someone came to see me—he said he was from Internal Revenue—to ask about my dealings with you. But I have a cousin who has a cousin in the Ministry: It's you they're after, and it comes from Switzerland."

Thus, even here, His Banking Highness was tracking me.

Knowing Rome better than I, Letta took me to dinner in the Trastevere, on the other side of the Tiber, in a "tipico" restaurant specializing in seafood and fish. I watched him as he polished off a sea urchin: when he was finished, you couldn't find anything left in the shell with a microscope. And a guy like that could find me five hundred thousand dollars in forty-eight hours, "Maybe sooner"! I smiled at him:

"What's your first name?"

"Adriano."

Besides Italian and French, he spoke Arabic and a little Spanish.

"Do you really speak Arabic?"

"Like French and Italian."

"Adriano, I need someone to take care of all my business in Europe . . . no, wait, in Europe and the Middle East, since you speak Arabic. Does that suit you?"

It suited him.

"But there's one condition: officially, and for some time yet, you will be only one broker among others and your dealings with me will merely concern brokerage. In other words, I want those people who are interested in me, who came to you to ask questions about me, to go on thinking that all I'm doing is selling a few apartments here and there. This business of the five hundred thousand dollars must remain secret—totally."

We came to an agreement, Adriano Letta and I: It was understood that the money from the ten buyers he was going to round up for me would go not to the Curaçao company, which had apparently been spotted by Yahl's spies, but to a different one in Lichtenstein.

"And we'll continue to use Curaçao for the brokerage deals?"

"Yes."

He understood everything, and I trusted him, since I could not do otherwise.

Two days went by, and I could have used them to make a quick trip to Paris to kiss Catherine and her mother, but that would have jeopardized the secrecy in which I had made my journey to Rome. I waited, walking endlessly in the gardens of the Villa Medicis. Forty-odd hours later, Letta had kept his word, and gathered his ten buyers together.

My plan was quite simple. Normally, I would deliver the money from these ten buyers to Adams and pocket my commission on the side. Instead, I set up a buyers' cooperative, and with the money I picked up the ten-million-dollar mortgage held by a Boston bank, which let me have it for half price. In order to throw Yahl and his dogs off the scent, I deposited the same amount of my "commission" into my regular account, as I would have done if I'd given these buyers to Adams.

From that moment on, I was no longer selling, apartment by apartment, a building that belonged to Henry Clay Adams' bank (after having assigned one to each of my Italians, naturally), but a building that belonged to me outright, for which, however, I had as yet paid only five hundred thousand dollars, which wasn't mine anyway, and for which I still owed the bank only four and a half million dollars. Which I had time to pay off. The bank was satisfied; it could write the bad deal off its books, while handing me "the baby."

Before, during, and after my Florida tour, once back in New York, I questioned as many people as possible, including the oldest brokers, who cried with one voice: "This real-estate slump won't last, it's impossible, even in '29 it wasn't like this."

The very bankers who dumped their mortgages on me used the exact same argument to convince me to substitute myself for them. Very well, I believed them, and at the time I bought my first mortgage, I believed them more than ever.

I was convinced that sooner or later the overbuilt situation would no longer exist, everything would go back to normal, and, with the traditional American clientele having resumed its habits, all those apartments now going to waste, practically on the scrap heap—because of that very American tendency to throw out anything that can't be used immediately—all those apartments would quickly find new buyers.

I had no way of knowing how right I was.

For now, one thing counted, speed. With each passing day and week, those same banks with which I dealt on two levels—on the one hand, directly selling their apartments and pocketing the commissions, and on the other hand, buying up the greatest number of their mortgages with the most complete discretion—those banks would realize that what I had done—seek customers outside the United States—they could do too, with vastly superior means, on an incomparably larger scale. Especially since the first signs of a recovery were already appearing.

Leonard Sussman—the very person who had first told me about the Slump, and had more or less put me on the track— was the first to warn me. They say that to get anything done in the Army, it is often better to know a sergeant than a general. Very well, Leonard Sussman was the sergeant of an army in which Henry Clay Adams was the general. Leonard just happened to manage that department of the Adams bank that handled real property. He was intelligent and sharp—to say the least. He was probably one of the very first New York experts to become convinced that the recovery was beginning. He passed that conviction on to me, very discreetly. "On one condition, Franz: let me go in on it with you." I agreed.

The next three weeks were crazy. At the time Leonard Sussman became involved, I had already cleared three mortgages. In three weeks, I would clear sixteen others.

The real figures were unrounded, of course, and more varied, but you could give a fairly accurate picture by saying that I thus acquired theoretical ownership of nineteen buildings, each one worth ten million dollars, which the banks handed over to me at half price, for ninety-five million dollars.

Ninety-five million dollars, of which I paid, according to the leverage principle, only about ten percent, or nine and a half million. And I found that nine and a half million through my buyers' cooperative, which put up about half the sum, at the end, through loans I took out from small banks Leonard Sussman had told me about.

Of course, it might not have worked, or at least, not so well. It was a deal written on sand with a feather. The touch of one harsh finger could bring the whole risky business tumbling down around my ears.

And then recession suddenly ended, and the recovery—as often happens in the United States, where the market reacts with insane speed—the recovery was lightning-swift. I would already have earned a lot of money if the nineteen buildings for which I owed the mortgages had merely regained their true value of ten million dollars each. In that case, I would have gotten five million dollars for five hundred thousand dollars down, or a thousand percent, which wouldn't have been bad.

But the recovery was accompanied by a price explosion, and very soon a given building on the Florida or California coast which nobody wanted for five million dollars six months ago—not to mention its real price of ten—was going for twenty, twenty-five, thirty million dollars. I saw people stand in line just to buy apartments which a few weeks before, Adriano Letta, or one of my brokers in Brussels or Geneva, even Hyatt, was having a hard time selling.

To resell a building for eighteen or twenty million dollars after paying five million for it seven months earlier, only a tenth of which had yet been paid—it happened to me, not once, but several times during that crazy time. On three occasions, I actually got back twenty-five million dollars for a five-hundred-thousand-dollar investment. And while the other buildings did not bring in as much, they still gave me huge profits.

I had wanted to move swiftly and I did. But events moved even more swiftly. Had I had another month, or some powerful protection, I could probably have made ten times as much, at least.

At the end of that wild adventure, which lasted nine months all in all, I added everything up, and it made my head spin.

All along the way, I had stuck to my initial decision: that is, I had clearly separated the official profits, as it were—those that would be reported to Martin Yahl, in any case—which I had earned as a broker for Henry Clay Adams due to my fifteen percent commission on all the money from my European or Asian customers (Hyatt acquitted himself well).

These profits amounted to a little more than one million four hundred thousand dollars in nine months. In addition to the three hundred-odd thousand I already possessed, they represented a total of one million seven hundred thousand, which was more or less my official wealth, of which Martin Yahl was surely aware. He must not have been worried about it. Eleven months earlier, when I had almost four and a half million dollars, before Robert Zarra's friends had dropped in, Yahl had apparently not been worried about the danger I might represent.

With only one million seven hundred thousand, I must have seemed perfectly harmless to him.

What he did not know—I would have sworn to it—is that I

had operated on two levels in the Sun Belt deal, carrying on two separate activities. With very different results. The truth was that the leverage principle had worked wonders.

And the assets of my Lichtenstein company amounted to seventy million dollars.

* * *

I have never played cards. Yet there is something I believe in. I believe there are times in life—a moment or two or three, if one has ordinary luck—when one possesses a kind of sixth sense for a few seconds. And if on top of that, one reaches the necessary higher state of intense concentration and even a degree of exaltation, at such times, you KNOW that the hidden card is indeed the fourth king you still need. You KNOW that that card will come, whatever happens, against all odds. You KNOW it.

I knew that I was going to be offered a way of revenging myself on Martin Yahl.

On that day, while we were still on the verge of that final explosion that finished off the Sun Belt operation, I was in an airplane taking me from California to New York.

Leo Sussman would normally have gone with me, but minor difficulties had appeared at the last minute concerning a building I was interested in in Santa Barbara, and he had remained behind. So I was alone, too worn-out to sleep, and in a seat next to mine was an elegant man, with one touch of sartorial eccentricity, a silk handkerchief up his sleeve like a Restoration dandy.

Were Leo Sussman present, he and I would probably not have stopped talking business throughout the entire trip, but my solitude was the necessary condition. With the American taste for socializing, my neighbor struck up a conversation. He offered me a drink, which I accepted. We spoke of air travel, of California, which we had just left, of New York, which we were going back to. He gave me his business card, showed me a photo of his house in Harrison, a very exclusive suburb of New York, his wife, his two children, and his dog.

He was a lawyer; his office was in Manhattan, and he had worked with McEnroe, whose young sons, it was said, were the hopes of the tennis world. All of which I couldn't have cared less about. He wore a pin in his buttonhole, and for a second,

I couldn't remember where I had seen one like it before. He laughed.

"I was graduated from Harvard."

And suddenly it came back to me: Martin Yahl usually wore the same pin. Martin Yahl was hardly a name I liked to utter, and yet I asked:

"Do you know a Swiss banker by the name of Martin Yahl, who studied at Harvard?"

The name was familiar to him; he had seen it among the names of alumni, but Yahl had been in an earlier class.

"As far as I can remember, he was there in the days of the famous Will Carradine."

"Nicknamed Scarlet."

He was amazed that, in spite of my age, I should know Carradine's nickname.

"Especially," he said, "since it's been years since he retired from public life."

Something leaped wildly within me.

"What do you mean, retired? I heard he was dead."

My companion stared at me.

"Dead? Who in hell told you that Scarlet was dead?"


# 19


The events of that period are so intertwined, and overlap with one another to such a degree, that it would be difficult to maintain chronological order even if I wanted to.

This happened before the end of Operation Sun Belt, and also before I learned that William Carradine, known as Scarlet, was not dead.

It was a phone call from Adriano Letta that set the ball rolling. Adriano had been instructed never to call me at the St. Regis.

"And what if I have something really urgent?"

I couldn't see what might be so urgent about selling apartments, but to make him happy, I told him he could get in touch with Leo Sussman, who spoke Spanish, which presumably would enable them to communicate.

"His Spanish is terrible," Leo told me, "but if I understood right, he would like you to call him immediately at the Hotel de Paris in Monte Carlo."

That Adriano would phone me was already a surprise, especially since he had paid for the call himself, and was, shall we say, thrifty. But to imagine him in a setting like the Hotel de Paris in Monte Carlo amounted to sheer fantasy. I called him right away; I got him; he told me I had to be there as soon as possible, that it was extremely urgent and important. He wouldn't say any more. From one plane to the next—there I was in France, or rather, Monaco. On the Côte d'Azur, on a day I remember as very cloudy and menacing, returning from the Nice airport where Adriano Letta had picked me up, he explained to me what had happened. He was, in fact, in the position of a cop who gives somebody a speeding ticket and discovers that he's captured Public Enemy No. 1.

"We began talking about investments in the United States. He let me talk, it seemed to amuse him, and I realized that something wasn't normal. But when I finished laying out my arguments, he said: "Fine. And now, supposing that instead of taking five of your apartments, I buy five thousand, or fifty thousand?"

That sort of thing takes you by surprise, Adriano said. I agreed; it surprised me, too.

"You haven't told me his name."

The most irritating thing about Letta was that he really did speak Arabic, perfectly. His pronunciation showed it. He uttered a stream of patronymics, of which all I understood was Aziz.

"He's a Saudi. I checked: he's fabulously wealthy. If he doesn't like the way they treat him in a casino, he's liable to buy the place."

An important asset, according to Letta: The prince (he was a prince, it seemed), Aziz, was the same age as I, and that might make things smoother.

"But he doesn't make decisions alone, or at least without asking advice from the man who accompanies him and acts as his adviser.

Watch out—that guy is part Lebanese, part Syrian; he pretends to speak English and French badly, but he really speaks them very well."

He was a financial wizard, about 60, formerly with Intrabank of Beidas. His name was Fezzali.

And that was how, two hours later, after barely having time for a shower and a change of clothes, I found myelf sitting across from two Arabs, a lobster soufflé, and the braised bass with lettuce for which the Hotel de Paris is famous. I had decided to use the tactic of complete candor.

I told them my story down to the last details, at least the more or less official part: Kenya, Hong Kong, the gold, the gadgets, what I called the real estate business in Paris and San Francisco; I told them how the Sun Belt deal had started, leaving out my skirmishes with Landau, Lamm, Hovius and Donaldson. Aziz listened to me with an almost complicit smile; it wouldn't be difficult for us to be pals. But the other man remained expressionless, neither sympathetic nor hostile. A man of marble, his blank eyes rested on me with an apparent lack of interest.

"You mean to say that you were the first to think of finding buyers outside the United States when the American market could no longer provide them?"

"It couldn't provide them for the time being. The recession won't last."

"But you were the first to think of that?"

"I defy anyone to prove the contrary."

The exchange was with Aziz, but I looked frequently at Fezzali, who ate his soufflé the way he would have eaten a handful of dates, with the same indifference. Even without Adriano Letta's warning, I would have distrusted him: that denseness, that seeming coarseness of a street merchant—especially in the sleek setting of Monte Carlo—would have put me on my guard anyway. It was he, too, perhaps he alone, who had to be convinced.

Something bothered me about him; the feeling that he knew something I didn't, and thus had an advantage over me. He seemed a hundred miles away from us as I told the story—as wittily as possible, making Aziz laugh, at least—of my first meeting with Henry Clay Adams, my first sales in Belgium and Luxembourg. I recounted how I had once or twice chartered a plane, filled it with prospective owners of property in Florida, and landed everybody in Miami to be greeted by Cadillacs, Cuban bands, and pretty girls in tiny bathing suits.

Aziz's eyes shone:

"Were the girls really pretty?"

"Superb."

We smiled at one another in complicity, Aziz and I. There was definitely a feeling of comradeship between us, and already the tacit prospect of wild "partying" together. That was when I decided to go for broke.

My choice at that moment was clear. I could, of course, confine myself to being a broker—with a lot of leeway, but a broker all the same, acting as a middleman between the American sellers and the formidable potential buyer that Aziz was. By doing that, I would undoubtedly earn a great deal of money.

Or, I could reveal that I was functioning on two levels in the Sun Belt operation: earning a commission *and* acting on my own behalf, and buying up as many mortgages as possible for an operation that, if successful—and I had no guarantee of that at the time—should bring in fantastic results.

By revealing the full scope of my activity, I ran a dual risk: first, that in some way or another, there should be a connection between Fezzali and Martin Yahl, who would then be alerted; second, that I would simply lose the biggest customer I would ever have. Why would Fezzali go through me to carry out operations he could manage alone, now that I had told him how to go about it?

My eyes riveted to the totally blank face Fezzali showed me, I decided to run that risk. He had registered nothing and had said practically nothing up to now, and the only time he had opened his mouth was to speak Arabic. But I was now in the process of explaining the lever principle, and he decided to take a more active role in the conversation after all. His questions in Arabic were translated into English for me by Aziz:

"If your prediction about the recession turns out to be valid, what will happen?"

And I again repeated my argument:

"Imagine a building mortgaged for ten million dollars. You now pay at most one-tenth of that amount to clear the mortgage. I am convinced that the end of the recession is very near, and that that same building will very soon be worth fifteen or twenty

*238*

million dollars, twenty rather than ten, which represents only the mortgage and not the real value of the building at the time of its construction. You sell the building for twenty million. Minus the nine million you owe, that leaves eleven. You have earned ten times the investment. And if you find banks that agree to let you have mortgages at half their value, twenty times the investment."

I had finished my fish, and my argument. I waited while my two listeners talked in Arabic. Fezzali's face was still as expressionless as ever, and since I didn't understand a word he said, I tried to interpret his tone of voice, which suggested nothing more specific. Again I had the strong feeling that he knew something I didn't, something crucial for me to know. And I though, out of sheer instinct: You've lost, Cimballi. You gambled and lost. That guy is against you, whatever you suggest. Maybe he's even in collusion with Martin Yahl, and maybe this meeting was set up for the sole purpose of pumping me. I was almost at the point of suspecting Adriano Letta of double-crossing me.

"Dessert?"

Fezzali ordered a huge dish of ice cream; for Aziz only coffee and a cigar. I never smoked, not even an occasional Havana for social reasons. Aziz lit a Davidoff Chateau Something-or-Other; I stared at the sea and the illumined coast. A memory came back: the Grand Prix of Monaco, which my father took me to, with red Ferraris on the track exactly like the one at La Capilla, but full-sized.

"Mr. Cimballi?"

The voice was not familiar to me, and yet, with the waiters gone, there were only three of us in the suite. I turned my head and realized that, for the first time, Fezzali had just spoken to me directly, in complétely fluent French:

"Mr. Cimballi," he said, "I knew your father very well. In fact, he was my friend. I would have attended his funeral if it had not been limited to the family. But to have been a man's friend does not necessarily mean placing one's confidence in that man's son. His Highness Prince Aziz wanted us to give you one hundred million dollars to invest in the business you are offering us. To make a further investment, especially in such a short period of time, would require certain arrangements. That's why our discussion took so long. But we have finally reached an agreement. The sum that will be placed in your hands, under my supervision, of course, will be two hundred fifty million dollars."

I stared at him, open-mouthed. And I could hardly keep from laughing: My instinct! Tell me about it! Cimballi, you're nothing but a young fool.

Aziz couldn't follow our discussion in French. He smiled at me, and asked in English:

"Is there something wrong?"

I shook my head, smiling at Fezzali, who seemed to have amused himself somewhat at my expense:

"Things could hardly be better."

I didn't know how right I was. It was not only that enormous capital, enormous for someone at my level. In a way, that was only a detail. The consequences of what had just happened did not become clear until later, and they were pretty damned spectacular, not to mention decisive.

*   *   *

The car I had rented was waiting for me in front of the main entrance of Caesars Palace in Las Vegas, where I had spent the night. I hit the road. It was seven o'clock in the morning. I drove along the Strip, turning left just before the Sahara. Despite the hour, the casino was humming. Left again, toward Reno. According to my map, I had nearly a hundred forty miles to go. I drove at a moderate speed, and it was after ten o'clock when I entered, for the first time, Death Valley.

The name alone fascinated me and made me uneasy, though it was only one of those Homeric nicknames bestowed by the pioneers. The New York lawyer I had met on the plane had told me: "Follow Salt Creek Valley Road, make a left toward Stove Pipe Wells, across the sand dunes. On the left again you'll see a road to Mosaic Canyon and the ghost town of Skidoo. It's on the right. Cross Titus Canyon, and three miles after Grapevine, you'll see the house. . . . You can't miss it; there are no others for miles around, it's in the middle of the desert, all by itself and rather dazzling; built in the Spanish-Moorish style, almost like Alhambra.

It was a long drive, and I had plenty of time to think and plenty to think about. First, that Yahl was onto me, and that he was having me shadowed by detectives, at least whenever they could catch up with me they shadowed me. Next, that Yahl, with his international financial empire, might at any moment find out—maybe he'd already found out—the speculations I was involved in, and their scope.

He was a formidable adversary; I couldn't wish for a worse one. And he loathed me . . . what were the words Veronique Varles had used? "A paranoid hatred of you, Franz." Yet, instead of avoiding Yahl, I was dedicating my life to catching up to him and finishing him off, in his own arena, on my own terms.

Was it Yahl who was trying to kill me? I hoped so. I'd sooner have all my vengeful eggs in one basket than have to deal with hostility on two fronts at once. Still, dead is indubitably dead, and I would have to be more careful. Thus far I had presented a moving target, harder to hit. I had been jetting from city to city, from one nation to the next. But I couldn't go on crossing borders for the rest of my life.

Oddly enough, even though I knew that my plan to get Yahl depended greatly on my keeping the lowest possible profile and remaining patient, like a snake who remains motionless until the bird hops close enough, even with that understanding, a great part of me wanted to rush to Switzerland and confront Yahl with my bare hands, and simply tear him to pieces. My youth, I suppose; patience is the enemy of youth.

But, because that wasn't possible, I felt frustrated. Fate, however, had cast something into my path to ease my frustrations somewhat. The restoration to life of a dead traitor, a brand-new enemy for my hit list. If I couldn't present myself in Switzerland to get Martin Yahl, I could present myself in Death Valley to get William Carradine, a/k/a Will Scarlet.

And there, suddenly, was the house: at the end of that puzzle trail studded with names that might have been made up by a screenwriter. It was there, and it did create a remarkable impression of solitude. "Franz, if you go there in the next few days, I'm sorry for you; the heat will be stupefying; it sometimes goes above 110 degrees in the shade."

Although my car was air-conditioned, I felt that incredibly dry ovenlike heat beating at the windows. And it hit me like a fist when I cut the engine after a slow approach on a dirt road, opened the door, and got out.

At least a minute went by in a silence like the beginning of the world, heavy as a woolen mantle. Yet I knew someone was there, and that someone would come; I had seen a silhouette. I waited, already streaming with sweat. The house itself was built around a huge inner courtyard with a mosaic floor and tiled fountain. Only one storey high, it was raised off the ground. A gallery ran along three sides of the courtyard, with the fourth side taken up by a huge domed porch. Flowers everywhere, abundant clusters of them climbing the walls. In the air was that peculiar smell of water flowing over sunbaked earth.

"This is private property."

I hadn't heard the woman coming. There was nothing surprising about that; she was barefoot, a detail that did not fit in with the rest of her outfit; she wore an absolutely spotless nurse's smock and cap.

"I know. I would like to see Mr. Carradine."

"Mr. Carradine isn't seeing anyone."

A movement on the right, this time: another nurse appeared, just as quiet as the first and about the same age: a harsh, unlovely fifty, marked by all the signs of a ruthless efficiency. The newcomer stood still, hands folded on her stomach, looking at me without the slightest expression. And out of the series of dark rooms beyond the gallery, white-painted but apparently windowless, came the apparition of a third woman, as ghostlike as the first two.

"He'll see me. If you give him this."

I held out the cardboard rectangle on which I had written a few words. I held it out to the empty air. None of the three women I could see made the slightest motion to take it. And I had the impression there were other women I did not see, likewise barefoot, wearing immaculate, you might say icy, smocks, likewise motionless, hands folded on the stomach in a purely feminine gesture. . . . I decided to take a few steps, I climbed the three stairs leading to the gallery that ringed the courtyard.

"Mr. Carradine sees no one. No one. There are no exceptions."

The difference in temperature between the crushing sunlight of the courtyard and the coolness inside the gallery was more than relative, it was real, and at least twenty-five degrees. I raised my eyes and saw the air-conditioning vents in the ceiling.

"Mr. Carradine will agree to see me. Give him this message."

Silence. I still held my card in my sweaty hand. I crossed the gallery and entered a huge living room furnished with oversize Spanish pieces that seemed magnificent to me; there were heavily carved coffers, and above all, a *vargueño*, a dark wooden cabinet that had been carefully left partly open to show the inside, filled with sculpted shelves and drawers. I dropped my card on an Aragonian chair.

"Mr. Carradine does not read."

"Then read it to him. I will not leave."

Suddenly, one of the women gave in. She came toward me, passed by me without giving me the shortest glance, snatched up the card as she passed, and disappeared into the series of rooms. At least ten minutes went by, in a sepulchral silence, and the other two, remaining there motionless, surveyed me coldly. Emerging finally from the darkness, the woman who had taken my card returned:

"Come!"

From the outside, the house seemed very large; it was, in fact, even larger than it appeared. But that was not mainly what struck me, nor was it the insane luxury and museumlike atmosphere. It was the smell.

It struck my nostrils once and immediately faded, so that I might have thought I had imagined it. And then one or two whiffs came back; soon it was a cloud that enveloped me. It was vicious, sticking to the skin; it was foul and stifling, absolutely abominable.

As soon as I realized that the smell got heavier as I went forward, I paused and nearly recoiled. And the woman leading the way for me obviously guessed what was happening. She stopped for a very brief instant and turned only part of the way around:

"And that's nothing yet," she said. "But you wanted to come."

We set off again, and the smell became downright suffocating. It was worse than anything I had ever smelled before, worse than anything I had ever imagined smelling. It was a stench that assaulted not only my nostrils but every inch of skin; you breathed it in like a gas.

"This way."

The final door that the woman opened for me made the stench literally roll forth like a ground swell. I was sure that nowhere in the world was there a charnel house that stank as badly as this hexagonal room I was entering. It was an extraordinary room: the walls—and the ceiling and floor as well—were hung with incredibly valuable paintings. I recognized Van Goghs, Renoirs, and Gauguins, next to other painters I didn't know. These paintings decorated five sides of the room, the sixth consisting of a rectangle opening onto the boundless panorama of Death Valley in all its remarkable beauty. Really opening: you could go out that way, and the air-conditioners were striving to beat back the heat that was determined to get inside.

However, the room's occupant, though he might contemplate his fabulous museum at leisure, could not even touch anything; we were in a glass cage that fitted the exact dimensions of the five decorated walls with a four-inch clearance.

And I understood the reason for this strange device, when, with a gulp of revulsion, I discovered the yellowish trails of pus smeared all over the glass.

The room's occupant was an entirely naked man slumped on a metal chair without any sharp edges, apparently specially designed to be doused with water. For the man's whole body was nothing but a huge abscess, a monstrous pus-filled wound. The face itself was partly eaten away. There were not three square inches of flesh that were not devoured by an oozing leprosy.

"Mr. Carradine does not read," the women had told me. Dear God, with what could he read? You could no longer even see the eyes in that horror mask of scabs and abscesses, and nowhere in the house was the smell as strong as in close contact with what remained of William Carradine, called Will Scarlet.

*   *   *

The woman, after showing me in, withdrew like a shadow. She had placed my piece of cardboard on one of the armrests of the metal chair. My visiting card was already stained; a yellow trace marked one of the corners.

The horrible ravaged face turned slowly in my direction. A long silence. And then the voice rose, fantastically clear and pure, tinged with an upperclass Boston accent.

"So then, you are Andrea's son?"

I stared at the card, so as not to have to bear the sight of the wreck that was his face. He said:

"Read me what you wrote, please."

244

*"I am the son of Andrea Cimballi. I challenge you to find a way of destroying Martin Yahl."*

The blind face moved slightly; you could almost have said there was a smile on it. But it remained aimed in my direction like radar.

"Your first name?"

"Franz."

"Birthdate?"

"September 9, 1948."

"Do you remember La Capilla? If you are really Andrea's son, you should remember it. Almost fifteen years ago, I gave Andrea's son a gift. Something big and red."

"A toy Ferrari."

"It had a license number."

"Seven."

Silence.

"You have the same tone of voice as your father. Do you resemble him physically?"

"Pretty much."

"Your height?"

"An inch taller than he," I said a little stiffly, and now there really was a smile, ghastly to see.

What was most astounding, for me, about this conversation was William Carradine's voice, a voice of perfect clarity and precise diction; it was the voice of a lawyer accustomed to the courtroom, the voice of a professor emeritus, perfectly measured. And yet coming out of that red and yellow, purulent, inhuman mash. How did this . . . thing . . . continue to live? More importantly, Why?

"How did you find me?"

"By accident."

"But you weren't looking for me."

"I thought you were dead."

Nausea was overtaking me as the seconds passed, even though, strangely, I was beginning to adjust to the smell. I took a few steps, crossed the room, and went out into the sun, nearly staggering under the heat that suddenly struck me. The voice behind me:

"I was figuring your age, Franz; you must be twenty-three or twenty-four. And you want to destroy Martin Yahl?"

"Almost twenty-five. Not Yahl alone."

I suddenly began to vomit, and it lasted a long while. Then I moved away and sat down on a rock, under a cactus, but actually close to the threshold of the room, about ten feet away from the cage.

"You mean that you're planning some kind of revenge?"

"It's already been taken."

The spectacle of Death Valley was breathtakingly beautiful, in spite of the shimmering heat, which blurred part of the landscape. My nausea faded.

"Revenge on whom, Franz?"

"Landau, Lamm, Hovius and Donaldson: for them, it's over. Bremer died, and escaped me. I'm left with Martin Yahl."

"And me."

"I told you I thought you were dead."

"I'm not."

"You might as well be. I'm not sorry for you. On the contrary, I'm glad to have seen you and to know what happened to you. When I heard of Bremer's death, I felt frustrated. Not now. I'm glad to know that you're nothing but human garbage."

A movement in the room behind me; a series of rustles, heaves, and disgusting slides. I pictured Scarlet leaving his metal chair and flowing toward me with the slow slithering of an ameba. He moaned and grunted. I did not turn around.

"All the others played only secondary roles." I continued. "Not Martin Yahl or you. You and he were the ones who organized everything. I don't know which of you masterminded it. It doesn't matter. Your goal was to dismantle what you yourself built at my father's request; you provided the necessary technique for the embezzlement, and you acted with such skill that even knowing about the theft, I still found it impossible to prove."

The loathsome slithering continued. He wept with pain and rage with every move he made. He was no more than six feet away from me. His stench enveloped me.

"What I most blame you for, Martin Yahl and you, what makes me hate you more than you can imagine, is not even the fact that you robbed us, my father and me. Not even that you betrayed a man's confidence to that extent."

Still three feet between us, but he was suffering agonies; every inch was torture for him. The slithering stopped. He wheezed in great hoarse gasps like a man on the point of asphyxiation.

"What makes me hate you most of all is what you put my mother through. I remember that waltz around her even while she was dying. Instead of letting her die peacefully, you kept her in her agony, barely legally competent to sign all the papers you tormented her with. You ignored her suffering; at that time, you didn't give a damn. I heard the doctors talking among themselves. That—Scarlet, or Carradine, or whatever your name is— I can never forget. Yahl and you. I hated you with a child's hatred, and that hatred has not grown less with the years, far from it. And you'd like me to sympathize?"

He still did not move. I turned. His hand—that kind of running stump that was his hand—was only six inches from me, in the red dust. He himself was lying face down across the cement and steel base on which ran the bay window that closed the room. He was stretched out, panting, all the pus that ran from his body imbibed by the desert sand. Judging by what welled up on his face where his eyes should have been, and by the sobs that shook him, he was crying. The thing was crying.

I rose and knocked on the windows of the neighboring room, where two women were sitting. After a few moments, they came, wearing plastic slippers and gloves, and I understood why they went barefoot. They lifted the body gently, sponged it, and injected a whitish substance into it with several needles, cleaned it as much as possible; at the same time, two other women doused the glass room with water, including the white metal chair, using hoses that spewed something that smelled like ether. They placed Scarlet back in his chair, and had hardly turned on their heels and gone out when the festering sores began to run again.

The sepulchral silence of Death Valley fell again, finally broken by that astonishingly clear, almost beautiful, voice:

"The idea was Martin Yahl's not mine. We were at Harvard together, and I owed him a great deal. He had helped me early in my career. He lent me money and introduced me to your father. I set up the first Curaçao company, in which your father held the shares. The years passed. I still had big money problems, and Martin Yahl was always there to help. And then, in 1955, the first abscess appeared.

"My doctor gave me antibiotics, but whatever it was seemed to feed on the drug, because it grew larger, and spawned other abscesses like spores. I went to a specialist, took tests, received injections, went to more specialists. Nobody had ever seen anything like it; it was a running sore, an open wound, and it wouldn't heal. It was agonizing.

"The laboratory tests could only reveal that it was a virus of some kind. But where it had come from and, more important, how it could be healed . . . this nobody could tell me. And it was spreading, from my face to my body.

"I had to keep myself in isolation in my own home. My sheets, my towels, everything that came into contact with my body, had to be burned. I was a contaminant, even though the virus wasn't communicable. My wife couldn't bear to look at me. Soon she would leave me, and I couldn't blame her."

I had always imagined Death Valley as an absolute white-hot desert. But the reality was quite different: the beauty of that place was stunning, and the life forms were infinitely varied: I saw insects, reptiles, dozens of furtive animals, including what seemed like a hare; and, a stone's throw away on my right, gushing out of ocher rocks in to a natural basin, was a clear spring. While William Carradine spoke, I picked up a rock and idly studied the line of metal ore that ran through it.

"In the spring of 1956 I could no longer appear in public; my cheeks were totally diseased. Martin Yahl came to see me. I needed money more than ever. He asked me if I could undo what I had constructed, if I could erase even the last traces of Curaçao One, as if it had never existed; and then, with the same assets, the same capital—creating them out of nothing, as it were—set up another company, Curaçao Two, of which he, Martin Yahl, would be the sole owner. I replied that there was one major obstacle: your father. Your father and all those who had been his close collaborators and knew the truth. It would be impossible to fool them."

"Landau, Lamm, Bremer, Hovius and Donaldson."

"There was also an Italian named Revere, but he was killed in an auto accident in '57. I never met either Landau or Donaldson. Did you see them?"

"I didn't need to see them. They're bankrupt, both of them, like Lamm. Bremer is dead, and so is Hovius." I added, "I didn't kill them."

Or had I killed Hovius?

"They were all obstacles. I told Martin Yahl that; he said he would take care of them, and that they would keep their mouths shut. I asked: 'What about Andrea?' Martin shrugged his shoulders. 'His heart will give out sooner or later. He's at the mercy of a violent temper.' When did your father die?"

"August 28, 1956."

"Natural death?"

"Heart attack."

"What was he doing when he died?"

"Talking on the phone."

"You don't know who he was talking to?"

"No. But he was speaking German."

I turned around and faced Scarlet. My hands trembled. The blind face wavered slowly from left to right, staring at me.

"You see, Franz? That must have been Martin on the other end of the line."

I was bathed in sweat. But I could now look at the dead eyes almost without repulsion:

"You really can't see any more?"

"A year ago, I could still see shapes. Not any more."

"Is Martin Yahl still paying you?"

"I live off the interest on the capital he gave me in 1956. I knew I couldn't manage my own money; I'm not allowed to touch the capital, I only get the interest. Martin Yahl is a smart banker. Martin Yahl never makes a mistake. He always knows what to do."

The contrast between the rottenness of the body and the sarcastic gaity of the voice was striking and dramatic. Scarlet remarked:

"I remember you as a child who played naked on the Pampelonne beach. Did you really revenge yourself on all those people?"

I began to relate not only how I had done it, but again the entire story of my departure from London, up to the very minute I had set foot in Death Valley. It was a tale that took some time, and I had to stop at one point, when the gloved and booted women, masked like surgeons, came back to repeat the earlier operation—a cleaning thorough but futile; the instant they departed, the pus began to run again, and the smell reappeared.

"Listen to me, Carradine. I want to get back at Martin Yahl."

"With money?"

"With money."

249

"How much do you have?"

"About seventy million dollars."

"That's not enough. Martin Yahl has easily three times as much, not to mention the resources of his bank. You can cause trouble for him, probably make him take a sizeable loss, but you'll bankrupt yourself, and that's all."

"So I don't have a chance, then, in your opinion?"

"Alone? Not a chance."

"And with your help?"

Silence. The horrible face pivoted slowly, as though following the line of the Grapevine peaks.

"With my help," he mused. "Did you know that five years ago, Martin Yahl came to see me just to talk about you?"

"How could I know? I thought you were dead."

"Of course. Yahl stood exactly where you are standing now, and for exactly the same reason, to get away from the smell. He couldn't escape it any more than you can.

"He crossed an ocean and a desert just to talk about a nineteen-year-old boy, whom he hated with incredible ferocity. You!

"There was nobody else in the world to whom he could confide his hatred but to me, his old accomplice. A man of his wealth, his power, his vaulting ambition, to be afraid of a child! A child whose only goal in life, it seemed, was to spend every penny of his inheritance as quickly, recklessly and foolishly as he could. I laughed at him, but inwardly I shuddered. There was something obsessive about his hatred, like the wrath in an ancient Greek tragedy, that brings down entire dynasties."

Sweat was streaming over my entire body; my clothes were wringing wet. But it was not the fearful heat that made my hands tremble:

"I can attack Yahl? With a hope of beating him? You'll help me?"

Scarlet sank shiveringly into his steel chair, folding his stumps of legs under him, with a motion that, coming from a monster, was strangely human.

"If we were playing chess," said he, "I'd tell you: mate in nine moves."

# 20

I began by going to Rome. On Letta's instructions, I met him in a small hotel on the Via Sforza, about midway between Santa Maria Maggiore and the Colosseum. Fezzali himself was not royalty, that much was clear. There was no restaurant, so he went to sit down over *gelati* at a small sidewalk cafe. Fezzali listened to me for several minutes, without a word. Finally, thoughtfully, he remarked, "It's a remarkable plan."

Then he shook his head, like a carpet dealer at the Fez market judging the competition's products.

"In your opinion is it workable?"

They brought him a giant ice cream, and he began to spoon it up greedily, shrugging his shoulders.

I said, "it's not my plan." Then I told him about my visit to Death Valley. It was one of the few times, during our many meetings, when I saw him express anything but a general distaste for humanity. His was the sadness of an old camel afflicted by age.

"I thought Scarlet was dead. I knew him."

"He knew you, too. He told me to ask you if you remembered the Bester business."

"I remember," Fezzali said.

He gulped the ice cream down with astounding swiftness and immediately ordered another. While waiting for it to appear, he stared at the sidewalk with intensity, and said:

"How much did you tell me you wanted?"

"Three hundred fifty million in New York, six hundred in Geneva. But you heard me perfectly the first time."

"That makes nine hundred fifty million dollars."

"I can count that far. And I remind you that in at least one case it only involves a shifting of signatures."

They brought him another ice cream, even larger than the first. He looked at it with poignant melancholy, then began to devour it.

"Obviously I can't answer you right away."

"Of course not."

"I'll have to consult the prince."

"I'll wait."

All between two gigantic mouthfuls of ice cream and candied fruits. I watched him: he had known my father, claimed to have been his friend, and, all in all, was the first person I had ever met to make that kind of statement to me; I would almost have believed that my father had lived only to be betrayed.

"Did you get along with your father?"

He took a mouthful of thick black coffee, and afterward a little ice water, gobbled up the ice cream, drank another steaming mouthful of coffee. He chose not to hear my question, glancing at my sundae, which I hadn't touched:

"Aren't you eating yours?"

"You can have it."

I rose.

"Call me in New York at the numbers I gave you. Not at the St. Regis."

"Have a safe journey home," he mumbled.

As I was leaving, he called me back, expressionless:

"You might at least pay the check."

"Excuse me."

"It's the least you could do," he said.

*　　*　　*

Fezzali phoned me two days later: "Okay on both operations. Good luck." I was in Leo Sussman's apartment, where Leo had had three more phones installed at my expense. We were sitting down to eat, Leo, his wife, Robin, and I . They both saw my face:

"Bad news?"

"No. No, just the opposite."

Another step. A dance step. Another decisive step. It had begun.

*　　*　　*

The tape arrived by messenger. I clicked it into the player.

Scarlet's clear voice, with its pleasant timbre, rose from the cassette:

*"First move: Make available to Martin Yahl the capital he will need later on. In this case, the key is obviously Fezzali. It's up to you to convince him. He will listen to you because he was a friend of your father's and because you've demonstrated a degree of talent to him in this*

252

*Sun Belt real estate venture. He will listen to you, but convincing him to get involved will be another matter, especially if it means committing such large sums; you don't do business on the basis of good will unless it's charity. No, Fezzali will agree because what you're proposing will benefit him—him and the turbaned emirs he represents. What's mainly at stake is that company he'll have a chance of acquiring. Fezzali knows it's an excellent investment. And he'll also agree because he'll see a chance to gain control of a Swiss bank, which is what the petrodollars have always been striving for without success. Once you have Fezzali's agreement, and the hundreds of millions of dollars you asked him for. . . ."*

* * *

I devoted nearly a month to subterranean activities, which were already complicated in themselves but were all the more so because everything I did was done secretly, behind the backs—or so I hoped—of the detectives Martin Yahl had hired to dog my footsteps. This game of hide-and-seek was fun at first, but it soon became exasperating.

So I did something daring and perhaps foolhardy, but something which made me laugh my old laughter. I sent Yahl a cablegram: CALL OFF YOUR WATCH DOGS BEFORE I THROW THEM A POISONED BONE. (signed) CIMBALLI. And it worked!

My wire must have startled Yahl, but after that I never saw a detective again. The first shot had been fired. I had acknowledged his existence and was forcing him to acknowledge mine, and the enmity that lay between us.

Nearly four weeks after receiving Fezzali's phone call telling me he agreed to get involved in the operation; and after making sure, of course, that the money had really been transferred to the account of my Lichtenstein company; and after establishing, as agreed, the new Panamanian company I was going to need; and finally, after having held numerous consultations with my three lawyers—after all that, I went down to that bank on Nassau Street in downtown Manhattan.

* * *

*"Move number two: Young Cimballi, the man you will see after getting Fezzali's agreement is a banker named Stern. He's an elderly man who's been wanting to retire for years now. He was expecting his grandson to take over from him, but the boy died, and Stern hasn't been the same*

*since. And I think he's ready to listen to any reasonable purchase offer, especially if the price you offer for his shares goes beyond anything he might currently expect from a buyer.*

*"Listen to me, Franz, and you'll see that all of this is very simple. On the day your father died, Martin Yahl began to direct Curaçao Two. Yahl has made it one of the most powerful multi-nationals in the world. Only one other conglomerate in our western capitalist world is larger, and that's UNICHEM. UNICHEM and Curaçao Two are competitors, at least in theory; in raw reality, they have a tacit nonaggression pact and share the largest part of the world market, again in their particular fields.*

*"The relationship of forces? UNICHEM is twice as large as Curaçao Two, give or take a few billion dollars. Are you following me, young Franz? Good. Now let's see what UNICHEM is composed of. It's a company in which forty-five percent of the shares are in the hands of small owners; so there must be—but you'll have to find out—nearly twenty-five thousand shareholders, most of them citizens of Free America.*

*"We'll come back to that. For now, let's look at that other fifty-five percent: the majority. That fifty-five percent is held by two families, represented by two banks, which are managed by two men, fifty-five percent representing six hundred seventy thousand shares. The largest of those large shareholders, who actually controls UNICHEM, is that same Mr. Aaron Stern. . . ."*

\* \* \*

Aaron Stern was facing me. Facing us, I should say. I was not alone. I was accompanied by my three lawyers, all three of them disciples and former pupils of Scarlet, whom they considered their spiritual father. What's more, it was Scarlet himself, risen from the dead, who had written them, asking them—in return for some hundreds of thousands of dollars—to dedicate themselves to my battle.

It was one of those three lawyers, Philip Vandenbergh, who made the introductions:

"Mr. Franz Cimballi and his counsels: James Rosen and Joseph Lupino."

Handshaking. We sat down. Philip Vandenbergh spoke, as agreed. He was a New Yorker, thirty-five to forty years old, a Harvard graduate as well, smart as Lucifer, cold as ice; it was easy to come off looking like a coolie in his eyes. Not likeable, but that was the least of my worries.

When I met him for the first time (and on top of that, he was six inches taller than I), he did not conceal that he would definitely have declined any proposal to do what we were doing if William Carradine himself—"but I thought he was dead"—had not personally intervened. "Though this strange battle we're beginning is, I admit, rather fascinating, solely from an intellectual point of view."

Vandenbergh had also pointed out to me that forming a team with him, Lupino, and Rosen amounted to assembling the best brains of the young generation. "Lupino and Rosen will duplicate my work, but I guess old Scarlet made us a team so that none of us could go over to the other side."

Philip Vandenbergh was still speaking. But it was me Aaron Stern was looking at:

"Whom do you represent, Mr. Cimballi?"

"Franz Cimballi. Myself."

"And you'd be willing to pay me three hundred fifty dollars apiece for shares that to this day have barely reached three hundred at most, and which right now are traded at less than two hundred thirty?"

"That's the reason I'm here."

"And that price is good for all four hundred ten thousand shares we own?"

I glanced at Philip Vandenbergh, who, as agreed, drew the certified check from his briefcase and placed it on the bare desk tray.

"Four hundred ten thousand times three hundred fifty dollars equals one hundred forty-three million five hundred thousand dollars," he said. "Cash."

I kept my gaze not on the eyes, but on the hands of Aaron Stern, which were trembling with excitement. I sensed that he was quite capable of saying yes immediately, and that would spoil everything. I had no intention of really giving him that money.

"I don't expect a hasty reply, Mr. Stern," I said peremptorily. "I understand that you need to think it over. Do so, by all means. But do it fast, for I have no time to lose. Today is Wednesday, May 7, and it's ten-twelve in the morning. I'll be in this office across from you tomorrow at eleven a.m. to hear your answer."

As agreed beforehand, Philip Vandenbergh registered the surprise and consternation my apparent tactical error caused him.

255

The charade was absolutely necessary to convince Stern that only my youthful impetuousness and also a certain presumptuousness had prevented the signing of an agreement which he was ready to sign then and there. To prevent him from opening his mouth anyway, I rose and went quickly to the door. I stopped on the doorstep, striking a haughty pose verging on parody:

"Tomorrow, Mr. Stern."

And I went out, while my three counsels, as though embarrassed by my impulsive stupidity, also withdrew, with blank faces barely tinged by irritation.

Fezzali had already transferred six hundred million petrodollars, supposedly in search of fruitful investments, to Geneva, to the Yahl Bank, and Fezzali himself had gone to the shore of Lake Leman; he had met with Yahl and spoken to him.

The second step: the visit I had just made to Aaron Stern, holding a certified check from the Bank of America for one hundred forty-three million dollars.

The third step. . . . The dance was beginning.

\* \* \*

*"Three: after Stern, you'll go see Glatzman, the other banker. The ideal thing would be for you to meet him the same day, say an hour after your appointment with Stern. Their offices are in the same neighborhood, anyway; Rosen will arrange that for you easily. Such haste will fit in perfectly with the role you're playing—that of a slightly pretentious young mad dog, somewhat dazzled by his own success, who doesn't look before he leaps.*

*"One can imagine how all that money acquired so quickly would go to your head. Fine, let's talk about Glatzman. There's a very different customer from Stern. Stern is old and wants to sell. Glatzman is twenty years younger, and won't sell unless he sees some special advantage. Above all, don't try to fool him. Go right to the point. Tell him why you absolutely must have those two hundred sixty thousand UNICHEM shares he holds."*

\* \* \*

Glatzman looked at Vandenbergh, then Lupino, then Rosen. And finally me. He raised his eyebrows:

"What is this? A parade?"

I smiled at him:

256

"Wait till the others get here, they couldn't find a cab."

He put out a small chubby hand and took the certified check for ninety-one million dollars.

"That's a lot of money."

"So I noticed."

"Did you go see old Stern?"

"We've just left there."

"What did he say?"

"He'll tell us tomorrow."

"But you think he'll agree?"

"Yes."

His eyes studied me, while his hand drew his desk top calculator nearer. He did his arithmetic without rushing, checking each calculation twice: four hundred ten thousand shares from Stern, two hundred sixty thousand from him, that made six hundred seventy thousand in all, at three hundred fifty dollars each. . . .

"Two hundred thirty-four million five hundred thousand dollars."

*"Franz, he'll ask you why you want to buy those shares. . . ."*

Glatzman asked:

"And why this frenzied desire to become the majority stockholder of UNICHEM?"

*"Whatever you do, don't lie, Franz. Tell the truth."* Scarlet's voice.

"Because my name is Cimballi, and the man who controls the other world monopoly besides UNICHEM is called Martin Yahl. And because I won't stop until I've massacred Martin Yahl. If you refuse to sell me your shares, you can still be a spectator with a ringside seat, but in that case you risk losing heavily. This is a battle to the death between Yahl and me. Only one of us will come out alive. . . ."

*"Franz, Glatzman is a businessman first. He'll resume the discussion because you intrigue him, he wants to know how far you can go, and also because that's his nature. You're offering him three hundred fifty dollars a share? He'll try to get more."*

"Let's say a hundred million for my two hundred sixty thousand shares," Glatzman said.

*"And you'll refuse."*

"No."

"Ninety-five and they're yours."

I rose, my face expressing—I did my best—a cold rage.

"It's a mistake to treat me like a boy, Glatzman! Ninety-one million or nothing. And make no mistake: I'll only buy your shares if they'll assure me control of UNICHEM. Of themselves they don't interest me. I only want them if I can also buy Stern's. I'll pay both of you three hundred fifty dollars a share. That's already too high a price. Stern is to give me his answer tomorrow morning at eleven. My representatives will be in your office half an hour later. I'll buy from the two of you, or I won't buy."

Back to the St. Regis. In the Mercedes 500 SEL I had rented, Lupino hummed, tapping his fingers in time to the song. Despite his Italian name, he was reddish blond, with that blondness they call Venetian. He winked at me as if to say: "Isn't this fun!" The youngest of my three counsels, thirty-two, Lupino already had earned a remarkable reputation.

The car slowly made its way up the Avenue of the Americas. Now that the battle was under way, I was scared. The vastness of the sums invested, hence the vastness of the risks involved; the power of the enemy I had engaged in this death struggle— all of this suddenly became clear to me, amplified further by my active imagination and my crushing fatigue. I felt like I hadn't really slept in days, and that was fairly true—I was so exhausted that I could hardly get to sleep, when I had time to try. I asked of no one in particular:

"Is anyone having lunch with me?"

With his usual icy politeness, Philip Vandenbergh declined. Rosen said he was already busy; Lupino accepted. Vandenbergh and Rosen left the car near Rockefeller Center.

Lupino chuckled as the Mercedes took off again:

"Rosen, Glatzman, Stern, Cimballi, Lupino—all in this together. To Vandenbergh, they're all peasants, swine. But the Dutch son of a bitch is a damn good lawyer and almost as foxy as I am, in spite of his Stone Age ancestry. Franz, you know that Scarlet put together a terrific team? This deal is one of the most incredible maneuvers in the history of finance. I'll make you an offer: you pay for the drinks, champagne with the meal, and the food; I'll pay for the coffee. What do you say?"

Cute. He was real cute.

# 21

Public Tender Offer.

That was the technical term. It was the same as publicly announcing—and you were bound by law to such publicity—that you were prepared to buy up all the shares of a given company, at a specific price that is higher than the current price. And to do so in a given period of time, without a limit on the number of shares. In other words, you officially make a tender offer for all the shares that are put up for sale.

Martin Yahl officially opened his public tender offer for UN-ICHEM stock on Thursday, May 8, at ten o'clock, Eastern Standard Time. The price per share offered to any bearer showing up within the prescribed period, three hundred eighty dollars. The period in which the offer would be valid: thirty days.

Or until Friday, June 6, at ten o'clock. Yahl was determined not to let me gain control of UNICHEM.

We learned the news in the office I had rented in the name of my new Panamanian company, on Fifty-Ninth Street. I'd taken precautions so that none of Yahl's possible agents would be alerted. It was one of James Rosen's assistants who gave us the news over the phone, from his post on the floor of the New York Stock Exchange.

When the news came, all four of us were there, Philip Vandenbergh, Rosen, Lupino, and I. We expected the announcement, but nevertheless it made us nervous. I stood up and began pacing. As I passed, Joe Lupino gave me his usual wink, Rosen scribbled something, and the icy Vandenbergh cracked a thin smile.

"He's fallen into the thick of it."

Philip Vandenbergh also got up and stared at me, with an expression in the depths of his clear eyes that I had never seen before, made up of curiosity, and something close to respect. As though he were seeing me for the first time. He said, in his Harvard voice:

"I had a lot of respect for Scarlet. I always did. In this particular case, I didn't think he could be right. Three hundred eighty dollars! My God! I would never have imagined a banker like Martin Yahl going that far. Scarlet's guess was correct: that Swiss has been carried away by his hatred for you."

He was a head taller than I. I asked:

"And is that what's bothering you?"

"Yes. Because you judge a person by his enemies."

"Then what do you make of this?" I asked. "I can't stand *you*."

* * *

On May 17, at five o'clock in the afternoon, I was in a completely anonymous Fiat, which, by the dubious grace of a taciturn driver, dropped me off behind a small hotel not far from Via Aurelia, in Rome. By appointment, I went to the room on the second floor. Fezzali was already there.

"Have a good trip?"

"Shouldn't we exchange code phrases, like, 'Watch out, the toilets are stopped up'? And you'd answer, 'I don't give a damn, I'm constipated.' Just in case I'm not me and you're not you."

Fezzali smiled:

"Still a chatterbox, eh? But we'll play another time. I'm supposed to be in a meeting in my suite at the Hassler, and I don't have much time. You know, of course, that everything went off like clockwork."

"You met with Yahl?"

"In Rome, at the Hassler."

"When?"

"Wednesday, at nine in the evening."

Three in the afternoon, New York time! Martin Yahl's reaction had been fantastically swift. Barely four hours after I had met with Glatzman and Stern, he had already contacted Fezzali, hired a plane, rushed to Rome, and launched into a negotiation, to block me from acquiring the stock.

"What did he offer you?"

"He first reminded me of the request that I—that Prince Aziz and I had made some time ago when we deposited six hundred million in his bank, a request for help and advice in making fruitful investments. He told me: 'The time has come. I have a deal for you.' And he offered to sell his control of his conglomerate for two hundred sixty million dollars."

"You agreed?"

"I refused. I suggested two hundred ten, so that we could bargain to two hundred thirty. And we came to an agreement on that sum—two hundred thirty million dollars with the proviso

260

that he continues to manage. I agreed with him that it would be difficult to find a better manager. In addition, we pledged to respect a noncompetitive pact between UNICHEM and his former group."

Fezzali gulped down at least a quart of ice cream with the greatest sadness. I sighed.

"You old camel trader, you are determined to make me squirm, it gives you so much pleasure. Okay, I'll ask. What about the part that concerns me?"

The animal—he took the time to swallow voluptuously enough *gelati* to float another Titanic. Finally, he threw me a melancholy glance:

"Mr. Yahl also asked us to promise to buy any share of UN-ICHEM that was put up for sale apart from the six hundred seventy thousand held by the Stern and Glatzman banks. I replied that in principle I had no objection whatever to making that pledge, provided my promise was ratified by the emirs I report to, of course. Two days ago, I called Geneva to confirm that my principals accepted the condition."

"But you didn't sign anything?"

"Nothing. We had a simple verbal agreement. After all, minus the two hundred thirty million dollars spent to buy the Yahl group, we still had three hundred seventy million dollars on deposit with that gentleman. I pointed out to Mr. Martin Yahl, anyway, that the risk of a large number of small shareholders putting their shares on the market between now and the close of his public purchase offer was minimal, in view of their dispersion, their atomization, rather."

Fezzali gulped down another large spoonful of ice cream, saving the maraschino cherry for last. He concluded:

"It was agreed that I spoke wisely."

Having finished his ice cream, he stared at the empty dish with eyes more melancholy than ever. He asked me:

"And on your end?"

"Stern and Glatzman sold all of their shares to His Banking Highness, who therefore now holds a majority within UNI-CHEM and is manager of the competing company. Lucky for him he isn't governed by American anti-trust regulations. As for me—poor innocent lad destroyed by his own recklessness—I had the pain of discovering that my mortal enemy had upped my offer and killed the deal I was dreaming of. It brought tears to my eyes."

"And the other operation?"

"The Vandenbergh, Rosen, and Lupino team have been doing fantastic work for more than a month now. It's going pretty well."

We exchanged a look. I was sure he could read on my face the real anguish inside me.

"Another ice cream?" Fezzali offered.

"Eat mine, as usual."

"As long as you're paying," Fezzali answered, amiably.

* * *

Another cassette tape arrived from Scarlet.

*"Young Cimballi, remember. In One, you got your Arab friends to make a payment of six hundred million to the Yahl bank and three hundred fifty million to your account. Two was your visit to Stern, and your offer of three hundred fifty dollars per share. Three was the same offer, this time to Glatzman. Fine. So much for your first three moves. At this point, if everything goes as planned, where are we? Well, theoretically, Martin Yahl should react, and quickly, if I know him. With his flanks covered by the six hundred million petrodollars in his bank's vaults, he has only one means of preventing you from buying the fifty-five percent of UNICHEM shares: to buy them himself in the framework of a public tender offer. He's a banker who worries about all the appearances of legality, and for him, a public tender offer is the only way to go.*

*"He doesn't have the capital necessary to buy, but he has a solution: sell his own conglomerate to the Arabs. I know Fezzali: Martin Yahl certainly won't get the two hundred fifty million dollars he's hoping for from him. The most he'll get is two hundred thirty. To beat the offer you made to Stern and Glatzman, he has to go up to three hundred seventy; it's my belief he'll go higher, to knock you out, in a way, and give you the proof of his omnipotence. Anyway, even at three hundred eighty dollars and change, he's not getting such a bad deal: UNICHEM is a healthy enterprise, which has nothing to fear but its sole competitor, the former Yahl Group . . . and Yahl is quite capable of asking to remain in charge of it. That's what I would advise him to do, anyway.*

*"Let's do our arithmetic, Franz the Dancer: six hundred seventy thousand shares at, let's say, three hundred eighty dollars makes two hundred fifty-four million six hundred thousand. Two hundred fifty, roughly. He'll get two hundred thirty from Fezzali, so twenty-four million six*

262

*hundred thousand are still missing. Yahl has them, if he dips into his private wealth. Which he does. So he buys up all of Stern's and Glatzman's shares. And that's where it gets interesting. . . .*

*"Because he's not crazy, you know. He knows that somewhere in the world, there are still about five hundred fifty thousand UNICHEM shares also included in his public tender offer. And he knows the law, old Yahl does: he knows that anyone who puts out a public tender offer is required to buy all shares that are put up for sale in response to the offer within the period defined by the offer.*

*"Of course those shares are dispersed, atomized, as we say, but why take risks? By putting out the two hundred fifty million dollars to buy up fifty-five percent of UNICHEM, Yahl has used up the largest part of his maneuvering power. He should have about fifty, sixty million dollars left, maybe a little more, I don't know exactly. Plus his bank, of course, but he would commit suicide ten times over before he'd allow the bank to go. And that money he's got in reserve isn't necessarily available immediately; it's working somewhere, or else Yahl wouldn't be a banker.*

*"If by a horrible coincidence, those five hundred forty thousand shares— the minority, let's call them—showed up en masse demanding three hundred eighty apiece, he obviously couldn't match them. Martin Yahl doesn't really believe in such an outcome, and, all things being equal, he's right. But he's prudent, very prudent. And before launching into the venture, he asks Fezzali to pledge to buy all the UNICHEM shares that are put up for sale which he can't buy himself. . . .*

*"That's move Number Four."*

\* \* \*

From Rome, despite the shortage of time at hand, I did not return directly to New York. I stopped off in Paris, not long, barely four hours between two planes. But that was enough to kiss Catherine, who picked me up at Roissy.

"You look tired."

"I am tired. But I haven't forgotten the promise you made."

The golden eyes sparked with provocative malice:

"I don't get it."

"Like hell. The first time, we were in the Bahamas, and you had on a sliver of a black bathing suit. The second time we were in Paris, and you were wearing a blue dress with flowers all over it. Both times you told me: "I'll marry you, darling Franz, light

*263*

of my life, without whom life wouldn't be worth living. I'll marry you as soon as you stop acting like an idiot, running all over the place and dancing your crazy dance."

"Are you sure that's what I said?"

"That was the general idea."

She suddenly stopped smiling, and her eyes became moist.

"Oh, Franz" she said in a small voice. "I was beginning to think you'd forgotten me!"

We drove quietly through empty country roads, Catherine holding the wheel with my head on her shoulder. I think we drove through Halatte Forest, climbed to the top of Aumont Peak, and took off again for Senlis, which was superb in that month of May. Afterward, she took me back to the airport without our having exchanged more than a few words, although thousands of kisses.

"Catherine, it won't be much longer now. The payoff is very, very near."

"How long?"

"Three weeks, perhaps less. Cimballi's dance is winding down."

"And then?"

"What happens when a dance is finished, when the violins are still? You go home. And you close your door and put out a sign: 'Please do not disturb.' "

\* \* \*

*"Move Five, young Cimballi. If everything has gone as planned, it is time to remember that three hundred fifty million that Fezzali agreed to transfer to your account while depositing another six hundred in the Yahl Bank in Geneva. You used that money once to back up the checks you waved under the noses of Stern and Glatzman. You also used it— this time in truth—for what I call Operation Round-up. Don't forget that you must constantly watch, instigate, start all of this again. Everything depends on its success. Check on it every day, every hour, urge the men on, don't give them a moment's rest. If they complain, overpay them. . . ."*

\* \* \*

Of course, you have guessed long ago that it was never my

intention to buy UNICHEM. Those certified checks I showed Stern and Glatzman, while quite genuine, were never intended for anything but show. My plan hinges upon forcing Yahl's hand, coercing *him* into an attempt to head me off by buying up UNICHEM stock himself, using his own capital and others', namely, the petrodollars from Fezzali's emirs.

It began even before I met Fezzali in Rome to ask him for nearly one billion dollars. The entire network was set up even before he gave his consent; it went into action as soon as the consent was obtained. What was it exactly?

\* \* \*

*"Franz, you have a choice of two possibilities. Either form a Small Shareholders' Protection Association, by hinting, for example, that a maneuver is in the works that would be harmful to the small owners. Or—and this is the best solution—whenever possible, buy as much as you can yourself, so that you can then sell it to the emirs if they wish, as you promised Fezzali. For the secret round-up of the stock, trust Vandenbergh, Rosen, and Lupino, especially Rosen, who has a genius for that sort of thing. Why do you think I chose those men? They're going to put two or three hundred brokers on the trail for you. The best. Nothing must leak out."*

\* \* \*

I was the one who paid the brokers, just as I paid an exorbitant price for Vandenbergh, Rosen, and Lupino, and their countless assistants. That was not my only major expense. I offered to sell Fezzali all the "minority" shares I acquired—that is,the shares that were not part of the fifty-five percent bought by Yahl. Fezzali agreed, gobbling his *gelati*.

"Okay. But the fact that your father was my friend doesn't mean I have to succumb to the wildest extravagance. I'll buy back everything you have to sell and deduct from my three hundred fifty million back-up loan. Worry not. Each share of UNICHEM is valued on the open market at three hundred twenty-eight and I'll pay you three hundred thirty."

"But to convince the small shareholders, I have to pay them more than three hundred eighty!"

"Your problem, my young friend, not mine."

And he gobbled his mound of ice cream.

"Three hundred thirty, Franz. No more. Make up the difference out of your own pocket."

* * *

Martin Yahl put forth his public tender offer on Thursday, May 8. That offer was supposed to close on Friday, June 6. As for the operation nicknamed Round-up by Scarlet, it had begun a month earlier. That was when the two hundred or so stock traders, lined up by my attorneys, went on the hunt. Their mission: to purchase as many shares as possible. Only where the owner refused to part with his shares, would he be invited to join the Protection Association.

All of this, of course, in the most absolute secrecy.

For the sole purpose of being able to follow the progress of the round-up minute by minute, I transformed the rented offices on Fifty-Ninth Street into strategic headquarters. No fewer than twelve operators were assigned to collate the news from the brokers. Some, in their eagerness, tracked shareholders all the way to their golden retreats in Jamaica, the Greek Islands, or Switzerland; even to Scotts Bluff, Nebraska.

In addition to their usual commission, they had been promised a bonus of a thousand dollars each for each chunk of twenty-five thousand shares purchased. That was Rosen's idea; he was generous with my money. Rosen was a small, sad, taciturn Jew, hardworking as hell, with a gift for organization and teamwork like Mozart's for music. He had a truly ferocious energy and tenacity.

On Wednesday, May 7, an hour before we went to Stern's office, Rosen gave us an initial report on the situation:

"UNICHEM shares have moved in a narrow range over the past five years. Except in special situations the bounty-hunting brokers were not offering to buy UNICHEM outright. More often, they offered exchanges for other, first-class shares: I.B.M., Royal Dutch, General Motors, and others, such as Hoffman La Roche, which we supplied them with."

"Give me figures."

"To date, thirty-one hundred shareholders contacted. Perhaps half agreed to sell. About twenty-five percent have joined the

Association. "We've managed to gain access to approximately one hundred and forty thousand shares."

"Out of . . .?"

"Five hundred forty-eight thousand."

"We've got a way to go."

"Don't judge everything from the figures. We've made more progress than is apparent. Up to now, we've only contacted the small owners. Since yesterday, we've unleashed all our firepower on the larger shareholders. These people will be easier to convince—they're more informed about market shifts—and as soon as we offer them ten percent over the tender price—"

"This is costing me a fortune."

A thin smile from Vandenbergh. I loved the guy.

"Revenge is a luxury," he said. "It's expensive."

It did indeed cost me a fortune. Eleven days before Yahl's offer was due to expire, the total number of minority shares I controlled, either by transfer or membership in the Protection Association, passed the three-hundred-thousand mark. Two days later, we were up to three hundred fifty thousand. After that, each hour changed the figures written on the blackboards Rosen had hung up in the Fifty-Ninth Street offices. The rise continued, with the inexorable power of a tide.

The "future public tender price" plus ten percent had been offered, on Rosen's orders, by the brokers to all shareholders who agreed to sell. That forced me to pay four hundred and eighteen dollars for shares. I would never be able to resell them for more than three hundred thirty to that old bastard Fezzali. Going over my accounts, adding in the salaries, bonuses, and expenses, the royal fees of Vandenbergh, Lupino, and Rosen, their assistants' salaries, the bonuses I had had to pay in order to buy hundreds of thousands of shares at a loss, the huge expenses I had had from everywhere, the bribes I'd had to dish out here and there—I came up with a grand total of thirty-two million six hundred thousand dollars gone, once and for all. Hell, it was only money.

But the result was there—fascinating in its incredible sharpness. Martin Yahl had made his public tender offer; he had spent—by selling the company he had stolen from my father— two hundred fifty-four million six hundred thousand dollars;

quite a bit more, in fact, with expenses. He had already spent twenty million of his own resources, which no longer amounted to more than perhaps sixty million. On Thursday, June 5, in the morning, at the very moment when I myself was going over my accounts in my room at the St. Regis, I enjoyed thinking that he might be going over his. In Geneva or in Zurich—I didn't exactly know where he was—he was probably already savoring his triumph.

* * *

It was six o'clock in the morning in New York. I hadn't slept the night before, and the previous nights had been just as restless, but I was much too nervous to even close my eyes. In Switzerland it was noon.

He was probably at his desk—he was a man of order, punctuality, discipline. I picked up the phone and dialed the number of the bank on Quai Général-Guisan in Geneva.

"I would like to speak to Mr. Martin Yahl, personally."

"Who's calling, please?"

The first name that came to my mind:

"Prince Henri of Orléans."

A few seconds, and then the icy voice, tinged with his German accent:

"What a pleasure to hear your voice, Your Highness."

For the first time, the voice of my enemy. I said nothing. I heard the silence that contained only his breathing. And he, at the other end of the line, became more and more anxious about that silence.

"Hello? Hello? Hello?"

I hung up. At a quarter to eight, I went out into the New York morning and walked up Fifth Avenue, unhurriedly, strolling, stopping to drink two cups of coffee, both lousy. The air was breezy and warm.

It was almost nine o'clock when I finally entered the offices on Fifty-Ninth Street. Rosen and Lupino were already there, or perhaps had been there all night. Rosen's dark eyes met mine, and he answered my question before I could even ask it.

"Three hundred thirty-nine thousand shares purchased, one hundred thirty-five thousand in the Protection Association. For a total of four hundred seventy-four thousand."

"Can that still change?"

"Not really. We've done out utmost, in my opinion."

For the hundredth time since the moment I decided I might as well get up, giving up on the sleep that eluded me, I consulted my watch; it was two minutes past nine o'clock in the morning. Martin Yahl's public tender offer would close in twenty-four hours and fifty-eight minutes. I sat down, my legs heavy.

"Four hundred seventy-four thousand shares at . . ."

The phone rang. Lupino answered and passed me the receiver.

"Franz?"

It was Fezzali.

"Franz, I'm at the Rome airport. My plane leaves in five minutes. My favorite uncle is very sick. He lives in the desert. He has no phone, no telegraph, no radio. I need two days to get there, two to spend there, two to come back. Six days altogether, during which no one can get in touch with me, no matter how important the business. No one can, Franz. Do you understand me?"

"I understand."

The line went dead. Philip Vandenbergh came in just then. He probably hadn't slept either, yet he was impeccably shaved and clean, unlike Rosen, who looked like a rumpled old bag. I told him and the others:

"No one can reach Fezzali for the next six days."

I didn't add: And Fezzali is the only one with access to the hundreds of millions of petrodollars deposited in the Yahl private bank. My listeners could weigh the importance of the news as well as I. Another piece of the trap had just fallen into place. I finished the accounting I had begun when Fezzali called me: Four hundred seventy-four thousand shares at three hundred eighty dollars each makes one hundred eighty million one hundred twenty thousand dollars.

Which Martin Yahl would be compelled by law to pay. And he would have to pay the huge sum between the time I decided to put those four hundred seventy-four thousand shares I was holding up for sale, and the time when his public tender offer would expire.

It went without saying that I would leave him as little time as possible. The final act would be played out in a few hours.

According to Scarlet, according to Lavater and his investiga-

269

tors, according to all the estimates we could make, Martin Yahl possessed, on that Friday, June 6, sixty million dollars at most—not all of it liquid. That would mean that he would have to find a hundred twenty million dollars in no more time than it takes to cross the street.

He had counted on Fezzali's help, even had Fezzali's money in his vaults. The unfortunate absence of the Lebanese, and the strict orders he had given his replacement—DO ABSOLUTELY NOTHING—would bottle up the capital Yahl was hoping to use.

\* \* \*

*"Move Number Six, young Cimballi: As little time as possible before the close of his public tender offer, offer up a very large number of shares as a block. Yahl will not be able to pay for them. He'll turn to Fezzali: Fezzali won't be there. Martin Yahl, despite this tough blow at the last minute, still has one hope—getting credit from other financial groups. He'll go after it. After all, he still has tens of millions of dollars, and above all, he has his bank. That's when you trigger the trap we discussed. . . ."*

\* \* \*

The trap was sprung that day. It took the form of stories that appeared simultaneously in *Le Monde*, Paris; *The Financial Times*, London; *The Washington Post*, United States; *La Tribune de Geneve;* the *Bild-Zeitung*, Hamburg (which headlined it across three columns on page one, with a photo of Martin Yahl), and the *Frankfurter Allgemeine Zeitung*. On the whole, they all more or less followed the theme of the dossier I had supplied: FORMER NAZI BANKER MAKES PUBLIC TENDER OFFER FOR AMERICAN JEWISH COMPANY.

The dossier had required Marc Lavater and me to finance nearly four years of research. It established, beyond doubt, the relationship, the collusion even, between the Yahl family—especially Martin Yahl—and Heinrich Meinhardt, the Nazi chief sent to Switzerland by Hitler in the spring of 1933 to recover all the German money, in particular the German Jewish money, squirreled away in Swiss vaults.

It gave proof of the commonality of ideas then existing between the young Martin Yahl and men such as the Swiss *Gauführer* Robert Tobler of Zurich, and the founder of the Swiss Fascist chapters, Arthur Fonjallaz.

*270*

It offered evidence that on at least one occasion, the Yahl Bank had agreed to a "repatriation" of German Jewish funds under entirely irregular conditions; namely, that it was willing to transfer to a German bank funds that had been entrusted to it by a Jewish banker from Hanover.

The dossier contained photos of Martin Yahl in the company of his SS friends during a 1941 trip to Nuremberg. It also contained a letter he had sent to an official of the *Volksdeutsche Mittelstelle*, the SS administration, in which he made a list—"rounding out the one I already sent you," he wrote—of his German Jewish clients whose capital might be "repatriated." And such a disclosure to third parties—whoever they might be, but especially if they were German Nazis—was in strict violation of Article 47 of the Swiss law on banks and savings associations—a regulation dating from November 8,1934, and establishing banking secrecy through the device of numbered accounts, precisely in order to protect assets such as those of the Jews.

\* \* \*

*"Young Cimballi, after the blow you have just given him, he must be aware that he is cornered. He knows perfectly well that no banking association, especially Swiss and especially within so short a time, will come to his rescue.*

*Place yourself in the financiers' place: at first they thought they were dealing with a normal public tender offer. But what has just happened—the sudden, belated emergence of hundreds of thousands of shares, the disclosures to the press—proves that what is really involved is a mighty contest between the Yahl bank and an unknown adversary. Who? No one knows. Who would meddle in such a fight without knowing the combatants, with less than twenty-four hours' notice? In finance, young Franz the Dancer, when a man goes under, you turn your head and look elsewhere. Yahl is alone. The Seventh Move has been well played by you. Let me take care of the Eighth. . . ."*

\* \* \*

The calm, cold, educated voice of Philip Vandenbergh, his surgeon's voice ringing in the silence of an operating room:

"Mr. Yahl, my name is Philip Vandenbergh. I manage a large law firm in New York. I am calling you on the advice of Mr. William Carradine, and am authorized—not by him, but by a client he represents—to offer you five hundred thousand United

States dollars in exchange for six hundred seventy thousand UNICHEM shares now in your possession. In exchange for such a sale on these express conditions, my clients will make a written pledge to take over your public tender offer and fulfill it."

Silence.

"You said what amount?"

"Five hundred thousand dollars. But I have something else to tell you, Mr. Yahl. . . ."

With the same surgical calm, Philip Vandenbergh unfolded a newspaper, so that the noise of the crinkled paper reached the ears, went through the receiver, and crossed the Atlantic in the same instant.

"Mr. Yahl, I have in front of me the photocopy of a letter we received yesterday by mail, dated February 11, 1935, which you sent to one Joachim Schaer, of the *Ausland Organization* of Berlin. That, of course, was the foreign chapter of the Hitlerian National Socialist Party.

What Philip Vandenbergh was really looking at was a review of an Off-Off-Broadway play which the critic considered disastrous.

"Mr. Yahl, your public tender offer will expire in two hours. You are not in a position to meet your obligations to the sellers who have presented stock; I urge you to accept my client's offer. . . ."

"Who is he?"

"I am not authorized to reveal that."

"Is it Franz Cimballi?"

"I give you my word that that is not the name."

Which was absolutely true. For once, I wasn't the one who was paying the five hundred thousand dollars; it was Prince Aziz.

"Accept the offer made to you, Mr. Yahl, and you can at least keep your bank. That's the advice Mr. Carradine told me to give you. If you wish to contact Mr. Carradine yourself, I can—"

"No . . . no . . ."

Martin Yahl's voice was low, nearly inaudible. Philip Vandenbergh's icy blue gaze left the spread-out newspaper and sought mine, with a question in the depths of his clear pupils: "What do you feel at the sight of a dead enemy?"

"Mr. Yahl," Vandenbergh went on, as cold as ice. "It is four minutes past the hour. Two of my associates in this matter, James

Rosen and Joseph Lupino, are in Geneva. They're a few hundred yards away from you, in the offices of the Swiss National Bank. They wait for your decision. They are authorized to guarantee you in return that our client will advance payment for the four hundred seventy-four thousand shares you cannot afford yourself. As soon as the sale is complete, they will contact me."

\* \* \*

*"Young Cimballi, by the end of the Eighth Move, Yahl will have resold for five hundred thousand dollars what he bought ten or twelve days earlier for two hundred fifty-four million six hundred thousand dollars. Gauge his losses yourself. He's not bankrupt, of course. Anyway, he still has his bank, which means more than anything to him, for which he agreed to lose more than a quarter of a billion dollars, and with which he hopes to make himself over again, or, at the very least, since he's more than sixty years old, maintain and redeploy some of his power.*

*"At that point, all that's required is the Ninth Move, and he'll be checkmated."*

\* \* \*

It was Marc Lavater who managed the Ninth Move. Marc had always maintained his friendships in Switzerland. He was especially close to a private banker in Basel, who, in keeping with tradition, headed the Swiss Banking Association. Marc, after making a phone appointment, appeared in the lobby of the Dolder Hotel in Zurich.

In an attaché case he carried was a deposition of William Carradine taken legally in Nevada. It dealt with the crooked maneuvers that had resulted in the transformation of Curaçao One and the subsequent birth of Curaçao Two. It was a tale of grand theft.

The next day, Martin Yahl himself arrived in Zurich, summoned by his peers assembled as a veritable jury. He knew what awaited him. What happened was exactly what he expected.

\* \* \*

*Young Cimballi, the Ninth Move will be the most terrible. Yahl will be there, before his colleagues who will also be his judges. Franz, you who have danced your dance of death around him, be content; the moment has come. Franz, there are many in Switzerland who have done as much and worse than Martin Yahl—with the money of Jews, Arabs, Black kings, dictators of all stripes, left or right, big drug dealers or arms merchants. But Martin Yahl was caught. His business is public; his dossier with my confession will be made public tomorrow, if he doesn't accept the conditions of the ultimatum we've offered him. He'll be forced to renounce for good all banking or financial activity having even a distant connection with Switzerland. Franz, you will not have bankrupted him; that was an impossible mission. But you will have destroyed him. As destroyed as I am myself, waiting for death so sweet. . . ."*

* * *

So. It was over, and I had won. Scarlet had been right; it *was* a chess match, a matter of moving pieces of unequal strengths around a board. Pawns, rooks, knights, even kings, but just pieces of wood after all. Yahl was finished, and I was left unsatisfied; unlike Hamlet, I had not killed my father's murderer with my own sword.

I had to see him with my own eyes. I flew to Geneva.

Yahl hadn't even been allowed to remove his personal papers from his bank; a seal had been placed on everything, and Martin Yahl himself was forbidden the premises. I found him in his house, a tall, marble-fronted building that spoke—now falsely— of great wealth and luxury within.

He was packing to go . . . where? Where on this earth could he go to? Whose hands would receive him? Whose roof would shelter him now?

He was old, that's the first thing I noticed, exulting. Old and wrinkled and suddenly feeble.

"It *was* you, Franz Cimballi."

"Who else could it have been? Of course, me." In my pocket, a small but powerful pistol.

"For some time, I've suspected that you would be coming after me. I've even feared it. At first, when I heard about Landau and Bremer, I was certain you were behind it. Then, when it was clear that Bremer had died naturally, I was lulled into a sense of false security. That changed with the business of Hovius and Donaldson. Then I was certain that you were crossing names off your list, waiting to get to mine."

"You tried to have me killed," I said without emotion, my hand in my pocket, lovingly fingering the ice-cold metal.

"Yes, that stupid, bungled attempt. It was foolish of me, and for that I apologize. Afterward, I realized that it was necessary for us to play the game out, move by move—"

I interrupted: "You killed my father and robbed my mother."

"Your father died because he lived too quickly on the thin edge of things. Perhaps I contributed to his heart attack, but his condition was the human condition. He died of ambition."

That thought had never occurred to me.

"But the embezzlement . . ."

"Ah, there you have me," and he gave me a wintry smile. "The money was there to be stolen, so I stole it. Let me tell you something about money, Cimballi. She is a whore, and will go with whom ever offers her the most. Money isn't inanimate, it has life and power and a language of its own. You've learned that language in just a few short years, Cimballi, and that means the money-whore will always go to bed with you."

"I scorn money!"

"Of course you do, and that's another reason she follows you. Because, like all whores, she despises herself. Now, if you've come to kill me, why not take that gun out of your pocket and get it over with? With money gone from my bed, I have little left to live for."

Slowly I drew the gun from my coat and held it out, aiming for his chest, directly at his heart. But my finger wouldn't tighten on the trigger, no matter how I willed it to.

It wasn't that I was reluctant to kill a human being, although that was part of it. Nor was it that I was afraid of the consequences, although *that* was a part of it, too. It was just that, looking at the pathetic shadow of a man, my hatred was dissipating. It was over, and none of it had mattered.

I put the gun in my pocket, and turned to go.

"For what it's worth, young Cimballi," his aged voice called after me, "for what it's worth, I wish you had been my son."

I had to get out of there.

\* \* \*

I lunched with Rosen and Lupino, Philip Vandenbergh not being free, of course. That evening, I took Leo Sussman and his wife Robin out for a farewell dinner. I came back to the St. Regis and drank champagne, alone, until sleep finally overcame me.

Fezzali called me the next morning.

"You'll have to see us, my friend."

I said: "Not right away."

"The prince and his cousins have plans for you. You've impressed them tremendously."

"Not now."

I hung up. The desk confirmed that my plane seat had indeed been reserved, and that my luggage would be picked up.

I looked out over the skyline of midtown New York.

I thought of Sarah and Joachim and Chandra, of Hyatt and Li and Liu, of the Turk and Ute Jenssen, of David and Leo and Robin Sussman, of Marc and Francoise Lavater, of Philip Vandenbergh, James Rosen, and Joseph Lupino with his complicit wink; I thought of Robert Zarra and of Sally Kendall, though there was a world of difference between the two of them; I thought of Mr. Hak. I thought of Sarah again, and I had tears in my eyes.

Would I ever see her again? It's true that I was in love with Catherine and would marry her, but in my way I had loved Sarah, too. She had carried my baby, and had disposed of it without even asking me. I should resent that, but I didn't. Somewhere in the world was a woman of great intelligence and independence, with mocking green eyes, a woman who had helped to turn a boy into a man.

The ringing echoed for a long time without anyone answering, and I imagined the women in their starchy smocks, hands folded flat on their stomachs, walking unhurriedly on their bare feet, in a sepulchral silence.

Finally, someone answered; I gave my name, I asked to speak to him, and was told he had already been dead for several days. No one knew how, but he had managed to drag himself onto the burning sand of Death Valley, around the Spanish-Moorish house, and as far as the garage, where he had found the gasoline he was looking for. He had doused himself with it, and ignited himself, thus putting an end to the pus flowing from his entire body, no longer able to survive the wait for that sweet death.

The voice of William Carradine, called Scarlet, which had guided me in this last battle, had come to me from beyond the grave.

276

# 22

"You're out of your mind. We'll never find a room in St. Tropez in July. Unless you want us to get scalped for outrageous prices. Do you think I'm a billionaire?"

"Yes," said Catherine Cimballi demurely. "You *are* a billionaire. Would I have married anything less?"

We had been married in that little burg, Fournac, because Catherine wanted her wedding there. First, we were married in the parish church, with Catherine all in white, like a sugar angel. Well, as a virgin, she'd a right to white. Then, a day later, we had the civil ceremony that French law demands. As a wedding present, I gave her a small statue of Buddha, made of obsidian. She looked puzzled.

"For luck," I told her. "It brought me luck, now you."

We had our wedding night in the family house, with the two old bats peeling potatoes downstairs. She was frightened; I was tender. I loved her so much I thought my heart would explode in my chest.

She was the sunlight, and I had been so long in the dark. The things that I had done, had been forced to do and had forced myself to do, had left me with a heavy soul. I was soiled, dirty, smelling of money. Catherine—her very name meant "a cleansing"—Catherine would wash me clean.

We got out of Fournac the following day, driving south with my wife at the wheel. She wanted to go St. Tropez, insisted upon it. For the honeymoon.

On July 2, as the sun was visibly planning to disappear, we entered St. Tropez—not exactly St. Tropez, though, since my wife took a right toward Ramatuelle. My head was on her shoulder, and I felt wonderful. I said, without opening my eyes:

"Watch out, in a hundred feet it gets really narrow."

"You know perfectly well where we're going. Lousy old billionaire, you're showing off."

"Ah, Catherine, you don't fool this lousy old billionaire. I knew a long time ago that your mother was a cousin of Martin Yahl, that she was the one who sent me that anonymous letter in Mombasa. I knew who you were and why your mother had so much regard for me and for us."

We kissed, and one of the Ferrari's fenders grazed a wall that jut happened to be passing by.

"These Italian cars don't hold the road," Catherine said. "And my mother was in love with your father from the time she was fifteen, so that when your father died and she guessed, that Cousin Martin was a terrible bastard, she bought the house in St. Tropez and kept it as it had always been."

"But that must have cost her a fortune!"

"Yes, but not her own money. Yours. Or rather, your father's. When he began to suspect Yahl, shortly before his death, he turned over to her enough money to purchase this villa for you and maintain it until you were old enough to take it over. So, you see, it's always been your home, never anybody else's."

"Hmmmmmm," I teased. "And do you think your clever mother would have turned it over to me if I hadn't fallen in love with her beautiful daughter and married her? Or would she have kept it in the family?"

"*Chien méchant!*" Catherine gave me a playful swipe on the ear, that stung like crazy. I'd have to watch out for that one.

We kissed again, and the left fender swiped a telephone pole.

"And our meeting in the Bahamas?"

"Didn't Marc Lavater tell you? He was the one who told Mama you were going to Nassau. I had just enough time to jump on the same plane as my English friends. I wanted to see what you looked like."

So Veronique Varles had been Lavater's "crystal ball." Now it was clear.

The road became narrower and narrower, and as we embraced again, the rear of the car hit a low wall.

"Am I driving too fast?"

The closer we got, the more she accelerated. It was a game, and an immense impatience, a feverishness, came over us both. The moment came when the asphalt simply stopped, and the road became a path, almost a lane.

"Stop."

She braked.

"I'd like to go the rest of the way on foot."

She nodded without a word, with that half-smile on her lips I was beginning to know so much better, which for her expressed a deep inner contentment.

I went around the car, took her by the hand, and we went off together, following the path. We both felt a little like crying and laughing at the same time, and we moved slowly, checking our impatience with delight, taking all the time that now belonged to us. We went through the rockroses toward the house that we couldn't see yet, on the sunny shore of the Pampelonne beach, but which we had long known was there, waiting for us.

We took the curving path, and soon I saw the high walls, with their velvety ocher, roughcast plaster.

A soft thud in my chest.

Catherine felt my hand tighten. She stopped smiling.

I stared at the house as I walked around it. The steps, the terrace, the garden and the pool, dead in this season. All the shutters were closed.

I let go of Catherine's hand, and went down the few steps. So many pictures, crowding one another in my memory. Laughter, too; at least, I thought so. Distant laughter. Children's cries.

I walked and came to the end of the dock, where the mahogany yacht bobbed peacefully.

I don't even know what I was thinking of. I looked at the Pampelonne beach, deserted but not lonely.

Another soft thud in my chest.

I sat down, and my feet plunged softly into warm water. Catherine was there, behind me, quiet. I was sure she wasn't even wondering why I hadn't thought to remove my shoes.

The sky turned indigo in the waning sun.

More pictures. Sharper. My father's hand, reaching toward me to lift me aboard a canoe. A beastly lump formed in my throat.

And then I heard my child's voice, murmuring:

"Papa."

*279*